T0058687

THE
DROWNED
GIRLS

OTHER TITLES BY LORETH ANNE WHITE

In the Barren Ground
In the Waning Light
A Dark Lure
The Slow Burn of Silence

Wild Country
Manhunter
Cold Case Affair

Shadow Soldiers
The Heart of a Mercenary
A Sultan's Ransom
Rules of Re-Engagement
Seducing the Mercenary
The Heart of a Renegade

Sahara Kings
The Sheik's Command
Sheik's Revenge
Surgeon Sheik's Rescue
Guarding the Princess
"Sheik's Captive," in *Desert Knights* with Linda Conrad

Romantic Suspense

Melting the Ice
Safe Passage
The Sheik Who Loved Me
Breaking Free
Her 24-Hour Protector
The Missing Colton
The Perfect Outsider
"Saving Christmas," in the *Covert Christmas* anthology
"Letters to Ellie," a novella in *SEAL of My Dreams* anthology

LORETH ANNE WHITE

THE DROWNED GIRLS

Montlake
Romance

Text copyright © 2017 by Cheakamus House Publishing, Inc.

Published by Montlake Romance, Seattle

www.apub.com

Amazon, the Amazon logo, and Montlake Romance are trademarks of Amazon.com, Inc., or its affiliates.

ISBN-13: 9781503941212
ISBN-10: 1503941213

Cover design by Rex Bonomelli

Printed in the United States of America

This one is for Marlin—thank you for sparking Angie's Victoria to life and for being a beta reader extraordinaire.

JANE DOE

Mirror, mirror, on the wall, who are you, for I know you not at all?

Day One

We all lie.

We all guard secrets—sometimes terrible ones—a side to us so dark, so shameful, that we quickly avert our own eyes from the shadow we might glimpse in the mirror.

Instead we lock our dark halves deep in the basement of our souls. And on the surface of our lives, we work industriously to shape the public story of our selves. We say, "Look, world, *this* is me." We craft posts on social media . . . *See this wonderful lunch I'm eating at this trendy restaurant with my besties, see my sexy shoes, my cute puppy, boyfriend, tight ass in a bikini. See my gloriously perfect life . . . see what a fucking fabulous time I'm having drunk and at this party with my boobs swelling out of my sparkly tank top. Just look at those hot guys draped all over me. Aren't you jealous . . .*

And then you wait to see how many people LIKE this fabricated version of yourself, your mood hinging on the number of clicks. Comments. Who commented.

But darkness has a way of seeping through the cracks. It seeks the light . . .

And then the narrative groans to a slow stop. Or the end comes violent and sudden . . . and the truth is there, written all over you, ugly under harsh fluorescent-white light. And there is nothing more that you can do to hide it from the detectives who will come looking.

I'm in a hospital bed . . .

I can hear the machines.

They're helping me breathe, trying to keep me alive. I can hear nurses whispering, two cops talking, but I can't respond. I can't move or feel anything at all. I'm unable to tell them what happened. I'm not dead. Not yet. But I can feel myself floating away on silvery threads.

A doctor comes in, argues quietly with the cops. Their words drift through me in fragments. *Sexual assault . . . gathering of forensic evidence . . . hospital policy . . . ethics . . . informed consent in absence of next of kin . . .*

They don't know who I am, I realize. They haven't found my mom.

I'm sorry, Mom. I am so, so sorry. I never wanted you to find out . . . And they *will* find out. As much as I want to protect you from this, from the shame that I know you will feel, the hurt, I do want them to learn what happened. I *need* them to learn the whole story. Find who did this. In order to save the others. Especially Lara.

He said Lara would be next. He wants us all. I need to warn Lara . . .

I slide away for a moment, and then I hear machines again, sucking and exhaling and beeping. I realize I will not make Christmas. I think about the tiny tree in our apartment living room, and I wonder if my mom will find the gift I've already bought. It's under my bed, in my room. I so wanted to see the look in her eyes when she unwrapped it.

At first, they'll say I just went to work—like I do every Saturday night, for my shift at the Blue Badger Bakery down by the water on the west side, where we prep for the big Sunday brunch influx. Always long lineups no matter the weather. One of the more popular brunch venues in a city fast becoming known as *the* brunch capital, the Badger bakes all its own breads and pastries. Even makes its own bacon.

Like most humans, a creature of habit, I routinely catch the 6:07 p.m. bus from Fairfield on Saturdays. The route takes me through the city and over the blue iron bridge to an area which is now a mix of scrappy dockyard industry and trendy gentrification—a millennial's holy grail of tiny, boxy, colorful, pet-friendly, "loft-style" condo complexes overlooking the Gorge and Inner Harbor and latticed with biking and jogging trails and boardwalks and boathouses storing kayaks and outrigger canoes and stand-up paddleboards.

But I never made it to work. I'd had a sense of being followed, of being watched for the past week or so. The new man on the bus last week seemed off yet vaguely familiar, but then this was Victoria—not a big city. We all move within six degrees of separation from one another. I'd probably just seen him around town. And he'd worn a dark wool hat, the collar of his jacket turned up against the December cold.

But it was him. He'd been stalking me, studying the habits of his prey, riding the same bus. Planning his trap. He'd found his choke point—the small, dark alley through which I take a shortcut.

My mind goes back, trying to replay the events, sort them into chronological order. Memories slice through me like sharp shards of a broken mirror . . . it was a windy night. Brittle with cold and thick with fog.

It had started to snow . . .

CHAPTER 1

There is none righteous, no, not one.

—Romans 3:10

SATURDAY, DECEMBER 9

Angie Pallorino looked out of the floor-to-ceiling windows that ran the length of her parents' living room. A sweep of manicured lawn rolled down to a pebbly beach, where her dad kept his boat in a small boathouse, and from where a dock jutted out into the waters of Haro Strait. But it was dark out. She couldn't see the beach—just her own distorted reflection and glimpses of whitecaps on the black, wind-whipped water.

Down the center of the strait ran the US-Canada border, and during daylight, the hazy-blue mountains of San Juan Island were visible over the ocean. Behind them, on a clear day, Mount Baker rose stark and volcanic white against the sky.

It was cold. Bitterly so for December on the island. For the past nine days an arctic outflow had been pouring air down from the north, and it had brought crystal clear skies and temperatures well below freezing. But now a fat, wet Pacific front was blustering in, and the precipitation was clashing with the frozen air and coming down as snow.

Flakes flecked with ice ticked against the windows.

Angie hated snow—the way it smelled. The subtly metallic scent unsettled her on a deeply profound level. It was a sensation she'd never quite been able to articulate, but it was there. Always when it snowed. Worse around Christmas. She rubbed her arms, her thoughts boomeranging back to her failure on a sweltering evening last July—her inability to save the life of a three-year-old toddler. How her focus on trying to resuscitate the little girl might have also cost the life of her partner.

Tiffy Bennett had died in her arms while her mentor and partner, "Hash" Hashowsky, had taken a bullet to the throat and bled out before EMTs could arrive. Then Tiffy's father, standing over the body of Tiffy's dead mother, had turned his weapon to his own head and shot out his brains. He'd been abusing his baby girl for just about her entire life, and a restraining order had failed to protect Tiffy and her mom.

Sometimes, Angie thought, the difference between heaven and hell was people. Sometimes, no matter how hard you tried, you made no difference at all.

"You look tired," her father said, coming up behind her.

She straightened her spine, turned to face him.

"All those new lines around your eyes," he said. "That job of yours, it ages you, you know?"

"You don't look so hot yourself, Dad—been a rough day all around. Here, give me that." She took the box that her father was holding, and she set it near the front door. It was packed with some of her mother's things that he thought she might want. They'd spent the morning moving Miriam Pallorino into a long-term psychiatric facility, and the afternoon cleaning out her home office and closets. The house felt hollow and huge.

"Why don't you quit, Angie? Especially after—"

"After what? Losing that kid and my partner?"

"You could maybe move to another department. Dealing with all those sex perverts who come through the special victims unit . . . seeing that sordid side of humanity all the time, it gets in your head. It's changed you."

6

Anger flared hot in her chest. It came with an urge for physical violence—a kind of ferocity for which there was sometimes no real justification, which just set upon her at the slightest of provocations. Which she worked very hard to control under a cool and seemingly detached exterior. She stared at her father. Standing there in his oversize sweater with leather patches on the elbows. His thatch of dense white hair, once so black. Behind him a fire crackled in the hearth, and the walls were lined with cabinets of books, pieces of art. A life of privilege. Dr. Joseph Pallorino, professor of anthropology at the University of Victoria. Born into an Italian immigrant's fortune hard-won in the mining industry. Given on a silver platter the wherewithal to indulge his personal academic passions. Her parents had always lived a rarefied life into which she never really felt she fitted.

"I deal with victims," she said quietly. "Survivors. Innocent and vulnerable women and children who never asked for what hurt them. I put bad guys away." She held his gaze. "And I'm good at it, Dad. Damn good. I make a difference."

"Do you?"

"Yeah, I do." She looked away, at the unlit Christmas tree in the corner with the gold angel on top, and a chill passed through her. "Sometimes. Yes. I do."

"Your mother, she thought you'd outgrow it. She always thought you joined the police out of some kind of rebellion."

Her gaze flared back to his. "Is that what you thought, too? That I'd get my kicks, find what I was looking for, then finally settle down in a nice Victorian character home with a picket fence and a little row of nodding daffodils out front?"

"Angie, you have a master's in psychology. You were top of your class. You could have gone into research, could have had an academic career—*still* could . . ." He wavered under the heat of her glare, cleared his throat, stuffed his hands deep into his pockets, and gave a resigned shrug. "I—we—just want you to be happy."

7

"Let it drop, okay? This is *not* the time. I'm going to order pizza—we can eat together before I go." She made for the phone on the kitchen wall as she spoke. She'd booked the weekend off, and she and her father still had Sunday to get through, to finish moving things. To check in on her mom again, make sure that she was settling in okay. She lifted the receiver. "Want anchovies?"

The pizza, dinner, prolonging the evening had been a mistake. Angie and her dad ate in awkward silence, lost in their own worlds without the bustling presence of Miriam Pallorino. Outside the wind howled and branches rattled against the eaves. Angie's thoughts turned to the small room in which they'd left her mother this morning. The locked doors in the facility. The white-coated orderlies. The confusion and, yes, the fear she'd witnessed in her mom's eyes.

She reached for her juice, sipped, cleared her throat. "How long, really, did you know that she wasn't well?"

Her father did not look up. "A while."

"Like . . . how old was she when you first noticed the onset of symptoms?"

A shrug. He picked an olive off his pizza.

"It has a strong hereditary component, you know?" she said. "The illness occurs in less than one percent of the general population, but it manifests in ten percent of people who have a first-degree relative with the disorder, like a parent." She waited. Her dad said nothing. Angie leaned forward. "I'd like to know when you first saw the signs, first became aware that something was . . . off."

He pushed the olive to the edge of his plate.

"Dad?"

He wiped his mouth and carefully folded the hem of his white linen napkin over the orange cheese and tomato stains. He tucked the neatly folded napkin under the rim of his plate. "She's been on medication for quite a long time now, Angie. Keeping things under control. The first indication I had that she might be experiencing hallucinations, delusions, came in her midthirties." He looked up. "We thought it was PTSD, from the car accident in Italy." He fell silent for a long while. The fire in the hearth flickered. "Images, sounds, smells—they can all trigger flashbacks that can look like psychotic hallucinations, you know? The emotional numbness, apathy, social withdrawal, low energy . . . the doctor said it could all be signs of post-traumatic stress disorder." He looked sad, broken, as if the bones of his large skeleton had suddenly crumpled inside him a little. He inhaled deeply. "She was formally diagnosed with schizophrenia when she turned forty-two. A mild form, one that could be successfully managed with medication. And it had been." He paused, a strange and distant look entering his eyes. "But now, combined with the early onset of the dementia . . ." His voice faded. Her mother had suddenly and sharply lost touch with reality. It was why they'd had to institutionalize her. She'd become a danger to herself.

Angie waited until his eyes met hers again. "Can you tell me about the early hallucinations?"

"Auditory and visual," he said.

"So she heard voices? Saw things that weren't there?"

"Just . . . minor at first. She didn't even know they were not real, or anything to worry about."

Angie's pulse quickened. "And you didn't tell me about it? Even though she's been suffering all these years?"

He pushed his plate to the side. "Well, you didn't notice either. It's not like you spent much time here lately."

Her jaw tightened. "You *could* have told me."

"And what could you have done?"

"I don't know! Understood, maybe, what was going on in her head. Been less short-tempered with her, with *you*. Come around more. Maybe I wouldn't have taken my mother's emotional distance so personally in my late teens. Maybe I would have had some context for why I so often felt locked out as a kid."

"Locked out?"

"By you and her."

"That's nonsense—all kids—"

"What else have you lied to me about?"

"It *wasn't* a lie, Angie—"

"By omission, yes it was."

He surged to his feet, his quick Italian temper puffing out his chest, coloring his cheeks, flashing into his dark eyes. "I don't know why you get so angry—always so damn angry about everything!" He flung his arm out in her direction. "It's that job of yours. Working sex crimes. It's made you suspicious about everything and everyone."

Coolly, she got up, started gathering the plates and cutlery. "I need to go. I'll wash up."

She carried the plates into the kitchen, dumped them into the sink. Bracing her hands on the counter, she lowered her head for a moment, a vise of anxiety squeezing at her temples. What was her dad going to do now, alone in this big empty shell of an oceanfront house? What about Christmas? She truly hated this time of the year—detested the thought of making an effort. The farce of it all.

Guilt weighed sudden and heavy on her shoulders. Guilt at her own selfishness—because she'd be obligated to come and visit her dad more often, and she didn't have the time. Or inclination, even. She did *not* want to listen to him going on about her work as a cop. But he was going to need her.

And what of his wedding anniversary, come January?

Aging parents, families, were never easy. There was always so much love, hurt. Regret. All muddled together. And now there was a sense of time lost. Somehow she'd let these past years flow under the bridge without noticing them. Really noticing. And now it was over. Her mother gone. Still here, but gone.

Inhaling deeply, she began to rinse off a plate, stilling as her thumb moved over the blue flower pattern along the edge. A memory, like a piece of bright-yellow sunlight, sliced into her mind—one autumn afternoon spent shopping with her mother for this crockery set at the big old department store downtown. The Hudson's Bay Company. Her mom used to love that store. Maybe in her more lucid moments she still did. Would her mother even be able to recall that day now, this set with the cornflower pattern that they'd bought together?

It had been eight years ago. Angie had promised to drive her mother downtown because her mom's car had been in the shop. But Angie had been distracted by a case—she'd just made detective, and all her mom had been fretting about was whether the thirty-two-piece dinner ensemble would still be on sale when they got there. It had irritated Angie—her mother's preoccupation with the inane.

And then suddenly life had passed her by. She'd woken up one morning and her mother was gone—lost in mind, a lifetime of precious memories erased from the hard drive of her brain. What did that do to the concept of "self"? Memories defined a person. Without autobiographical memory, the face in the mirror was a stranger's. One became an alien, flailing around in a constant, unrelenting present with no touchstones to guide one into the future and out of the past.

Angie flattened the thought, rinsed off the second plate, and stuck it in the rack. She dried off her hands and returned to the living room to get her coat.

She found her dad sitting by the fire, his big frame crumpled into an old leather La-Z-Boy, which her mom had tried forever to persuade him to ditch. Yet there it still hunkered in its corner next to the hearth, like a dinosaur relic of some past era among her mom's plush cream sofas and chairs. He'd put the tree lights on, and a fat glass of whiskey rested on the table at his side. Flames were dying to glowing embers in the hearth. He was paging through an old photo album, his head bowed.

Angie went to his side, placed her hand on his shoulder, gave a small squeeze. "You going to be okay?"

He nodded. He was staring at an old photo of the three of them, taken the first Christmas after the car accident that had occurred during his sabbatical in Italy when Angie was four. The legacy of that accident was evident in the fresh pink scar pulling up the left side of Angie's lip—the photo had been shot before further surgery had restored her mouth to a more even, but never perfect, shape.

He turned the page. Another photo of Angie with her mother. This one taken when Angie was maybe six years old. Spring. Lush green grass. Cherry blossoms. The sun was gold and angled low. The rays threw a halo of copper around her mother's strawberry-blonde hair, and it made Angie's darker hair gleam like burnished red cedar. The O'Dell Irish legacy, courtesy of her mother's genes.

A tightness began to build in Angie's chest.

Her father glanced up, something unreadable and strange entering his face. "Take it," he said, closing the album and looking away.

"I . . . I don't think so, Dad." She didn't have time to sit and page through these memories, these little pieces of their lives that had been trapped in time under the protective plastic sheets on the thick pages of the album. She had another Justice Institute exam to take. She was registering for as many courses as she could to bolster her bid to join the elite of Metro PD's integrated homicide unit.

"Please," he said, voice thick. "Take it away, with the other boxes. Just for a while. It'll stop me from looking, kitten." Angie's heart beat a little faster at his use of her old nickname. Her father hadn't used it since she was maybe ten. She came around, sat on the ottoman at his side, took the leather-bound book of memories from his big hands. She opened it at the beginning. Her mother pregnant. Her tummy growing. The day Angie was born.

"She made it for you. Your life from the minute she knew you were on the way. It's . . . too . . . painful right now, you know, for me to look at these things."

Angie gazed upon the image of her mom in a hospital bed, wearing a blue gown, cradling her newborn. The haze of dark-red hair already evident on baby Angie's head.

"You were so tiny," he whispered, turning his face toward the dying coals. She heard the catch of emotion in his words. She knew there were tears in his eyes. The tightness began to intensify in her chest.

She turned to another page. The day of her baptism—her mom and dad holding her as a baby in a long white, lace-embossed gown. The priest in his ornate robes at their side. Another photo showed them all at the beach. She skipped forward several pages. Emotion whammed through her chest. She caught her breath and gently touched the image. She could almost hear her mother's voice from that day, feel the warm summer breeze against her cheeks, taste the rich, sweet taste of plump Okanagan cherries. Slowly, Angie turned the page. There were pictures of more family holidays, Angie's first day of school, her first Holy Communion, learning to sail at camp, her prom, graduation.

A picture of Angie in her brand-new police uniform, her mom standing proudly at her side, long hair billowing in the breeze.

Gently, Angie moved her fingertips over the contours of her mother's face.

"I'll miss her."

"I already do," said her father.

She closed the book. "I'll borrow it," she said. "I'll bring it back by Christmas, how's that? What are you doing for Christmas, Dad? You want me to get a turkey?" Shit. She'd said it. Committing. At one of the busiest times of the year at the station. Perverts—bad guys didn't take holidays. In fact, things got worse at this time of year.

13

He rubbed his brow. "I'll figure it out."

An errant log caught flame, and the fire crackled. Wind moaned.

She nodded. "I'll see myself out." She got up, hesitated. "Go easy on that whiskey, okay? Get an early night."

He nodded, his face still averted from her gaze.

"Night, Dad."

Angie loaded the boxes and album into her car. Outside, wind tore at her hair, and fog came in thick off the sea. She could hear the crash of waves on rocks down below.

The snow was coming down heavily and sideways.

CHAPTER 2

Angie rounded the corner and hit the unprotected strip of Dallas Road that ran along Ross Bay. Wind and driving snow slammed into her. Waves crashed and boomed along the concrete road barrier, and fog billowed in over the bay. Leaning forward for better visibility, she slowed her unmarked Crown Vic, her wipers struggling to clear arcs in the snow smearing over her windshield.

As she neared the lowest dip in the road, her tires entered a stream of seawater spilling over the wall. Debris and foam hurtled across her windshield. The beams of her headlights bounced back at her in the fog and silvery snowflakes. She rounded the curve, and something dashed suddenly out into the road in a swirl of mist and foam. A blur of pink entered the glow of her beams. Angie slammed on the brakes, her Crown Vic skidding sideways as it planed on the seawater that had puddled in the dip.

A small girl in a pink dress stopped right in front of her car, then spun around and disappeared up into the dense, leafless tangle of roots and branches that grew tightly up against the side of the road.

She stared, heart hammering, skin hot. Clouds cleared for a moment, but the child was gone. No other vehicles—not one other soul in sight. *What the . . .*

She pulled over to the side, flicked on her police lights, grabbed her flashlight, and removed her Smith and Wesson 5906 service pistol from the lockbox mounted in her console. She loaded her weapon. Blue and red light pulsed in the fog as she opened her door, got out. She drew the hood of her jacket up against the driving wind and snow pellets.

"Hello!" she yelled into soup of fog. "Anyone there?" Wind snatched her words, tossing them up into the hedge of tangled trunks and branches that screened the old cemetery above. A strange, eerie sensation filled her.

She walked a few meters up the road, panning her beam through the twisted branches along the embankment. "Hello!"

A voice, soft and susurrating, whispered . . . *Come playum dum grove . . . Come down dem . . .*

Angie froze.

She spun around.

Come playum dum . . . come . . .

The eerie sensation turned to ice in her chest. She swallowed, walked a little farther along the road, ducking as debris blew at her. No sign of the kid on either side.

She climbed back into her car and rubbed her wet face hard with the palms of her hands. And for a while she just sat there peering into the mist, her police lights still strobing into the storm. But the child did not reappear.

Pink dress? About four or five years old? Shit. No kid would be out in this weather, alone. Especially not dressed like that. And how could she have heard that whisper over the crash of waves and howl of wind? Angie realized her hands were trembling.

Her father's words filtered into her mind.

The first indication I had that she might be experiencing hallucinations, delusions, came in her midthirties . . . We thought it was PTSD, from the car accident in Italy . . .

Cold, she told herself. Just wet and cold. And exhausted—worsening insomnia since July taking its toll. She hadn't slept for four nights straight now. That's why she was shaking. She flicked off her lights, reengaged the gears, and pulled off slowly, wipers clacking.

A drink. She needed a stiff drink.

She needed to get this shit out of her head. She glanced at the clock on the dash. She'd promised herself she'd tone things down—it's why she'd booked time off work. It's why she was making an effort to help her mom and dad this weekend. She'd thought focusing on family affairs might help settle the urge in her. But once the thought had entered her head, Angie knew where she was going. What she would do. In spite of herself.

She'd do what she always did when she hit a bad hurdle, when she needed to find a way to cope—to blow off steam. Just the thought of it made her feel better already.

CHAPTER 3

We all lie . . . We all move within six degrees of separation
from one another.

Angie knew the instant he walked into the bar that he was the one.

Slowly, she sipped her drink, keeping her eyes trained on him as he
sifted through the gyrating crowd—it parted for him like the Red Sea
to Moses beneath the sparking disco ball. He moved with a commanding presence. She could feel the techno thump of the music resonating
up her bar stool, and the pulse matched the beat of her heart as she
watched him.

He stopped a moment, scanning the bar patrons as if searching
for someone. He stood a head taller than the crowd, his shoulders
broader than average. Light danced off his hair, which was ruffled and
the dark blue-black of a raven's feathers. His skin was pale. His eyes
. . . she couldn't see the color from here, but they were wide set under
dense brows. Strong features, she thought, ones that hovered between
handsome and interesting. There was an otherworldly air about him, a
vaguely worn yet incredibly alert look.

He turned, caught her eye.

A sense of trepidation rustled through her—he didn't quite belong.
Not here, in this club. There was something slightly off about his

presence. But this only fueled her interest, her adrenaline. He held her gaze for a moment, and when she did not look away, he started to come toward her seat at the bar. Warning bells began to clang deep inside her mind as he neared. Heat rose in her body. Angie swallowed.

Don't think. Just feel. Stay in control. Rule # 1: Always stay in control.

The Foxy Club was Angie's hunting ground. It was located just off Highway 1—the road out of town that led over a mountain pass and up the island. From the outside the Foxy was a bleak, square building squatting on a cracked parking lot. A big billboard with flashing lights promised adult entertainment to motorists passing by. Tonight happened to be "Seventies Disco Night" with "Big Bad John" spinning bass-laden tunes under period disco balls. On the long and narrow stage behind the bar, female strippers in white patent leather go-go boots, tiny thongs, and silver wigs made seductive love to their poles. On this night they were paired with a male dancer who'd poured his muscular body into a tighty-whitey disco suit. He undulated his way between the strippers and their poles, thrusting his hips to the beat and pointing to the sky like something out of the old *Saturday Night Fever* movie . . . *stayin' alive . . . ah ha ha . . . stayin' alive . . .*

Yeah. Story of our lives. Just trying to stay alive—to live a little and fuck a few people along the way.

Because, as Angie knew all too intimately, at the heart of all life, and death, was sex. She was acutely aware of how sexual proclivity ran the gamut from "normal," to deviant, to deadly. And the Foxy showcased sex in many of its forms. It was a place men came to buy it. And a place she could get it for free. Her own personal game of Russian roulette. Her own way of flipping a bird to mortality, the sometimes apparent futility of it all.

Her own way of *stayin' alive . . . ah ha haaa . . .*

The club's motel on the opposite end of the parking lot rented rooms by the hour. She'd already paid for one upon her arrival. The lights dimmed suddenly and shifted from hot reds to blue as the song changed. She knocked back the rest of her drink, relieved to finally feel the beginnings of a nice fuzzy buzz. She motioned to the bartender for one more as her target approached her stool.

He smiled, and Angie inhaled, a zing spearing down into her belly. Even better up close. Nice white teeth, incisors a little lower than the rest, giving him a deliciously feral air. Creases fanned out from eyes that were such a dark blue they almost looked purple in this light. *Fuck, he's fucking beautiful.* But still a little beat-up looking, just the wrong side of perfect.

Quite simply, he stole her breath.

And somewhere, far off, those mental warning bells started to clang louder—five alarm. And in the recesses of her consciousness she heard the words, *Don't touch.*

Not this one. Too attractive to you. Not the profile you've set for yourself. Never take one that makes you feel vulnerable in any way . . .

"Hey," he said.

She nodded and took a deep swallow of the fresh vodka tonic that the barkeep had just placed in front of her. *Just stay in control. Leave first. Leave early. No names.*

"Can I buy you a drink?" he said, bracing his right hand on the bar, leaning across her, his mouth close to her ear in order to make himself heard over the music.

She held up her glass. "I'm good."

"A dance, then?" He held her gaze. She didn't blink. Slowly, she set her drink down on the counter and came to her feet, closing the space between them. He straightened up but did not step back. It forced her to look up at him. He was even taller than she'd anticipated. Broader.

"How about a room?" she said.

Now he blinked. And she noticed a flicker of unease pass quickly through his eyes. Angie smiled, turned on by her own power to put that glimmer of wariness into a big man's eyes. It shifted the traditional balance of power. In her line of work, the victims were nearly always female. Or children. Innocent children. And the aggressors were nearly always male. She continued to meet his gaze, waiting for him to process her question. When he did not reply, she grabbed her leather jacket off the back of the stool and started to negotiate her way through the throbbing dancers toward the red exit sign above the rear door.

His decision to come after her was swift. He caught up to her and grabbed her arm, stopping her, applying a little too much pressure. Large hand. Iron grip. A slight fear washed through her, and it excited her, awakened her. Slowly, she breathed in, calming herself, and then she turned to face him. Her heart skipped a beat at the sexual tension she saw tightening his features now, the darkening of his already dark-blue eyes.

"What do you mean?" he said.

"What do you think I mean?"

His grip remained firm on her upper arm, and his gaze lowered, taking her in—all of her. Her breasts, her hips, the length of her legs, her black biker boots. His pulse became visible at his carotid. Lifting his free hand, he touched her hair, which she wore long and loose tonight. Gently, he felt the texture of it, and then he lifted a fall of it to expose her neck. And he cupped the side of her neck, tracing his thumb along her jawline. Her vision blurred, legs felt weak. He lowered his head, bringing his mouth close to hers. "You're cheap," he whispered. "Why?"

Her lids flickered. "You . . . don't trust me because I'm free?"

"I don't trust anyone."

"If you'd rather waste your cash, try one of the ladies up on the stage." She turned to leave.

But his grip only tightened on her arm. "Fine," he murmured in her ear. "Let's go."

Red light pulsed into the motel room from the neon sign in the parking lot outside, setting the thin drapes aglow like a beating heart, like a crucible in a devil's basement. *Thrum. Thrum. Thrum.* The bass of the music from the club could be heard through the thin walls, felt through the very floorboards, and it matched the throbbing pace of the neon. Somewhere, far off, a siren wailed. Ambulance, maybe cops, or fire. Society taking care of its citizens, policing.

The headboard thumped as Angie rode him in time to the bass thud coming through the walls, her blood hot, her skin slick. He was naked under her, and she'd zip-tied his wrists to the headboard above his head. Their clothes pooled on the old carpet, boots scattered across the room. She dug her nails into his skin as she fucked him with all her might, panting, sweating, breasts bouncing, obliterating all thoughts of the past months from her mind . . . all the things she couldn't do to save the kids . . . her limits, her vulnerabilities. The toll this unit took on cops. The depravity she'd witnessed over the years. And just when she thought she'd seen it all, the job dished up yet something more.

He was blessed with a fucking big dick and she loved it, let it fill her. The hair on his chest was rough and dark, his body honed, skin pale like alabaster, carved marble. A Michelangelo masterpiece. That buried voice rose again into her consciousness. *Something's wrong here. Who is he? Why does he want this? Why did he come to this place when any woman would probably throw herself at his feet? No band on his ring finger, but a faint, telltale indentation of paler skin. Recently out of a relationship? Hiding it? Whichever way, this is not a man without history. Without relationships. What is wrong, deviant about him . . . ?*

Angie shut out the voice, opened her thighs wider, and sank deeper onto his dick. She rocked her hips faster, filling herself, making herself hurt. She was close, so close, and he could feel it. He bucked under her, wilder, wilder, thrusting his cock up into her. She tried to pull back, to deny him full pleasure, but suddenly she froze, her entire body going rigid, as if in rigor. Her breath caught in her chest, and she held still a moment, red lights pulsing, bass beating. And suddenly, she came, her vision blurring, a cry suffocating in her throat as her muscles contracted and released in hot, rolling waves. She collapsed onto him, her breasts against his rough chest hair. He was still hard inside her as aftershocks continued to ripple around his erection.

A noise sounded in her jacket on the floor. Her phone—the familiar ringtone she'd set for Holgersen. *Shit.*

Angie tried to focus. She wasn't on call. Not tonight. She'd booked the weekend off to help her dad with her mom.

The phone rang again. She reached down and groped along the floor for her jacket.

"Leave it." His command was husky. Velvet on gravel. Surprisingly authoritative. "Untie me," he said. "My turn."

She closed her eyes for a moment. The call went to voicemail.

"Untie me."

Angie looked up into his face. Something in his eyes whispered "danger." The phone started to ring again. It had to be urgent. Holgersen, her new partner, would not contact her on her night off otherwise. Angie slid off the man's cock and padded over to her jacket. She extracted her phone. Pushing a tangle of thick, damp hair off her face, she connected the call.

"Yeah," she said, not using her name. She hadn't given Mr. Big Dick her name, and had no intention of doing so either, so she wasn't about to mention it while answering the phone.

"Party's over, Pallorino," came Holgersen's oddly accented voice. "You and me got us a Jane Doe over at Saint Jude's. Young—mid to late teens. Sexual assault. Paramedics picked her up in Ross Bay Cemetery. Critical condition. Nonresponsive."

She glanced at Mr. Big D. He was watching her intently, listening, his hands still bound above his head. She turned her back to him, moved naked to the window. "What about the others?" she said quietly. "Dundurn and Smith? They're on tonight."

"Dundurn wants to pass it on. He and Smith have been on seventy-two hours straight with this flu bug hitting the department. And they're still winding down on another call." A pause. "He said you might want it. Could be your guy from the Fernyhough and Ritter cases. Except this time the mark has been carved into her forehead."

Everything in her body went stone still. Her and Hash's old cases. An unsolved thorn in Hash's side—a repeat rapist who'd first come to their attention four years ago in the sexual assault of sixteen-year-old Sally Ritter, and then again a year later in an attack on Allison Fernyhough, fourteen. They never found him. "I'll be there in twenty."

"What are you, like in the States, or what? You coming by bicycle?"

"Handle whatever you can until I get there. Twenty minutes."

She killed the call, grabbed her jeans, rammed her feet into the legs, and shimmied them up her hips. Pulling her shirt on quickly, she scooped her hair back and twisted it into a tight ponytail at the nape of her neck. Angie yanked on her boots, reached for her leather jacket, and paused, looking at the man tied to the motel room bed. His sheathed penis glistened, not near going flaccid. Nice. A warm rush flushed through her. Her gaze tracked up his body. He was watching her—analyzing her. Oddly calm and in control for a man bound naked to a bed. She met his eyes.

He jerked his chin to his groin. "We have unfinished business," he said.

She moistened her lips. From the back pocket of her jeans she took the carbon-fiber Sebenza 25 knife that she carried everywhere. Sharpest blade she'd ever met. She opened the knife, leaned over, and sliced through the hard plastic ties binding his wrists. He continued to hold her gaze as he lowered his hands. The skin on his wrists had been rubbed raw.

"Give me your number?" he said. "For next time."

Again, she felt that whisper of unease—a faint sixth sense of warning that maybe this time she'd bitten off a bit more than she could chew, or control. Because she wanted to do him again. He was like the first taste of a potent, addictive drug. And she didn't like the feeling—she didn't want to *need* him. She'd made that mistake once before.

Do it. Do it again. He's like medicine. He took all your cares away . . .

Angie hesitated, her brain racing through the options. One more time couldn't hurt—could it? She moved quickly to the small table next to the bed and scrawled her private cell number onto the hotel pad. It was for a burner phone. She could get rid of it anytime she wanted. She shrugged into her jacket as she made for the door.

He called after her. "You got a name there, warrior princess?"

She paused, hand on doorknob, and the devil on her shoulder whispered, *Yes, you can control this. You can stop anytime you want to . . .* Besides, she was only human. She could have a life. It wasn't as though it was forbidden to have a relationship. As long as she held the reins, all the control.

"Angie," she said.

Silence.

"You?" she asked.

He smiled slowly, one side of his mouth curving slightly higher than the other. "I've got your number." He paused. "Angie."

CHAPTER 4

*Wherever he steps, whatever he touches, whatever he leaves, even
unconsciously, will bear silent witness against him.*
—Locard's exchange principle

SUNDAY, DECEMBER 10

Snow came down in big fat flakes now, swirling between the city buildings and settling on the night streets. It was 3:00 a.m. Sunday when
Angie turned off Douglas, her wipers carving arcs on her windshield.
An unarticulated anxiety filled her as she peered at the shining store-
fronts filled with Christmas fare. Twinkling lights had been strung
over the streets in the older, touristy parts of town. Across the black
waters of the Inner Harbor, the legislature buildings shimmered like a
Disneyland palace outlined with fairy lights. An old Bing Crosby rendi-
tion of "Silver Bells" came on the radio . . . *city sidewalks . . . dressed in
holiday style . . .*

Irritably, Angie jabbed the button, switching the station to a news
channel. *New mayor-elect Jack Killion and his council will be sworn in
on Tuesday . . .*

She hit the OFF button.

VOTE KILLION signs from the civic election two weeks ago still lingered on the occasional lawn. Killion had managed to oust mayoral
incumbent Patty Markham by a mere eighty-nine votes. Apparently

that was all it was going to take to usher in a new tough-on-crime-clean-sweep-the-police-board policy. Long live democracy. And if Killion was true to his election mongering, he'd start the ball rolling for change from the second he and his slate of councilors were sworn in on Tuesday.

Make this city great again.

Whatever that meant. What it did mean for Angie and her colleagues in the Victoria Metro Police Department was an irascible chief constable growing ever more testy over Killion's threats of radical change. It had created an internal climate of festering unease and finger-pointing over crime stats, budgets, overtime allowances, staff costs, and case closure rates. And then there was the speculation that Chief Gunnar's own head would eventually roll and that he'd be replaced by one of Killion's lackeys.

Angie found a parking space outside Saint Auburn's Cathedral, which rose dark and gothic beside the similarly designed buildings of the adjacent Catholic-run hospital. She removed her service weapon from the lockbox, holstered it under her leather jacket, pulled on her black woolen skullcap, and exited her vehicle. As she hurried through the snow toward the red-lit emergency entrance, gargoyles peered down at her with stone eyes.

Holgersen was slouched in an orange plastic chair near the nurses' reception area, looking more like a recovering street addict in need of medical attention himself than a major crimes detective. As he saw Angie approach, he pushed himself up to his lanky six-foot-two height.

"So what kept you, Pallorino?"

"Where is she?"

He eyed her for a moment, then made a sign with his finger under his eyes. "Your mascara is running."

"Where is she, Holgersen? What have we got? Any ID on her yet?"

"She was still in surgery when I arrived. They're moving her into ICU now. The uniform upstairs will brief us—she and her patrol partner were the first responding officers. They arrived on scene at Ross Bay Cemetery just after two paramedics had started working on her."

"She regain consciousness at all?"

"Nah." He started for the elevator, saluting the admitting nurses with two fingers as he went. Angie kept pace with him. The antiseptic smell of hospitals always made her oddly edgy—even more so tonight.

He pressed the elevator button. "One of the docs said they actually lost her for a few minutes in the ER."

"Lost her?"

"As in, she died. They brought her back. Twice."

Going up in the elevator, Angie peered at her distorted reflection in the metal sides and rubbed under her eyes, trying to remove her smudged mascara. Holgersen observed her in silence.

"What?" she said. "It's snowing out. I got wet. Makeup runs."

"I didn't say nothing, Detective."

If he had said something, he'd probably have said, *Yeah, in the three weeks since I've been partnered with you, I've not seen you wearing makeup once.* He might look like a washed-up junkie, but Holgersen didn't miss a beat. His mind was razor-sharp, and he was weighing her, filling in puzzle pieces from the first day they'd met, building a mental image of her.

He'd worked years in narcotics, both up north from whence he came and locally, with several stints undercover. His lazy speech and weird syntax fooled most, and Angie suspected he liked to keep it that way. At least he was easier to bear than the last asshole they'd tried to pair her with. Plus Holgersen deferred to her. Most of the time. She liked that. She didn't know much about him otherwise—a closed book. And she didn't pry, either, because she preferred to keep her personal life personal, too.

As they exited the elevator, a patrol officer waiting on a chair farther down the corridor came abruptly to her feet. Sometimes it felt like yesterday that Angie had been a beat cop herself. Other times it felt like decades.

"Detective Pallorino—sex crimes," Angie said, introducing herself. "And this is Holgersen."

"Constable Tonner," said the uniform, opening her notebook. "My partner, Hickey, and I were the initial responding officers. I rode in the rear of the ambulance with the victim and have been at the hospital since. Hickey remained on scene to secure the area and interview witnesses."

Small mercies. "Where's our survivor now?"

"They've just moved her into the intensive care unit."

"Who initially called it in?" Angie said.

"A ghost tour guide." Tonner checked her notes. "Name's Edwin Liszt. He and a group of four clients found her lying on one of the grave plots. They made the nine-one-one call."

"Ghost touring? In *this* weather?" Holgersen said.

Angie glanced at him, thinking of the image she'd thought she'd seen on the road below the cemetery.

"Apparently it's on nights like this when an infamous female apparition appears around midnight," said Tonner. "We arrived after the EMTs were already working on her. Victim was soaked, hypothermic, nonresponsive, bleeding from a face wound and from her vaginal area. Her skirt had been pushed up, her stockings had been either ripped or cut away from her pelvic area, and her legs were splayed open. She was still wearing her boots."

Silence hung a beat.

Angie cleared her throat. "We'll need contact details for the paramedics, and for Liszt and his clients."

"Got them. Hickey officially ID'd all the witnesses and took initial statements."

"Her clothing?" Angie said.

"Logged and bagged." Constable Tonner nodded to the paper evidence bags on the chair behind her. "Pair of Francesco Milano boots in there. Skirt was a designer label, too."

"And no ID—wallet, phone?"

"Negative."

"Rape kit?" Angie said.

A strident female voice sounded behind them. "Our primary commitment was patient survival." They all spun around. A doctor in green surgical scrubs approached them. She was tall with a clean, strong face. Bright eyes, but they were lined with what Angie read as fatigue, stress.

"Dr. Ruth Finlayson." She held out her hand. Angie reached forward and shook it. Firm grip.

"Angie Pallorino. And this is Kjel Holgersen."

"There's always an ethical problem when an unconscious patient presents with signs of sexual assault," said Dr. Finlayson. "Performing a forensic exam without consent can make patients feel an additional loss of control once they regain consciousness. However, I am trained to administer a forensic examination, and our hospital policy does allow leeway to gather evidence if the collection occurs during necessary emergent care. So we did what we could. Usually we hold on to that evidence kit until consent for release is obtained, either by the patient or a surrogate decision-maker such as a family member, guardian, or judge."

"I'm aware of the policy," Angie said. "How is she? Can we see her?"

The doctor held her gaze for a moment, then inhaled. "Come this way." As she took them down the corridor, she glanced over her shoulder. "If you could turn your mobile phones off—they can interfere with equipment in the unit." Angie and Holgersen powered off their phones as they entered the intensive care ward, and the doc led them to a room. She slid the glass door open.

They stepped inside. Machines beeped and hissed. Angie's attention shot to the girl lying on the bed. Ventilator tubes were plastered to her mouth, and drips fed into her veins. Monitoring equipment was strapped to her arms, pasted to her chest. A loose dressing covered her brow. She was a brunette, young, and there was a strange tinge to her skin.

"She's . . . blue," said Holgersen. "What's with the color? That from cold?"

"Cyanosis," Dr. Finlayson said quietly, her gaze upon her patient. "It can occur when the blood oxygen level drops too low. She had no heartbeat when she arrived. It's a miracle she's even alive. The next twenty-four hours will be telling. However, if she does manage to pull through, there will likely be permanent neurological damage. Of the near-drowning patients who do present without a heartbeat, thirty-five to sixty percent die in the emergency department, while almost all of those who do survive are left with permanent disabilities."

Both Angie and Holgersen's attention snapped sharply to the doc.

"Near *drowning*?" said Angie. "What do you mean?"

"She'd been submersed in water. Usually when drowning begins, the larynx closes involuntarily, preventing both air and water from entering the lungs. In ten to twenty percent of cases, hypoxemia—a reduced concentration of oxygen in the blood—results because the larynx spasms and stays closed. This is called dry drowning. But in her case, it was wet. Her larynx released, and a small amount of water did enter her lungs."

Angie stared at the doc, then turned to Holgersen. "Was she found near water?"

"No water bodies in Ross Bay Cemetery that I know of. Just the ocean across the road at the bottom end."

"It wasn't seawater," the doc said. "The physiological mechanisms that produce hypoxemia in wet drowning are different for freshwater and saltwater. Freshwater in the lungs is pulled into pulmonary circulation by osmosis. Diluting the blood this way leads to the bursting of red blood cells. Potassium levels shoot sky-high and sodium levels plummet, which alters the electrical activity of the heart, usually causing ventricular fibrillation. This can cause cardiac arrest in two to three minutes. Saltwater, on the other hand, is hypertonic to blood. It does the opposite of fresh. Osmosis will instead pull water from the bloodstream into the lungs, thickening the blood. Which requires more work from the heart, leading to cardiac arrest in eight to ten minutes. No matter the saline content of the water, either way, technically, she could still drown," Dr. Finlayson said.

Angie stepped closer to the bed, and her chest tightened. Just a kid. A girl all of maybe fifteen years old. Like Allison Fernyhough. Like Sally Ritter. Except this victim was slightly on the plump side. Her hair had been wiped back from her brow and held traces of dried blood. A loose dressing covered her brow. The skin around her mouth was raw, red.

Angie's attention moved slowly down the body of the girl. Purplish ligature marks marred her neck and her wrists. Her nails had been ripped, a few torn right off. One of her fingers was in a metal cast. Cuts and contusions patterned her forearms. She'd fought. For her life.

"Can I see the wound on her brow?" Angie said quietly.

The doctor hesitated, and then her mouth tightened. Gently, she lifted the dressing.

The wound had been cleaned and sutured. And it was in the perfect shape of a crucifix, the bottom of the cross ending right between the girl's eyebrows.

"Carved into her flesh with a fine-edged blade," said Dr. Finlayson. "Like a razor or scalpel or box cutter. He pressed deep, right down to the brow bone."

Angie stared, feeling hot. Fernyhough and Ritter had also been marked with a cross on their foreheads. Same size and shape as this one—the base of the cross terminating between the eyebrows. But theirs had been drawn onto their foreheads with red permanent marker ink. Not sliced into flesh.

Angie leaned forward to better examine the girl's brow and hairline. Her pulse quickened as she found what she was looking for. "She's had a lock of hair cut off, right at the center of her brow."

"Dundurn was right," Holgersen whispered. "He's back, and he's escalating."

"*If* it's him," she snapped quickly under her breath. "I prefer to delay any speculation until we have hard evidence."

"I'll just keep my ignorant observations to myself, then," he muttered.

"Signs of intercourse?" she said to the doctor. "This bastard leave any calling card?"

"Semen was not immediately apparent, but it was difficult to see because of the bleeding." She met Angie's gaze. "Her genitals were mutilated with a blade." The doctor hesitated. Her eyes burned brighter. "She was circumcised."

Angie felt blood drain from her face. "Meaning?"

"Clitoral hood, clitoral glans, and labia minora have been excised."

Angie's heart began to pound. "We're going to need a detailed forensic exam," she said quickly. "Photographs—"

"We photographically documented the mutilation while in surgery, Detective. We collected the fluids. We've taken blood samples, vaginal swabs, saliva, scrapings from under her nails. Now you need to do your job and find her next of kin before we lose her." Her features tightened as she spoke, and Angie recognized the emotion in the doctor's face for what it was—a quiet and barely controlled fury. It was an emotion Angie, with her own anger management issues, understood all too well. It was the same aggressive energy that drove her. It's what had gotten her into the special victims unit. It's what had her gunning for a promotion to the homicide team. "Promise me," the doc said softly, almost below audible range. "Promise me that you'll nail this bastard."

Angie's mouth turned dry. And it tasted bad—sour from the vodka she'd consumed earlier in the night.

The door behind them slid suddenly open, and a nurse poked her head into the room. "Dr. Finlayson, Dr. Nassim needs an urgent word."

"If you'll excuse me," the doctor said.

Angie and Holgersen nodded, and Dr. Finlayson exited the room.

Angie returned her attention to their Jane Doe. Gently, she touched the girl's hand. Her skin was ice-cold. Angie turned over the hand. Defensive wounds were evident on her palm and forearm—looked like they'd been made with a blade, sharp. The deeper cuts had been sutured.

Who did this to you, sweetheart? How did you end up here? What were you doing in the cemetery on this stormy night?

"What's left of her nails shows a gel manicure," Holgersen said at her side. "Highlights in her hair are recent. She takes care of herself, has pride. And those boots of hers—Francesco Milanos—those'll set you back over a grand a pop."

Angie glanced up at him. "How do you know that?"

"I know stuff, Pallorino."

She studied him. His goatee. The pale, sunken hollows under his cheekbones. Haunted eyes. *How much do we know anybody? How much can we know anyone?*

"Alls I'm saying," he said, "is our girl has some mega-expensive taste. And a means to indulge it. This is not some homeless junkie. Somebody's gonna be missing her."

Angie nodded, turned, and made for the door.

"We going somewhere, Pallorino?" he said, following her out into the hall.

She took her phone from her pocket. As soon as she pushed through the doors exiting the ICU ward, she dialed the station. Tonner still waited down the corridor by the chairs. Angie strode toward the female cop, phone pressed to her ear.

"Pallorino!" Holgersen called behind her. "Hey, wassup with this—where are we going?"

"Cemetery," she snapped over her shoulder. "I want a forensics team out there."

"In the dark?" he said, catching up to her, matching her stride.

"To be ready first light. The longer we wait, the more this weather will destroy any trace evidence." While waiting for her call to connect, she addressed Tonner. "Get those evidence bags to the lab stat," she said. "Log it properly. Watch that chain of custody—" Her call picked up.

She ordered a forensics ident team to meet them at the Ross Bay Cemetery ASAP. She then placed a call to the Metro PD's missing persons unit, leaving a message that gave a description of their Jane Doe, and asking if anyone matching their victim had been reported yet. She then left a message for the sergeant in charge of Metro's high-risk offender unit, asking if any new sex offenders had moved into the area. *If* this was the same perpetrator from her and Hash's crucifix rape cases, he'd been lying low for the past three years, or, possibly, his assaults had gone unreported. When she returned to the station, she'd have this MO run through ViCLAS again—the country's violent crime linkage system—to see if there had been similar attacks elsewhere. She strode toward the elevator as she spoke into her phone, the heels of her biker boots echoing down the sterile hospital corridor. Adrenaline and bottled rage fueled her.

She was going to get him this time. She'd nail this bastard's ass to the wall. She'd do it for Hash. For the doc. For all the Jane Does out there. She jabbed the elevator button.

"So, we're still like partners here, Pallorino?" Holgersen said, coming up beside her.

"What?" The door opened.

She stepped inside, but Holgersen clamped his hand over the door, holding it open. "We still partners, right?"

"You coming, or what?"

He ran his gaze over her outfit, then stepped slowly into the elevator, allowing the doors to slide shut behind him.

He watched the floor buttons lighting up in succession as they descended, and he said, "Your mascara—it's still smudged." A hint of a smile tugged at his mouth. "Alice Cooper lite—suits you. 'Specially for a graveyard visit. Dark side and all that." He turned and looked down at her. "We all have a ghost in the mirror, don't we, Pallorino?"

Angie met his eyes, and a subtle sense of challenge swelled between them.

"Our survivor goes and drowns, then what?" he said. "This shunts over to homicide?"

She said nothing.

"So far as I knows, where death is imminent, it's attempted murder, and hom—"

"This is ours," she snapped. "The doc did not say death was imminent. She said only that the next twenty-four hours would be telling, that's all."

The elevator hummed, then bumped to a standstill.

"This is ours," she said again.

He regarded her for a beat. "Why do I feel working with you is not going to be a win-win situation?"

A bright flare of light turned snowflakes silver, blinding both Angie and Holgersen as they exited the hospital. Then came another flash.

"Shit," said Holgersen, shading his eyes as an elfin woman in a voluminous raincoat emerged from the shadows carrying a large camera. "It's that little pit bull from that tabloid trash of a newspaper."

"Detectives," the woman said, breathless, her cheeks pinked, her face wet from snow under the bill of her black ball cap. "Merry Winston, *City Sun* crime repor—"

"What do you want?" said Holgersen.

She raised her camera lens, clicked again.

"Jesus," Holgersen said, shoving her camera away from his face. "Where do you people get off?"

"You have a young female who was admitted to Saint Jude's—the victim of a violent sexual assault, I understand. She was found nonresponsive in Ross Bay Cemetery earlier tonight. Can you give me any details?"

Angie and Holgersen exchanged a fast glance.

"And you, what? Just happened to be sitting around listening to the scanner at three a.m. on a Sunday morning?" Holgersen said. "You ain't got no life, or what?"

"I drove to Ross Bay, saw the ambulance, saw the paramedics treating a woman, then a Metro PD cruiser arrived, and I saw two uniformed cops talking to one of those ghost tour groups. I got photos. I know the victim was brought here. Now you guys arrive—sex crimes. Do you have an ID? How old is she? What happened? Is the perpetrator still at large? Are others in danger?"

Angie glared at her, then turned and stalked toward her vehicle.

"What is her status?" the woman called after her. "She was alive, from the way the paramedics were working on her! What was she doing in the cemetery? Any suspects? Any words for the new mayor on how another sexual assault will impact the city and his new tough-on-crime mandate?"

Angie reached her Crown Vic, beeped the lock.

Merry Winston came scurrying after them. "Look, I'm going to run with what I do have, so—"

Angie whirled around and took a fast step toward the woman. The reporter fell silent, stepped backward.

"Hold your photos," Angie said quietly, up real close and in the woman's face. "Hold your story, okay? Do that, and . . . we'll give you an exclusive."

"Hold until when?"

"Until we've notified next of kin. At least."

"So you *do* have an ID on her?"

"Yeah," Angie lied.

"Is she Annelise Janssen, the student who's been missing for two weeks?"

"You coming, Holgersen?" Angie got into her vehicle, slammed the door, and palmed off her wet skullcap. Holgersen slid into the passenger seat beside her and swore as he shut his door.

"Freaking ambulance chaser. D'you think she'll hold off on the story?"

"No." Angie engaged the ignition, shoved the car into gear. She pulled out of her parking space.

"Well, our Jane Doe is no match to the photos and description of Annelise Janssen, that's for sures—you could have said that much."

"I don't talk to the press."

"You just told her we had an ID and that she'll get an exclusive."

"To shut her the fuck up."

Holgersen cursed and put his head back as Angie drove, wipers squeaking. After a while he said, "She's kinda cute, though, all that spiky black hair, pale skin, if not for those bad teeth and all."

Angie shot him a glance. "How would you know about spiky hair? She was wearing a ball cap."

"Seen her around."

"Didn't know you had a type, Holgersen."

"Ooh, Pallorino's getting nosy now."

Irritation tightened her hands on the wheel. "Someone's been tipping that woman off. No way she could get the stuff she does without a source on the inside."

"What? It's not *me* who's tipping her off—you heard her. She got the scoop from the scanner."

"I heard *you* say she was listening to a scanner."

CHAPTER 5

Holy Mary, Mother of God, pray for us sinners, now and at the hour of our death. Amen.

One of the uniforms handed Angie a coffee from the 7-Eleven across the street.

"Cream, no sugar," the officer said.

She took it and absently sipped while trying to form a mental picture of what had happened here last night. The day was dawning dark and bitterly cold, low with cloud and mist blowing up from the sea and sifting through the gnarled graveyard trees. Yellow crime scene tape cordoned off the various cemetery entrances and flapped in the icy wind.

The Ross Bay Cemetery, opened in the late eighteen hundreds, had the oldest surviving formal landscape design in the province. Angie knew this from her father. It was, he'd told her, a prime example of a Victorian-era burial ground with its winding carriageways, unusual flora, and intriguing marble, sandstone, and granite monuments, all standing sentinel over the dead.

She'd ordered a covered staging area to be set up right outside the stone perimeter walls. It would serve as a consultation space for the crime scene techs and other personnel, and for their equipment.

She'd also established a secure temporary storage area for any evidence that might be found, in accordance with chain of custody protocol. She was the primary investigator on this case, and she was working fast to put her stamp on this. As Holgersen had so succinctly noted, this could turn into a full-blown homicide investigation, and if so, she was going to push to stay on the case.

Angie had called her sergeant in charge of the sex crimes unit, Matthew Vedder, at his home, and she'd given him the rundown. He'd okayed her request for overtime if necessary, and allowed her as many uniformed officers as she might need. He wanted a full briefing when she returned to the station in a few hours. Already she'd sent patrol cops out with questionnaires to start canvassing residents who lived adjacent to the cemetery. Most of the stores in the shopping complex across the street behind her were still closed, but she'd have officers in there as soon as they opened. Depending on their business hours, someone might have seen something last night. A person behaving oddly. A vehicle. A man carrying a heavy load. Perhaps someone heard something—a woman's screams. She also had a uniform inquiring about the closed-circuit surveillance system at the 7-Eleven. She'd noted a camera outside the store, and there was a chance it had picked up something along this road.

Holgersen was on his phone with the hospital, checking on their Jane Doe's condition. He killed his call and came over.

"Not looking good," he said. "Still unconscious and vitals going downhill."

Damn. She didn't want Jane Doe to die yet. Not until she had her claws firmly into this case.

"And still no ID?" she said.

"Nah. No active missing persons cases match, either, and no new reports have come through. Her prints and DNA are not going to be much use unless she's in the system. Same with dental records—pretty damn useless unless yous gots something to match them with."

40

"It's still early," she said. "Parents, friends, might not have noticed her absence yet. By the time schools open and the day gets under way, we could start getting calls."

"Or when news of our mutilated, comatose cemetery girl hits the front page of the *City Sun*."

She glanced sharply up at him, then checked her watch, urgency twisting through her. One of the forensics techs approached them. "We've established a path of entry," he said. "You ready for a walk-through?"

"Let's do it." She handed her unfinished coffee to a uniform, tugged on crime scene booties, and turned her collar up against the cold. They stepped out from under the makeshift cover and she walked alongside Holgersen into the teeth of the frigid salt wind, grateful that she lived downtown and that she'd managed to swing by her apartment for a change of clothing. She'd also quickly scrubbed off her makeup.

Constable Hickey—the patrol officer who'd responded with Tonner—met them at the stone entrance. He stood shivering in his waterproof poncho, which flapped in the wind. He wore a plastic cover over his hat. The young man had been out in the cold most of the night. Angie had already interviewed him, as well as the EMTs. The ghost walkers and their tour guide, Edwin Liszt, would be coming into the station later.

They signed the crime scene sheet offered to them by a patrol officer and entered the cemetery grounds, Hickey and the tech leading them down the path. A fine layer of snow crunched beneath their covered boots. They passed white marble cherubs on plinths, the milky eyes of the statues seemingly tracking their progress among the gravestones.

"At least the precip is holding off, for now," Hickey said, ducking as pinecone debris was flung at him in the wind.

"Global warming," said the tech. "There'll be more and more like it. Increasingly violent weather."

"Thought the globe was supposed to be getting warmer, not *colder* and stormier."

The tech shrugged.

"You think our perp chose last night because of the storm?" Holgersen said. "Because he could use it to hide? Because everyone was locked up cozy indoors?"

Angie did not reply. Instead, she stilled a moment, trying to breathe it all in—the dark, wet tombstones. A mausoleum to her right. Dead flowers, some in plastic cones, poking through the layer of snow on the interment plots. A black stone angel peered down at her, wings hanging like a vulture. The trees around them were gnarled and twisted giants, some coniferous, other deciduous, their bare branches draped with green witch's hair. With several entrances to this cemetery, Jane Doe's attacker could have come in from several directions.

"Wouldn't catch me doing no ghost tour in this crap," Holgersen said, turning in a slow circle beside her, following her gaze. "When did the city last have a snowstorm like this one anyway?"

"It's because the wet front coming in is clashing with the colder air from the arctic outflow that's been locked over us since late November," she said quietly. "The snow won't last long now as the warmer front moves in."

Officer Hickey and the tech started back down the path, taking them toward the twisted, leafless hedge of trees that bounded Dallas Road and the ocean below. Here the wind was icier, angrier, and the sound of waves crashing in Ross Bay grew loud. Angie's coat snapped sharply about her calves. Her eyes watered in the cold. Her thoughts turned again to the little girl in pink she'd seen on that road below last night. An involuntary shiver chased through her.

"This is where Constable Tonner and I found the paramedics working on her," Hickey said, stopping in front of a grave site. "The ghost tour group had come down via that entrance." He pointed. "And stumbled across our vic lying here."

The ground was a slushy mess, tracked out with prints and pinked with blood. Forensic ident personnel in white Tyvek jumpsuits had started working the area around the interment plot, scraping back snow, searching for trace evidence, photographing and sketching the scene.

The tech said, "The scene was compromised by the paramedics, the ghost group, the first responding officers, a *City Sun* photographer who apparently arrived later—we'll be lucky if we find anything uncontaminated."

Angie's gaze tracked up from the bloody slush on the ground to the granite pedestal upon which a large stone statue had been mounted. She read the inscription on the pedestal below the statue.

Mary Brown, 1889–1940.
Though I walk through the valley of the shadow of death,
I will fear no evil,
for you are with me.

Her attention moved from the epitaph and up to the statue itself. The blank stone eyes of the mother of God gazed sightlessly down at the ground where the victim had lain. Sculpted robes draped her body, and she held her arms out slightly at her sides, palms up. Suppliant. Angie's blood turned cold at the symbolism.

"Our circumcised Jane Doe was left at the feet of the Virgin Mary," she said softly. Turning to Hickey, she said, "How exactly was she lying?"

"On her back, face up," Hickey said. "Her head was there, right at the base of the pedestal, and her arms were folded over her breasts, one hand atop the other, like this." He placed his hands over his heart.

As if in prayer . . .

"And her legs were splayed open, displaying her bloodied crotch." He cleared his throat. "She was drenched. And the snow was starting to settle on her. How she survived, I . . . I don't know." He coughed and cleared his throat again.

"She was posed," Holgersen whispered, staring at the bloodied snow.

A noise like a gunshot cracked behind them. They all jumped and spun around. A tree branch came crashing down in the wind, bits of bark and moss exploding off it as it hit a gravestone and then tumbled to the snowy ground.

"Shit," Holgersen said, shaken.

Hickey looked white. He was shivering harder.

"And there are no ponds or anything nearby?" Angie said, her attention moving from the broken branch back to the grounds.

"Negative," said Hickey.

"So she had to have been immersed in freshwater somewhere else, then brought here, where he carefully arranged her as if in prayer at the stone feet of the virgin mother of God." Angie's mind went to the Ritter and Fernyhough cases, the crucifixes that had been drawn onto their foreheads after they'd been sexually assaulted by a masked assailant. In both cases the girls had been drunk, and they were vulnerable because of it. They'd both left social gatherings solo. Both had been attacked from behind, smashed down into the ground, and raped facedown, a knife held to their throats, before receiving blows to the head. Both remembered their assailant saying the same words as he fisted their long hair with a gloved hand and held his blade to their throats.

Do you reject Satan, father of sin and prince of darkness?

Do you reject Satan and all his works . . .

He'd forced them to say *I do . . .* before he penetrated them from behind.

She and Hash had discovered that those exact words formed part of the Catholic church's baptism rite. The girls had both come around to discover a red crucifix had been drawn on their brows with a permanent marker. And a lock of hair had been snipped from each of their heads.

Those words, the crucifix on their brows, the missing hair—it had all been holdback evidence, so the similarities between those sexual assaults and this new one was unlikely to be the work of a copycat.

He was back—it was her guy. The guy she and Hash had been after. She felt it in her bones.

Angie raised two fingers and touched them to her brow. "In the name of the Father"—she lowered her fingers, touched her sternum—"and the Son"—she touched her left shoulder, then right—"and the Holy Ghost," she said quietly, then turned to Holgersen. "He immersed her in water, and he marked her with the sign of a cross. He assaulted her, then he defeminized, desexualized her, and posed her here to die under the watch of the Virgin Mary. This is not rape. It's ritual—he baptized her."

The others stared at Angie.

The wind howled suddenly, switching direction. Ice pellets began to spit from the sky.

"Fucking freak," whispered Holgersen. "We gots us a Baptist. And this . . . this sure as hell ain't this guy's first rodeo. He's done it before, and he's going to do it again."

CHAPTER 6

"Still no change in our Janie Doe's condition," Holgersen said, killing his second call to the hospital. "And still no ID."

Angie's fists tightened on the wheel as she took a corner on Fairmont. She was driving them to the station, and adrenaline hummed through her blood. She itched to get her hands back onto the case binders for Fernyhough and Ritter. Their Jane Doe just had to hang on long enough for her to get her teeth fully into this, and the sooner they obtained an ID, the better, because without knowing who she was, they were hamstrung in their investigative approaches.

One of the most significant factors in this kind of attack was victimology—what was Jane Doe's personality, where did she go to school, did she have a job, hobbies, where did she live? The bottom line was: What had she been doing at the time of her attack? What had brought her into the orbit of her assailant?

"So, wanna wager how long it takes for this to go to homicide?" Holgersen said. "Sexually motivated, yeah, but our perp leaving our vic there like that—he *intended* to kill her. That's attempted homicide. Perhaps he even thought she was dead already. And she got lucky."

"Lucky my ass." She shot him a hot glare. "I want this case. Don't fuck it up for me."

"Crap, Pallorino. We both want it, okay? I'ms just saying—"

"I want this for Hash, okay? It always bugged him to hell that we never solved those serial rapes. If this guy is the same suspect as in those other cases—"

"Ooooh, I get it—it's personal." He turned to look out the window. "Dangerous, Pallorino," he said quietly. "Verrrry dangerous. When things get personal, you lose objectivity."

Her jaw tightened. She pressed down on the accelerator.

"Pull over," he said suddenly. "Right over there, that mall."

"*What?* Why?"

"I need a coffee. A decent one."

"Are you *serious*?"

"I've been up, since, like the whole night, so yeah, I need caffeine."

"You always like this?"

"And you?"

Angie cursed and swerved into the parking lot of a small strip mall that boasted a Starbucks on the far corner. "Make it fast," she said. "Vedder's waiting."

As Holgersen loped his gangly way over to the coffee shop, Angie fisted the wheel. With shock she realized she was trembling slightly, her whole body. She put her head back against the headrest and closed her eyes a moment, trying to steady her breathing. Instead, a pulsing red image pounded into her brain—her rocking naked on Mr. Big D. The rhythmic boom of the bass from the club. The pulse of red light behind the drapes . . . then suddenly a little girl in pink running through mist as her car careered down onto her. Angie's eyes snapped open, her breaths coming short and fast.

Not good, not good. Stay focused . . . She stared at the coffee shop door, impatient for Holgersen to exit. Wind gusted. Sleet started ticking again on the windshield. Suddenly she saw him inside, through the misted window, moving back and forth. He appeared to be talking on his cell phone. And that's when she noticed his cell phone lying on the passenger seat beside her.

She frowned. Had he wanted her to stop so he could make some kind of urgent call? On a private phone?

Holgersen exited the Starbucks, returning to the vehicle with two cups and a brown bag. He got in, placed the cups in the holders, then fished into his bag. The scent of food and coffee filled the vehicle. "Here," he said, holding something out to her.

"What's that?" she said.

"Egg and bacon on an English muffin. Figured you might also be hungry."

Her stomach clenched. She took it from him, and he unwrapped his own breakfast sandwich and bit into it.

"You can go—you can drive now," he mumbled around his mouthful as he reached for his coffee.

She studied his face, trying to read him.

He paused chewing. "What? You vegetarian? Vegan? Gluten intolerant?"

"Who did you phone inside there?"

He stilled his chewing, and slowly his eyes narrowed. He swallowed, cleared his throat, and said, "I didn't phone nobody. Left my cell in the car."

She continued to hold his gaze.

"Besides, Pallorino, even if I did, it's none of your fucking business. I got a life, even if you don't."

She swore softly, dumped her wrapped sandwich onto the dash, engaged the ignition, and accelerated out of the parking lot, making him spill his coffee as she swerved into the street.

"Is this what you did to the other guy?" he snapped as he tried to dab up the spill on his jeans with a paper napkin.

"What other guy?"

"Your previous partner—how long did he last with yous? Alls of three months?"

"He didn't have what it took. Not my fault."

"So, he wasn't Hashowsky. I *get* it, Angie."

"That's Pallorino to you."

"Yeah, yeah, okay, Pall-or-eee-no." He turned to look out the window, sipped his coffee, then said, very quietly, "I intend to keep this job, Pallorino. I'm gonna make sergeant someday—okay? I got stayin' power your other dude didn't have. So pace yourself."

CHAPTER 7

James Maddocks shook out his umbrella and inserted it into the holder by the door of the Blue Badger Bakery along with all the other wet umbrellas. They'd finally gotten seats. The place was choked to the gills, and the line outside was still growing despite the blustery weather.

Their server, wearing a funky short skirt and long red boots, led them to a tiny table with chairs that were not designed to accommodate the frame of someone Maddocks's size. Outside the window, tables and chairs on the wooden deck glistened wet and empty. Beyond the deck, gunmetal-gray water rippled with wind.

Ginny had insisted on brunch, and she'd insisted on the Badger. *It's the cool thing to do in Victoria, Dad . . . they make a great eggs benny.* Maddocks could think of a lot of "cooler" things to do with Ginny that did not involve standing in a line outside in gusting wind and sleet for half an hour. Or plunking down a fortune for eggs he could fry up himself in his yacht galley. These places didn't take reservations, either. What was so cool about eggs benny? But his goal in moving here was all about Ginny and trying to salvage what he had left of a family. Maddocks wanted a second chance with his daughter before he lost her altogether, so when she'd been accepted at the University of Victoria, he'd started looking for a job here, too.

Ginny shucked off her coat and draped it over the back of her chair before sitting. Maddocks shrugged out of his own gear, wondering if Jack-O needed to pee. The old dog had been in the car for almost an hour already. As he hung his coat over his chair and seated himself, he noticed ink poking out of his daughter's T-shirt.

"Is that a tattoo?" he said.

Her eyes flared up to meet his. "So what if it is?"

"When did you get that one?"

"Mom doesn't mind. I don't see why you should. Everyone has them."

He wasn't a prude. He was okay with tats. Just not indelible ink on his baby girl.

"You might like having it now," he said, "but in years to come—"

"Dad."

He inhaled, and they perused the menu in silence while chatter rose from the tables around them. Maddocks was almost bumping elbows with the guy seated beside them. He dutifully ordered the ranch benny with bacon and sausage. Ginny went for the low-carb option, sans bagel. He knew better than to ask. His kid had long struggled with her weight, although he thought she looked beautiful. Their server brought coffee.

"How's school?" he said as the server left.

"Fine."

He poured cream into his mug, stirred. Ginny sipped hers straight. He wondered how long she'd been taking her coffee unsweetened and black, and whether it was part of her perpetual attempt to slim down. Guilt feathered into him. He'd been realizing since he moved here just how little he did actually know about his daughter, how much he'd missed of her childhood, her growing up.

51

"Want to tell me about the new courses?"

She blew out air.

"I'm trying, Ginn. Cut me a break."

She moved a fall of dark hair back off her face. "It's . . . just so obvious, Dad. So fake."

"Hey, I'm here, aren't I?" He smiled. "How many old dads do you see standing in that line out there in the sleet?"

Her lips curved in spite of herself. "Okay. You win."

Baby steps. He was going to win this with baby steps. It wouldn't be simple—his daughter was still so full of old triggers and her mother's poison—but he was here. He was showing up. And yeah, a shrink might have a field day with him and all his reasons for relocating, including the battered old yacht he'd bought and was trying to renovate, and in which he lived at the West Bay Marina. An analyst would probably also find meaning in the fact that he couldn't look at, let alone sign, those divorce papers his wife's lawyer had sent him. But for now he'd secured a job locally—no mean feat since it was a highly coveted position. He started tomorrow.

This was going to work. He was going to pull it all back together. Sort of.

While they waited for the food, which was taking forever, Ginny prattled on about her new semester and how she wanted to eventually get into law. He was proud of her, and he told her so. And she warmed further, telling him about the college choir she'd recently joined, how they sang on Thursday nights at the Catholic cathedral downtown with its amazing acoustics and stained glass, and how they'd all gone out after a practice to a karaoke club downtown last Thursday. "It's actually a gay bar," she said. "Owned by a gay couple."

Maddocks nodded and finished the last of his coffee. As much as Ginny was relaxing into her conversation with him, there remained an underlying and subtle need in her to provoke her father. He was not taking the bait.

"Our singers rocked the place," she said. "We got standing ovations. And then I stayed on by myself, after the group had all left, because I still wanted to perform a solo. I sang that one from *Les Miz*. You know, the one where—"

"Me? Know anything from a musical?" He laughed.

She fell silent. And he knew she was thinking of her mother's new prick of a boyfriend, who apparently loved opera. She looked down and picked at her napkin. Under the table he fiddled with his wedding ring, which he wore mostly for Ginn, to give her the idea of hope, show her that he was trying to hold on to some half-baked notion of family and long-ago promises.

"How did you get home from the karaoke club, then, if you were on your own?"

She shrugged. "Walked. It's only, like, five blocks."

"What time was that?"

Her gaze darted up, and defiance crackled back into her eyes. Eyes so like his own. Dark blue against her pale skin. His Welsh heritage showing in his progeny. His chest tightened with a protective surge, the rawness of a father's love.

"It's a totally safe city, Dad."

"No it's not. No city is 'totally safe,' Ginny."

"Compared to Surrey, or the downtown east side of Vancouver, it is."

"I know exactly what goes on in this city. It's why I have a job."

"That's the trouble with your job, you know that? You see so much bad shit—you constantly see such an ugly, ugly side of humanity that you forget there's even goodness and kindness in people."

"Ginny—"

"I don't care what you say. You think everyone is bad. You never laughed at home. You never just enjoyed a weekend with me and Mom. Never went hiking or camping or just had the neighbors around for a backyard barbecue. *Those* were the things Mom wanted from you. That *I* needed from you. You barely even smiled at me when you did actually come home—"

His cell buzzed in his pocket. She fell silent, stared at him. It buzzed again. He ignored it. The waitress was coming over with their plates of food. The call kicked to voicemail. And almost immediately his cell started to buzz again.

He removed it from his pocket, checked the caller ID. His new boss. He frowned. He wasn't due to start until Monday morning.

"I need to take this," he said softly.

Ginny glowered at him.

"Maddocks," he said quietly into his phone.

"It's Jack Buziak," came the voice. "Sorry to disturb your Sunday, but homicide has just caught a case, and it has the potential to blow politically, considering the new mayor-elect's posturing. I'd like you as lead on this one from the get-go."

He glanced at his daughter. She was watching him intently. "What have you got?" Maddocks said.

"Floater. In the Gorge under the Johnson Street Bridge. Looks like a female. They're pulling her out now—coroner, pathologist, and indent crew is on scene with Detective Harvey Leo. We've got uniforms securing the area—" A pause as Buziak spoke to someone else, then came back on line. "Looks like our DB has been in seawater for some time. There's speculation that she could be the missing UVic student, Annelise Janssen. Can you get down there? Can I let Leo know to expect you? I've told him you're the primary on this."

The food arrived. "Ranch benny?" the waitress said, holding the heavy white plates. Maddocks turned his back to her slightly, lowering his voice further. "Where exactly?"

"Johnson Street Wharf, right under the bridge off Wharf Street."

"Be there in ten."

"You're not going to leave, are you?" Ginny said as he killed the call.

"Ginn. I . . . I'm sorry. We can do this again some other time."

The waitress was still standing there. "Ranch benny," she said, louder.

"Why don't you stay, finish your breakfast—"

"Forget it." Ginny turned to the waitress. "Take it away. We don't want it."

"Would . . . you like me to bag it for you?" the server said.

"No," Ginny snapped, pushing her chair back, bumping the woman seated behind her. She grabbed her coat. "This—see? *This* is why Mom couldn't stand it. Whenever she tried to make family time, someone went and got themselves murdered. It's your fault that Peter is in her life—your fault she's taken a boyfriend. You care more about dead people than your own family!"

The patrons around them fell quiet.

She punched her arms into her jacket, yanked her sling bag over her shoulder, and made for the door. She shoved through it. Maddocks quickly dumped a wad of cash on the table, grabbed his coat, and hurried outside after her.

"Ginny!" he called. "I'll give you a ride—"

"I don't want a ride. I'm going to see a friend."

He watched his daughter stride up the sidewalk slick with dead leaves. The wind tore at her coat. She rounded the corner where a lamp standard was still plastered with an old election poster. He inhaled deeply, stuffed his hands into his own coat pockets, and made for his vehicle.

Maddocks unlocked the car and opened the driver's side door. The stench of dog pee was instant.

"Oh, Jack-O, what in the hell?"

The old Jack Russell sleeping on the backseat lifted his head and stared benignly at him, the scar from where his back leg had been amputated still pink from a more-recent second operation. The dog had gone and peed on the newspaper lying on the floor of the front passenger side. Maddocks swore, climbed into his vehicle, and wound down the windows in spite of the sleet and cold. He didn't have time to find a place to dispose of the wet newspaper right now. He put his car into reverse. "You couldn't have waited another second or two, Jack-O boy?"

The dog gave a little sigh, closed his eyes, and went back to sleep on his blanket.

And Maddocks drove to a murder.

CHAPTER 8

The Metro PD sex crimes unit operated out of a large cubicle that had been partitioned into four smaller work areas through the arrangement of metal desks. Adjustable shelving units around the periphery of their cubicle housed their case binders and files. Angie was one of the sixteen detectives in sex crimes, and they were divided into teams of four. The detectives, along with a training officer, a ViCLAS coordinator, an analyst, and two project assistants, worked under Sergeant Matt Vedder, whose glass-walled office was one of several in a corridor that ran down the sides of the various bullpens.

The place was empty when Angie entered her work area. Dundurn and Smith—the other two in her and Holgersen's team of four—had punched out from their night shift. She hung up her coat, palmed off her wet hat, tossed it onto her desk, and made straight for the shelf with the Fernyhough and Ritter case files. She located the file box, hefted it onto her desk, and opened it.

"Pallorino!"

She glanced up. Sarge Vedder, her superior, was standing in his office doorway, a newspaper in his hand.

"Where's Holgersen?" he said.

"Washroom or having a smoke—don't know."

"Get in here," he said with a jerk of his head. "Come catch me up."

She abandoned the files and followed Vedder into his glass-walled office. He closed the door behind them, slapped a copy of the *City Sun* onto his desk.

"You just caught this case last night. It's not even nine thirty a.m., and you're all over the front page. I already have Fitz on my back, and Singh is on his, going all the way up the chain of command to Chief Gunnar. You talked to the *Sun*?"

Angie's gaze dropped to the paper on Vedder's desk. Across the top of page one a big, black, blocky headline blared:

Violent Sexual Assault in Ross Bay Cemetery—
Young Woman Left in Coma

Beneath the headline was a photo of the two paramedics wheeling their Jane Doe into the back of an ambulance. Beside it was another image—her and Holgersen exiting Saint Jude's, she in her black wool cap, hair pulled back, face tight and complexion ghost-white in the light of the harsh flash. Her mascara-smudged eyes and overly red lips gave her an aura of a haunted addict. Holgersen fared no better—looking just as much a narc user with his hollow cheeks, sharp bones, mad eyes. She snatched up the tabloid and skimmed through the story.

Metro sex crimes detectives have identified the victim and are notifying next of kin. No word yet on whether the woman could be Annelise Janssen—a UVic student and daughter of prominent Victoria industrialist Steve Janssen. The student mysteriously vanished from campus a fortnight ago . . . adding to the growing crime statistics that new mayor-elect Jack Killion has vowed to stem . . .

"You're kidding me?" She looked up from the paper. "She's dragging Killion into this?"

"The rest of the city media will have picked the story up and be running wild with it within the hour. Who told this reporter it was a sexual assault anyway?"

"She appears to be in possession of a scanner. She went to the cemetery and saw for herself. Perhaps she spoke to one of the EMTs, someone at the hospital—I don't know."

Vedder heaved out a sigh and dragged his hand over hair that had started to thin over the last six months. "Okay, so what have you got, what do you need? Who is the victim?"

"We don't have an ID on her yet."

"So what's this reporter saying, then? Did you tell her that she'd been identified?"

"I didn't deny it." Angie tossed the paper back onto his desk.

He swore. "Way to notify next of kin, Pallorino. This is somebody's kid. Somebody's sibling—"

"Like I don't know that," she snapped.

"And let me tell you something else." He jabbed his fingers on the photo of her and Holgersen. "You can bet your ass that Gunnar isn't too happy about seeing *your* face on the front pages again—I sure as hell am not. You're becoming like the poster child for things gone wrong with Metro PD, *my* unit in particular."

Anger stabbed fast through her. She clenched her jaw. "Don't. Don't you dare, Vedder. What happened with Hash—that was not my fault. I was cleared in—"

"Okay, okay." He raised both palms in surrender. "You're right. I'm sorry." He cursed again and smoothed his palm over his hair once more before turning to face his window. He stood in silence for a moment, his back to her, watching the sleet against the panes. Tension shimmered between them. Angie's heart thumped. Her neck was wire taut.

"All due respect, sir," she said quietly, straining for calm, "I didn't run this story. That woman shanghaied us outside the hospital. I frankly don't see that it's such a big deal, anyway. Half the stuff in that piece of tabloid trash is either fabricated, slanted, or unsubstantiated, and people know it."

He nodded slowly, turned. His eyes met hers. "Apologies, Angie," he said, softening his voice. "We all miss Hash. Tensions . . . are just running high right now. Everyone's expecting Gunnar's head to roll, and who knows who's going with him—could be me next." He paused. "You doing okay? Holgersen working out?"

"It's early yet."

"He's good. Make it work."

She inhaled. "Yeah."

"So what've you all got? Catch me up."

"The cemetery assault could be linked to the old Fernyhough and Ritter cases." She quickly gave him a rundown, hitting at the similarities, but before she could finish, a knock sounded on the door.

"Come in," Vedder called.

The door opened. It was one of the uniforms. "We got Jane Doe's mother," the cop said, excitement hot in his eyes. "She's at Saint Jude's right now. Lorna Drummond. She saw the newspaper headlines this morning and rushed right over, hysterical because her kid hadn't come home from her Saturday night shift at the bakery."

Way to inform next of kin, Merry Winston . . .

"What bakery?" Angie said, voice clipped.

"Blue Badger. Other side of Johnson Street Bridge. Staff say the kid never showed up for work and never answered her cell when they called to check on her."

Angie pushed quickly past the uniform and exited Vedder's office. "Holgersen!" she yelled out over the cubicle partitions as she grabbed her coat from the hook near her desk. "Where in the hell's Holgersen?" she called out loudly as she punched her arms into her sleeves and grabbed her sling bag.

"He was outside having a smoke," came a male voice from the other side of a cubicle.

Dammit. She checked her watch, turned to the uniform. "If you see him, tell him to meet me at Saint Jude's."

She left the building without her partner. As she got into her vehicle her phone rang. She answered it on the hands-free as she put her car into gear.

"Pallorino," she barked, reversing.

"Angie?"

Her father. Shit. She'd forgotten—they were going to move the rest of her mom's things today. She was supposed to have been there an hour ago.

"Dad, I . . . I can't make it today, I really can't. Just landed a big case—"

"Right, right," he said. "I didn't think you would come. Running. Always running from something, Angie."

He hung up.

Her eyes burned as she pulled into the street.

CHAPTER 9

Maddocks drew up to the police barriers and wound down his window.

Metro PD cruisers lined the length of Wharf Street, bar lights flashing. Sleet was coming down hard as cops in bright-yellow visi jackets diverted traffic away from the waterfront and up into town. A crowd of onlookers was gathering along the barricades.

He showed the patrol officer his new Metro PD badge, which he'd picked up when he'd signed the official HR paperwork last week. Jack-O barked. The officer peered inside at the dog.

"New K-9 reporting for duty, sir?"

"Mascot. 'Scuse the pee smell."

The officer gave an unsure smile, stepped back, and moved the barrier aside. "Down that way, sir." He pointed. "That small lot just before the Johnson Street turnoff—it's been cordoned off for crime scene personnel. The wharf access is down the embankment behind those brick buildings."

At the parking lot barricade, Maddocks flashed his badge again, and another officer entered his name into a crime scene log. He parked behind a forensics van and glanced at Jack-O.

"You be good now. I'll come and let you out in a bit, okay? Tomorrow you'll have a sitter."

No response.

Leaving the windows open slightly for the animal, Maddocks dug into his glove box for a ball cap—he'd forgotten his umbrella in the stand at the Blue Badger. He tugged on the cap, exited his vehicle. Wind tore instantly at his coat. Sleet slashed cold against his cheeks. He walked past a dark sedan with a CORONER ON DUTY sign displayed on the dash alongside an open box of half-eaten Tim Bits—fried doughnut holes. Breakfast of champions. They reminded him he hadn't eaten. So much for the ranch benny and a date with his kid.

He made his way around the brick buildings. They were abandoned—boarded-up windows, moss smothering the walls, graffiti, big FOR LEASE signs. Detritus of the homeless littered the recessed doorways—broken glass, an empty vodka bottle, beer cans, cigarette stumps, cardboard, a piece of unidentifiable clothing.

He paused a moment in front of the buildings, absorbing the scene in the choppy Gorge waters below. Two Metro fire-rescue vessels—bright yellow with rigid black hulls—bobbed on the far side of an L-shaped dock that jutted out into the water. Officers in all-weather gear and ball caps hung over the gunwales, fishing for something with grappling hooks. Another officer appeared to be working a line that fed into the water—he had a dive partner down there, Maddocks guessed. On the shore side of the dock, logs jostled in a boom floating upon calmer water.

The big blue Johnson Street Bridge loomed over the whole scene like an iron leviathan rising into the mist. Traffic hummed and clunked over it.

A tall, slender male and a squat woman—both in black jackets marked *Coroner*—stood on the dock, also wearing ball caps against the sleet, which was now turning to heavy, gelatinous rain. Beside them hunkered a sturdy man, his hands in his coat pockets, a shock of white hair atop a square head. Detective Harvey Leo, Maddocks figured.

The grass growing on the bank that sloped steeply to the water was slick underfoot as Maddocks started to make his way down to the water's edge. A foghorn sounded. A large vessel piled high with scrap metal churned under the bridge, sending a succession of swells surging toward the dock. The dock swayed as the swells hit, and the logs in the boom rolled and bumped against one another. Water slapped along the shore.

"Jesus fuck!" the white-haired man bellowed, gesticulating at the scrap vessel. "Can someone get a patrol boat out into the Gorge and stop that goddamn marine traffic! We almost had her—now she's been pushed under again." He turned and stared at Maddocks as he approached along the dock.

As Maddocks reached them, the man said, "So, you're the new guy from the horsemen?"

"Horsemen?" Maddocks feigned ignorance at the dig as he continued to survey the scene.

"Mounties—Mounted Police, that little blue horse logo on the sides of your cruisers?"

"Right. I'm Sergeant James Maddocks." He extended his hand. "You must be Harvey Leo?"

The older cop assessed him for a moment with clear blue eyes. Slowly, he reached out and accepted Maddocks's hand.

"The one and only," he said. His skin was cold, rough. Iron grip and a craggy face to match.

"This here is Charlie Alphonse—city coroner." Leo gestured toward the tall skinny guy. "And pathologist, Barb O'Hagan. We figured we'd get O'Hagan down here personally for this one."

Alphonse was a lanky man with a small head, beaked nose. O'Hagan looked to be in her late sixties, built like a little barrel, short with coarse salt-and-pepper hair sticking out of her ball cap. Bright brown eyes. Maddocks exchanged greetings with them.

"What've we got?" he said, turning to watch the rescue vessels as they started to come around the dock and into the calmer waters on the shore side where the log boom surged on the new swells made by the scrap vessel.

"Our floater came up far side of the pier, then just as they'd almost snagged her with those hooks, a tug went by, sending a bunch of waves that shoved her back below the surface. Had to call in a diver. Now that scrap boat has washed her under the dock and through to the calm side. We think she's somewhere beneath that boom of logs now. Tide's pushing in hard, too." Maddocks could see it from the ripples and chop in the channel.

"You certain it's a female?"

"Negative. Our DB was floating facedown, but the hair was long. Brunette. Just assuming she's female," Leo said, watching the dive tender feeding his line into the gunmetal-gray water near the rolling logs. "Dangerous shit that, diving under a boom. Worse than diving under ice. Need a tandem team with one guy working the surface, or the diver could come up inside the confines of a boom—those agitating logs would crush him."

"Probably several feet of silt and other detritus at the bottom, too," Alphonse said as his phone rang. "'Scuse me." He walked back along the dock and stopped under the protective cover of the bridge to take his call. After a brief conversation, he called out, "Barb! Got a vehicle pileup on the Malahat because of the snow at that elevation. Multiple fatalities—I need to get out there, stat. Can you handle this from here?"

"Go. We're good," she called back.

Maddocks got down onto his hands and knees and peered under the dock. Pylons were encrusted with slimy muck, mussels, and oysters. Sharp edges.

"They say the Gorge is clean enough to swim in now," O'Hagan said, watching him.

"My ass," said Leo. "Sewage is still pumped raw out to sea. How d'you know the currents and tide aren't washing it all back into the Gorge? Like it probably washed this floater here in."

Maddocks came to his feet. He moved to the outer edge of the dock and visually scanned the surrounding area. The city lay behind him. The harbor with its marinas and float plane terminal stretched to his left, and the bridge and kayak club were situated at his right. Across the water apartments rose into the dense mist.

"So, not only did you jump the homicide queue, I hear Buziak wants you as the lead on this," Leo said, coming to stand beside him.

"Didn't know there was a queue," Maddocks said, his gaze tracking up the bridge toward the massive counterweight in the sky.

"At least six guys at the station champing at the bit to get that slot in homicide, all locals who know this city like the backs of their hairy ol' hands. Plus a female detective in sex crimes who's been rattling at the doors, like, forever."

Little did they know.

This was not a career jump for him. It wasn't even a lateral move. Logistically he should be moving up, managing things from behind a desk. He'd been pretty much Buziak's equivalent back on the mainland. But he'd taken this job to be near Ginny. To make a break. To get away from the boyfriend issue with his wife, the messy divorce proceedings. To get down and dirty in the trenches. Maybe it was avoidance or plain self-distraction. Whatever, he *needed* this.

Barb O'Hagan cut in. "Not that *she* stands a chance with all you union deadwood plugging up the place, sitting there at your desks, shaving pencils, solving your daily jumbles, drinking bad coffee, and scratching your fat butts, eh, Leo?"

Leo snorted and tilted his head toward the squat little pathologist. "Crusty old morgue doc here can talk. When *you* up for retirement, anyway, Barb?"

"And what would you do without me to solve your murders for you, Detective? I figure Pallorino would whip your fat asses if she got half a chance."

"Yeah, right. She's not a team player, okay? She's a . . . a misanthrope, a misandrist. It's why you two get along so well, now, isn't it? Barb?"

"Big words, Leo, big words. You looked those up for your daily jumble this morning?"

Maddocks mentally filed the tone of their banter. This pair was going to be interesting. Or trouble. He walked toward the bridge, looked up. It was maybe nine meters high on the west side, but more than twenty on the huge concrete counterweight side. "Who called it in?"

"Homeless guy camping on the bank under the bridge," Leo said. "He saw the floater, went berserkers, alerting the bridge operator who works way up in that box there." He pointed. "Operator's in charge of raising the bridge for marine traffic. We got his statement and one from the homeless wingnut. Got him in a vehicle up in the lot."

"Jumper, you think?"

"Not a chance in hell. She's trussed up like a sausage in plastic— wait till you see this one."

"Yo!" A sharp whistle issued from one of the officers on the vessels. "We got her! Diver's bringing her up!"

They all swung around to watch the boat with the dive team maneuver around the logs, the tender carefully reading his buddy's line. A soft wet mist shrouded the water. The sleet doubled down as rain. Yet another vessel chugged along the marine channel under the bridge, sending a bigger surge and more waves slapping and chuckling under the dock. The logs rolled and bumped together.

"Fucking idiots!" yelled Leo. "Where's that backup harbor unit? Can't they stop these damn things? Going to kill our diver down here."

The diver's neoprene-covered head suddenly emerged outside of the boom in a smooth, mercurial swell of gray water, his goggles glistening. He brought a plastic-shrouded shape up beside him, and he started to swim it toward the dock. Maddocks, O'Hagan, and Leo went to the edge. Silence befell them. Their floater was still facedown. She surged and rolled in the swells, hair undulating with seaweed around her head. As the diver brought her closer, they could see two parallel striations— deep gashes—across the back of the victim's skull, as if her head had been hacked open with an axe. From the neck down she was bound in what looked like a thick polyethylene tarp, opaque. Wound tight with rope. Another long piece of rope attached to her neck floated several meters out into the water.

"You weren't kidding when you said she's been trussed up like a sausage," Maddocks said quietly as he snapped on latex gloves. He crouched down at the edge of the dock as the diver brought her near. O'Hagan put on her own gloves, squatting down beside him. Leo stood slightly to the side, watching, his hands firmly in his pockets. A chill washed through Maddocks as he got a closer look at their floater.

Under that plastic sheeting she was naked, her skin fish-belly white, like something alien. A grub.

"Get that photographer down here," Maddocks said to Leo, who in turn bellowed for the guy. The photographer, who'd been sheltering under cover of the bridge, came running along the dock, almost slipped, regained his balance.

"Bloody rookies," Leo mumbled, hands still tucked deep in his pockets. The photographer began to shoot images of the floater in the water. Two morgue guys came along the dock, carrying a metal litter basket and body bag.

"Take a close-up of the back of her head here," Maddocks said to the photographer, pointing to the bloodless gashes in the victim's skull.

The flash went off. A foghorn sounded as mist thickened.

"She could have been slashed by a boat propeller," O'Hagan said, leaning in for a better look herself. "Not uncommon in drownings, especially if she went over the side of a boat and caught the props at the rear. Wasn't a very big vessel if that was the case, or she'd have been dismembered, chopped into tiny pieces. Propellers from craft like tugboats tend to space the lacerations farther apart." More photos were snapped—a close-up of the rope around the victim's neck and the ropes binding the tarp.

"Or she didn't go overboard but resurfaced after a period of submergence due to gas production," O'Hagan said. "And then she was chopped by the prop of a passing boat. When that kind of refloat occurs, in most instances, the body comes up in a facedown attitude, like this one, and the damage will nearly always be to the back of the head, shoulders, neck, buttocks. Okay, let's get her out."

"Some more hands on deck here, please," Maddocks said. The coroner's guys laid the body bag out on the dock and helped heft the floater out. They placed her gently on the body bag. Water pooled around her. The rope around her neck stretched about three meters long and was frayed at the end, blackened by what looked like engine grease.

More photos were taken. They rolled her over.

"Holy *fuck*," Leo said, taking a sharp step backward.

They stared.

A skull that was barely covered with a layer of raw, ragged flesh grimaced up at them. Eyeballs, opaque, protruded from hollow sockets. All the tissue around them was gone. Eaten. Nose gone. Holes in the cheeks. No lips at all softened the bare grin of her jaw.

"Jeezus fuck, I hate floaters," Leo whispered.

"Anthropophagy," O'Hagan said quietly, still on her haunches, studying the face closely. "The ingesting of a human body by any multicelled organism—fish, reptiles, crustaceans, animals, invertebrates—is a natural phenomenon, but it can be truly shocking to a novice diver to recover something like this."

A small creature slithered out of the mouth.

"Fuck," said Leo.

"How long to do that kind of damage?" Maddocks said. "Any idea how long she's been down there?"

"Depends on several factors—like where she went in, from where she drifted, temperatures, currents, and what kind of sea life got at her. Sea lice are voracious feeders, for example. They'll enter the body through any orifice—anus, mouth, ears, nose, open wounds—like those on her skull—or they'll go for the soft tissue, force their way in around an eyeball, eat eyelids, lips, ears, nose. Once inside the body they continue to feed until the source of nourishment is consumed, or until they're disturbed. Shrimp could have done this within sixteen hours, can reduce a body to a near skeleton within a week. I'll need to get her onto my table for a better idea. And more context would help."

From the ravaged face, there was no immediate way to tell if this DB was male or female, but through the plastic Maddocks could make out the swell of a bare breast, dark nipple. He swiped rain from his wet brow with the back of his sleeve.

"Doesn't look like too much damage under the tarp yet," he said.

"Clothing usually serves as a barrier for at least the first twenty-four hours," O'Hagan replied. "Her torso appears to have been pretty well insulated by that polyethylene. It's tightly secured around the neck. I'm guessing she hasn't been in the water that long."

"Why wrap her body up like that but leave the head exposed?" Maddocks said, more to himself than anyone else as he touched the plastic with his gloved fingertips, trying to better see what was under it.

O'Hagan shone a small Maglite into the exposed jaw. "Extensive cosmetic work—all her teeth have been veneered, some bridgework immediately apparent," she said. "She's not in rigor. I'll need to cut away some of the tarp or make a hole to get an internal temp."

"This tarp, those ropes, what's inside—it's all crime scene. I'd prefer not to tamper with anything until we get her into the morgue," Maddocks said.

O'Hagan pursed her lips, considering her options. Leo continued to watch in heavy silence. Thick rain beat down on them.

"Can we get another close-up of the end of this neck rope here?" Maddocks indicated to the photographer. "Looks like it could have gotten caught up in a propeller or something. Maybe she was dragged into the inner harbor before the rope frayed and severed, then the currents and tide did the rest of the work."

"She could have gone into the water anywhere in that case, come from anywhere," Leo said. "If she refloated, then got caught up in a vessel . . ."

"Okay," O'Hagan said, closing her bag. "Establishing postmortem interval is going to be a bugger any way you look at it, without knowing more."

"Right, guys, let's take her in." Maddocks came to his feet. The body guys zipped the bag up around the tarp cocoon and the ragged skull, and then they lifted their DB into the stainless steel litter basket. They carried her down the dock to where a gurney waited on the bank.

"See you guys at the morgue when I open her up, then," O'Hagan said, pushing herself up onto her feet. She followed the body, her bag in hand.

Leo watched them go, hands still in his pockets. "Got your first day on the job cut out for you, eh, boss man?"

Maddocks glanced down at him. Those cool blue eyes looked up, met his, and Maddocks had a niggling feeling that he could go down as a scapegoat in this department if they failed to close this case, and soon, given the mayor's posturing. Maybe it was the reason Buziak wanted the new investigator as lead on the case from the get-go. He was being positioned as the potential fall guy.

"Get a full recovery report from the dive team, Leo," he said coolly. "Everything the diver saw down there. Opinions are of value, too, but they should be attached and noted as such." He snapped off his gloves, and a burn of pain along his wrists reminded him suddenly of the raw ligature marks from his sexcapade at the Foxy, how a mysterious redhead named Angie had cuffed him and fucked him. He'd not been able to get her out of his mind, to the point he'd called her number first thing this morning before going to meet Ginny. No answer. He'd left a message and was probably an asshole for doing so. He wasn't even sure why he'd gone to the club in the first place. Again, a shrink would have a field day with that. Didn't matter now. Leo was on the money. He had his days—and nights—cut out for him for a while. He shoved her out of his mind and began to move swiftly along the dock.

"I tell ya, I really hate floaters," said Leo, clumping along the dock after him. "One time we called in a family to make an ID on a DB that had been covered in clouds of the sea lice. Some of the bugs slithered out of an orifice right there on the table. I tell ya . . . gotta plug up those orifices in cases like that before calling in family. Mother fainted right there, on the spot. Cracked her head on the morgue floor. God, I hate floaters."

CHAPTER 10

Angie watched the woman in the ICU room through the glass. She sat hunched forward, holding her child's hand, her back to the door, dark wavy hair pulled up in a tangled ponytail.

Angie's thoughts turned to her own mom, to the burdens all mothers faced in keeping their daughters safe, how her mother had spent a lifetime caring for her. Guilt rushed hot into her chest. She should be with her mom now—looking after her, the tables turned. Again, Angie felt the hollow sensation of time lost, of years swept away under a bridge. The image of the Mother Mary statue shimmered into her brain. A Madonna supposedly untainted by sex, pure in body, yet fertile with child—the farce of it all. It angered her—these mixed messages that society dumped on females, the notion that sex, the act of propagation, the enjoyment of intercourse, was somehow foul, came from the gutter. *Filthy* girl. *Dirty* books. A flash of red filled her brain. Blood—she tasted it suddenly in her mouth, felt it hot and sticky upon her face. Pain seared through her lip. And suddenly the little girl in the pink dress was standing in the ICU room beside the mother. Angie's heart started to stammer. The girl slowly turned her head and looked directly at Angie, but she had no face. Just a luminous white blur framed by long, dark-red hair. The child reached her hand out to Angie, and those words whispered through her brain . . .

Come playum dum grove . . . Come down dem . . .

The hallucination vanished. Fear was ice in Angie's chest. She took a second to gather herself before sliding open the door and stepping into the room. The hissing and beeping sounds of the machines greeted her.

"Can you hear me, honey?" the woman was saying. "Please, squeeze my hand if you can hear me, Gracie. *Please.*"

Angie came up to her side, cleared her throat. "Mrs. Drummond, I'm Detective Angie Pallorino from Metro PD."

The woman glanced up, white-faced and hollow-eyed with shock and grief. It was a look Angie knew all too well in her job. The horror, the disbelief, degradation, powerlessness that could hit when violent crime intersected with everyday life, and suddenly an ordinary person going about an ordinary life had to face cops, doctors, coroners, questions, media scrutiny, criminal lawyers, people they never thought they'd have to deal with in their lifetimes.

"I . . . I didn't know that she wasn't at work last night until I saw the news this morning. I . . . went into her room, just to be certain that she . . . she was there. How could this have happened? How could I not have *known?*"

Compassion washed through Angie. On the back of it came a raw, furious burn to nail this repeat offender who she believed had slipped through her and Hash's hands. If they'd gotten him three, four years ago, this woman, this child, might not be in this hospital room.

"I'm so sorry," she said.

"The doctor told me what that monster did to . . . to my baby . . ." Emotion choked off her words, glistened in her eyes.

"The nurses told me that your daughter's name is Grace."

The woman's shaking hand went to her mouth. "My Gracie—we call her Gracie," she said, tears spilling down her cheeks. "Gracie Marie Drummond. She's sixteen. She's turning . . ." A sob racked her body.

"It's okay." Angie tentatively placed her hand on the woman's shoulder.

But the mother soldiered on. "Seventeen. She's turning seventeen on December twenty-ninth. When she first started to work at the Badger, I had to write her a letter of consent so that she could get that job at the bakery. She . . . wanted the money. I mean, we are just getting by. I should never have let her do it, at night, catch the bus by herself. But the city is so safe, and the bus stops right outside our apartment around six in the evening. That's not so late, and she's safe inside the bakery until five the next morning, after which she catches the bus home, and a mother wants her daughter to have nice things, you know? I can't buy nice things for her, let alone myself. I thought it was okay, and it was, for over a year . . ." Her hand pressed down hard over her mouth, as if to keep it all in, stop herself from collapsing completely.

"Can I get you a coffee, Mrs. Drummond?" Angie said. "Some water?"

Lorna Drummond shook her head.

"I need to ask you some questions, Mrs. Drummond. There's an alcove down the hall we can use. It's probably better if we speak there."

"I don't want to be too far from Gracie. She's been in here all alone."

"We'll be right across the hallway. You can see the door from there."

The mother got up and exited the room woodenly. Angie escorted her to a group of chairs beneath a window, helped her sit. Seating herself opposite the woman, Angie took out her notebook. "Can you tell me when you last saw Gracie, Mrs. Drummond?"

Lorna Drummond pushed tangled strands of hair off her brow. "It was Friday morning. Before I went to work. I work a twenty-four-hour shift at a nursing home downtown. I start at four on Friday afternoons and end at four on Saturdays." She worried her lip. "So I usually see Gracie before she leaves for her shift at the Blue Badger on Saturday evening, but I . . . I had a date last night—I've just started seeing someone—and I got home in the early hours of Sunday morning, went straight to bed. I woke later than usual this morning, then I . . . I heard the news. I went to check on Gracie. She wasn't in her room. Her bed was still made. I . . . you must think I'm a terrible mother. I shouldn't have gone on that date. But I was finally feeling like I was getting my life back." She fumbled in her pocket for a Kleenex, and she blew her nose hard. It was red. Swollen. Her eyes puffy. "You think you have all the time in the world, and then . . . then you wish you'd . . ." Her words were swallowed as her body heaved with a racking sob.

"I know," Angie said. She waited until Lorna Drummond was able to look up again. "So Gracie works every Saturday night at the Blue Badger?"

"In the bakery, yes. Night shift."

"Do you know of anyone who regularly catches the same bus as Gracie, perhaps, someone who might have seen that Gracie got both on and off the bus at the bakery stop yesterday, Mrs. Drummond?"

"No. I . . . I don't know. I think it's usually the same bus driver, though. She's mentioned him before. Gary, I think his name is."

"Why did she mention Gary specifically?"

"Because he's friendly. He always greets her by name."

"Which school does she attend?"

"Duneagle Secondary."

"Did she mention any concerns, whether anyone has been following her in the last while, bothering her?"

"No, I . . . don't think so. I shouldn't have let her work nights. I shouldn't have. She was working because I'm a single mom, right."

"And her father—where is he?"

"We're divorced. He remarried. Moved up island, but where exactly I couldn't tell you. Can't remember when I last saw a maintenance check from him."

"You've been separated long?"

"Since Gracie was nine."

"Does she work anywhere else?"

"Just that one day a week at the Badger."

"Did her father perhaps send her money directly?"

She glanced up, eyes widening for a brief instant. "No, why?"

Angie held her gaze. "Your daughter was wearing some very high-end designer boots last night."

"She . . . must be paying those off herself. Through her work—that's why she's working. Like I said. To buy nice things."

"Do you know how much a pair of Francesco Milano boots costs?"

"No—what is this about, exactly?"

"They cost upward of a grand, I believe."

Lorna Drummond paled. Her eyes flickered. "Maybe she got them on consignment. She buys a lot of things secondhand. Maybe she was borrowing them. Oh God, I haven't been paying attention."

"Who is your new partner—your date?"

"You don't think—"

"Just for the record."

"Kurt Shepherd. I met him four months ago, when he lost his mother at the nursing home where I work. He lives in Esquimalt. He's a mechanic at Barney's, a really good guy. He's been so nice to me."

"We'll need to come to your house, take a look at Gracie's room. Is that okay?"

"Yes, yes of course."

"Does Gracie have a cell phone?"

"An iPhone. I've been calling it ever since I saw that terrible stuff on the news. It just kept flipping to voicemail."

"We'll need her number and the name of her service provider."

"I . . . uh . . . her plan is with ClearWave, I think." She gave Angie her daughter's number. As Angie jotted it down, she caught a flash of movement in her peripheral vision. She glanced up to see a flurry of activity outside Gracie Drummond's room.

A voice, calm, came over the ward paging system. "Code blue, room twelve. Code blue, room twelve."

Angie's heart kicked. Lorna Drummond whirled around in her chair. "What is *that*? What does that mean?"

The double doors at the end of the corridor blew open. Nurses and a cardiac team in green scrubs came rushing through the doors and down the corridor. Dr. Finlayson ran behind them.

Lorna Drummond lurched to her feet. "Oh my God—that's Gracie's room! They're going into her room—" She lurched in a wild stumble toward them.

"Mrs. Drummond!" Angie surged up and went after her. "Lorna! Wait, please!" Angie caught hold of the woman's arm outside the room windows, halting her from entering. Through the glass they could see a nurse pumping Gracie's chest while the defibrillation paddles were being readied.

"Stand back," another nurse ordered. The paddles were applied to her body. Gracie's frame juddered as they fought to shock her back to life. But nothing happened. The line on the machine ran flat, not even a blip. They tried again. Again. Again. Still nothing.

Lorna wrenched free of Angie's grasp and burst into the room. "Oh my God, Gracie—" A nurse stopped her.

"Please," Lorna Drummond sobbed. "*Please* tell me what's happening!"

The nurse placed her arm around Lorna Drummond's shoulders and led her back out into the corridor. "You need to wait here, Mrs. Drummond. Let us do our job. You'll just be in the way. Okay?"

"Come, Mrs. Drummond," Angie said gently, trying to steer the woman away from the glass.

But Gracie's mother broke free again and pressed both her palms flat against the window. "Gracie! Oh my God, Gracie . . . Please, please, don't die. Not now."

Inside the room, Dr. Finlayson met the eyes of the nurse with the defibrillation paddles. The nurse shook her head. Dr. Finlayson checked her patient, then glanced at her watch and said something. Angie's heart sank. The doc was pronouncing time of death.

A strange, thin, inhuman wail issued from the throat of Lorna Drummond. She whirled around and attacked Angie, slapping at her chest and arms and face. "You—*you* did this! *You* took me away from my baby's bedside. You let her die without her mother there!"

Angie braced against the feeble assault, emotion hot in her eyes. For a moment she was unable to move, unable to bring herself to grab hold of Lorna Drummond's wrists and halt the distraught woman's blows. It was as though Angie *needed* to be hit, to be punished by this mother. For her neglect of her own mother. For whatever wrongs she'd done in her life.

Finally, a spent Lorna Drummond slid down the length of Angie's body and crumpled onto the floor at Angie's biker boots, her body racked with sobs. Two nurses came running to their aid.

Angie swallowed and stepped away, thankful that hospital staff was taking over. Shaken, she made her way down the corridor and stepped outside the ward. She stopped and caught her breath. Then, mouth dry, she called Vedder.

"She passed—she's dead," Angie told him when he answered. "Her name was Gracie Marie Drummond. Sixteen years old. In her final year at Duneagle Secondary. Would have been seventeen in a few days." As she spoke, she caught sight of Holgersen loping angrily down the corridor toward her.

"What the fuck, Pallorino?" Holgersen demanded as he reached her. He pointed his finger at her face. "You do that to me one more time and—"

"She died."

He stilled. His hand lowered slowly to his side.

"She drowned. Right there in her hospital bed." Angie's gaze remained locked with his. "Some things don't wait for you to take a piss or a smoke."

CHAPTER 11

It was 11:15 a.m. in the newsroom when Merry Winston's cell phone rang. She checked the caller ID. Unknown. She answered.

"Merry here."

"She's been identified, and she just died." The voice was distorted, sort of electronic-sounding. Neither male nor female.

Her heart kicked. She glanced around the newsroom. Quiet. Sunday morning—the majority of the staff was off for the weekend, out on a break, or chasing down a story. Merry didn't take weekends off. She had something to prove and no life outside of her work. Her wet rain gear hung drying over a chair at the empty desk next to hers. She'd gotten soaked trying to get information down at the wharf this morning, but she couldn't get past the police barricades this time. Cops weren't saying anything. But some gawker in the crowd said he'd heard that a body had been found floating in the Gorge, under the Johnson Street Bridge. She'd come in to make some calls in an effort to get information.

"You mean the Jane Doe at Saint Jude's?" She clicked the record button on her phone as she spoke.

Silence.

Tension, adrenaline crackled through her. This was not the first time her mysterious informant had called with proprietary information. He—she did believe the distorted voice belonged to a male, although she couldn't say why, because it was just very well disguised—had previously offered her tips that could only have come from inside the Metro PD.

"Who was she?"

"Gracie Marie Drummond. Sixteen. Student of Duneagle Secondary."

Merry's pulse raced as she jotted the information down. "What else can you tell me? Cause of death?"

"Drowning."

"*What?* In the hospital?"

"She'd also been mutilated. Genitals. And a crucifix carved into her face."

Something inside Merry stilled like stone. For a moment she couldn't find her voice. She cleared her throat. "Can you repeat that?" she said quietly.

"She had a crucifix carved into her forehead. She'd been circumcised with a sharp blade. Her assailant took a lock of her hair."

"Where . . . where did you get this?"

The call went dead.

"Wait! You bastard." She glanced toward the editor's desk. The weekend editor was not there, either. Shit. She got up, paced, sat back down, got up again. She was shaking. *Shitshitshit.* She needed to verify this.

What did he mean, drowned?

Circumcised?

The hair.

And the crucifix . . .

Is he trying to mess with me? How could he know? A voice from the past serpentined up into her memory, escaping from a locked door in the basement of her soul . . .

Do you reject Satan, father of sin and prince of darkness?
And all his works?
Do you reject the glamour of evil and refuse to be mastered by sin?

Sweating, she quickly dialed the Metro PD press liaison. Her call kicked to voicemail. She left a message, then phoned the hospital. As expected, they wouldn't give out information. She searched online for the name "Gracie Marie Drummond," found a Facebook page, but privacy protection had been engaged—she couldn't see who Gracie's friends were. Or any of the posts. There were a few online mentions of a Gracie Marie Drummond in connection with Duneagle Secondary school choir performances, but that was about it.

She tried the Metro PD press person again. Once more her call went to voicemail. She left another message.

Merry paced, waited.

No one returned her calls. The clock ticked.

Was he back? Was it possible? She needed to file this story. She wanted to get it out there bad. Technically, she couldn't until she verified the information from her anonymous source. But this deep throat hadn't let her down yet. What his agenda was she did not know, but his information had been 100 percent solid to date.

A kind of desperation rose inside her. The kind that had always preceded her need for a fix. She hadn't felt this kind of twitchy desperation in years, and it only fueled the maelstrom that had exploded inside her body and her brain with the mention of the crucifix. The hair. She seated herself at her desk, bit her lip.

Foot jiggling, she opened her Twitter account. Twitter was where she routinely plugged her personal crime blog—the *Winston Files*. Her private blog was where she piqued and provoked and raised questions that she couldn't under the auspices of the *City Sun*. One day she hoped to put podcasts up. She was planning to do a true crime series, like that famous podcast *Serial*. It was a very, very fine line she treaded on her blog, by newspapers' standards, but so far the *Sun* brass had let her have at it, because it was sensational. Because it had brought readers directly to the *Sun*. And part of the ailing *City Sun*'s mandate was to salvage itself and grow readership by going more trashy, sensationalist. Other journalists now followed Merry's Twitter and blog accounts—reporters from respected radio and television news shows. She was getting to be a fucking independent social media crime star in her own right. A long way from her life in foster care and on the streets. *This* was what she had to prove to the world. *This* was her agenda. She'd once had to sell herself, her body. For the crystal meth.

Do you reject Satan, father of sin and prince of darkness?

It was after the rape that she'd started to come right. It was like a final wake-up call. Pastor Markus at Harbor House had helped steer her onto course and had picked her up when she'd fallen off the wagon. Missing kids, abused females, addicts, sex workers—yeah, she had stories and things to prove. Now she sold other people's misfortune instead of her own. She rubbed it all into mainstream society's face. It was her fuck-you back at the world, and the fresher and more salacious the stories she could find, the better, and it was paying her bills.

But still, she hesitated . . .

Do you reject Satan, father of sin and prince of darkness? Say it! Say, I do!

She swallowed, steeled her jaw, and started typing out her tweet:

#CEMETERYGIRL Duneagle student Gracie Marie Drummond, 16, raped @Cemetery has died.

Merry paused. Sweat prickled above her lip. She added:

Circumcised. Crucifix cut into face. Lock of hair taken.

She squeezed her eyes shut, trying to block out the disjointed snippets of memory this information was flaring through her brain. She remembered his eyes—had seen them through the slit of a ski mask. And those words. He'd said those words, a blade pressed to her throat as he'd kneed her into the ground. And she'd woken up in weeds and garbage at the bottom of a ravine with a red crucifix on her forehead, bleeding. In terrible pain. No pants. A missing lock of hair from the center of her hairline.

Rage, fear whammed through her. She opened her eyes, sucked her breath in deep, and stabbed ENTER.

The tweet went live.

She started typing up a blog post.

CHAPTER 12

The new thin-screen television mounted on the wall in Zach Raddison's office was tuned to the local twenty-four-hour news channel. Zach's office adjoined the mayor's, and he kept an eye on the news as he directed the guys with the special Sunday delivery of the mayor's new desk.

The *City Sun* had this morning run a shocking front-page article about a violent attack on a Jane Doe in the Ross Bay Cemetery, and the reporter—that pugnacious little Merry Winston—had dragged the mayor's office into it already by mentioning Killion and crime stats, and by mentioning missing UVic student Annelise Janssen. It was tabloid trash, sensationalist scare-mongering at best, but Zach knew firsthand what a powerful tool that kind of fear-mongering garbage could be. He'd used Merry Winston himself during the campaign—quietly feeding her information that would hurt their opposition.

But now this was happening on Killion's watch. *That* was a problem.

Plus there'd been a police incident at the Johnson Street Wharf this morning, slowing city traffic to a snarl—a woman's body had been found in the Gorge. This news in particular worried Zach. He told himself it couldn't be *her*. It wasn't possible. Still, he was on edge as he followed the breaking story.

"Over there, near the window," he instructed the men hefting the desk.

Mayor-elect Jack Killion would be sworn in as the lead lawmaker of the city in just two days, and as Killion's successful election campaign manager, Zach had now been hired on as Killion's "special advisor," a right-hand man whose key objective was to keep the Killion brand going and growing. It was a cut-to-order position for him and would evolve over time.

They called his father—Jim Raddison of Raddison Industries—the King Maker, and Zach was the King Maker's son. He'd tasted his first big win with Killion now. He'd gotten his hands dirty in the campaign trenches, and he'd loved every minute of it. He was twenty-eight years old, and he'd helped put a man in office.

He would be a king maker himself.

"No, no, angle it more to the left, for the light," Zach instructed. The delivery guys inched the desk a little more to the left.

The ousted incumbent was a woman—Patty Markham—and it had showed in her office decor. Zach was remedying this. He wanted to depict Killion as a man's kind of man. A powerhouse. A business leader and innovator who did not mince his words.

The paint job had been completed and the new images hung—sleek black-and-white photographs of Victoria's architecture dating from the eighteen hundreds to images of buildings currently under construction, including Ray Norton-Wells's big waterfront development. The works had been shot by a top photographer, and they depicted power. The past and the future. Control. Growth. Jobs. That, and Killion's tough-on-crime approach, had been what eked them into this office door. They now had four years to prove themselves and to better the results next time around, because Killion had set his sights way higher than the mayor's office. He had his eye on provincial, then federal political balls, and Zach planned on going with him all the way.

A BREAKING NEWS banner flashed suddenly across the bottom of the television screen. The show cut to the anchor in the studio. Zach stilled, pulse quickening.

"A warning: the following information is graphic, and it might be upsetting to our sensitive viewers," she said. "The young victim of last night's brutal sexual assault in Ross Bay Cemetery has died from her injuries. She's been identified as sixteen-year-old Gracie Marie Drummond, a Fairfield resident and student of Duneagle Secondary."

What the fuck . . . ?

Zach grabbed the remote, jacked up the sound, heart hammering. This was not good, not at all. He barely noticed the delivery guys taking leave as he glued his attention to the breaking news.

"Drummond's cause of death is, mysteriously, drowning, according to her mother, Lorna Drummond, who was contacted by VNN reporters this morning following a disturbing leak by a crime reporter on Twitter. Metro police are not commenting other than to say their investigation is ongoing. However, Lorna Drummond has confirmed to VNN that her daughter had been immersed in water, sexually mutilated—circumcised—and that the shape of a crucifix had been carved with a blade into her forehead. A lock of hair had also been cut near her hairline." A school photo of Gracie Drummond appeared at the top right of the screen.

Zach stared, a sick dread building in his stomach.

"Drummond was left unconscious and bleeding at the feet of a statue of the Virgin Mary in the Ross Bay graveyard, during one of the coldest snaps on record . . ."

His cell phone rang. He kept staring at the television as he answered it. "Yeah?"

"You see the news?" It was Killion.

"I'm seeing it now."

"We need to handle this. Before it handles us. Before this whole tough-on-crime thing blows up in our faces from day one. What is this leak on Twitter that they're talking about?"

"I . . . don't know." Zach moved to his computer, clicked on his Twitter bookmark. *Shit.*

"It's her," he said quietly. "Merry Winston from the *Sun*. She came out with that tweet at eleven forty-five this morning."

CHAPTER 13

Death, the great equalizer.

"Media shit-storm breaking out there," Leo mumbled around a wad of cinnamon-scented gum as they watched the two dieners weighing the bagged body of their floater. He glanced up at Maddocks. "You heard, right?"

Maddocks nodded.

It was almost six hours since their decedent had been retrieved from the Gorge—and here they were, already in the morgue at 4:00 p.m. on a Sunday. The room was cold, windowless, with tiled walls and floors, stainless steel tables, sinks, and backsplashes. Unforgiving fluorescent lighting hummed softly overhead. Banks of glass-fronted cabinets housing tools of the trade—bone-cutting devices, disposable face shields, other equipment—lined the back wall. Lab coats, once pristine white but now soiled with brownish-red stains, hung loosely on a stand beside a pair of electronically controlled doors that hissed softly when they opened.

There lingered in the room an odor that Maddocks associated with all morgues. The scent was one of raw meat, blood, formalin, and disinfectant, and it reminded him of a butcher shop he'd once visited with his grandfather as a boy.

In this jurisdiction an autopsy was usually performed within forty-eight hours of death. But a rush had been put on this one. The coroner's office fell under the purview of the office of the attorney general, and given the breaking news, the possibility of an internal Metro PD leak, the twitchiness of the police chief, and pressure from the new mayor and police board, word had come right from the assistant deputy attorney general herself to expedite this medico-legal autopsy stat.

If ordered by law, next of kin consent was not required for a postmortem. Besides, they had no idea who to inform yet, anyway, not until they'd opened the tarp up and unwrapped what was essentially part of a crime scene. Maddocks and Leo were present to witness that process and to take delivery of any evidence that came out of it. They did, however, already know that their DB was not Annelise Janssen, the missing student, as the newspaper had speculated.

The Janssen family had provided Metro PD copies of their daughter's dental records along with DNA samples when she'd first been reported missing. From those records it was evident that Annelise Janssen had undergone very limited dental work in her lifetime, and nothing cosmetic. Their lipless DB with her exposed jaw, on the other hand, had clearly undergone extensive dentistry, both cosmetic and repair—a bridge, implants at the front of her mouth, ceramic fillings in nearly all her real teeth. Her mouth had once been a mess.

Dr. Barb O'Hagan put music on, and the sounds of soft cello rose in the sterile room while she checked her microphone above the stainless steel autopsy table and made notes, comparing the information on the body bag seal with the authorizing paperwork to make sure this was the right body. She wore voluminous green scrubs under a disposable plastic apron, booties over her shoes. The autopsy techs wore rebreather devices. O'Hagan did not. Maddocks knew pathologists like her—old school. They preferred to use their noses. Smell was important in a postmortem. It could tell you a lot.

"Could have been anyone, that leak," Leo said as O'Hagan snapped on her latex gloves.

Down came the zipper on the bag. They watched the assistants lift the plastic-cocooned body with its ragged head and long strands of wet hair. They positioned her on the stainless steel table, which was slightly canted and equipped with running water to rinse fluids into the drainage holes at the bottom. Leo avoided looking at the head as he rubbed wintergreen oil under his nose. He offered the container to Maddocks.

"Thanks." Maddocks dabbed some of the ointment under his own nostrils. O'Hagan might need to smell the corpse, but he did not. He returned the container.

The victim's brown hair was still entangled with seaweed. Photos were taken before anything was touched.

"It could have come from one of the EMTs," Leo said. "Or someone in ER, any one of the nurses. Even one of the docs. Christ, the mother herself might have told any number of people that her kid had been mutilated like that. It's upsetting. It's something people need to get out, you know?"

He was motormouthing. Maddocks suspected this was Detective Harvey Leo's coping mechanism, his compartmentalization tool. They all had one or two such tools in their arsenals, but he wished Leo would shut the fuck up.

"It *could* also have been internal," Maddocks countered coolly as he watched the assistants carefully checking the empty body bag for trace that might have shaken loose during transport to the morgue and gotten left in the bag.

"Yeah," said Leo. "And that's *exactly* the conclusion everyone is gonna jump on. Kick at the cops. Pallorino and Holgersen's case—I tell ya, she's in shit street now. First there was the Hashowsky shooting five months ago, and the death of that little kid and her parents, and now this? I tell ya, if Gunnar is looking for heads to roll, if the board is looking for a fall guy, her tight little ass is a damn fine target about now. She's toast, I reckon."

Maddocks glanced down at him. A glint of glee actually flickered in the man's eyes. Detective Leo clearly had a hate-on for the female cop working the cemetery case. Or he was using this as a diversion from the gruesome sight on the table in front of them. Maybe a bit of both.

O'Hagan glanced up from the body. "We're about to begin, gentlemen." She held Leo's gaze pointedly. Maddocks could feel the ice in it. The doc, on the other hand, clearly appeared to like the female detective. She reached up, clicked on the mike that hung above the table, and stated time and date and that she was commencing a preliminary external visual examination.

She spoke her observations out loud, starting from the head, as her assistant meticulously took more photos from all angles.

"The more vertical slope of the forehead and size of the head is indicative of a female. Smaller mandible and maxilla. We'll have the odontologist look at the dental work if necessary, but extensive cosmetic dentistry is immediately apparent. Anthropophagy on face is extensive. From the feeding patterns, likely primarily saltwater shrimp, perhaps some other crustaceans and invertebrates. First site of attack appears to have been the softer tissue of the lips, eyelids, ears."

Maddocks stepped forward for a closer look. Leo fidgeted behind him, paper crackling as he opened another stick of gum. O'Hagan brought her magnifying glass down by an extendable arm and peered closely at the decedent's opaque, bulbous eyes. The strings of the cello rose.

"Petechiae," she said quietly, bringing the magnifier with its built-in light closer. "Tiny pinpoints. Clusters."

Maddocks was intimately familiar with the term for the small red or purple spots—hemorrhages—that occurred when blood leaked from the tiny capillaries in the eyes. The cause of the ruptures was usually due to increased pressure on the veins in the neck when airways were obstructed. If petechial hemorrhages were present, it was a strong indication of asphyxia by strangulation as cause of death, whether by manual strangulation, hanging, or smothering.

"Looks like multiple events," she said.

"As in tightening, releasing, tightening again?" Maddocks said. "As in erotic asphyxiation, or breath-control play for sexual arousal?"

"Possible," O'Hagan said. "The presence of petechiae does not prove strangulation, and their absence does not disprove it. They're simply a marker of increased cephalic venous pressure. But in eighty-five percent of manual strangulation cases, petechial hemorrhaging presents. Takes only about thirty seconds of sustained pressure."

She moved her light again and looked into the other eye. "When the carotid arteries are compressed, the sudden loss of oxygen-rich blood to the brain and the accumulation of carbon dioxide can lead to feelings of giddiness and pleasure, all of which will heighten sexual sensation. Combined with orgasm, the rush is said to be no less powerful than cocaine and highly addictive."

The cello music rose to a crescendo, then fell to a seductive whispering as the dieners combed through their Jane Doe's hair, removing seaweed, other vegetation, small invertebrates, and foreign particles, meticulously bagging and documenting each piece of trace. The fauna and flora trace in her hair might help determine postmortem interval, or PMI. It could also help determine where their Jane Doe might have entered the water and from where she could have drifted.

"A lock of her hair has been cut," said one assistant suddenly. "See? Right at the hairline, near the center of the forehead."

Maddocks shot a glance at Leo. Both knew about Gracie Drummond's lock of hair. It was all over the media now. Photographs were taken of the cut sprouts of hair.

O'Hagan turned her attention to the victim's neck.

"The rope securing the tarp to her neck looks to be the same kind of rope used to bind up the rest of her body. Knots also appear consistent."

She measured the length of the loose end. "Three point nine five meters from the knot cluster at her throat."

"Looks like polyester, maybe three-strand," Maddocks said quietly. "Common marine equipment that you can buy anywhere. Recently bought several meters exactly like it myself. And those look like reef knots. Any mariner, climber, Boy Scout, Girl Guide, or fisherman knows how to tie those knots to join pieces of rope."

"You got a boat?" Leo said.

"Hmm." Maddocks watched closely as O'Hagan moved her attention to the plastic tarp, checking for external trace—hairs, fibers. She reached suddenly for forceps and carefully extracted something minute from the fibers of one of the knots.

"Looks like some kind of hair has been trapped inside some of the knots and caught in the rough weave of the rope." She brought her magnifying glass back down close again and began to painstakingly remove and examine the evidence. "Some as long as two centimeters. Some blondish, others dark brown. A white one. Coarse." She fell silent a while. "Quite a few. Not human. More like the outer guard hairs of an animal. And what appears to be softer, finer fur."

"Dogs? Cats?" Leo said.

"We'll get the lab to tell us," O'Hagan said. "Hairs are composed primarily of the protein keratin. Each species of animal possesses hair with characteristic length, color, shape, root appearance, and microscopic features that will enable our forensic techs to identify one species from another."

The hairs went individually into paper envelopes and were labeled by the dieners.

"Might help associate her with a crime scene," Maddocks said quietly. "On land—because I'm guessing that's not hair from a sea creature."

The cello notes fell, almost silent now, creating a kind of tension in the room before the anticipated next crescendo. The minutes ticked by.

Maddocks began to feel hot in spite of the cold in the morgue. Stainless steel instruments clacked against the sink.

"There are some scratches in the tarp fabric," O'Hagan said. "Could be traveling abrasions from being dragged along by the current." These breaches were noted, photographed. "Let's flip her over then, shall we?"

The assistants aided O'Hagan in hefting the cocooned Jane Doe onto her stomach.

"Striations on the back of her head are almost four centimeters deep and nine centimeters apart." O'Hagan picked a tiny, wiggling shrimp out of one of the wounds. It was bagged.

"Eating into her brain. Shit," mumbled Leo.

Maddocks inhaled slowly to reach for calm, but he regretted it instantly because it filled his nasal cavity with the briny smells of the woman's death and the morgue.

More photographs were taken. Again, O'Hagan worked her external examination from head to foot. Deep-purple marks were visible under the plastic.

"Lividity?" said Leo.

"Or other contusions," O'Hagan said. "We'll know more when we unwrap her in a few."

With her visual external examination complete, the assistants helped O'Hagan roll the body back onto its back.

"So maybe she was involved in some kind of erotic breath-control game that went wrong," Leo said quietly. "Or was plain old strangled, then trussed up in the plastic sheeting and dumped into the water somewhere. Then she drifted with currents and tides along the bottom, finally gassed up, refloated, was hit by a prop, went down again, and then she came up in the Gorge somehow, up under the Johnson Street Bridge."

"Why don't we wait to see what we find inside?" Maddocks said.

Leo eyeballed him, his mouth flattening.

"Okay, let's open this up then," O'Hagan said.

The cello strings clashed in angry discord, growing ever more strident.

"Wish she'd turn that fucking thing off," Leo muttered, fishing for his gum again. "Yo-Yo Moo, or Mah, or something or other. She plays the same bloody thing every time."

Carefully, O'Hagan sliced open the thick layers of opaque tarp, peeling it back as if a chrysalis to reveal the pupa therein. A pupa that would now never grow into the butterfly she was once destined to become. Her skin was a translucent white, blue veins evident beneath, the nipples of her breasts small and dark rose in color. A gold ring looped through the left nipple.

"Remarkably well preserved considering the extent of anthropophagy on the head," O'Hagan said, revealing a flat stomach upon which the decedent's hands appeared to have been folded, one atop the other. O'Hagan cut away more rope and stripped back more of the thick plastic.

The tattoo was instantly evident.

Everyone fell silent.

"Well, fuck me," Leo whispered, coming sharply forward to the autopsy table in spite of himself.

Writhing serpents twisted across their victim's lower abdomen—the snakes coming from a Medusa's head, and the Medusa's screaming, open maw with fanged teeth was positioned right over the victim's shaved pubic area, as if the Medusa's mouth opened to the vagina and that anything inserted into that Medusa's throat would be swallowed alive. O'Hagan stilled, frowned. A sense of foreboding swelled into the room.

The doc bent closer, gently opening wider the labia majora with two gloved fingers, as if revealing the pink insides of the mouth of the Medusa.

The cello strings softened to barely a whisper.

She looked up, eyes clear and serious. "The clitoral hood, clitoral glans, and labia minora have been excised," she said quietly. "She's been circumcised."

They stared at the doc.

The doors hissed open, and everyone jumped.

"Hey, Doc. Anyone for some supper or snacks?" Leo and Maddocks spun around to see a cherub-cheeked blonde who'd entered the morgue pushing a food trolley. The detectives stared at her as if she represented the outside world that had somehow just invaded their alien alternate reality of horror and cold and dead.

THE BAPTIST

Behold, I was shapen in iniquity; and in sin did my mother
conceive me.
—Psalms 5:15

It's Sunday evening when he places three rolls of duct tape and a box of
extra-thin blue latex gloves into his shopping cart at the Druggie Mart
in James Bay. He's run out of gloves, and he likes to keep a pair in his
pocket at all times, like a detective. He once tried to become a cop.
But upon application, he learned that he suffers from a red-green color
vision deficiency. Normal color vision is one of the minimum require-
ments listed to join the Metro PD. Until his application, he hadn't even
known he was partially color blind.

But he's learned to think like a cop nevertheless, in the same way
police learn to think like criminals. He slows at the aisle with protein
powders, selects a tin of his favorite complex. Expensive, but worth the
cost. His body is his temple.

Self-care is a sign of self-respect, Johnny boy . . .

He runs at least forty Ks per week, works out using the outdoor
gym equipment in the park down the road. It keeps him sharp. Focused.
Strong. He likes the way exercise makes him look. Women appreciate it,
too. He sees the way they stare at him when he works shirtless in the sun.

He enters the cosmetic aisle, finds the lipstick he's looking for—
Cherry Blush Red. He takes his purchases to the checkout. The store is

located on the corner just down the street from their house, and he likes to walk. The vehicle is for his more private nocturnal activities, when he needs to transport bigger things, and he keeps it safely locked away in the garage.

"How's your mom doing?" says the store owner, Oliver Tam, beginning to ring in the purchases. The Druggie Mart is a small family-run business, and Tam often works the checkout himself. His mother likes Tam, likes to support local businesses that have not been gobbled up by major chains.

"Good," he says, setting the lipstick on the counter, then the protein powder. "Getting much better." But his attention is suddenly riveted by the headline on the newspaper on the rack beside the checkout. His hand stills.

Violent Sexual Assault in Ross Bay Cemetery— Young Woman Left in Coma

It's the first he's seen of this news.

He was up late last night. His work made him so tired that he slept most of today, waking only around 5:00 p.m. Tam nods toward the *City Sun* front page. "Terrible attack on that young woman," he says. "That's this morning's issue, but latest on the radio is that she died. Only sixteen years old. Drowned. How in the hell does *that* happen in a hospital?" He moves the first bag of goods to the end of the counter. "They said on the radio that she'd been mutilated, a crucifix carved right into her forehead. And then there was the body found this morning floating under the Johnson Street Bridge. All bound up in plastic or something. Apparently she could be that missing woman from two weeks ago. Fine way to head into Christmas—that new mayor better live up to his promises."

He looks up from the headline. "What missing woman?"

"UVic student. Eighteen years old. Clean vanished off campus and into the blue about two weeks ago. Annelise . . . Janssen, that was it."

He takes the paper from the rack, reads the first paragraph, then studies closely the black-and-white photo of the two detectives from the

Metro PD sex crimes unit. They look like haunted things in the swirling snowflakes under the glare of the flash. Behind them, a shadowy gargoyle face is carved into the stone wall.

"Those officers look as scary as the bad guys they hunt, eh?" Tam says. "You want that copy?"

"Yeah." He places the paper on the counter. "And a pack of menthol lights."

"You should tell her to stop smoking those things," Tam says with a smile as he reaches behind him for a packet of cigarettes and plunks it on the counter.

He meets Tam's gaze and returns the man's smile with a big, high-wattage grin of his own—his is a smile that makes people trust him. Forced or not, it comes with dimples that can melt the logic in a certain kind of young woman's brains. He has a keen radar for that kind of woman. Something . . . needy in them. "That'll be the day that she listens to me," he tells Tam. "Oh, and I'll take a lotto Quick Pick." The sign outside the store declares the prize is up to fifteen million this week. He could do with winning a few million, especially given his work situation now.

Tam rings up the total and hands over the lottery ticket. "Tell your mom I say hi."

"Yeah, I will." He picks up his bags.

The walk home is blustery and cold. When he returns to his mother's neatly painted little early nineteen hundreds house, he shakes out his coat, hangs it carefully on one of the hooks near the front door before unpacking his bags. He then lights the fire, puts the television onto a recorded episode of *Coronation Street*, and he sits down to read the paper.

So, she was found alive.

That was a bad slip. He supposes he panicked a little, thought she was dead when he left her in the cemetery. He'll have to make certain next time.

Sloppy Johnny, stupid peeping Tommy, stupid, stupid child . . .

He gets up, paces, clenching and unclenching his fists. He picks up the paper again and peruses the story further, taking note of the detectives' names. Angie Pallorino and Kjel Holgersen. He tries pronouncing their names out loud. *Kell? Key-yell? Kay-gel?*

Angie. That one's easy.

A kind of power, arousal, spreads through him.

Game is on, detectives . . . you can't catch Johnny, watch Johnny run, no one has caught Johnny, peeping Tommy, because for years Johnny's had fun . . .

But it's more than fun now. It's a calling. Now he has a higher purpose.

Save the Bad Girls, Johnny . . . make them Good Girls, Tommy . . .

He reaches for the new tube of lipstick on the table, opens it, and applies the color carefully to his lips. He then opens the new packet of menthol cigarettes, puts one between his lips, lights it, then balances it at the edge of an ashtray on the kitchen table where it continues to burn, releasing a tendril of smoke like incense into the air. Atmosphere. It arouses him. He fetches the sewing box from downstairs and places it upon the kitchen table, where he seats himself before opening the box. Inside are spools of colored thread, needles, buttons. A small bottle of resin. His ultraviolet pen flashlight.

Beneath the bottom tray is the lock of hair he was too tired to fix last night.

He removes it. A lovely walnutty brown.

Humming to himself, he opens his bottle of UV resin and dips the end of the lock into it. The strong scent makes his eyes water and his nasal passages burn. He shines his ultraviolet flashlight onto the resin to dry it, and the tip of the lock goes smooth and shiny-hard within three seconds. This will ensure the hairs stay nicely together. Until recently he used clear nail varnish to finish his trophies, but then he had to find a way to clamp the locks of hair so that the varnish could air-dry. It took time, and it sometimes got messy and stuck to surfaces. Then he saw this fly-tying documentary on the sports channel where the angler used UV resin for his flies. It works like a charm.

The scent of the resin itself is becoming a trigger now, a delicious neural shortcut firing straight from his nose to his groin. He's going hard already, and he opens his thighs wider to better enjoy the sensation. He picks a spool of mauve embroidery thread from his mother's sewing box, and he ties a tiny bow around the fixed lock of hair.

He runs the strands softly across his upper lip. Ticklish, silky. He closes his eyes, and her scent fills him. It's as if she's with him again. He can taste her, can see her lashes soft and dark upon the swell of her cheeks, can feel the satiny texture of her skin. He moans quietly as his penis hardens to an exquisite, almost-painful peak. A gentle girl. Who had to be punished before she could be saved . . .

The sound of Her voice mingles with the fragrance of menthol smoke, the *Coronation Street* theme tune playing on the television . . .

Save the girls, Johnny . . .

Johnny is a bad boy. Peeping Johnny likes to peep like a peeping Tommy . . . a very bad boy, Johnny, to look at the good girls, to want the girl . . . we need to scrub Johnny . . .

His breathing becomes shallow. His vision narrows. His heart races so fast he's going dizzy. He lurches up, knocking over the kitchen chair as he hurries to the bathroom to find the exfoliation mitt. Slipping it onto his hand, he unzips his pants and takes himself into his mitted fist. He watches his eyes in the bathroom mirror. Photos of naked Gracie are taped down the sides of the glass. He begins to work the coarse mitt up and down, up and down, in time to Her words, harder, harder, faster, the pain growing into an unbearable pleasure . . . *scrub, scrub, scrub . . . clean Johnny . . .* his eyes are watering with pain, with pleasure. Braided together. *Scrub, scrub, scrub it raw . . .* his vision blurs into scarlet . . .

CHAPTER 14

"Bad timing?" said the cherub-cheeked woman with the snack trolley.

Maddocks cleared his throat and caught Doc O'Hagan's eyes. The unspoken subtext—the echoes of the so-called "Cemetery Girl" case—simmered heavily in the dead air between them all. The doc looked up at the clock, clicked off her mike.

"This one's going to take a while," she said. "Shall we break before we open her up, gentlemen? Resume in, say, forty-five?"

"That's probably a good idea," Maddocks said quietly, checking his own watch, adrenaline fizzing hot through his veins. "I need to loop Buziak in. Leo, see if you can get anyone to pull some extra hours working the databases for a possible match to the Medusa ink on our DB. There's a chance something like that could be in the system."

And Jack-O was still in his vehicle. He desperately needed to find the animal a sitter while he worked this case. The one he'd arranged for when he was due to start work had fallen through.

"What you got there for sandwiches, Hannah?" O'Hagan said to the food trolley woman as she snapped off and trashed her gloves, then turned on the tap in the sink to wash her hands. Water drummed against steel.

"A chicken mayo, a couple of turkey salami and cheese, all on white. And a vegetarian, gluten-free hummus wrap. Sorry, that's all that's left."

"Always the morgue for last, eh? Dregs," the doc said, drying her hands. "Bottom of the barrel in the basement."

"Hey, it's hospital food. You say you hate it, anyway."

"I do. Just don't find the time to ever get out of here."

"Want me to put it on the counter?" Hannah said, holding up a wrapped sandwich.

"Thanks, and a coffee—cream, two sugars. And a Snickers bar—got Snickers?"

Leo, who was using his cell to quickly snap some photos of the Medusa tattoo to send back to the station, crooked up his brow. "Plenty of calories in them Snickers, Doc."

"Long night ahead. This job is physical, especially when you start wielding the saw."

"How about you guys?" the food woman said. "Want anything, detectives?"

Maddocks hesitated at the trolley. "Ah, yeah. I'll take that turkey salami."

She handed him a wrapped sandwich. "On the house," she said. "Would go to waste anyway. How 'bout you, Detective Leo?"

"No," Leo said quickly, his complexion looking a little green as he pocketed his phone and passed the trolley on his way to the exit. "I'll snag something hot from the cafeteria upstairs." The automatic doors hissed open, and Maddocks and Leo departed the morgue.

"How the fuck can she eat in there?" Leo said.

"Let me know if you get a hit on the ink," Maddocks said as he turned to head down the length of the sterile basement corridor toward a fire escape. Fluorescent lights flickered. Air conditioners and other machinery hummed in the bowels of the hospital.

"Where are you going?" Leo called after him.

"Stairs. Got to give my dog a bathroom break. I'll call Buziak from the parking lot."

"You got a dog? In your car?"

Maddocks ignored him and pushed through the fire escape doors. He climbed the stairs two at a time instead of using the elevator, needing to work his muscles and get the cloying scent of death pumping out of his lungs. He shoved out of the hospital doors into brittle air. The sleet had stopped, and Maddocks drank the fresh oxygen down into his lungs as he strode for his Chevy Impala.

He beeped the lock, opened the door, and peered in. Jack-O lifted his grizzled little head.

"Hey there, old man," Maddocks said, reaching in and ruffling Jack-O's coat. "Com'ere. Let's get you outside." He hooked the dog's lead onto the collar, and he lifted the animal down into the crystalline slush covering the ground.

The dog hobbled awkwardly on three legs and peed on the left front tire of the Impala.

Maddocks snorted. "See? You don't even have to lift your leg now. There's an upside to everything."

He got out his phone and called his superior while Jack-O led him across the parking lot on a little sniffing expedition.

"Buziak, it's Maddocks. We could have an active serial on our hands." Quickly, he briefed his boss on the ominous similarities between his floater case and the cemetery case that was being splashed all over the media.

Buziak was silent for a long moment. Maddocks looked up at the windows of the hospital building. Christmas tree lights flickered in one.

"Any sign of a crucifix?" Buziak said.

"Can't rule it in or out yet. Couldn't tell from the preliminary external—facial tissue was severely scavenged by invertebrates. The internal, X-rays, could reveal more."

Buziak instructed Maddocks to keep him immediately apprised of any new developments, day or night. Meanwhile, he was going to get authorization to set up a task force and have a dedicated incident room ready first thing in the morning.

Maddocks killed the call feeling truly energized for the first time in a long, long while. He checked his watch, then lifted Jack-O's tubby little body up from the snow. He carried him back to the car and got into his Impala with Jack-O. He laid a spare jacket on the passenger seat and set the dog upon it. Temps were dropping as night crawled in. He found the water bottle and bowl he'd tossed into his car this morning, and he filled the bowl, which he placed on the floor on the passenger side. He then unwrapped the turkey salami sandwich. He hand-fed Jack-O the hospital fare, breaking off pieces and delivering them to the critter's mouth. The dog's breath was smelly, and the rascal was clearly starving.

"So, what's your story, huh?" Maddocks said to the animal for the hundredth time, as if the three-legged canine might suddenly answer one day. "Should've called you John Dog. Like John Doe, eh." The animal burped.

"Never mind. You going to be good now? Catch some Zs?" Maddocks smoothed the dog's head. And be dammed if that funny little tail didn't thump against the car seat. Maddocks smiled. It was the first time he'd seen Jack-O's tail wag, and it gave him an odd punch to the heart. It had not been his choice to rescue a dog, but their paths had collided in the dark of one night, and say what one might, it made him feel good to have made a difference, to see Jack-O's tail finally wag. Maybe that's all it took to feel human—to know that you'd made a difference in the life of another.

He shut Jack-O inside, leaving the windows open a crack. He still had enough time to join Leo in the cafeteria, where he might find something hotter and more nourishing than a stale sandwich.

An extra bite fueled his stride as he made his way toward the hospital entrance. Day one on the new job and he'd landed a doozy of a case, maybe even a serial. Complete with media fireworks. He knew from experience that this kind of thing was a career maker. Or breaker, but he was not about to let that happen. He'd made the right decision coming here. Felt it in his gut.

He was going to make this work. With Ginny. With everything.

He phoned Ginny on his way in, but got voicemail. "Hey, kiddo, just checking to see how the rest of your day went. Sorry about this morning. Landed a whopper of a case. This is going to work out. We . . . we need to talk about Christmas—plans. Give me a call, okay?"

CHAPTER 15

Angie and Holgersen crossed the blue iron bridge over the Gorge and turned into the gentrifying area along the water.

It was 6:07 p.m. on Sunday, and they'd been pushing sixteen hours straight now, amped on caffeine and junk food. Angie had barely slept since Thursday. Her brain felt odd—light and buzzy. She slowed her Crown Vic as they approached the bus shelter where, according to the driver on shift yesterday evening, Gracie Marie Drummond had gotten off, as usual, for her Saturday night shift at the Blue Badger Bakery.

Earlier, Angie and Holgersen had visited the bus depot, spoken with the manager, located the Saturday route driver, and gone to his house. Gary Vaughan, a veteran transit operator, had been both helpful and horrified. Angie replayed the driver's words as she pulled off the road next to the bus stop and came to a halt.

Gracie was such a nice person, always so friendly, always a smile for everyone. Fairfield is an early stop on my shift. I do the first part of the night on Saturdays. Yes, she got off at the stop nearest the Blue Badger yesterday. Yes, I'm sure.

"This is it," said Holgersen, peering through the rain-streaked window. "Vaughan said he made this stop around 6:37 p.m. Saturday."

I was running late. I usually am by that point. I always have trouble keeping up to the posted schedule because of constant construction, traffic. The weather. It's getting close to Christmas—always more congestion on the roads around that time, and on weekends.

"So," Holgersen said, "Gracie Marie boards the bus right outside her apartment building in Fairfield. She takes her usual seat, right-hand side of the bus, near the front door, and she has white earbuds in her ears, listening to something on her phone, as she always did, according to the driver." Holgersen turned to Angie. "Gary Vaughan there seems to have taken real special notice of our Gracie. What you make of him?"

"Not sure yet." She mentally replayed more of their interview with Vaughan.

Did anyone else get off with her at that stop on Saturday?

Two guys. Wait, no, it was just the one. Week before, I think, it was two guys.

So this one guy who got off with her on Saturday, he's a regular?

Yeah. Usually it's Gracie Marie and the one guy. He's on his regular home commute, it seems. Keeps to himself. Doesn't make eye contact. Short. In his fifties, maybe. Asian looking.

And the other guy from the week before, what did he look like?

Tallish. Fit-looking. Dark clothes. Toque pulled low . . . didn't really see his face.

"There's street lighting—sidewalk is pretty well lit." Holgersen tugged at his goatee. "Something happened to Gracie between this stop and the door of the Badger. From here, her phone goes dead. The staff call, get no reply. Nada. Vanished. Until she winds up in Ross Bay Cemetery at the feet of the Virgin Mary."

Techs had been trying during the afternoon to trace Drummond's cell phone, but no luck. Battery was either dead or removed. They'd acquired her recent call records from her carrier, which was being cooperative, and a tech was presently going through those. Next step would be a visit to the Drummond house and taking into evidence any other electronic equipment she might have used. But the clock was ticking fast. Angie figured she had until tonight to catch a break, because by tomorrow morning this case would probably be in the hands of a homicide team.

Technically speaking, a primary crime scene was where the victim was found. In this case, the cemetery was the primary scene. However, an assault like this began at the point where a suspect first changed intent into action, and it included any other location where physical or trace evidence might be located. She hoped to find something here.

Shutting off the engine, she pulled on her skullcap. But as she reached for the door handle, her own cell rang. She checked the ID. Her dad. She let it go to voicemail as they got out of the car.

"Okay, let's walk it through." Angie turned in a slow circle, surveying the surrounding area. Fog was thick, and sleet spat from the low sky. "She gets off the bus here. And the Blue Badger is down by the water over there, around those brick buildings."

"Abandoned," said Holgersen, shining his flashlight along the side of the closest structure. "Derelict gasworks from the eighteen hundreds. About to be redeveloped, according to those rezoning application signs plastered to the walls."

"How'd you know they were gasworks?" she said.

"I told you. I know stuff."

She crooked a brow and panned her own flashlight over old rail ties that ran alongside the building perimeter. The ties were overgrown with weeds that were covered in a light layer of slush.

"So, Drummond starts walking this way." Angie headed off down the sidewalk. Holgersen followed. "Her shift starts at six thirty, and the bus was late, so she's hurrying. It's cold, windy, snowing that night. She has her head down, earphones plugged in. Unaware of her surroundings."

"Plenty traffic going by," said Holgersen.

"But it was stormy," said Angie. "Weather like that turns people's attention inward. Drivers' attention was probably focused on the road directly in front of them." She checked her watch as they reached the corner at the end of the block. "It takes her maybe two minutes tops from the bus shelter down to this corner." They rounded the corner and entered a neatly paved parking lot with standing light fixtures reminiscent of the gaslight era. Ahead of them was the bakery and café with a blue neon caricature of a badger in the window. Bright, warm lights inside illuminated patrons at small tables. "And we're here." They climbed the stairs to the patio, made for the glass doors.

Angie stopped on the deck. "Except Drummond *didn't* get here. Something happened *before* here."

As Holgersen reached for the door handle, something compelled her to turn and stare into the shadows across the parking lot. The two brick buildings hulked dark and ominous, side by side, windows boarded up. Wind gusted suddenly, sending a thick shroud of fog swirling up from the water, and there she was. At the entrance to the narrow alley that led between the brick buildings. The little girl in pink. Luminous, almost floating. Her back was to Angie.

The child turned slightly and glanced over her shoulder. White face glowing in the dark. She held out her right hand. In her left was a small basket.

Come playum dum grove . . . Come down dem . . .

A kind of terror rose inside Angie. The child was beckoning. She could feel the pull deep inside her, as if invisible strings tugged inside her chest, drawing her toward the shadows. Almost not of her own volition, she took a step toward the apparition.

"Pallorino? You coming?" Holgersen stood there, door open in his hand, music and laughter seeping out into the cold.

"Ah, yeah . . . Why don't you go ahead, see if anyone saw Drummond yesterday? Ask the usual—was she having any problems, had she recently expressed any fears, made any complaints about patrons, personal situations, fellow workers. I just want to go check . . . something out over there." She moved quickly across the patio and back down the stairs.

"Pallorino!" he called after her, then cursed as she disappeared into the swirl of sleet and mist. She made for the alley.

Come, come playum . . .

The whispering inside her head grew louder, the tug in her chest fierce. She began to race toward the black opening between the buildings even as every molecule inside her body screamed for her to flee.

Run . . . Run! . . . Uciekaj, uciekaj!

The strange words filled her head. Some sounded like mangled English, like the odd utterings of a toddler, and those seemed to beckon her to come and play, to do something nice. While the others seemed to be in a foreign language, yet she seemed to understand instinctively what they meant—*Flee! Run away! Fast!*

She entered the alley, heart hammering. And stilled. The child in pink was suddenly at the far end—a soft, impossible wash of shimmering pink. The girl's arm reached out again.

The mist swirled, cleared, and she was gone.

Angie swallowed. Sweat prickled across her upper lip. The shadows were like ink inside the brick corridor. Soot and lichen blackened the walls. She clicked her flashlight on again. Old rail ties. Glint of broken glass. A bottle. All sticking out of the fine layer of slushy snow. She entered slowly, gravel and frozen slush crunching and squelching beneath her boots.

Her beam bounced off the walls and flickered in crevices, making shadows dart. Something scuttled across her boot. She gasped, swung her beam as her hand shot instinctively toward her holstered sidearm. A small shape disappeared into a drainpipe tucked into a little alcove in the wall. Just a rodent. Gathering herself, she made her way to the end of the corridor where she'd seen the toddler. The alley spilled out into a wide, vacant lot—clumps of grass and brambles poking out of the slush. A foghorn moaned out on the water. She ran her flashlight across the lot. No child.

Of course there was no child.

She was fucking hallucinating, like her mother . . . it was starting. She was getting sick. What on earth had even compelled her to follow something she *knew* to be an apparition, a figment of her own mind? *That's* what frightened her most. The fact that her hallucinations could exert such powerful control over her own sense of logic. She turned to quickly return to the warmth and lights of the Blue Badger, and suddenly she saw the rear end of the bus shelter up the bank, her vehicle parked beside it. And it struck her.

She spun back to face the alley. This was a shortcut. Drummond could have taken this route through the alley between the abandoned gasworks buildings. A vehicle could have been waiting in this empty lot, accessed from a side road nearer the water. There was no lighting down here.

Angie scanned the ground with her beam. Whatever vehicle tracks might have been made last night were covered with slush. She started to retrace her way back toward the alley, examining the ground inch by inch with her flashlight as she walked. Nothing jumped out at her. She reentered the alley and stood there for a moment, imagining that she was Drummond, just alighted from the bus, hurrying down the bank from the shelter. The kid probably had her head down against the weather, her body hunched into her coat, collar up against her cheeks. Her hat pulled low. Listening to her music. She'd surely have been moving fast through this alley, given the fact her bus was late and that fear in a dark and lonely place like this was instinctive.

Maybe she cut through here weekly, if, as Vaughan had said, his bus was always running late. Maybe someone knew her routine and was waiting for her last night. A crime of choice, not chance.

Angie put her head down, as if she might be Drummond, and walked, examining the ground with her flashlight as she went. She stilled as her beam caught something shiny. Her earlier footprint had exposed an object lying in gravel. Angie crouched down, snapped on her gloves, and picked up a set of small white earbuds attached to a broken cord. She glanced up. She was crouching adjacent to the recess in the wall into which the rat had scuttled. The alcove was set back enough to accommodate an assailant pressing himself against the bricks. He would have been

114

totally hidden. He could have stepped out as Drummond approached or struck her from behind as she passed. The earbuds could have been ripped out of her ears, the cord broken in the violence of an ensuing tussle. Judging by the defensive wounds she'd seen on Drummond's body, she'd fought for her life. But Drummond would have screamed, surely?

Angie came to her feet, and she cried out, testing sound in the canyon of brick. Her scream fell flat, deadened by moss and lichen and by the layer of slush on the ground. Even if Drummond had managed to scream, no one would have heard her in the storm, in the dark. She'd have been all alone. Completely vulnerable.

"Pallorino!" came Holgersen's voice. "Hey! Who's there?" A flashlight bobbed at the end of the alley. Footfalls sounded, running, coming closer. The beam shone in her face, and she saw that her partner had his service weapon drawn.

She dangled the earphones up in her gloved fingers. "Bus driver said she was plugged in. Mom said she had an iPhone. These are standard Apple buds. There's a vacant lot at the rear of this alley, big enough to park a vehicle. He could have planned this—been waiting right here in this alcove. Knowing she would come. Jumped her, knocked out the buds. He planned this. He picked Drummond for some reason, Holgersen. He *hunted* and trapped her. She fit his fantasy, and we need to find out why."

"What the fuck, Angie?" He holstered his service weapon. "You *screamed*. I thought you were in danger. Jeeezus. I was looking for you, and then I heard—"

"Sound," she said, glancing up at the walls, "it's muffled in here. Go back exactly the way you entered, Holgersen. Retrace your footsteps to minimize further contamination. We need to cordon this place off, get a uniform to stand guard until we can get a forensic team in here in the morning. *This* is our abduction site. I'd stake my life on it. Go!"

He muttered a curse, started retracing his steps. She followed directly in his footprints.

"What did the staff at the Badger say?" she called out from behind him. "You get anything?"

He stopped, turned, glared down at her, anger and adrenaline still simmering off him. "Shift staff that she usually worked with was not there. But the manager said Gracie was a quiet, sweet girl. Empathetic. Private. Didn't talk much about friends, dates, whatevers. Diligent. Had not expressed any fears, so fars as they knew, nor any problems with other staff. She regularly took a shortcut through this alley. The Badger's night-shift boss is a stickler for punctuality, so she cuts through here to save like three minutes walking along the lighted sidewalk around the buildings."

"Good. So we—"

"Good? For crap's sake, Pallorino. You scared the scat out of me."

"Go. Keep moving."

They reached the end. "Go get the barrier tape from the vehicle," she ordered. "I'm going to call this in." As she reached for her cell, it rang.

"Pallorino, Metro PD."

"It's Vedder."

"I was just about to call you." She mouthed to Holgersen, "Vedder," and made a scooting motion with her hand for him to go.

"We found—"

"I need you to drop what you're doing—"

"What?"

"I need you to stop what you're doing, and—"

"No. Wait, we just got a break. I—"

"Pallorino, stop. Right now. You listening to me?"

"Sir. Yes."

"Homicide caught a case this morning. Young woman found naked and wrapped in a plastic tarp, floating in the Gorge. She's been genitally mutilated. Lock of hair removed."

Angie quickly ducked under the cover of an eave. "Crucifix on her brow?" she said.

"Too early to tell either way, but—"

"This and the Drummond case could both be linked to the Fernyhough and Ritter cases," she said quickly. "You can't pull me off now, Vedder. I worked *both* those sexual assault cases with Hash. I know them inside out. You have *got* to let me see this through."

"Dammit, Pallorino, just hear me out, will you? Buziak is setting up a task force as we speak."

"Fuck," she whispered, kicking at stones in the slush. It was all going to homicide.

"You're being temporarily seconded to that force."

She went stone-still.

"Buziak agrees that the Drummond, Fernyhough, and Ritter cases could be linked to his floater case, and since you're intimately familiar with those sex cases, he wants you to get over to the autopsy currently under way on the Jane Doe found in the Gorge, to observe and to inform the team of any other similarities you might see emerging."

Her hand tightened on her phone as adrenaline and excitement smashed through her system.

"The lead on the floater is Sergeant James Maddocks. You'll be temporarily partnered with him. He's attending the postmortem now. The Drummond PM is scheduled for first thing in the morning."

"Who's Maddocks? I've never heard his name."

"The new guy."

"*New* guy? In homicide?" Her brain reeled. "What do you mean, *new* guy? The position has been filled already? When did this happen?"

"It's not my unit, Pallorino. I don't know."

"You have my forms on your desk, Vedder, my application. Did you sign off on it? I've done all the Justice Institute courses and then some. I—"

"This is not the time—"

"It's exactly the time." *I can prove myself on this case. This is my big chance to break in.*

"Angie."

She stilled at his use of her first name.

"Look, I'm not stalling on this. I told you, I *need* that psych eval in hand before I can put you forward. You must see a police psychologist for debrief after losing a partner. It's MVPD protocol, and Buziak isn't even going to look at you for his permanent team until you get that clearance. So if you want this, do it. Go get that eval."

Excitement shifted into anxiety. A psych eval—a shrink figuring out that she was having visions of a toddler, or that she'd become addicted to anonymous sex as a coping mechanism—was the last thing she needed. She could lose her job completely. Holgersen arrived with the tape.

Focus.

She cleared her throat, spoke low and level. "I believe we've found the site of the initial assault on Drummond. An alleyway between the Blue Badger and the bus shelter where our vic got off the bus."

"Okay, good. Leave Holgersen to secure the scene and get yourself over to that autopsy. Briefing of the new task force will begin at seven thirty a.m. tomorrow. Good luck. And Angie—" He paused. "Be nice. If you play nice, Maddocks might put in a word of recommendation when the time comes." Another pause. "Violent death is not a one-person mission."

Vedder's warning was clear. He knew her well—how irascible she could be. Her issues with anger management and borderline rage at times. Her propensity to work solo. She was fully aware that a good homicide detective was a team player and that team playing was something she'd always had a problem with. Even at school. In college. She knew also from her meeting with Vedder earlier today that she already had a big fat department target on her back.

She had everything to lose.

And everything to win.

And some new guy called Maddocks was going to have a say in her future.

CHAPTER 16

Angie's boot heels echoed along the basement corridor. She knew the first thing that would hit her when she entered the morgue would be the smell. It would make her edgy. Hospital smells always did, although she'd never really figured out why—it's not like she'd ever had a bad personal experience in one.

She'd found a small jar of eucalyptus ointment in her glove compartment from when Hash had a bad chest cough. She hadn't had the heart to throw any of his stuff out. As she neared the morgue doors, she opened the container and dabbed some of the ointment under her nose.

Mistake.

The ointment burned like hell, and her eyes watered as the double doors hissed open. She entered, blinking. Cello music played against the click and clatter of instruments and the sound of water drumming in a sink. The decedent lay naked on her back on the stainless steel table—her body ghostly white, her head a bloodied mess with a bared jaw, bulbous eyes, dark strings of hair.

In spite of her mental preparation, shock washed through Angie.

Barb O'Hagan was the attending pathologist. This pleased her. The doc glanced up, a scalpel in hand. Two detectives stood with their backs to Angie. Leo's chunky frame and shock of white hair were instantly recognizable. The guy beside him stood far taller, maybe six foot four—shoulders twice as broad as Leo's. His hair was thick and glistened blue-black under the harsh fluorescent lighting. Something inside Angie went stone-still.

"Detective Pallorino has joined us," O'Hagan said into the mike, and she gave Angie a nod.

The two detectives turned. Indigo eyes met hers. Her heart started to stammer.

Mr. Big Dick.

Tall, dark, and just the wrong side of handsome—the guy she'd handcuffed to a motel room bed and fucked to her heart's pleasure last night. *He* was the new homicide guy? *He* could have a say in her future? A loud clanging began in her ears.

Angie inhaled deeply, but the eucalyptus ointment fumes made her cough. Her eyes watered even more, and her nose began to run, which made her sniff and cough again.

"Leo, Barb," she managed to say between her coughing fit.

Leo frowned. "What're *you* doing here?"

O'Hagan reached up and turned her mike off.

Angie wiped her eyes with the base of her thumb. "'Scuse me. I, uh . . . got . . . something in my eyes." She cleared her throat, sniffed again. "I've been seconded to this case. Buziak just assigned me to the task force."

Cello music crashed.

Leo stared, eyes flat. "This is James Maddocks," he said. "He's lead on this DB for now."

"Angie Pallorino," she said, looking up and once again meeting those deep-indigo eyes. Heat washed over her skin. Her set of sex rules raced through her mind.

Never sleep with a colleague. Never kiss. Leave first . . . Always stay in control . . .

Control was the last fucking thing she was in right now.

"The Drummond case is mine," she managed to say, wiping her nose with her sleeve. "Her assault might be linked to two earlier unsolved sexual assaults that I worked with my former partner, Hashowsky, three and four years ago. Similar signature in all three. I've been asked to observe this postmortem and to identify any other similarities that might come to my attention, based on my older cases."

Slowly, his gaze locked on hers, Detective James Maddocks extended his hand. Angie took it. Firm—very firm—grip. Big. The memory of his hand on her arm last night as he'd steered her out of the club punched through her. It was followed by an image of him stark naked on the bed, hands above his head. His chest, armpit, and groin hair black as night, skin pale and honed like marble. Like alabaster . . . that dick, erect, sheathed. She swallowed.

"Pleased to . . . meet you, Detective," he said, holding on to her hand a fraction too long, the hint of a smile playing over his lips, a deadly seriousness in his eyes. When he released her, she swiped again at her nose with her sleeve.

O'Hagan eyed them both a moment, exchanged a glance with Leo, and then said, "Got tissues on the counter over there."

Angie went over to grab a wad of Kleenex. "Thanks. I used some ointment that Hash left in my vehicle. Burns like hell." She tried for a light laugh. "His last joke's on me, as usual."

Shit shit shit . . .

She took her place beside Mr. Big D. and noticed that on this occasion he wore a gold wedding band. As she suspected. Her stomach balled tighter. Men. Out in the dark, hunting on the quiet in various ways, driven to satisfy the most basic of urges over which some had little or no control. But then she couldn't judge. She hunted on the quiet, too.

The fact that he was married could actually work in her favor.

It could give her leverage. She held on to that thought, cleared her mind, and returned her attention to the body on the table. Surprise washed afresh through her as she caught sight of the ink that covered the woman's lower abdomen and shaved pubic area.

"You're just in time," O'Hagan said. "We're about to open her up." She reached up and reengaged her mike.

CHAPTER 17

Jack Killion slotted his key into the lock and opened the door. The lights inside had been dimmed. Candles flickered next to an open bottle of wine and two glasses that had been placed on a coffee table in front of the floor-to-ceiling windows. Beyond the windows it was dark outside, the lights of the legislature buildings twinkling across the bay. Music, jazz, played softly.

He hesitated, tension balling between his shoulder blades. Perhaps he should leave, stop this. But he entered, closing the door quietly behind him.

"Hey." She came around the corner, startling him. She took his briefcase and set it on a chair, and then she curled her hands around his wrists and drew him close, kissing him on the mouth. She tasted of wine.

When he didn't respond in the way he usually did, she drew back and narrowed her eyes. "You okay?"

"Yeah. Yeah, it's just . . ."

"The swearing-in on Tuesday? The breaking news?"

"Fine timing, huh? Whole bloody stamp-out-crime angle could backfire on me now."

"Come—sit. Fire is on, wine is open." She padded on stockinged feet into the living area and seated herself on the sofa. She patted the cushion next to her. "Talk to me."

"Joyce, maybe we should stop for a—"

"Sit." Her features turned serious. "I can help, Jack." She had the ability to switch her business mind on or off in the blink of an eye, toggle back and forth. It made him wonder sometimes who the real Joyce Norton-Wells was at any given time, what she was really thinking in that calculating brain of hers. "Chief Gunnar called me at home to apprise me of what's happening," she said as she reached for her glass of wine. "It looks serious."

"Hell yeah—"

"No, I mean big, Jack." She inhaled deeply and crossed her gorgeously honed legs. "We could have a serial killer on our hands."

He lowered himself slowly onto a chair near the window, preferring—needing—to keep a little distance between himself and her, for now. She leaned forward. "As you know, the office of the attorney general is entitled to be told in advance of potentially major or difficult prosecutions."

A sense of foreboding rose inside him as he measured Joyce's dark eyes. They showed a glint of excitement. She had a taste for ugly battles. And he knew that whatever she was about to say, it was regarding a fight that was looming, something he didn't want as he took office on a very slim mandate.

"Go on."

"We ordered a rush on the medico-legal autopsy for the body found floating in the Gorge this morning. The PM is being performed as we speak—"

"At night? On a Sunday?"

"Extraordinary circumstances." She hesitated. "Something came up in the preliminary external examination."

The sinister feeling inside him furled deeper.

"A lock of her hair had been cut off." She paused. "And she'd been circumcised."

He stared, pulse quickening.

"Metro PD feels her case is linked to that of the young woman found in the cemetery and possibly to two earlier sexual assaults that they know of." She watched him, as if gauging his stomach, his stamina for something like this. "A ritual lust killer, Jack, someone who has escalated from rape to murder and who might be devolving very fast, given the apparent back-to-back timing of these two very recent homicides."

"I don't need this."

"Maybe you do. When the MVPD catch this guy, and they *will*, our prosecution of him is going to be sensational. It'll garner international attention. Gunnar is looping my office in from the start so that Crown counsel will be well prepared and apprised of all facets of the investigation—we want to ensure no balls are dropped, no legal holes left. I'm working to have a team of top prosecutors ready to clear their slates for this. We cannot afford a misstep."

He surged to his feet, strode to the floor-to-ceiling windows, and stared out over the lights of the harbor. *His* city.

"Jack?"

"You get off on this, don't you? You actually *want* this. You *like* it that young white girls are being sexually mutilated and killed in this city because you think it will further your career, shine the limelight on your office when it comes down to prosecuting him."

"Jack—"

"Eighty-nine votes," he said, still facing the view. "That's my mandate. *That's* my 'victory' over Patty Markham. It's all I got. And polls show that it was my zero tolerance on crime policy that won me that slim margin." He turned to face her.

She'd kicked off her heels, curled her legs under her butt, and was watching him intently. She reminded him of a Rene Russo type in looks. Sexy as all get out in an older woman kind of way that spoke of experience and confidence in her own sexuality. And power. Assistant Deputy Attorney

General Joyce Norton-Wells knew how to break men's balls with a smile and her intellect—and sometimes a calculated display of cleavage or calf.

Outwardly sophisticated and cool, yet inwardly ferocious, a blisteringly intelligent lawyer, leader, activist. Was it the penumbra of her power and genius that he loved to cloak around himself? Was it feeling part of a secret team, the sense that they belonged to an inner sanctum, that they both were going somewhere big in this country? Was it the sex? The titillation, the salaciousness of a clandestine relationship?

Whatever it was, it aroused them both. He was quite simply addicted to her.

"What makes you think they'll get him soon?"

"Because he's an addict. He's *compelled* to act out whatever sex-based fantasy he holds in his head. And his need is growing. If Metro is correct, his cooling-off period appears incredibly short, which means he's devolving astoundingly fast. He'll crash, make mistakes." She angled her head and smiled. It shot a spark of irritation through him. "Come here."

"Joyce—"

"No, listen to me. This *is* a good thing, Jack. It's a powerful tool. Think about it. You get Zach and his team to spin these terrible sexual assaults as the legacy of a Markham government lax on crime, too friendly to the homeless, not tough enough on street drugs. You tell them that *this* is what a corrupt and inept police board and MVPD has allowed to breed. Four years—" She held up four fingers. "*Four*—that's when this rapist apparently first came to the attention of the Metro sex crimes unit. Then another attack a whole year later, and still they did not apprehend anyone in those cases. And now this same repeat offender, if it is him, has been allowed to kill, maybe not once, but twice. Bad closure rates leading to further and more serious crime. You tell your constituents that *this* is why they elected you—to clean up the Markham-Gunnar mess—and you use this as your justification to act harshly and swiftly to sweep the police board clean, to appoint new members who are in synch with your policies. Then, when the MVPD gets close to apprehending this perpetrator, you find cause to axe Gunnar, and you put Antoni Moreno in his place, like you've been wanting all along." She pushed a fall of thick hair off her brow and smiled. "Then, an MVPD under Moreno's stewardship arrests the serial killer."

He looked away, inhaled deeply.

"It's a game plan, Jack," she said softly. "You have to have a game plan. It's a way of handling this before it handles us."

He turned back to face her.

Us.

"We're good together," she said.

He gave a derisive snort, but a smile pulled at his mouth nevertheless. "And then," he said slowly, "a sensationalist sex killer is convicted under *your* tenure as ADAG."

She angled her head and gave him a sly grin.

"You really are gunning for it," he said. "Minister of justice. Maybe even the premiership."

"No, Jack, premier is yours down the line." She came to her feet, padded over to him, lifted her skirt, and straddled him. She cupped his face, angled her head. "Supreme Court will suit me just fine." And she pressed her warm, open mouth over his. Heat washed into his groin. "We've got an hour before I need to be home," she murmured against his lips.

He slid his hand up the inside of her thigh, and his fingers met bare skin. His heart kicked. She was wearing suspender tights, no panties. He cupped her shaved pussy, and his vision blurred as she moaned and rocked her pelvis gently against his hand. With two fingers he parted her labia. Inside she was smooth and warm and wet and her little nub of a clit was erect. He slid a finger up inside her and massaged, searching for the elusive G-spot, the place that could explode her in an instant. She put her head back, arching her spine, opening her thighs wider, tilting her hips toward him, giving him deeper access as she groaned in pleasure.

✝

CHAPTER 18

Maddocks stepped out into the chill night air with Leo and Pallorino, his mind racing, adrenaline still thumping through his blood. Along with something deeper—a crackling hot sexual energy that had everything to do with the woman who'd walked into the morgue and shocked the nuts off him. What were the fucking odds? Angie—a *detective*? The woman he'd so badly wanted to screw again, the woman he'd phoned first thing this morning, was now working a case with him that he couldn't afford to screw up.

It was close to eleven, and the world felt quiet, waiting, breath misting from their mouths as they walked to their cars. Despite the pristine air, death clung to the fabric of their clothes, to their hair. It was inside their nasal passages and on their skin. It was a scent nigh impossible to get rid of, Maddocks knew from experience. Downstairs, O'Hagan and her assistants were winding things up. Once the doc had peeled back what remained of their victim's face, she'd found fine lines scored into the bone of the forehead in the shape of a cross. Additional ligature marks had presented around the neck, wrists, and ankles—marks that had been made antemortem—and there was severe anal and vaginal tearing, which appeared to have occurred both ante- and postmortem.

Their decedent had been through a rough time before she died from strangulation.

Inside the tarp cocoon O'Hagan had also found fragments of dried leaves, a few soil grains, and what looked like grass seed, plus sheep maggot evidence, which implied the victim had been dead on land and had possibly lain outdoors, likely under shelter, before going into the sea. This all might help narrow down location.

Establishing time of death, however, would remain tricky without the context of location and given the extreme below-freezing temperatures of late, which would have delayed the decomp process. As it stood, even in deaths with the same cause and identical environmental conditions, one body could show advanced putrefaction, while another could show little change, O'Hagan had explained. Maggot larvae could even go into a period of suspended animation if conditions did not warrant further development.

Once they'd opened up the body, things had taken a pretty standard timeline of around three hours for the rest of the autopsy. Tox, serology, entomology, odontology, and other forensic lab tests analyzing combings from head and pubic hair would obviously take longer, but they were being expedited, as per the ADAG's direction. O'Hagan would start the Drummond postmortem at dawn and have a preliminary report for them later tomorrow.

"Anyone up for a late beer and steak at the Pig?" Leo said, pausing to light a cigarette. He inhaled deeply and blew out a long stream of smoke. It made Maddocks wish he still smoked. It was better than the stink of death. And he was on edge tonight, as if needing some kind of fix.

"Not me," Pallorino said. "Been on over twenty hours straight. Need my sleep." Her eyes met Maddocks's in the dimly lit lot, and she glanced quickly away. She knew that he knew exactly why her sleep had been compromised and what she'd been doing last night when she'd gotten the call for Cemetery Girl—riding him at the Foxy Motel.

"I'll take a rain check," he said to Leo.

"Catch you both at the butt crack of dawn, then," Leo said. "My wheels are this way." He hunkered down into his wool coat and headed around the building to another parking lot.

Pallorino made for a Crown Vic parked alone under a light standard.

"Angie?" he called after her.

She stilled, stood motionless for a moment, her back to him, car keys jiggling in her hand.

"We need to talk."

She turned. "We do?" Her complexion was pale in the parking lot light, a black woolen hat pulled snug over her sleek, dark-red hair. The scar across the left side of her mouth was shadowed in this light, and it offset her obvious fatigue, which gave her an oddly sexy badass appeal mixed in with a vulnerability. Goddamn if he didn't find it appealing.

"Is this going to be a problem?" he said, coming closer.

"This?"

"You, me." He paused. "That club." Wind gusted, icy, lifting a fine spray of crystals.

"There is no you and me, Detective," she said quietly. "It never happened, okay? And it's Pallorino." She held his gaze. Unflinching.

He swallowed. Yeah, she really did it for him on all levels. Which gave him his answer—this *was* going to be a problem.

Her gaze shifted slowly, pointedly down to his left hand. He realized with a shock that he was fiddling his thumb against his wedding band.

"Married," she said quietly. "I suspected as much."

"It's . . . not what you think."

She gave a snort and took a step toward him so that they stood almost toe to toe. "If you don't want your spouse to find out about your extramural activities, Detective Maddocks," she said softly, "you won't mention 'us' to a single soul back at the station. Or anywhere."

He watched her mouth. An urge came over him to bend down, kiss her lips, explore that scar with the tip of his tongue. His groin stirred at the memory of her naked, straddling him, breasts bouncing, her head thrown back, long hair spilling over her shoulders. He inhaled slowly, deeply. "That a threat?"

"Consider it whatever you want."

A slow smile crossed his lips, and he angled his head.

"Don't mock me," she said. "And don't try me—you'll regret it." She turned her back on him and beeped her lock. "I should've made you for a cop," she said, opening her door. "I was a fool not to have seen it." She got into her car and reached to pull the driver's side door closed. But he clamped his hand on the door, stopping her.

"Yet you gave me your number. Your name."

She glanced up, meeting his gaze. "See you in the morning, sir." And she yanked the door out of his grip, slamming it shut. Her engine started. Exhaust fumes boiled white into the cold air.

He stepped back as she revved her engine and took off at a clip, skidding slightly on ice as she rounded the curve out of the parking lot. His breath clouded around his face. His heart, he realized, was thumping in his throat. He dragged his hand over his hair. Yeah—this was going to be more than a problem.

CHAPTER 19

Angie drove home, nerves crackling like live electrical wires. First the hallucinations and those weird words in her head that seemed to come from the child. Now Mr. Big Dick—her superior. Her temporary partner. A fucking cop. A ferocious urge rose in her to cut a U-turn and speed for the highway out of town, hit the club, even as exhausted as she was. She wanted to fuck her brains out, blow off steam with someone other than Maddocks. Overwrite her sexual experience with him, forge fresh neural pathways in her brain. Wash him clean out of her head with something hotter, wilder. Better.

Yet a little voice in the back of her brain said there wasn't going to be anything better than James Maddocks.

James—what kind of name was *James*, anyway?

Hi, I'm James . . . James Bond. She put on music. AC/DC. Pumped up the sound, amped the bass. *You . . . shook me . . . all night long . . .* She banged her palm on her wheel in time to the beat, the sound slamming through her skull as she turned onto Wharf.

She lived in one of those new "loft" condo developments right on the Gorge waterway at the bottom of Chinatown, "loft" being Realtor-speak for license to charge a fortune for postage-stamp footage that barely accommodated one bedroom. But it suited her—close to work, good investment, new, no-hassle appliances, easy resale. And it had rental potential should she want to travel. Or . . . get a life, or . . . something.

As she wheeled her Crown Vic down onto Dock Street with its steep incline to the water, the memory of Vedder's words hit her.

Be nice. If you play nice, Maddocks might put in a word of recommendation when the time comes . . . Violent death is not a one-person mission . . .

Great. Just great. She waited for the underground parking security gate to open.

After all these years of trying to get into the elite unit, it came down to this? The guy she'd screwed to blow off steam, to escape from her work, now *was* her work? And she had no choice but to cooperate, because making homicide was her one big life goal—a holy grail toward which she'd been gunning for the last six years since she'd made sex crimes. His dark-blue eyes, his words sifted into her memory as she entered the garage.

Is this going to be a problem? . . . You, me. That club . . .

Her hands fisted on the wheel. There would likely come a day in the not-too-distant future where she'd have to smile and be nice when she met his wife. She'd made this mistake once before in the not-distant-enough past—sleeping with a married man. Someone close to her work. In Angie's mind it had been a fling. Not in his. It had gone wrong—badly wrong—hurt too many people. Cost his marriage. She'd vowed it could never happen again. That horrible misstep was the reason behind her sex rules. It was why she'd started hitting the club. A good fuck. No strings attached. And she'd grown increasingly addicted to this fix, the latent danger, the taste of power, both physical and mental. There was something about using men that felt good, felt like payback for all the sick cases she worked where males hurt, abused, and used vulnerable females, children. It gave her control. It was a little secret that made her strong.

But now she felt suddenly off-kilter.

Angie parked in the space allotted to her apartment and caught the elevator up to her corner suite on the top floor.

Inside, her living space was sterile. Chrome and black. Bare wood floors. Easy to clean. No knickknacks. No pets to worry about. No plants to die under her neglect because of the hours she clocked on the job. She turned up the heat, shucked off her coat and hat, and kicked off her boots. She placed her service weapon, holster, and two phones on the table, and she tugged the hair tie out of her hair.

Massaging her scalp, she went to the kitchen, got a glass out of the cupboard, and the vodka bottle from the freezer. She poured herself a shot of ice-cool alcohol and sucked it back in one burning go before topping her glass up with a second. A drink or four might actually numb her into a few hours of sleep before she had to face the new task force and Detective Big D. in the morning. She put on the television and listened to the news while she warmed some leftover pasta takeout in the microwave. The twenty-four-hour station was running yet another rehash of the Drummond case. An image caught her eye as she took her plate from the microwave. Angie stilled, stared. Her heart started to stutter.

Someone had dredged up and was broadcasting a file photo of her taken last July—on a steamy evening. In the image she was carrying a limp and bleeding and dead toddler in her arms, her own face a twisted study of anguish. Blood covered her clothes, her hands . . . It was the evening Hash had died.

Angie set her plate down slowly and moved woodenly toward the TV. She grabbed the remote, bumped up the sound.

It was MVPD Detective Angela Pallorino and her new partner, Kjel Holgersen, who responded to the Ross Bay Cemetery attack last night, where Duneagle student Gracie Marie Drummond was found unconscious and bleeding. Drummond, sixteen, had been sexually assaulted and mutilated . . . Pallorino, who last made news when . . .

Rage slammed through Angie. She killed the feed. What in the hell did they need to do that for—drag up the thing with Hash? Fucking twenty-four-hour news, the need to feed the round-the-clock beast—that's what this was about. Reporters desperate to find material, mucking about and putting out old shit, trying to build a story out of blocks that were not connected at all. Vedder was right. She *was* going to look like the poster child for disaster at the MVPD if this continued.

Already there was the problem with the serious leak of what was supposed to be holdback information on *her* case.

She sucked back her vodka and poured a double. Carrying her dinner and drink to her computer, Angie's thoughts about the leak shifted to Holgersen—the phone call she was convinced she'd seen him making inside Starbucks, his denial, him suggesting that Merry Winston had picked up the cemetery call on a scanner: *She's kinda cute . . . all that spiky black hair, pale skin . . . seen her around . . .*

Distaste filled Angie's mouth. She did not want to doubt her fellow officers, let alone her own partner. She preferred to believe the Drummond case leak came from the paramedics or hospital staff or one of their family members—but it had knocked them all off ease at the MVPD, and it was breeding a simmering sense of mistrust, suspicion—the last thing they all needed right now with Killion and his team taking aim at the force.

She was going to have to watch her back.

Booting up her desktop, she delivered a forkful of pasta to her mouth and chewed while her emails loaded. She clicked through them. Nothing of interest.

She then googled Gracie Marie Drummond, found a social media page for the teen. Smart girl had activated her privacy settings. Angie couldn't see her posts, nor who her friends were. They'd need the techs to get on that. On impulse, she ran a quick Internet search for "Sergeant James Maddocks."

A few images and several news pieces came up—Maddocks at press conferences, Maddocks outside the RCMP station in Surrey, Maddocks in formal red serge at the funeral of a colleague, looking dapper in his Stetson and high brown Strathcona boots with spurs. She scrolled through the stories as she sipped her drink. He'd clearly been a big shot with the integrated homicide investigations team on the mainland—roughly Buziak's equivalent in rank and position. His experience prior to joining iHit appeared to have included working on the large interagency task force that finally resulted in the arrest of Vancouver's most infamous serial killer—pig farmer Robert Pickton. Angie's curiosity was further piqued—so he *was* familiar with major serial crimes. Now here he was with the MVPD, a smaller jurisdiction, working in the trenches under Buziak. His move to Metro PD was a step down by all appearances.

She finished her food as she studied the image of him in formal dress, irked that she found him appealing. Irritably she clicked the page shut, then checked the messages on her landline.

There was one. From her dad. She hit PLAY.

"Angie, I've been trying your cell all day. Maybe you'll get this message when you get home. You need to visit your mom. Soon." A pause. "She . . . uh . . . she *needs* to see you. She's having a real hard time settling in, and the nurses . . . Just try and visit her tomorrow, okay?" A clearing of the throat. "Please." Then a click as her father hung up.

Self-recrimination washed hot through her chest. She rubbed her brow. It was almost midnight. Too late to call him back. She hoped her mother was okay. Her attention went to the box of her mother's things that she'd left by the door before heading out to the club.

It seemed like ages ago.

She got up, lifted the photo album off the top, carried it to the sofa. Curling her socked feet under her, she sat and opened the leather-bound book of memories to the photographs of her first birthday. She then skipped forward a few more pages to the images shot in Italy, the year of her father's sabbatical. She turned to the photo of the three of them— their little family unit sitting in front of a decorated tree, the one her father had been studying earlier. It was taken their first Christmas after the car accident that had marred her face.

She touched her fingertip to the scar on her mouth as she studied the picture. A sudden flash of red exploded through her mind, and pain sliced across her mouth. She heard tires screech, the crunch of metal. She tasted blood. Angie sucked air in sharply—the visions, the sensations, were so sharp, so visceral they felt real. Pulse pounding, she got up, paced. Was that a memory? Was she remembering the accident? She had not recalled anything of the car smash until this very moment. Was she beginning to have some recall—possibly triggered by losing Hash and the toddler five months ago? Or was she extrapolating images and sensations from that terrible incident with Hash and imposing them on the photographs and the stories of her past that she'd been told? Arms wrapped around herself, shivering despite the fact the heat in her apartment was cranked up, Angie went to the mirror by the door. She stared at her reflection. Again, she touched her scar with her fingertips. An old rhyme came to mind . . .

Fractured face
in the mirror,
you are my disgrace . . .
a sinner . . .

Then other words, sounds, images, smashed through her brain.

Run . . . Run! . . . Uciekaj, uciekaj! . . . a shrill scream . . . fighting. Dark. Cold. Snowflakes. A woman . . . a familiar woman . . . Wskakuj do srodka, szybko! She yelled . . . A flash of silver . . . then blackness . . .

Angie's breaths came shallow, rapid. What the . . . ? Was this what PTSD looked like from the inside? Or worse, was she falling mentally ill? Genetics taking their toll?

She returned to the album and shut it. But as she did, one of the Italy photos slid out from under the protective plastic sheet on the page and wafted to the hardwood floor. Angie picked it up, started to reinsert it into the book, but then she noticed the tiny scrawl of her mother's hand on the back.

Rome. Jan. 1984.

Angie frowned. She peeled back the plastic sheet covering the Christmas photo—the one taken the December after the car accident, after they'd returned from Europe. She dislodged it from the page, turned it over.

Christmas 1987. Victoria.

That couldn't be right. She'd been told it was '86 that they were in Italy; 1986 was the year of her dad's sabbatical. March '86 was when the car accident occurred, when her mouth had been slashed open. The year she'd been four going on five. As far as she knew, they'd returned to Canada before Christmas. This photo should be dated "Christmas 1986." She removed another of the Italy photos and flipped it over.

Naples. Feb. 1984.

She needed sleep. Nothing was making sense. She left the album and photos on the coffee table, finished her drink, started clicking off lights. But as she reached for her Smith and Wesson to lock it away, she saw that her burner phone lying beside it was blinking with a message. She frowned and played the message.

"Angie," said a male voice, deep, resonant. Velvet on gravel.

Him.

"About our unfinished business . . . I'd like to finish it." A pause. "Can't stop thinking about you. Call me." He left a number.

Her mouth went dry. She pressed her hand to her brow. Then, quickly, she checked the time of the message. He'd called at 8:35 this morning. Mere hours since she'd left him and his erection at the Foxy Motel. He'd wanted to see her again, to be with her again . . . to complete their sexual act.

Until they'd met at the morgue.

138

CHAPTER 20

Angie entered the incident room hefting her case files and still wearing her coat. She was drenched and late. She'd been stuck in traffic, and her head was thumping from too much vodka and too little sleep.

"Thank you for joining us, Pallorino," Buziak called out as she kicked the door closed behind her. He stood at the far end of the room in front of a whiteboard that ran the length of the wall, looking like a small Al Pacino, which made Maddocks, who was standing beside him, appear even taller than his six feet four inches.

A group of about twelve detectives were seated in chairs facing Buziak, Maddocks, and the whiteboard. Heads turned to look at her as a quiet befell the room. All male, she noted, and older, some with paunches, tired-looking shirts, badges hanging by lanyards around their necks. The only other female Angie could see was Bettina, a ViCLAS coordinator. It was Bettina's job to run info through the Violent Crime Linkage Analysis System in an effort to link sex and violent homicides across the country together. She was in her late fifties. Also present was a project assistant and a young analyst.

Angie gave a brief nod to Holgersen, who was leaning against a pillar near the door beside Leo. The white-haired cop gave her a long and brazen look, then mumbled something quietly to Holgersen. She ignored him and offloaded her files onto a vacant table near the back. Finding a chair, she shrugged out of her wet coat, draped it over the back, and took a seat.

The tension in the room was palpable. Thirteen days to Christmas, a new mayoral regime taking the oath of office tomorrow, and the pressure was coming down from the top. Even Inspector Frank Fitzsimmons, head of major crimes, was present, seated up front and just off to the side. Angie hoped he was simply observing, because brass sticking fingers directly into an investigation always spelled trouble. Fitz caught her eye, but his features remained expressionless. Fitz had personally grilled her over the loss of Hash's life, and over Tiffy Bennett's and her parents' deaths. While she'd been cleared of any breach of department protocol, Angie believed that Fitz wasn't buying it—he was personally holding her responsible for the death of one of the MVPD's finest and longest-serving detectives. And he wasn't alone. He was probably thinking about the leaks now, the media fiasco with her face being splashed all over the front page again. A chill of foreboding slid down her throat. She broke the eye contact and turned to focus on Buziak.

He was busy sticking photos of the two recent homicide victims onto the whiteboard. He also added headshots of Fernyhough and Ritter. Then, with a black Sharpie, he scrawled LIMPET across the top of the board, and he underlined the word with a swift stroke of his hand.

"Operation Limpet," he said, turning to face the group. "That's what we're calling this investigation. It's a word totally devoid of particular relevance to this case, and one that stays out of the media. I'll be functioning as your team commander. Detective Maddocks is lead investigator. Salinger will serve as file coordinator. Given the media hysteria already developing, plus the fact that the two recent homicide victims were found within such a narrow timeframe, we need to hit this hard and fast, before our subject kills again."

He paused, meeting the eyes of each member of his task force. "I don't want to believe there is a leak in our institution, but given the level of confidential detail that has found its way into the press, nothing, and I mean *nothing*, goes beyond that incident room door that is not authorized for release directly by me. And no one talks to media for any reason at all. Refer all press queries to our media liaison officer. The MVPD will be holding a press conference this morning in an attempt to allay fears and to try to mitigate the damage already done out there. Do I make myself clear?"

Murmurs and nods.

"We follow a strict chain of command. Everything comes back to me, and I will relay information and make assignments as required. A seven a.m. daily briefing will be held in this room where possible. And again, where possible, a debrief and handover to the night shift will be held at the end of day. My directive is to keep overtime to a minimum without losing an eye on the ball. Which means coordinated around-the-clock rotation starting with who we've got in here. More hands will be enlisted if and when the need arises. The clock has started ticking, people, and time is not our friend."

Right, thought Angie. *Cut back, but deliver fast.* Gunnar's stamp was all over this speech—their chief was clearly buckling under pressure from Killion's election promises to cut costs while still increasing closure rates.

"Okay, we've got two DBs. Female." Buziak pointed to the first photo on the board. "Gracie Marie Drummond, sixteen, Caucasian, five feet six inches, shoulder-length brown hair." He ran through the details of her case so far. "Tentative COD for Drummond is that she was immersed in freshwater and succumbed to drowning in hospital. A postmortem is being performed as we speak." He tapped the back of his Sharpie on the second image. "Faith Hocking, nineteen, Caucasian, five feet seven inches, slight build. Also long brown hair."

What the—? The floater had been ID'd?

Angie shot a glance at Holgersen, Leo, then Maddocks. But all attention was focused on Buziak. Tension started to crackle inside her, and her unease deepened.

Buziak selected another photo from the table in front of him and stuck it on the board. "Hocking was identified late last night by this tattoo." The photo showed the Medusa ink with its hydra head of serpents.

"Shit," said someone.

"Wouldn't want to stick my dick in there," whispered another seated near Angie. She turned and shot him a hot glare. He crooked a brow back at her.

"Hocking is in the system, was picked up on a meth-related charge three years ago, when she was sixteen. According to the report made at the time, she was a runaway and had been a street kid since the age of twelve. Crystal meth user, and a small-time prostitute to fund her habit. As of now, last whereabouts or place of domicile unknown. But at the time of her arrest she was known to occasionally bunk down at a shelter for homeless kids and young addicts called Harbor House on Songhee Street. It's run by a volunteer known as Pastor Markus—Markus Gilani. COD for Hocking, tentatively, is asphyxiation due to strangulation with ligature. Official autopsy reports and lab results are pending, but so far several key common denominators have emerged in both homicides—evidence of violent rape and sodomy, followed by precise genital mutilation—the clitoral hood, clitoral glans, and labia minora were excised in the same manner in both cases." He paused. "Female circumcision."

Murmurs came from the almost all-male group.

"Also, a mark in the shape of a crucifix was carved with a sharp blade into the foreheads of both victims, and from each, a lock of hair was cut from their hairlines at the center of their brows." He tapped his Sharpie against his palm. "A keepsake, a trophy." Another pause. "We believe we're looking at an active serial."

More murmurs.

"So, two deaths makes a serial killer, then?" came a comment from one of the detectives.

"Whatever official definition of a serial you choose," said Buziak, "these two sexually based homicides look to be the work of the same offender, someone with a very particular signature, and one with strong religious overtones. This is a ritual that means something to him beyond simple sexual assault. It's also possible that the Drummond and Hocking homicides are linked to two violent sexual assaults three and four years ago. Allison Fernyhough, fourteen, and Sally Ritter, sixteen, were both raped and sodomized, also in the greater Victoria area. Detective Pallorino from sex crimes worked those cases with the late Hash Hashowsky."

Some of the men turned to look at her. Angie shifted slightly in her seat, wondering if it was blame that she could read in some of their eyes, or if it was her own mind putting it there, because on some level she would always wonder whether Hash might still be alive if she'd read the situation differently, if she hadn't been so hotheaded.

"What links the Drummond and Hocking homicides to the assaults on Fernyhough and Ritter, then?" came Leo's gruff voice from the back.

"I'm going to let Pallorino walk you through those cases. Pallorino?"

Angie got up and went to the front with her files. She set them on the table. Clearing her throat, she pointed to the photo of Ritter on the whiteboard, an attractive teen with long brown hair, petite build. "Sally Ritter was assaulted in August four years ago after leaving an outdoor concert to relieve herself in the woods nearby. By her own admission she was severely intoxicated. Once in the trees, out of sight from the concertgoers, she was grabbed by her assailant from behind. He held his arm tightly around her neck and pressed a knife blade to her throat. She remembers a male voice, dark clothing, and a ski mask. She believes her assailant was Caucasian, about five feet eleven inches tall, lean, very strong. Probably in his twenties or early thirties. He dragged her deeper into a bushy area, where he forced her facedown to the ground.

He pressed her face into the dirt, and, holding the blade to her neck, he yanked up her skirt and ripped off her underwear. He ordered her not to scream or he'd slice her throat. He then said these words: *Do you reject Satan, father of sin and prince of darkness?* Fisting her hair, blade to her throat, he forced her to say *I do*. He then penetrated her with his penis from behind, vaginally and anally, leaving tears. Ritter was sixteen at the time."

Angie paused, feeling Maddocks's eyes on her. She resisted glancing his way and focused instead on the men in front of her. "He then struck her on the head, she thinks with a rock, rendering her temporarily unconscious. When she came around, she made her way back to the concert, where friends asked her what she had on her face. Her assailant had drawn, in red waterproof Sharpie, a crucifix on her brow, and a lock of her hair had been cut from just right of center of her hairline."

Angie pinned up a photo of the red cross on Ritter's forehead. "This photo was taken by her sister—Ritter reported her incident three days after the fact. The size and shape and positioning of the cross matches the ones carved into Drummond's and Hocking's foreheads. The lock of hair was cut from the same area."

She pointed to the photograph of Fernyhough. "Allison Fernyhough was fourteen at the time of her assault. She was leaving the Tudor Bar downtown in early September three years ago where she'd been drinking under a false ID. On a deserted street, she was attacked, also from behind, an arm around her neck, knife to the throat. She was pulled into an alley and behind a dumpster, where she was forced facedown into the paving and told not to scream or her throat would be cut. Her assailant ripped her clothing and repeated the same words: *Do you reject Satan, father of sin and prince of darkness?* He forced her to say *I do*, then raped her in the same manner as Ritter before rendering her unconscious. Fernyhough didn't remember much about her assailant— she also admits she'd had too much to drink and was vulnerable. She only discovered the red crucifix on her forehead and the missing lock of hair after she returned home that night and looked in the bathroom mirror." Angie pinned up the photo of Ritter's brow with the crucifix. "Again, same shape, size, positioning. This photo was taken by her friend. Ritter reported the incident six days later, at her friend's, then her mother's insistence. Neither Ritter nor Fernyhough had rape kits done. Their clothes had been washed in both cases, and their assailant, they believe, wore a condom. We found no witnesses, nothing, other than both victims admitted to having felt they were being 'followed by a man' in the two weeks preceding the attacks. There were no further assaults reported, nothing matching this MO on ViCLAS, nothing from the high-risk offender unit matching this offender's MO, either."

"So if this is the same perp, where's he been?" came a question from the group.

"Possibly in prison, or offending elsewhere, or there've been additional cases that have gone unreported." She met the eyes of each man and the one woman in front of her in turn. "Those specific words," she said, "are part of the Roman Catholic baptism ritual. Given those words, the crucifixes, the references to sinners, and the fact that Drummond was immersed in water and posed at the feet of the Virgin Mary, and that two of the victims were defeminized—had parts of their bodies removed that serve no other role in human biology other than to experience sexual pleasure—it's possible that our offender believes he's punishing the girls for their sin of female sexuality. Or for stimulating lust in himself. He—"

Buziak came sharply to his feet. "Thank you, Detective. Let's gather the facts and not speculate at this point." He checked his watch. "This is all very preliminary. We're waiting on final autopsy reports and lab results, including the results of tests being conducted on what appears to be animal hair and seeds found on Hocking's body. We'll be seeking further entomological, botanical, and odontological interpretation on that trace. We'll also be soliciting meteorological and ocean current expertise. Our techs are combing through the results of the canvass that was conducted around Ross Bay Cemetery, including examination of footage secured from a 7-Eleven security camera across the street from the graveyard. And we'll be doing further interviews with Blue Badger staff and a canvass of the surrounding area."

Chairs scraped back, and detectives gathered around while Buziak assigned investigative tasks.

"Leo, you and Holgersen go to Harbor House—see if anyone there can tell us more about Faith Hocking. And take these." Buziak handed Holgersen a pile of flyers with Faith Hocking's mug shot. "Maybe someone in that area has seen her around recently.

"Maddocks, you and Pallorino head to the morgue, see what O'Hagan has for us on Drummond." He glanced at his watch again. "After that, visit the Drummond residence and see what the victim's living conditions can tell us. I'll be sending patrol officers with questionnaires to canvass residents in the area around her residence. Maybe they'll locate someone else who got on that same 6:07 p.m. bus at the stop outside the Drummond apartment block."

Fitz said nothing, just watched like a dark hawk on the side.

Voices rose.

Buziak banged the base of an empty water glass on the table. "Listen up." Chatter quieted.

"We solve about eighty-five percent of our homicides in this country, and there's a simple reason for that—most people are attacked by someone they know. But as soon as we have stranger-on-stranger crime, that nexus between victim and offender is broken. Find that nexus, and we'll find him."

Fitz unfolded himself and rose from his chair. He came to Buziak's side in front of the whiteboard. As tall as Maddocks, he was as narrow as Buziak. Beak of a nose. Long face. Sensual lips. Hooded, lugubrious eyes that belied a crackling sharp intellect and temper.

A heavy quiet settled over the room.

"Statistically," Fitz said in his oddly high voice, "this offender *will* strike again, and soon, if this current time span between Hocking and Drummond is anything to go by. We're not going to let that happen." He paused. "I want this suspect in custody before Christmas."

Buziak added with a clap of his hands, "So, what're you all waiting for? A hug goodbye? C'mon, let's get started already."

CHAPTER 21

Angie stepped outside and ducked under an overhang to call her dad. While she waited for the call to pick up, she watched Leo and Holgersen exit the building and make for cover farther along the building. Holgersen bent forward as Leo lit his smoke. She turned her back on them as her call connected.

"Dad, it's me. How's Mom today? Any better?"

Her father sighed heavily. "It's not going to get better, Ange, only worse. She got all hyper and stressed and disoriented with the move. They have her heavily sedated at the moment."

Her heart ached. He sounded so defeated. Lonely. She glanced over her shoulder at the guys smoking, laughing. What was she doing with her life anyway? What was family to her? Suddenly these questions were big and real. Her mind went to Lorna Drummond, her brutally murdered child. The sense of lost time.

"I'll try to go—" She hesitated. "No. I *will* stop by today. I promise. When I get a moment."

"Yeah, Angie. Yeah."

She bit her lip, jiggling her car keys. "By the way, Dad, what year was your sabbatical in Italy?"

"Why?"

"I . . . was going through all those old photos you gave me and wondering."

He fell silent for a moment. "I'd need to look it up—I don't recall exactly."

"But it was the year of the car accident, right? We never visited Italy any other time, did we?"

Another beat of silence. "What's going on, Angie?" She noted a shift in his tone.

"It's nothing. Just that Mom had written 1984 on the back of a photo taken in Rome, and again on a shot from Naples, but I thought we were there in '86 and that that was the year my face was cut."

Another odd beat. "Your mother was probably confused. It . . . the symptoms—they'd started."

Angie said goodbye, killed the call, and regarded the rain for a moment, unsettled by the tone in her dad's voice. But it made sense. If her mom had already been losing touch with reality and time.

Maddocks exited the station, and Angie's attention snapped to him. He looked arrogant and striking as all get out in a black wool car coat, crisp white shirt, and burgundy tie. He moved with that same commanding presence that had snagged her attention—and libido—in the club. Yeah, she should have recognized that swagger and made him for law enforcement, military, or some allied profession.

"Doc O'Hagan is expecting us," he said as he approached her.

"I'll meet you there." She stepped out into the rain and headed for her vehicle.

"We can take my car!" he called after her.

She hesitated, turned. "I always drive."

"Fine," he said, coming up to her and holding out his keys. "You can drive mine."

"What's wrong with my vehicle?"

"You want dog pee in yours?"

"What?"

149

"My dog sitter fell through. I won't have another until tonight, so Jack-O needs to hang out in my vehicle until then. Sometimes he pees in there. And his blanket and bowl and other trappings are in there."

"You're kidding me."

He tossed her his keys. She caught them. "It's the Chevy Impala over there." He strode toward the car.

She stared after him in disbelief. Holgersen sauntered up behind her and chuckled. "Good luck with the control issues, Pallorino."

"Oh, fuck off."

"You sure you haven't met him before?" Holgersen said. "Old Leo back there reckons you two got history. Said you both looked like you'd been slammed with an RPG when you locked eyes on each other in the morgue."

Angie swore and stalked toward Maddocks, who was waiting by his vehicle, hands in pockets, rain forming diamond droplets on his jet-black hair. Beeping the lock, she tossed the keys back at him. "It's fine," she snapped. "You drive." She climbed into the passenger seat. A little mongrel growled on the backseat.

"Oh nice, it really does stink," she said, turning to check out the mutt. Ugly critter. Some kind of Jack Russell cross, and it appeared to have recently had its back right leg amputated. It growled again, baring yellowed little teeth.

"Like I said, only until I get a sitter," he said, getting into the driver's seat. "Then I can get the car detailed." He shut the door and pulled on his seat belt. In the closed confines of the vehicle the pee smell was stronger, and Maddocks's body was suddenly too close, the space too intimate. His eyes met hers, and the memory of their sex together swelled through her. His pupils darkened, and she knew he was thinking of it, too.

About our unfinished business . . . I'd like to finish it . . . Can't stop thinking about you . . .

150

Quickly clearing her throat, she said, "What's with the dog, anyway? What happened to its leg?"

He fired the ignition and backed out of the parking space.

"Hit-and-run. Happened right in front of my eyes. Truck crushed his leg. I stopped and pretty much peeled him off the road, took him to the vet. They couldn't save the leg, so amputated. No one claimed him." Maddocks shrugged. "Maybe his owner didn't want to pay vet bills, or couldn't. Maybe he was just a stray. So I paid, and then I couldn't have them just dump him at the shelter, poor guy." He glanced at her. "So I took him. He needed follow-up surgery anyway. He's just getting over that second op now."

"What kind of name is Jack-O?"

The hint of a smile toyed with his mouth as he pulled into the road. "It was Halloween night when he was hit. He was trying to eat a shattered pumpkin on the road." He shot Angie another look, and his smile deepened, lighting his eyes. "Besides, he's a scary-ass-looking little thing, don't you think? And he's partially orange, like a pumpkin. I think it fits."

She weighed him, her preconceptions turning on top of themselves in her mind. So, the good-looking homicide cop blessed with a beautiful big dick also rescued orphan animals.

He turned the heat up. Wipers squeaked as he drove. Her gaze lowered to his wrists, where his sleeves were pulling back to expose the red ligature marks left by the friction of her restraints and their hot sex. Her mouth turned dry, and her focus settled on his wedding band.

"Why doesn't your wife look after Jack-O—she also work full-time, or what?"

A flash of those eyes. His mouth tightened. Ah, she'd hit a sore spot. Curiosity deepened.

"She lives on the mainland. I moved here to be near my kid. Ginny just started school at UVic." He stopped at a red light, tapped his fingers on the wheel. "I was actually with Ginn at the Blue Badger Bakery when I got the call for the floater. Trendy spot where Drummond worked."

More questions about this man, his wife, his kid, rolled through Angie's mind. She looked out of the rain-streaked window. She didn't want questions, or to feel interested, or to know that he could be available despite that wedding ring.

"Buziak was a bit of an ass back there, cutting you off," he said as the light turned green and he entered the intersection. "Sorry about that."

Surprise rippled through her. "It's not for you to apologize." Then pride whipped up her spine. "It's not like I was fazed. Buziak is like that."

"What were you going to say?"

"Are you trying to indulge me?"

"Is that what you think? Look, if you're going to be partnered with me, I want to hear your theories. All of them. And you're gonna hear mine." He turned onto the slipway that led onto the highway that would take them to the morgue. "Besides, you and Hash worked those earlier rape cases. I read the files, but there's nothing like a firsthand account."

"When did you read the files? Last night?"

"Early hours of this morning."

She stared at him. She was beginning to feel like her old cases, plus everything she'd already done with Holgersen on the Drummond investigation, were being sneaked out from under her. "Why didn't you guys call me when you got the Hocking ID?" she said.

He smiled. "Because you needed your beauty sleep."

"Fuck off, Maddocks," she said quietly. "If you're going to patronize me—"

"Hey, if you've got a chip on your shoulder and want to think that everyone is somehow patronizing or indulging you because you're female, or some kind of misandrist, that's your problem, not mine."

His eyes turned serious. "Because I don't play those head games. Understand?"

"Tell me one thing," she said coolly. "Since we're clearing the ground here. Why did you take this job? It's a step down, from what I can see. You were pretty much Buziak's equivalent with the RCMP, yet here you are, taking orders from him, getting your fancy tie and wool coat dirty in the trenches. You fuck up on the old job, or what?"

"I told you. I came here to be close to my kid."

"And you just left your wife back there? Yet you wear your ring."

He shot her a hot glance. "It's complicated." The warning in his features, in his voice, told her to back off. "And personal."

She studied his profile—the aggressive thrust of his forehead, dark brows, strong nose. Wide, sculpted lips. Long, thick black lashes. An image of his dark groin and chest hair came to mind. In spite of herself, she felt a spark in her groin. She looked away. Yeah. Personal. They'd gotten real personal at the club.

This *was* going to be complicated.

Dangerous, even. If she wanted that homicide job.

CHAPTER 22

"Jayden? What's the matter? You look positively white."

He clicked off the television news in the kitchen. His heart galloped in his throat. They'd identified the Cemetery Girl. *Gracie.* There had to be a mistake. *How in the hell could it be Gracie?* He felt like he was going to throw up. "Nothing."

"You certain?"

"I'm fine," he snapped as he pushed his uneaten breakfast aside.

His mother's eyes flickered between him, the television, and the kitchen clock. A frown creased into her brow. "Aren't you supposed to be at the law faculty thing this morning?"

Without answering, he got up and hurriedly left the kitchen, almost bumping into his father on his way out. As his dad entered the kitchen behind him, briefcase in hand, Jayden heard his dad say, "I don't know why that kid still lives with us. He's going to be thirty in two years, for heaven's sake."

Jayden stilled, eavesdropping as his parents discussed him.

"Because he can focus on his law degree without worrying about looking after his own place and buying and cooking his own food," his mother said.

"He's too soft and simple to be a lawyer. Too . . . I don't know—he should've been a social worker or artist or something. Don't know where that kid came from. Not yours or mine by temperament."

"A law degree will help him, Ray, as will his anthropology degree."

Jayden heard the television come back on. The anchor was still talking about the Cemetery Girl and an unidentified body found floating in the Gorge.

He began to shake as fear noosed around him.

"Anything new on those cases?" his dad said, obviously watching the news.

"MVPD is holding a press conference this morning," said his mom. "They've identified both victims and are keeping my office looped in. This thing is going to spiral out of control unless the MVPD gets a handle on it and tamps down the budding hysteria." A pause, the sound of crockery going into the dishwasher. "I have a meeting tonight." His mother's voice. "Will you be home for dinner?"

"Got a late business thing for the new development on the waterfront. Probably be back around ten." Another pause. The sound of his father clicking his briefcase shut. "Have a good day—see you later."

Jayden quickly ducked around the corner. He heard his father's footfall on stone tiles, the thud of the front door. He hurried along the passageway to his suite in the west wing of his parents' house, which was far too big for just the three of them.

Once inside his suite, Jayden stood at his window, watching his father's bronze Jaguar wind down the driveway as he made his call.

It was answered in three rings.

"So, you heard—you saw the news?" came the voice.

It was enough to undo Jayden. His shakes turned into great big palsied shudders, and sweat began to dampen his body. In an effort to steady himself, he dragged his hand up over his brow and pressed his palm down hard on the top of his head, as if he could somehow bottle it all back down, as if he could make this all go away as long as he could just keep it inside his skull. "What . . . what happened to Gracie? *How?*" he managed to say.

"How the fuck do *I* know what happened?"

Jayden swallowed, and his voice cracked. "And the body in the Gorge—who's that?"

There was a beat of silence. "Jeezus, Jay, how in the hell would I know? C'mon, what's going on with you?"

"I . . . I'm just wondering if this is . . . connected. I mean with—"

"Listen to me. This has got nothing to do with us. Neither of these deaths do."

"What're we going to do?"

"Nothing, Jayden, nothing. I told you this has *nothing* to do with us."

"But on the back of—"

"Are you hearing me? It's *not* linked. Understand?"

"What if the cops come looking?"

"Why *would* they?"

"I was going to be with Gracie. I . . . I . . . I was going to help her. When she had enough. We had plans to—"

"Jayden, listen to me, very carefully. Is there *any* record of you helping her? Anything at all? Financial records? Did you buy her anything on your credit card?"

"No. I . . . I don't think so."

"Then the police will not come looking at you. And if they do, if you fuck up and you talk, we *all* go down. You hear me? You'll take your mother down with you. Your father. All the others. A scandal of epic proportion. You'll do prison time. That's how serious this is. So you just shut the fuck up and lay low. Go away if you need to—take a holiday out of country."

"I got exams coming up—I want this degree."

"Then focus on what you do want. And listen, I don't know what you were thinking getting messed up with that girl in the first place—you can do so much better—but I am sorry for you. You have my condolences. Now let it—her—go."

Several reporters glanced Merry's way as she entered the newsroom. They'd clearly all been talking about her, about her brazen tweet, her blog.

"You okay, Merry?" It was Dwaine, a colleague whose desk abutted Merry's.

"Fine," she said as she hung her jacket over the back of her chair and seated herself at her computer.

But she was not okay.

For the first time in five years she had a bad need for a hit of crank, and it scared the bejeezus out of her. She'd cracked at the idea that *he* might be back—and it proved that she was still just a junkie tweaker. It was spiraling her out of control. She needed sleep. Had lost her appetite. Had consumed too much caffeine and was overcome by jitters.

Another reporter's voice came from the other side of her cubicle partition. "Want a bet they fire your ass before the hour is out, Winston? Career suicide by Twitter." He chuckled dryly. "You wouldn't be the first. Who was that politician, put a photo of his prick on Twitter? And the MVPD chief, tweeting sweet nothings to the wife of another officer under his command, thinking it was private? Just watch Killion use *that* when he eventually fires Chief Gunnar's ass. It's the same psychology—like getting behind the wheel of a car . . . you're removed from face-to-face responsibility and you think reality can't bite you in the butt."

"Fuck off, Steve."

"Merry!" The editor in chief, red-faced, stalked into the newsroom and jerked his head toward his office door. "My office."

"Whooo," the reporter said from behind the wall. "What I tell you?"

Quickly, she began copying her files onto a memory stick. Once they'd been moved over, she started deleting everything she'd ever written on her workstation computer.

Dwaine watched her. "They'll find them," he said. "It leaves digital footprints."

"Nothing worth finding," she snapped, pocketing the memory stick along with the saved digital files of the recordings she'd made of her deep throat's calls. She wasn't going to leave her hard-won work and contacts if they fired her.

She got up, squared her shoulders, and walked to the gallows, half expecting to see out the corner of her eye the security guys arriving with a cardboard box to pack up her things while she was inside the editor's office.

"Shut the door," her boss said as she entered. She closed the door and seated herself slowly in front of his desk.

"I had a visit from two MVPD officers at my home early this morning. They want to know who your source is."

Merry cleared her throat. "My sources are good. I verified the information given to me by those sources," she lied. "And don't ask me to reveal them, because they'll stop talking."

"The MVPD is looking for a possible internal leak."

"Then that's their problem, not mine, not ours."

His gaze tunneled into her. "What you did—putting information out like that on Twitter, on your blog—"

"The info wasn't wrong—it all checked out. The MVPD has a media conference coming up this morning, and nothing I put out there is being denied."

"You're treading a very fine line here, Merry. If they do come back with a court order—"

"Then let them. With all due respect, sir, freedom of the press is a good fight. And look at the publicity my blog and Twitter account has brought the *Sun*. Every reporter, every news station out there was onto it and running with their own versions. It's been picked up by the wires, even. It's me who'll get sued for my personal blog and tweets if I'm wrong, not the *Sun*. You get all the glory plus my follow-up stories. And if the MVPD does come after me for my sources, we *become* the news. Even better." Her mouth was dry, her pulse racing, but by the look in her boss's eyes, she was winning.

He heaved out a big sigh. "Okay. You're on thin ice. Proceed cautiously. Because if the editorial board does decide to cut you loose, you're gone, Winston. No benefits, no letter of reference, zip. And I will not back you. I took a risk hiring you in the first place, and the *Sun* took a chance in unofficially allowing you to run your crime blog on the side to begin with—we're feeling our way in this new and ever-changing digital landscape."

"You know why the editorial board has *not* shut me down? Because I'm moving print newspapers. I'm bringing new readers. Wasn't that the mandate when Raddison Industries bought the outfit—build readership? Go lowbrow and trashy?"

"Be careful," he said quietly. "I like what you bring to the paper, Merry—there's a feisty rat-pack quality to your approach. I like your energy. But if there's someone or some persons inside the MVPD feeding you information on the side, they're using you as much as you are using them. They have some kind of agenda." He watched her in silence for a beat. "You could get yourself into hot water, and we will not be able to help you out."

Gracie Drummond's body was draped in a white sheet, her head exposed. Her features were almost serene. She reminded Angie of a patchwork doll, with the stitched crucifix wound on her brow and the thick line of black sutures from where Barb O'Hagan had sliced and peeled back her face to remove her brain from her skull.

Angie stood beside Maddocks once again as O'Hagan ran them through her preliminary report.

"COD was drowning in freshwater," O'Hagan said as she folded back the sheet to reveal the top of the Y-incision on Drummond's young chest. "Note these contusions here, along the sides of her neck and on her shoulders, and this line here, across the bottom of her ribs." The pathologist pointed to a fat line of dark blue-and-red bruising.

"She could have been forced over something, like the rim of a bathtub," said Angie, "or a trough of some kind, while her head and shoulders were held under water and she struggled to free herself."

O'Hagan nodded. "Drummond also presented with vaginal and anal tearing indicative of rough sexual penetration. And I found small traces of powder residue in her vaginal vault—same as with Hocking."

"So he used a condom," Maddocks said. "In both cases."

"Drummond's circumcision occurred antemortem, as we know. But Hocking was circumcised postmortem," O'Hagan said.

Angie and Maddocks exchanged a glance. "So he switched MO?" Angie said.

"Or he's refining it," Maddocks replied. "Or he thought Drummond was already drowned and dead when he did it."

"Appears that it was definitely executed by the same hand in both cases—same size blade, same direction of cuts, same parts excised." She shook her head, staring at Drummond's dead, calm face. "What people do to each other in the name of sexual gratification. The mind is the largest sex organ—whatever can be imagined can be enacted, and often is. And there's nothing like an orgasm for positive reinforcement of an idea."

Angie felt hot and overly conscious of Maddocks beside her. "And the crucifix markings on her brow?" she said.

O'Hagan led them over to a light box on the wall containing X-rays. "This is Hocking's skull. You can see faint scoring on bone here." The doc pointed to very thin lines in the shape of a crucifix on the brow bone. "And this is Drummond's skull. Same scoring depth, same shape."

"Again, looks like the same hand," Maddocks said. "He exerted the same pressure with the blade in both cases."

"Drummond was in otherwise healthy condition," O'Hagan said. "Whatever other trace might have been left on her body was likely lost in the hospital."

"Her clothing is still with the lab," Angie said. "Maybe we'll get something off it that could tie these two victims together in terms of location—perhaps some clue as to where they were abducted and then assaulted."

"Her teeth?" Maddocks said.

"Very good shape. No evidence of cosmetic work there. The odontologist will be taking a look at Hocking's dental work later this morning. There's evidence of very poor oral hygiene and serious decay in Hocking's past, which has been remediated by some rather high-end dental wizardry."

"We now know that Hocking was a crystal meth user for several years," Maddocks said. "Her tooth decay, or meth mouth, would thus be consistent with her drug use." He paused. "It's like she was cleaned up."

"And had the finances to do so," O'Hagan offered.

"Or, more likely, someone paid to have her cleaned up," Angie said.

CHAPTER 23

"Yo, yous got some spare cash?" A rake-thin woman, scabby face, rotted and missing teeth, accosted Detectives Kjel Holgersen and Harvey Leo as they strode down the sidewalk past a thrift store with its fake Christmas tree and tangled tinsel in the window. Kjel ran his gaze quickly over the sorry creature. She wore fingerless gloves, jeans, a filthy denim jacket. Her wet hair clung in ratty, dun-colored strings against her hollowed cheeks, and her mad eyes darted up and down the street.

She grabbed at Leo's jacket. "C'mon, gramps, *you* got cash. Spare some for the season of joy, a time of giving." She shot a paranoid glance over her shoulder, her tongue darting in and out of her mouth.

"Get your hands the hell off me, you meth-ho," Leo snapped as he shook her off and sped up, leaving Kjel in his wake.

"Asshole!" she shrieked after Leo. "Fucking prick. Yo, man, you . . . I'm talking to *you*, grampa! Come back here. *Look* at me. Look in my face. I seen you around. I know yous. You want some pussy, man? Merry fuckin' Christmas!"

"She stinks," Leo muttered as Kjel caught up to him. Rain, icy, pattered down harder on their shoulders, splashing into puddles forming between mounds of melting brown slush. "Fucking tweaker. Sky-high on crystal meth, oozing chemical scabs."

Kjel cast him a sideways glance. But he bit his tongue. For now. He'd barely been getting a handle on Pallorino, and now he had this asshole to deal with. Harvey Leo came with a different kind of chip on his shoulder than Pallorino, but he was a bona-fide member of the old boys' club back at the station. Kjel figured he'd do well to stay on the right side of that bunch.

"You know the difference between a crackhead and a tweaker?" Leo said as they rounded the block on their way to Harbor House. "Crackhead will steal your shit and bounce—tweaker will steal your shit and then help you look for it." He chuckled throatily at his own joke, finishing with a rattle of a smoker's cough. "Can bang like rabbits for hours, those tweakers."

Kjel said nothing.

"What kind of name is Kell Holgersen, anyway? Like Scandinavian, Nordic, what?"

"It's Kjel."

"That's what I said."

"No, yous said 'Kell.' It's pronounced like *Hh-yell*. Like you was saying the 'H' in the word 'huge.' But most English folk can't say it like that, so they use *Sh-yell*."

"Yeah. Like I said, what kind of name is that, anyway?"

"My pops's family came from Norway."

"That why you talk funny?"

He gave a slow smile, his gaze darting into shadowed doorways, trying to see into the faces of the homeless who crouched there. Victoria was full of them. And yeah, he still thought he might one day see the eyes of his father looking back at him from some dark doorway or cardboard box. It's why Kjel had become a cop. Why he'd worked narcotics up north, and undercover. He liked to work the streets, walk the walk. Talk the talk. If he hadn't become a cop, he'd probably have ended up like his pops, anyway. His badge was the fine line between one side and the other. Or . . . maybe it wasn't.

"I come from a place up near Bella Coola, near the Alaska border. It was settled by Norwegian fishermen forever ago. Got pretty isolated and hardscrabble once the fishing industry dried up, though."

"So . . . you what? Came down to sunny Victoria to further your career as a cop?"

"Sunny, my ass." He wiped rain from his brow.

"Warmer at least. It's why half the homeless end up here. They call it the San Diego of Canada. I heard you worked UC?"

"You got a lot of questions, Leo."

"It's why I'm a great detective." He grinned.

"Yet you never made sergeant? Your age and all."

A dark shadow crossed the old cop's face.

"Hey," Kjel said with a shrug. "I got questions, too." They arrived at the entrance to Harbor House. Kjel banged with the base of his fist on the door. Third time knocking, the door opened to reveal a dark-skinned man dressed in baggy brown corduroy pants and sporting a goatee. He kept his hand on the door, holding it half-closed as he regarded them with gentle-looking liquid-black eyes.

"Pastor Markus Gilani?" Kjel said.

"Who's asking?"

The detectives showed their badges. "Kjel Holgersen and Harvey Leo, Metro PD. Can we ask you a few questions?"

"About what?"

"Do you know this young woman?" Kjel nodded to Leo, who held out a damp flyer with Hocking's mug shot.

Gilani stared at Hocking's picture. Kjel watched the man's eyes narrow. A small vein swelled at his temple.

Hand still on the door, Gilani said, "Look, the kids who come here, they don't want to be found. They just sleep here, get a hot meal. Trust is a big issue for them. They don't trust the system, but they do trust they will be safe here, because we don't give out information."

"So you do know her?" Kjel said.

The pastor's jaw tightened.

Kjel scratched his wet head. "See, here's the thing, Pastor Gilani—yous a real pastor, by the way?"

Silence.

Kjel nodded. "See, thing is, your kids might not *want* to be found, but Faith Hocking here *has* already been found. Dead. And we kinda want to know how she gots to be that way."

The man paled visibly under his brown skin, and his eyes flickered. "What . . . what happened to her?"

"So, yeah. You do know her," Kjel said.

"She hasn't been here in a long time. Three years maybe." The man flicked a nervous glance at Leo, who was still holding out the wilting flyer.

"Can we come inside, Pastor?" Kjel said. "Kinda wet out here. Water's dripping down the back of my neck, see."

Reluctantly, the pastor opened the door wider to admit them. He shut and locked it behind them. "Come through this way. We don't open up for the kids until six sharp in the evenings, when we offer a volunteer soup kitchen. While we generally have enough food, thanks to volunteers and donors, we never have enough beds for all of them, so we run a nightly lottery while they're eating, and the ones who don't win—we have to put them back out into the cold."

He led them into a mess room with a kitchen. The walls had been strung with paper-chain Christmas decorations, the kind Kjel had once made in kindergarten. An ornamental Christmas tree decorated with odds and ends brightened up a corner near an empty hearth, and a banner above a serving table blared:

REPENT AND YE SHALL BE FORGIVEN
THE LORD LOVES ALL HIS CHILDREN

A selection of religious pamphlets were fanned out on a shelf beside copies of today's newspapers. Leo continued to let Kjel do the talking while he ambled around the room, hands in pockets, checking out the religious slogans on the walls.

"What happened to Faith?" the pastor asked again, and Kjel caught the fast dart of the man's eyes toward the newspapers as he spoke.

"You read the morning news, Pastor?"

The man swallowed, looking ill. "She . . . she wasn't the . . . the one found in the Gorge, was she?"

"Yup. Naked. Wrapped in plastic. Big-ass tattoo—a Medusa head with serpents for hair—inked right over her shaved pelvis." Kjel made a circular motion with his hand near his groin.

The pastor reached for the back of a chair, and Kjel figured the man had either seen Hocking's tattoo himself, or he'd heard about it.

Leo snagged a pamphlet off the religious pile. "What denomination is this place, anyway?" He glanced up at the pastor.

"We're an ecumenical, Christian-based volunteer organization. In addition to providing the lost with a hot meal and a bed where possible, we also open to them a route unto the Lord. Some have chosen that path and come clean. Left the streets."

"But which is *your* church?" Leo paused, those clear blue eyes steady, intimidating. "Pastor."

The man cleared his throat. "I worship at Fairfield United—my wife and I do."

"Worship? Not preach or administer or whatever it is that pastor persons do?"

"Technically, I'm not exactly a pastor. The kids just call me that. And they have for years, ever since I first started volunteering here."

"And when would that be?"

"Eight years now."

While Leo was taking his turn needling Pastor Markus, Kjel walked over to a corkboard that was pinned chock-full with photographs that had clearly been taken over the years. Various seasonal and religious holidays. Several of the pastor laughing or engaging with kids, his arm around them in some images. Nearly all the street kids on this board were female. Young. There was one with a young woman sitting on his lap where the "pastor" was dressed as Santa. Then one photo in particular caught Kjel's eye. His pulse quickened. He peered closer.

"You like the girls young, don't you, Pastor?" he said quietly.

"Excuse me?"

Kjel moved away from the board, picked up a newspaper. Him and Pallorino on the cover. Him looking like a freaking tweaker himself. Thing about meth is that people who did it long enough, even when they did quit, they were left so damaged that they retained the characteristics of a tweaker for the rest of their lives. Fidgety, darty. Paranoid.

"All on the streets are vulnerable, boys and girls, both."

"But the girls, they's . . . special."

"In our society, unfortunately it's the females and the young who are especially vulnerable and at most risk, and in need of safe sanctuary—"

"So, you likes to save them?" He nodded at a slogan on the wall: **SINNERS SHALL BE REDEEMED**. "You gets them to renounce Satan and all that."

"What do you want from me?" The pastor shoved his hands deep into the pockets of his loose brown cords, his neck muscles showing tension.

"Faith Hocking. I want to know where she went after she used to stay here."

"She came clean. She got a job."

"What job?"

"McDonald's on Main. For a while."

"Where did she go after Mickie D's?"

"I don't know."

"How about some of the other kids—they seen her around, talk about her maybe? Mention how nice her expensive, fixed pearly whites look?"

"What?"

"Her teeth."

"I—" A knock sounded on the door. "Look, I really need you to go. I've got to prep—"

"That a yes, a no?"

"I have *not* seen her. And I don't know anyone who has." He marched to the door as he spoke, opened it into the passageway, and headed for the front entrance.

"And you wouldn't tell us if you did know," said Kjel following the man, Leo coming slowly behind them.

Pastor Markus unlocked and opened the front door. Wet air blew inside. "I told you, these kids eschew bureaucracy. The system has let them down. Most have been bounced in and out of foster care their whole lives before landing on the streets. They don't want to go back. Won't even go to a clinic to see a doctor if they need to, because it could land them back in the system." He paused. "And cops, especially—they won't talk to cops." He met and held Leo's steely blue gaze a moment. "Not all cops are good cops, and they know that, too."

"You do realize this is a homicide investigation," Kjel said. "You could be withholding information that in turn could help save other victims. More of your kids, even."

"Then do your work, detectives, and let me do mine." He showed them out, shut the door, and watched them from a window.

Kjel paused under the eaves to pull up his collar and light a smoke, cupping his flame against the wind. Rain pattered into puddles and dripped off the eaves.

"What's your take on him?" Leo said, lighting his own cigarette. "Fake pastor. All that religious shit about sinners, saving girls? Don't trust weirdos like that."

Kjel watched the rain for a moment. "Did yous see that board of photos in there?" he said quietly as he blew out a stream of smoke. "Faith Hocking was pictured in two of them. In one she looked just like her mug shot, crappy teeth, scabby. Skinny. In the other she was all nice white teeth and clean hair, and she was with that young woman we saw earlier."

"That tweaker ho?"

"Yeah." He started to walk.

168

CHAPTER 24

"This is Gracie's room," Lorna Drummond said, opening the bedroom door.

Maddocks allowed Pallorino to enter ahead of him and to ask the questions while he observed. He wanted a better handle on this detective who'd so brazenly propositioned and slept with him, almost leaving him cuffed to the motel bed for the night. He'd also been asked by Buziak to keep a close eye on her performance because of an application she was making to join the homicide unit. She was going to get resistance, though—he'd heard enough from the guys already, especially from Harvey Leo.

Part of him didn't want her in homicide, either. Why? Because that part of him was still thinking he might enjoy the challenge of getting her back into bed. And having a relationship with someone in your unit, or worse, with your partner, was a no-go. Relationships like that screwed with objectivity, clouded judgment in high-risk situations. And if she so desperately wanted to get into homicide, she wasn't likely to risk blowing it by having sex with him again.

Mostly he just liked to watch her. Lithe limbs, a catlike quality to her movements, long, dead-straight, dark-red hair hanging in a ponytail down her back. Pale, translucent skin. And those cool gray eyes that gave away nothing. She intrigued him—a very attractive and accomplished female who hunted heinous sex offenders by day and sought anonymous sex by night. How often, he wondered, did Angie Pallorino actually hit that club? How safe was her habit? What in the hell had *he* been doing there, anyway? He should have left when his buddy hadn't shown up, not gone with her to the room.

He stuck his hands deep into his pockets, remaining near the door while he took in Drummond's bedroom.

It was neat and feminine, decorated in tones of green with dark-pink accents. On her bed a mountain of colored pillows had been topped with a stuffed bear. Above the bed, motivational slogans had been mounted on poster board, and on the wall near her desk a calendar hung alongside a wooden crucifix with a bronze Jesus nailed to it, the Lord's head bowed under his crown of thorns. Atop the desk was a hardback novel, a MacBook, an iPad, and what appeared to be a necklace of pearly beads plus a thin gold chain with a gold pendant attached. The closet doors were sliding mirrors, and one side was plastered with photographs.

Pallorino walked over to the desk, touched the gold pendant, then moved the beads gently with her fingertips, exposing a pearly white cross. It was then that Maddocks realized it was a rosary. His partner's attention went from the rosary to the crucifix with its Jesus on the wall, then to the motivational slogans. She moved over to a map mounted above a bookshelf at the base of the bed.

Gracie's mother wrapped the ends of her long sweater closer over her chest. She wore jeans, no makeup, hadn't showered or fixed her hair. A secondary victim—the survivor of the crime—the one left behind.

"Gracie wanted to travel," Lorna Drummond said as Pallorino leaned closer to examine the pins in the map. "She stuck pins into all the places she was going to visit. She . . . she wanted to see the whole world. She had plans. So many . . ." Lorna Drummond sniffed, wiped her nose with the base of her thumb. "So many plans."

Pallorino trailed her fingertips over the spines of the books on the bookshelf. "All alphabetically arranged," she said. "And nearly all of them hardcover. Gracie obviously liked to read."

Lorna Drummond cleared her throat and nodded. "She loves . . . I mean, she loved her books. Took really good care of them. Could swallow a whole tome in a day—mostly big fantasy books, which she reread often."

"Did you buy these for her?"

"No, she bought them herself."

Pallorino went to the iPad, opened the cover. "It's one of the newer ones with fingerprint ID." She glanced at Lorna Drummond. "We're going to need to take these electronic devices into evidence—"

"Why? Why do you need them?"

"Personal records including phone calls, emails, addresses, voice-mails, contact lists, calendar entries, and websites that she visited could all be vitally important. They could tell us what Gracie was doing, where she was going, how she might have encountered the person who decided to hurt her." Pallorino opened and closed desk drawers, then went over to the closet and slid open the mirrored door.

She moved the hangers, taking note of the victim's clothing. "Your daughter liked designer clothes, Mrs. Drummond. There are some really high-end labels in here, price tags still on a few." She looked over her shoulder. "Where did she get all these clothes?"

"I . . . I don't know. Online shopping mostly?"

"She was only sixteen—did you authorize use of a credit card?"

"No. I . . . I don't know how. She had a job. She bought things."

"You never asked her about her clothes?"

"Not really."

"And the iPad, laptop—she buy those, too?"

Maddocks noted that Drummond was beginning to look panicked, rubbing her arm.

"You said she just worked the one shift a week at the Blue Badger?" Pallorino said.

"Yes."

"You sure Gracie wasn't getting money from somewhere other than her work at the bakery?"

"Look, I don't see why you people need to be in here anyway. This is my daughter's space. *Her* privacy. Shouldn't you be out there looking for her killer, not in here going through her closets and judging me as a mother?"

Pallorino's eyes softened as she turned to the victim's mother. "I'm sorry, Mrs. Drummond. I know how tough this is." Her voice gentled—her whole persona seemed to morph in front of Maddocks's eyes. A chameleon. Most good detectives were shape-shifters, could mix with anyone, from high society to scum on the street. But who, he wondered, was the real Angie Pallorino when she was home? The babe in the club? The cold and dispassionate cop? The accomplished female detective—a calculating interrogator trying to squeeze the most out of her subjects to meet her own ends?

"I know you said that she hasn't seen her father in a while, but is there a chance he, or someone else, might have authorized a credit card for her? Without her telling you?"

"No. No . . ." Lorna Drummond buried her face in her hands and scrubbed her skin hard. "I don't know. I . . . I don't." She looked up, complexion raw and blotchy. "Gracie worked hard. I work hard. I got her through school. She got good grades. She went to church on Sundays. She could sing like an angel. She's . . . she was a good, decent girl."

"Things are not always what they seem, Mrs. Drummond. There are most likely things you don't know about your daughter." Pallorino paused. "We all have our secrets."

"So that's what you do—come into people's bedrooms, peel their lives apart? Expose their secrets?"

"Come, why don't we sit down for a bit?" Pallorino seated herself on Gracie's bed, and Lorna Drummond reluctantly lowered herself onto the edge beside her. Maddocks took the opportunity to go study the photographs on the mirror.

"When did you first notice these nice things appearing?" Pallorino said, her voice calm, soothing. "The fancy clothes, the laptop, iPad?"

"Slowly, I think. Six to eight months ago, maybe. Or . . . less. Certainly it was after she started working at the Badger."

"Which was when?"

"Just over a year ago now."

"Did you notice any other changes in Gracie around that six- to eight-month time frame, in her appearance, her mood?"

"She seemed happier. She started to lose some weight. She'd always been on the plump side as a child and struggled with diets."

Maddocks's thoughts turned to Ginny, and his chest tightened. Gracie looked an awful lot like his Ginn in some of these photos, too. He had his own guilt about not being present during his daughter's growth. Would *he* have noticed nicer clothes?

"Gracie was always a bit bullied at school, but things had definitely started to change. She appeared more confident, started wearing makeup. I thought she was just growing up, getting over her awkward, geeky stage." Drummond blew her nose.

"She have a boyfriend?"

"She used to go out with a boy from school—Rick Butler. They broke up."

"When?"

"I . . . uh, it was maybe eight months ago. Or nine. Or . . . I've lost track of time."

Pallorino took her notebook from her pocket and wrote down the kid's name. "Amicable breakup?"

"No, it was quite nasty. Gracie was devastated. But then she met someone new at the Oak Bay Country Club, where Rick goes for tennis coaching. He's an excellent player but would never be able to afford that club. A European coach, Serge Radikoff, sponsors his membership there. He's kind of a mentor as well as Rick's coach. Gracie used to go watch Rick practice."

"So she was currently dating this new guy from the club?"

Drummond heaved out a chestful of air. "I'm not sure how official the relationship was. After initially mentioning him, she didn't really talk about him again, but he did come pick her up here once when I was home. Drives a small black BMW."

Pallorino and Maddocks exchanged a glance—*the source of Drummond's money, fancy things?*

"And his name?" Pallorino said.

Guilt flickered through the woman's face. "Oh jeeze, I don't know. I've been working too much. Jack. John. No, John Jacks, that's it."

Pallorino recorded the name in her book.

"Is he in any of these photos here?" Maddocks said.

Drummond pushed herself to her feet and came over. Pallorino joined them. Drummond peered at the photos, and a sob hiccupped through her. She covered her mouth with her hand, tears pooling in her eyes. She shook her head, took a moment to gather herself, then said, "No. I don't see him. But that's Rick Butler there." She pointed.

"And these other photos?"

"That one was a beach picnic for the Blue Badger staff last summer. That's Gracie with her choir group from Duneagle Secondary—they went on a trip to Toronto last year."

There were several pictures of Gracie with a brunette, lots of curls, cute smile, dimples. They appeared to have been friends over the years.

"And this person, she looks like a close friend?"

"Lara. Sings like a nightingale. She's a year and a half older than Gracie and is now a student at UVic. They met in the school choir when

Gracie was in grade three and have been friends since. Lara introduced Gracie to a college choir, and she's been singing with them."

Maddocks shot Lorna Drummond a keen glance. "Even though she's not at college she sings in a college choir?"

"The choirmaster accepts some high school teens with special talent, especially if they're planning on attending college the following year."

"Do they happen to practice at the Catholic cathedral downtown?" he said. "Thursday nights?"

Surprise flittered through Drummond's features. "You know it?"

An unspecified anxiety tightened through Maddocks, his thoughts boomeranging back to Ginn and their conversation at the Blue Badger. "I recently heard mention of it. Was Gracie at practice last Thursday?" he said, wondering whether his daughter's path had intersected with that of Gracie Drummond four days ago.

"No, not last Thursday. She said she was going out with a friend instead."

"John Jacks?" he said.

"I'm sorry," she said softly. "I . . . don't know. I went out with Kurt that night."

"Kurt?"

"Kurt Shepherd, my new partner. I was trying to have a bit of my own happiness. I thought Gracie was on track, old enough to be left alone more . . ." Her voice cracked. She blew her nose again, her Kleenex turning ragged.

"Which church did Gracie attend on Sundays, Mrs. Drummond?" Pallorino said from the other side of the room. She'd moved back to the desk and was closely examining the gold pendant and chain.

"The Catholic cathedral downtown, same place she sings. Our family was fairly religious when Gracie was little, but we let things lapse after her father left, the divorce and all." She inhaled shakily. "Gracie got back into the faith in a serious way after she started singing at the church. The choir is not faith-based itself, but it put her back into that environment, and she liked it."

"Her joining that choir, her going back into the religious fold—did this perhaps coincide with her more upbeat change of mood that you noticed?" Pallorino said.

Drummond pushed a tangle of hair back from her brow. "Possibly. She joined the choir last June, the summer before she entered her final year of high school."

Pallorino held up the little medallion that had been lying on the desk. The chain was broken. "It's a Saint Christopher," she said. "The patron saint of travelers, often worn on a chain or a bracelet, or carried in a pocket, or placed in a vehicle to keep the owner safe on journeys."

"She wore that regularly. I guess she didn't have it on Saturday night because the chain is broken."

"It's engraved on the back," Pallorino said, turning over the medallion. "It says, *For Gracie, with love, J.R.*" She looked up. "Who is J.R.?"

"I . . . I didn't know that. I can't think of anyone with the initials J.R."

"How long has she been wearing this?"

"A while."

"You don't know exactly?"

She shook her head. "Last several months. At least."

"And this wall calendar here—there's a circle around last Tuesday. It says, *Lara P., Amanda R., B.C. @ eight.* She go out last Tuesday?"

"Yes. She went to Lara's place. She said they were going to cook dinner, catch a chick-flick—sleepover."

"Who's Amanda R.?"

"I don't know."

"And B.C.?"

She shook her head.

"I see there's another Lara-Amanda-B.C. date marked the week before, also on Tuesday. She do that fairly often, sleep over at Lara's?"

"Regularly. Like I said, they go back, have been friends forever."

"If you recall anything about those other initials, Amanda R., B.C., or J.R., will you give us a call, Mrs. Drummond? Anything at all, okay?" Pallorino handed the mother her card, then said, "Lara got a last name, address, phone number?"

"Pennington. She stays in an apartment right near campus." Gracie's mother scribbled down the address and number, handed it to Pallorino.

"And Rick Butler?"

"He graduated from Duneagle in June. He lives with his parents a block down from the school." She wrote down the address.

"Can you provide us with contact details for Kurt Shepherd as well?"

"Why? You really don't think—"

"Just to cover all bases, rule out as many people as possible."

Lorna Drummond wrote her boyfriend's details down, her mounting frustration evident in the sharp strokes of her pen. "I was with him," she said, her voice becoming clipped as she handed Pallorino Shepherd's address. "I was with my boyfriend when my daughter was raped, sodomized, and mutilated. Brutalized. He had nothing to do with it. I'm the one at fault. I should have been home."

"Is Lara aware of what happened to Gracie?"

"Whole damn world knows what terrible things were done to my baby, thanks to the newspapers. So yeah, Lara knows. She called me this morning. She's a wreck, too."

"We're going to have a unit come in to collect some of your daughter's things and take them into evidence. They'll document them properly, okay? You going to be home for the rest of the day?"

She nodded, her mouth set in a grim line.

✝

177

"A latchkey kid," Pallorino said, matching Maddocks's stride along the hallway of the old building. He could scent food in the air. The carpets smelled damp.

"Gracie lived a full life outside of her mother's witnessing it—buying clothes, electronics, dating," she said.

"Or this John Jacks from the swank Oak Bay Country Club with his BMW gifted her those things," he said.

"How often have kids used that sleepover ruse as a cover while they go do something else?"

He shot her a glance. "You have kids, Pallorino?"

Her pace faltered, the hesitation so brief it was barely noticeable. "No. But I was a teenage girl once," she said quickly. "I'm betting Lara Pennington is going to be able to tell us a helluva lot more about Gracie Drummond than her mother could." She then moved suddenly in front of him and trotted down the stairs at a clip. She shoved out of the building doors ahead of him.

Grateful for the blast of fresh winter air upon exit, Maddocks followed Pallorino to his vehicle, where Jack-O waited.

"A rosary is used to say prayers in penance for sins," she said as she reached the Impala. "After confession, the priest assigns a certain number of Our Fathers and Hail Marys, depending on the severity of the so-called sin, and then the sinner uses the prayer beads to keep count."

He beeped the locks, and she opened the passenger side door. "One of the versions of the Hail Mary goes, *Holy Mary, Mother of God, pray for us sinners, now and at the hour of our death, amen.*"

"You Catholic, Pallorino?" he said, settling into the driver's seat and strapping on his seat belt.

"Agnostic."

He smiled. "You like to keep your options open, then?"

"Maybe there's a God, maybe there isn't. I believe it can't be proved either way."

"Like I said, keeping options open." He started the ignition, put his Impala in gear, and pulled into the street.

"I was raised Roman Catholic," she said after a while. "My father's Italian family had a strong religious background. My mother comes from Irish Catholic heritage, so it's from both sides."

"But it didn't work out for you?"

She hesitated, and he shot her a questioning glance.

"I've said my share of Hail Marys in life. And I know the baptism ritual." She fell silent a moment as he drove. "We just stopped going to church one day. I don't really recall why, come to think of it." She cleared her throat. "Anyway, the nexus we're looking for—it could be that church, that choir. We should pay the cathedral and priest a visit."

"Pennington first," he said. "Then the club."

CHAPTER 25

Kjel and Leo found the woman who'd accosted them earlier shivering in a doorway not far from where they'd left her. Kjel held the mug shot flier out to her. "Do you know her? Her name's Faith Hocking."

She shook her head, picked at a scab on her cheek, eyes avoiding his. He judged her to be in her late twenties, although she could be much younger and just ravaged by drugs and the homeless life.

"What about this tattoo?" Leo asked, holding out his phone with the picture he'd taken of Hocking's Medusa tat. Kjel shot his partner a hot glance.

The woman's head snapped up. "Where'd you get that picture?"

"The morgue. Belongs to Faith Hocking. When did you last see her?"

She turned away from Leo and huddled into the corner. Kjel made a motion with his head for Leo to get out of sight. Leo scowled at him, then removed himself to a location a few doors down, where he ducked under an awning and lit another cigarette.

Kjel removed his pack of smokes from his breast pocket and tapped one out. "That was rough. I'm sorry. But see? I know yous seen that tat before, because I's seen those photos back at Harbor House of you and Faith, looking all buddy-buddies. One was taken pretty recently, too, with alls her new pearly whites and her nice new hairdo and sharp clothes." He offered her a cigarette as he spoke. She glanced up at him, then took the smoke. Cupping the flame with shaking hands, she allowed Kjel to light it for her. Shivering, she dragged hard on the cigarette and then blew out a long stream of smoke, relaxing just a fraction. Leo was on the money. She smelled rank. She was wet, too thin, obviously cold, and probably in need of medical attention.

"When did you last see Faith?" he said softly.

She sucked deeply on her smoke again, as if it were a lifeline. Her gaze returned to the mug shot. "What's in it for me?" she said.

"We don't bust your skinny ass," Kjel said.

"Go to hell, PoPo." She jabbed her cigarette toward him. "You don't got shit to bust me on."

"Okay, okay." He held up both hands, the pack of smokes still in one. "You gots me. I'm gonna leave now."

She eyed the pack of smokes in his hand. He turned as if to go. "Hey, you guys still, like, you know, pay CIs for info?"

"You wanna be a confidential informant, you gotta come down to the station so we can set up some paperwork. What's your name, sweetheart?"

"Nina."

"Nina who?"

"Just Nina."

"Tell me when you last saw Faith, just Nina."

"She's really dead? You really get that tat photo in the morgue?"

Silence.

She looked down, shifted from foot to foot. "Where'd you find her?"

"Floating in the Gorge."

"Fuck, man, fuck. Fuck, no . . ." She rocked backward and forward, wrapping an arm over her chest, then she kicked at the curb, eyes glittering. "The Cemetery Girl also drowned. Was the same done to Faith as to that cemetery girl?"

Kjel eyed her for a moment but didn't reply.

"Fuck. Fuck it. Fuck."

"We need to find her friends, family, tell the people who cared about her what happened. And we need to find the guy who did that to her."

Fear flashed into her eyes. "She don't got no family. No one that I know who cares."

"No one who cares, eh? So Faith makes this big-ass jump from meth-head and street pro to fast-food chain worker all on her own? Then suddenly she's sporting these real pretty chompers, capped all nice and pearly white, no more meth mouth. Where'd she get those teeth done, huh? How'd she fund fixing them chompers?" He tucked two twenty-buck notes into the box of cigarettes as he spoke, his back to Leo, ensuring his action went unobserved by his partner.

She wild-eyed the box, the money sticking out, and she scratched at her sleeve. "Pastor Markus helped Faith detox. Helped her get a regular job, like he did with some others."

"Pastor Markus help pay for her new teeth, too?"

"Don't know where she got dough for that. I ain't seen her in a while."

"How long?"

"I don't know. Lose track of time."

He nodded, handed her the box of smokes. She snatched it and squirreled it away inside her grubby denim. Her gaze jerked nervously up and down the street, as if someone might come and steal her score off her.

"Here's the thing, Nina," Kjel said. "If we want to get this killer dude off the streets, we need to know more about Faith—like where she was living, who she was hanging out with. You can help us. You can help Faith get justice."

Conflict warred in her face—raw fear, street loyalty, a desperate drive to score cash for more drugs fighting with an urge for justice for her friend. Kjel could read it all. He *knew* it.

"She stays in an apartment."

Adrenaline spiked in him. "Where?"

"Esquimalt. A block up from the water, place called MontBlanc Apartments—can see the mountains across the water from there." Sadness washed over her face. "Real nice."

"You been there?"

"I heard."

"From who?"

She looked away.

"Pastor Markus, he tell you?" Some guys were approaching down the street. It made her even more squirrelly.

"Maybe. Maybe not."

"Was it some john setting her up in a love crib—all for himself?"

"I gotta go."

Kjel watched her scurry off into the rain, Christmas lights flicking in the thrift store nearby. Wind gusted, and the sky darkened with lowering cloud. Daylight hours were short this time of year. Life on the streets could be real rough. Cold. Not like rest-of-country-cold, but nevertheless.

Leo rejoined him, and Kjel filled his partner in as they retraced their route to their vehicle.

"What did she mean when she said that she's seen your ass around?" Kjel asked as he opened the driver's door. Pallorino might never have relinquished the wheel, but Leo was happy to sit back in the passenger seat and let him drive. He kinda liked that.

Leo met his gaze over the roof of the sedan. "I'm a cop. I'm around."

"She got something on you?"

Leo held his eyes. "What the fuck are you asking? You want to know if I come down here for a blow job? What is wrong with you?"

"Wanna call it in—tell Buziak we got us a domicile for our vic?" Kjel said, getting into the car.

In silence they drove to Esquimalt, to MontBlanc Apartments.

✝

From the shadows, Nina, shivering, watched the detectives drive off. She needed to find her supplier, score now that she had some cash. But she was scared. She'd seen the newspapers in Harbor House, and she knew what had been done to the girl in the cemetery. The rape. The crucifix. Merry Winston's byline was on that story. She'd also heard about the female floater in the Gorge. *Faith?* Christ.

She ducked back into the rain and made her way quickly through the city streets to the stone building near the inner harbor that housed the *Sun*. Heavy fog roiled off the water and fingered into the cobbled streets and brick alleys. Foghorns sounded out at sea. She pushed through the revolving glass door and made her way over the gleaming marble floor to the reception desk.

The woman behind the desk told her to get lost or she'd call the cops.

"I got information. For a story," Nina replied, scratching her arm nervously. "Gotta see that reporter, the one who wrote the story on the Cemetery Girl."

The receptionist looked doubtful but paged Merry.

Merry came down. Shock registered on her face. "Nina? What the fuck? What're you doing here?"

Nina's eyes flickered around. She had noise in her head suddenly. She pressed her hands to her temples.

"Come, I'm going to get some coffee and hot food into you. Let me fetch my coat."

Merry came back downstairs with her coat on and a spare jacket in her hand. "Get that wet denim off you and put this thing on."

Nina acquiesced. The jacket was dry and warm, filled with pad-
ding, and she was grateful. "You can keep it," Merry said as she took
her around the corner to the entrance of a little pub.

"I don't want to go in there."

Merry weighed her, then nodded. She understood.

"Come, I know somewhere."

"No . . . I need to go. I need to score some Crissy. Had to see you
first."

Merry's face changed, her eyes filling with empathy, pity. Nina
hated it, hated who she was. Hated how people saw her.

"Don't fucking judge me, okay, Merry, just because you got out.
We go back, you and me."

"I'm not. I'm not judging you at all. What's the matter? Why'd you
come?"

"It's Faith."

"What do you mean, Faith? What are you talking about?"

"She's dead. Drowned. It was her they found in the Gorge. Some
cops was around Harbor House talking to Pastor Markus, asking about
Faith's family, who to tell that she was dead." Her gaze snapped down
the street. She was nervous that maybe the cop had followed her or
something. "She was *killed*, Merry, and rolled up in plastic, dumped
in the sea."

Blood drained from Merry's face. "You sure?"

"Cop showed me a photo of her body in the morgue—her tattoo.
What if he's back? What if it was *him*? I read what was done to that
Cemetery Girl—it's him. Gotta be him."

Merry looked waxen. She grabbed Nina by the shoulders, eyes shining. "Did that cop say anything about a crucifix on Faith?"

She shook her head. "But it could be him."

"Why do you say that?"

"'Cause I asked that cop if the same was done to her as to the
Cemetery Girl, and he looked at me weird, and he didn't deny it."

"Listen to me. When did you last actually see Faith?"

Nina scratched at the scabs on her face. "Like a while ago. Maybe five to eight months. She was with that pimp of hers from way back, Damián, and some other blond guy—rich prick who was driving a small, black BMW. Young, like in his twenties."

"You sure it was a Bimmer?"

"Christ, I know cars. I know where my best scores come from."

CHAPTER 26

"Like I said, we had a month-to-month lease, and the tenant gave notice at the end of November—eleven days ago. It was a Thursday. Her movers arrived the next day with cash from her, so she's paid up for December."

Kjel walked slowly across the bare hardwood floors to the window. Dust spots and darker areas marked the wood where rugs and furniture had rested. The view looked out over new construction toward the water. They'd located the property manager and had showed him Hocking's mug shot. He'd recognized her and said she'd lived here almost two years. Always paid cash. Now her place was cleaned out.

"She give the notice herself?" Leo said as Kjel continued to stare out at the view, his brain running through the possibilities.

"She phoned it in."

"You certain it was her?"

"Female voice. I had no reason to doubt it."

"What moving company did she use?" Leo said.

"I don't know. There was a truck here, white, but no company logo or anything on the sides."

"And the guy who gave you the money for her last month's rent—he give you a name?"

"No."

"What he look like?"

"Dark hair, average height, I dunno, maybe in his thirties. Ordinary guy."

"He have a uniform, a logo, this ordinary guy?"

"Just jeans, a dark jacket."

Kjel went into the kitchen and opened cupboards one after the other while Leo spoke. All empty. He looked under the sink for a garbage bin. Cleaned out. He opened the fridge—just an open box of baking soda and stains. He closed the door and started to move the fridge from out of its pocket between the cabinets.

"What're you doing?" Leo said.

"People stick contact numbers, appointments, notes up on the fridge. At my house stuff always falls down between the sides of the fridge and the counters, or sometimes it goes underneath. Give me a hand here." They shoved the fridge out while the landlord watched with mild interest.

A comb nestled in the thick layer of dust and grime beneath the fridge along with a scattering of old peanuts, a paper clip, and other unidentifiable bits of food. Plus a once-white, stained business card. Kjel fished the card out of the dust.

Dr. Jon Jacques. Cosmetic Dentistry.

"Bingo," he whispered, wagging the card in Leo's face. "I think we might have found us the dentist who fixed up Hocking's nice new pearly whites." He wagged the card in Leo's face. "Follow the money, I always says. Bet she didn't pay *him* in cash."

Finding nothing else, Kjel and Leo left a contact card with the rental manager and rode down in the elevator. As they walked into the lobby, they saw a woman outside the glass entrance doors, pressing a button on the door panel.

Kjel cursed. "It's her. That reporter."

They exited the doors, and she glanced up sharply, then swallowed. She was ghost-pale, eyes like deep black holes. She looked a mess.

"Merry Winston," Kjel said, eyeing her carefully.

She scanned the street, fear raw in her features. Something quickened in him. He moved to the intercom panel and saw that Faith Hocking's name was displayed in the box. "You come to visit Faith often, then?" he said.

"Was it her?" she said, voice hoarse. "Was it Faith who was found in the Gorge?"

Kjel exchanged a fast glance with Leo. "What made you think this?" Leo said.

"Just *tell* me." She was shaking now.

Kjel frowned, suspicion darkening inside him. "What brought you here to Faith Hocking's address at this point in time?"

"Just . . . following a lead."

"And where'd you get this lead?" he said. "'Cause it ain't from the scanner this time, is it, Winston?"

Silence. Kjel edged closer to her, towering his height over her. She took a step back. Leo watched. "Who told you about Faith Hocking? How'd you know wheres to find her? Who's giving you all this information?"

"I'm a good reporter, okay? I do the legwork."

"Obstruction of justice is a serious offense. If we find—"

"Then arrest me. Charge me." She shot an involuntary glance back at the panel.

"You're not going to find any Faith Hocking here, Winston," Leo said. "She's gone. Her stuff has been cleared out."

Paling further, she took another step back. "I don't believe you."

Leo shrugged.

"Who cleared out her things?" she said.

"Oh, your source leave that bit out, then?" Kjel said.

She glowered at him, then spun around and hurried down the sidewalk. She climbed into a lime-green Volkswagen Beetle parked under a leafless cherry tree several yards down the road. They watched as the Beetle engine coughed to life. Winston pulled out into the street, turned right at the intersection, and disappeared.

"How in the hell did she get that?" Kjel said, staring after her. "We just learned Hocking's ID ourselves this morning, and about this apartment right now—but Winston knew exactly whats she was looking for on that intercom panel."

"Fucked if I know," Leo said.

Kjel frowned, thinking. "What you say we call this in, and then we go visit us a dentist?"

CHAPTER 27

Lara paced behind the drawn sheers of her living room. She felt like she was going to throw up. Gracie was dead—the Cemetery Girl. And now Faith wasn't answering her phone. She should've listened to Gracie when she'd said two weeks ago that she felt she was being followed, that some guy had been lurking in the shadows outside her house one night, watching her window. Gracie had thought this same guy might have gotten onto her bus Saturday before last and off at her same stop. She'd thought that he could be one of *them*. And now, outside, across a street plastered with wet oak leaves, a black Lexus with tinted windows was parked under the gnarled branches. It had been there since dawn, engine running intermittently, probably to keep the occupant warm. Lara was certain that she'd seen the same Lexus outside the church last Thursday when she'd walked down the street to catch the bus after choir.

Lara dialed Faith's cell again, got voicemail again.

"Faith, it's me. Just . . . call, okay?"

She paced, then made another call, this one to Eva. Relief gushed into her chest when the call picked up.

"Eva, it's Lara. I . . ." She felt silly suddenly. "It's just . . . Gracie and that horrible news. And now I can't reach Faith. Have you heard from her?"

"She's probably just not checking her phone." Eva sounded curt, as though she was in a hurry.

"She always answers her cell—she's never without it." Lara opened the sheers slightly with the back of her hand as she spoke. The Lexus was still there. "Gracie said she might have been stalked, and there's someone outside my apartment right now—maybe it's one of them."

"Why would it be?"

"Have you seen anything . . . weird?"

"No. Look, it's probably fine. Whatever you do, don't go talking to the cops or there'll be shit. They could kill you if you talk, remember? It was part of the deal—no talk. Ever. And don't call them, either. They call you."

"Maybe Gracie *did* talk," Lara whispered. "Maybe—" Lara stilled as a dark-blue sedan drew up right outside her window. The car doors opened. Lara quickly killed her call, her hand tightening around her phone.

A tall, dark-haired guy and a woman with a long red ponytail got out. Black coats. They came up her path, and she heard their footsteps coming up the stairs.

They knocked. Loud.

Lara hesitated, fear swamping her.

They knocked again. Louder. She went to the peephole.

"Who is it?" she called, peering through at their faces.

"Metro Victoria police," came the man's deep voice. "Detectives Maddocks and Pallorino. We'd like to speak to you about Gracie Drummond."

Lara swallowed, hesitated, then opened the door a crack. She eyed them through the security chain. "You got some ID or something?" She had no idea what to look for or any way of telling what ID was genuine, but she figured she should ask.

They both showed badges.

"Are you Lara Pennington?" said the female cop.

It was then that Lara recognized the woman's face from the newspaper. A bad taste filled her mouth. "I don't know how you could have let Gracie's mother find out like that," Lara said. "Letting Gracie's name get out all over the news."

"Can we come in, Lara?" the female cop said, her face showing no reaction.

Lara unhooked the security chain, opened the door. She showed the detectives into her humble living room, which was furnished with old secondhand sofas over which she'd draped sarongs that came from Bali.

Lara seated herself on the edge of a chair. The female cop took the sofa. The male detective remained standing, surveying her apartment—the drawn sheers, the empty bottle of tequila—and it made her uncomfortable, even more edgy.

"I'm sorry for your loss, Lara," said the woman. "I understand that you and Gracie were very good friends."

Lara said nothing. A ringing started inside her skull.

They asked her all sorts of questions, and it just blurred. Mostly she declined to reply for fear of saying the wrong thing.

"Did Gracie spend the night here on Tuesday?"

"No."

"On her calendar she'd marked last Tuesday, and several Tuesdays previous, with the names Lara P., B.C., and Amanda R. Who is Amanda R.?"

The ringing inside her head grew louder. She really was going to throw up. "I . . . I'd cover for Gracie sometimes. She'd go out."

"Where did she go? Why always a Tuesday?"

"I don't know."

"Are you sure?"

Her eyeballs kinda wanted to roll back inside her head. She pressed her shaking hands down hard on her knees. "She didn't tell me."

"A close friend like Gracie? She didn't tell you?"

Lara looked down at her toes. She focused on the chipped polish, telling herself she needed a pedicure, anything to stop the noise in her head.

"What do the initials J.R. and B.C. stand for?"

She glanced up sharply, then regretted her slip. "I don't know," she lied.

The female cop studied her in silence, then exchanged a quick look with the male detective. He moistened his lips, walked slowly to the window, parted the drapes, and looked out into the street. Lara wondered if the Lexus was still there. The female cop consulted her notebook. "And what about John Jacks?"

She shook her head. "I don't know anyone by that name."

"Do you know where Gracie went instead of to choir practice last Thursday?"

"No."

"You were at that practice?"

She nodded.

The detective leaned forward. "Are you certain that you don't know a John Jacks? Because Gracie has been seeing him for a while, according to her mother. He drives a small, black BMW. Does that jog your memory? Maybe he gave her a lot of really nice, expensive gifts, or he bought her a pair of Francesco Milano boots, for example?" The cop paused. "Gracie Drummond was wearing those boots when she was attacked, Lara. They're at the forensics lab with her clothing."

"Oh God . . . I . . . I . . ." Tears spilled suddenly down her face, and she couldn't stop them.

"Talk to me, Lara. What can you tell me about John Jacks?"

"I . . . uh . . . It's—it was—more like an informal thing he had with Gracie."

"Where will we find him?"

"I don't know where he lives."

"He's a member of the Oak Bay Country Club. Isn't that where Gracie met him? While she was watching Rick Butler play tennis, before Rick broke up with her?"

Lara wiped her face with her sleeve. "I think so. Rick would know more."

"Why are you keeping information from the police? Who are you trying to protect?"

The ringing in her brain grew so loud that she felt dizzy. She was going to faint. The cop's voice sounded very far away, and Lara couldn't hear what she was saying any longer.

"Lara, Lara, look at me. Whoever did this to Gracie is still out there, and as long as he is, he could hurt someone else. We *need* to find him, and fast, and withholding information from the police is going to put lives in danger. If you have any information—"

"I don't, okay? I just don't!"

The woman nodded and tucked her notebook into her leather sling bag. "We'll be going through Gracie's emails, social media accounts, contact lists, phone records, so we'll be wanting to talk to you again if something comes up." She handed Lara her card. "In the meanwhile, if you do think of something, anything that could be relevant, no matter how small, please call me. Anytime." She paused again. "It would be better than having us bring you down to the station if we do find electronic trace that proves you know something."

As they were leaving, the woman cop turned suddenly and said, "Oh, one more question, Lara. Do you perhaps know Faith Hocking?"

Lara reached for the back of a chair. She swallowed. "No."

Both detectives eyed her.

"You've never met her?" the female detective said.

"No—I don't know anyone named Faith."

"Right," she said quietly. "Call us if you think of anything."

"She's lying," Angie said to Maddocks as they reached his Impala.

"Yeah, and terrified, but why? About what?"

Angie glanced back at the window. She could see Lara Pennington's shadow behind the sheers. The young woman was watching them.

"Let's see what the others give us and what Drummond's electronic devices yield," Angie said, opening the passenger door. "We'll bring Pennington in for formal questioning later—it'll be more productive if we have something we can use as leverage."

Angie seated herself inside the vehicle. While Maddocks led Jack-O along the grass verge for a bathroom break, she watched Lara Pennington's silhouette moving back and forth behind the drawn sheers. The teen really was scared shitless. Rolling possibilities through her brain, Angie turned her attention to the other side of the road. A gleaming black Lexus, recent model, tinted windows, slowly pulled off.

THE BAPTIST

He sees the cops outside Lara's place. Excitement crackles through him as he recognizes Detective Angie Pallorino with her long red hair. But it's not Detective Kjel Holgersen that she's with. It's some other guy, a little older, jet-black hair. This one's got swagger. The thrill deepens as it strikes him—this game truly is on. Real. Up close and personal. But it also means he will have to act faster with Lara now, if they're already questioning her. Thoughts of Lara Pennington fill his brain—plump-pussied Lara, bigger-breasted-than-Gracie Lara. Nice rounded-dimpled-butt Lara. He moistens his lips with his tongue, and he grows hard with anticipation. Because after Lara comes Eva—eager-beaver-wetter Eva. But along with the heat in his groin, along with the faster breathing and the galloping of his heart, comes a whisper of trepidation. He doesn't want to get caught. *No sirree, never get caught, Johnny. No-no, Tommy.* He's going to finish this job with these girls. And then there will always be more girls. Bad girls. The world would always be full, full, full with bad, bad girls. Other places. Faraway places. Over the seas and far away. He'll just have to be more cautious, smarter, now that they've come to Lara.

And Peter said unto them, Repent ye, and be baptized every one of you in the name of Jesus Christ unto the remission of your sins; and ye shall receive the gift of the Holy Spirit.

CHAPTER 28

"Dr. Jacques is with a patient," the receptionist said, eyeing the badges that Leo and Kjel held out to her.

"We can wait—have a few questions for the doc."

She glanced up and met Kjel's eyes. Conservative dresser, he noted. Good haircut. Understated makeup. Expensive-looking designer frames.

"I'm sorry, but his schedule is fully booked today," she said. "And he already has a waiting room full of patients, as you can see."

"Like I said, we can wait." Kjel turned and made a show of taking in the rather plush-looking waiting area. "So if you wants two cops here all day, that's okay by me." He began to squeeze himself into a narrow space on a sofa between two well-heeled women, who rapidly moved apart to accommodate him, like he had lice or something.

The receptionist hurriedly pushed her chair back. "Just give me a minute." She scurried into the back and returned a few seconds later. "Dr. Jacques can spare you exactly ten minutes," she said curtly. "This way, please."

She showed them into an office behind the reception area. Big, gleaming desk and shelves. Fancy art on the walls. Framed photos on a chest of drawers. Kjel picked one frame up. The photo was of a man with a thinning blond comb-over that had been sprayed fiercely into place. With him was a slender, dark-haired woman in a very low-cut wedding gown. She looked half the man's age. A shoo-in for a Victoria's Secret catalogue if he ever did see one, what with her pouty, collagen-filled lips and cat-slanted eyes. He set down the frame and snagged up another—this one displaying a photo of a young man, maybe in his early twenties. Also blond. Comb-over's son, he guessed. "I'm figuring child of a first marriage, and this here is the second wife," he said, showing the photos to Leo. "This woman doesn't look much older than the kid."

"Third marriage," came a voice behind them.

They swung around, Kjel still clutching the framed photos.

"Dr. Jon Jacques," Comb-over said, declining to offer his hand. He instead inserted his hands into his pants pockets and remained standing in the doorway. "What can I do for you, detectives?"

"Faith Hocking, she was a patient of yours?" Kjel said, setting the frames carefully back on top of the chest of drawers.

"I have many patients. I don't recall all their names."

Leo took the flyer from his pocket, showed it to Dr. Comb-over. "This woman," Leo said.

The dentist declined to look at the image. Instead, he met the eyes of Leo, then Kjel, and said, "Why don't you get to the point, gentlemen? I'm a busy man."

"Just want to know if you fixed her teeth, and who paid for it," Leo said.

Dr. Jacques lowered his gaze momentarily to the flyer, his features unreadable, then he checked his watch. "Look, forgive my irritation, but you of all people, detectives, should know that I cannot discuss patients, nor give out financial information. Now, if you will excuse me."

But Kjel and Leo remained unmoving. "She's a homicide victim, Doc. Anything you can tell us would aid in the investigation."

"I'm terribly sorry to hear that. But—"

200

"This woman," Kjel said, taking two fast steps toward the doc, who, up close, smelled of cologne, "came off the streets with a meth-mouth, and you know it. You don't forget a mouth like that. Just tell us who paid yous for the nice pearly whites, Doc, and we'll be out of your . . . uh, hair?"

The doc flashed a quick and feral smile with his own straight, pearly whites while his eyes turned flat and cold. "Like I said, patient information is confidential."

"Maybe we'll just come back with a warrant."

"Then you do that. Goodbye, gentlemen."

Kjel and Leo exited Dr. Jacques's practice through the waiting area, the doc's patients ogling them with brazen curiosity.

As they walked out into the street and rain, Kjel said, "That guy gives me the jeebies."

"But it looks like we got our dentist," Leo said. "And an ex-meth-head ho sure as hell can't pay cash for an apartment as well as afford the likes of Dr. Jon Jacques—not unless she's turning some seriously upmarket tricks."

"A pimp coulda footed the bill—had her cleaned up. Put her out to work the cost off. I mean, from that more recent photo at Harbor House, Hocking actually cleaned up pretty darn good."

Leo glanced up at him and cocked a brow. "Johns paying big bucks to put their dicks into that fanged Medusa mouth? Now there's a thought."

As they reached their vehicle, Kjel beeped the lock and said, "Well, we ain't gonna gets us a warrant for Dr. Comb-over's financial and billing records without some probable grounds."

"Then we find grounds." Leo opened the passenger door. "Because someone paid for those teeth, and I bet my ass Jacques knows who."

By the time Angie and Maddocks arrived at the Oak Bay Country Club, the afternoon was darkening—the hours ticking down to the shortest day of the year—and the white indoor tennis domes glowed with light like alien space pods in the winter gloom.

"They're not going to spill member details without a warrant," Angie said as they entered the big glass doors. The reception area was tiled, and soft piped music was punctuated by the rhythmic *thwock* of tennis balls meeting taut rackets. A statuesque, bronzed blonde working the reception desk looked up and smiled with a perfectly straight row of whitened teeth. Angie guessed her tan came courtesy of the club's tanning beds.

While Maddocks went up to ask Miss Sweden about John Jacks, Angie gravitated to the sound of the balls.

"Hey." She smiled, greeting a coach who was coming out of one of the court enclosures with a group of young teens. He looked to be in his late thirties with the ripped body of a tanned Adonis, designer sports duds, brown hair streaked surfer blond. She checked out the nametag on his shirt. "Serge Radikoff. Good to meet you—I hear you coach Rick Butler."

He ran his eyes up and down the length of her and smiled, the directness of his gaze brazen. She'd guessed right. Serge was a ladies' man. "He's very talented, one of my special ones." His accent was Eastern European.

"I hear that he's your protégé, that you're sponsoring him."

He wiped his face with the end of the white towel hooked around his neck, drank from his water bottle. "Rick has talent. He's going places with his game, and he'd never afford this place and my lessons otherwise."

Angie took a few steps up to the fence and watched some young guys taking turns with the ball machine. "So you'd make a name for yourself with Rick. And John Jacks—" She turned to face him. "You coach him, too?"

Radikoff was silent for a beat, just the hollow *thwocks* of the balls. One slammed into the fence right near her face, and she tensed with the surprise.

"I'm the club coach," he said, caution entering in his eyes. "I'm paid to teach whoever wants lessons." Another pause. "Who wants to know?"

"Angie Pallorino," she said, deepening her smile and extending her hand. "Metro Victoria police. I hear Jacks played with Butler."

He glanced quickly over his shoulder. "What is this about?"

"Jacks dated Butler's ex-girlfriend, Gracie Drummond. Gracie was murdered, and we're trying to figure out her movements in the weeks preceding her death."

He stared, and his jaw opened. "Not . . . not the Cemetery Girl, the one in the news?"

She held his gaze. "Drummond used to come here to watch Butler practice. It's how she met Jacks, I understand."

"What has this got to do with me?"

Out of the corner of her eye she saw Maddocks approaching. "Where can I find Jacks?" she said.

His features shuttered instantly. "If you'll excuse me—I'm not permitted to fraternize with members or club guests. Nor talk about them, as per my contract." He snagged his kit bag and rackets off a bench and strode off. She watched him go. Nice legs. Very nice legs. And ass.

Maddocks came to her side and followed her gaze. She glanced up at him, and those indigo-blue eyes held hers. A strange, palpable energy rolled off him in waves.

"And if *he* had walked into that nightclub?" he said.

"Don't," she said quietly, "ever raise that again." She strode rapidly for the exit, her pulse suddenly racing. An odd mix of defensive anger and something akin to shame churned through her. She hated that he knew about that side of her, that he judged her, that he'd brought it up again within a work context. More so, she hated that she actually cared what he thought, and what that might mean.

It wasn't until she was outside and waiting in the rain at his vehicle in the dark that he came out. She was drenched by the time he reached and unlocked the car. She didn't say a word as she got in. He let her sit there, engine running, heater blasting, while he took his little mongrel on a walk down the curb. When he returned, he took his sweet time giving the animal water from a bowl he'd fished out of the back of the Impala.

"And what did *you* get from Miss Sweden?" she demanded as he climbed into the driver's seat.

"Crickets. And you from Tennis Boy?"

She tightened her jaw, looked out the window as he pulled into the street. "John Jacks is a member of the club, as we suspected. Serge Radikoff coaches him. Once he found out I was a cop, he clammed up. We'll get more when we interview Rick Butler."

Instead of taking the road that would lead them back to the station, Maddocks turned left, and at the same time he groped behind him for something on the rear seat, his eyes fixed on the wet road ahead.

"Where are we going?" she said.

"Can you reach that for me?"

"Reach what?"

"The blanket behind my seat. Drape it over Jack-O. Temps are dropping, and he doesn't handle cold with his shaved fur. And since the second op on his leg, I think his immune system is down."

She frowned at him, then reached into the back for the blanket. As she covered the dog, it growled and snapped at her. Angie jerked her hand back. "Stupid little mutt. He tried to bite me."

A smile curved Maddocks's lips.

"What? You think that's funny?"

"Maybe he senses you don't like him."

"I don't. What's there to like?"

He cast her a sideways glance.

"No, tell me, really, why do you like this animal?" she said.

"Truth?"

"Yeah, truth."

"Because he makes me feel good. He makes me feel like I made a difference in his life." He shrugged, turned another corner, stopped at the lights, looked at her. "Which is more than you get from this job sometimes."

Her own earlier conversation with her father filtered into her mind.

I put bad guys away. And I'm good at it, Dad. Damn good. I make a difference.

Do you?

Yeah, I do. Sometimes. Yes. I do . . .

Angie's thoughts turned to Tiffy, and how she'd failed the child. To Hash, and how she might have failed him, too, and how much she missed him. She thought of the anguish and accusation she'd witnessed in Lorna Drummond's eyes, the wailing sound that came from her throat as she'd slid down to the floor. The weight of it all was suddenly heavy on Angie's shoulders.

"Where are we going?" she asked again, more quietly.

"To drop Jack-O off—Buziak is springing for pizza tonight while we debrief, and I finally found another sitter, one of the old guys at the marina who'll take him at least until this case winds down a bit."

"Marina?"

"West Bay. I live on an old schooner there. Trying to renovate it. Without much luck, I might add. Every time I fix something, a new problem comes up. It'll be easier when the weather warms again—I hope."

"So, you sail?"

He gave a soft snort. "It was always a retirement dream of ours, for after Ginn left home—me and the wife on a boat. Sailing up the coast, stopping at whatever little inlet took our fancy. Kayaking, fishing." He was silent for a few blocks. "Then our marriage fell apart. This job can be hell on a relationship."

Curiosity won the better of Angie. "You separated?"

"Going through a real messy divorce. Maybe that's another reason the dog is growing on me—dogs don't quit on you." He fell silent again, and Angie felt as though she'd just glimpsed a very personal, private part of this cop. Too personal. She didn't want to know more. She didn't want to care, to feel the things she was beginning to feel, but she couldn't stop herself from asking the next question.

"Why do you still wear the wedding band?"

"For Ginn. I put it on before we went out for brunch Sunday. To show her . . . I don't know, to show her that I was still trying to make it work. She blames me for breaking up the family." He gave a laugh, but it sounded hollow. "Sometimes I think a shrink would have a field day with me trying to salvage things that I know are irreparably broken—that old boat, that retirement dream, that old notion of family I once had."

Angie's heart beat hard in her chest. So he hadn't removed the wedding band to make a conquest at the club. He'd just put it back on for his kid, right before he got called to a murder and embroiled in this case.

"This is why you should have let me drive my own vehicle," she said crisply. "I could have gone back to the station myself while you went and did . . . whatever personal thing you need to do with that mutt."

CHAPTER 29

As Maddocks turned onto the road that would lead them down to the harbor, the Mount Saint Agnes institution loomed suddenly into view. Angie tensed and checked her watch. Her mouth turned dry as she fought herself. "Wait!" she said suddenly as they neared the gates. "Turn in here, please."

Maddocks glanced at her, slowing his Impala as he neared the entrance to the institution with its high walls and big iron gates. "Why?" he said.

"I . . . there's someone I promised to visit today. I only need about thirty minutes—you can drop your dog off in the meanwhile, then pick me up after."

Maddocks shot her another glance and wheeled his vehicle slowly in through the entrance to the Mount Saint Agnes Mental Health Treatment Facility. He drew to a stop under the portico in front of the double doors. Angie hesitated and rubbed her knee, nerves suddenly biting at her. As much as she loved her mom, part of her was afraid to face squarely up to what was happening to her mother's mind. And she knew this anxiety was in part because she feared the illness was beginning to manifest in her, too. This big concrete building with its stone walls and gates and white-coated orderlies possibly lurked on her own horizon in the not-too-distant future.

"Who's in there?" Maddocks said, regarding her with an intensity that made her feel naked.

"It's personal," she said crisply. She reached for the door. "I'll be no more than thirty."

"Take more time if you need it."

"I won't." She opened the door, got out, slammed it shut, and did not look back as she strode toward the entrance.

A nurse showed Angie into a large room where several tables and chairs had been positioned in groups. A few patients occupied some of the chairs, some fidgeting and muttering, others looking totally vacant and alone. An orderly stood by the wall, watching over them. In front of one of the windows a Christmas tree glowed with soft lights.

"She's over there, by the bay window," said the nurse, pointing to a bent figure sitting motionless in a cane rocking chair, facing her own reflection in the dark windowpanes. Shock dropped through Angie. Her attention shot to the nurse.

"Why is my mother in here? Why isn't she in her private room, with all her things?"

"I'm afraid she had a bit of an episode, being left alone for the first time. It happens—the unfamiliarity in a new place, the fear of not knowing where she is, who everyone is. She's here under observation for a while." The nurse paused. "Your mother has been heavily medicated, Ms. Pallorino. She's not terribly lucid, but seeing a familiar family member might help. If she does get upset, however, please just step away quietly and alert the orderly."

"Who authorized the medication, the dosage?"

"Her doctor, in consultation with her next of kin—her husband was here most of the day."

Emotion, guilt, slammed into Angie with such blunt force that it stole her breath and she had to concentrate on inhaling. "Thanks." Slowly, she made her way over to the window. Her mother's whitening hair looked more pastel orange than the deep strawberry blonde it once was. A white bathrobe draped her bony shoulders, and her mom was devoid of her customary makeup. Her skin looked blotchy, dry, lined. It seemed as if her mom had aged decades in the hours since Angie had last seen her.

"Mom?"

Her mother started rocking in her chair, faster, faster.

Angie pulled up a stool and sat facing her mother. "How are you doing?" She smiled.

Her mom stopped rocking and peered at Angie as if she didn't recognize her. Her eyes weren't focused. She wasn't fully there. "Who are you?" she said, her speech slightly slurred. "Do I know you?"

"It's Angie."

"Angie?" Her mother frowned and sat awhile, just staring at Angie. Then a slow, sad smile crumpled her face. "I had a little daughter once—called Angie. Such a beautiful little girl. Such a wonderful child. Then . . . just like that she was gone." She began to moan and rock again, her features twisting as if in pain, her hands gripping the armrests tightly. The moan grew louder, the rocking wild.

Angie leaned forward and covered one of her mother's hands, slowing the motion.

"It's okay, Mom. I'm here."

"The angels brought her back. They did. She didn't belong there. They returned her."

"Who? Who are you talking about, Mom?"

"Angie."

A dank sense of dread trickled into Angie. "Where didn't Angie belong?" she said.

"Heaven. In Italy. With God. They made a mistake. She wasn't ready to go with God. So they brought her back." A sad, wistful smile crossed her mother's face, and she stopped rocking. "Christmas Eve. That's when she was returned. I was singing at the cathedral . . . such a beautiful cathedral. It was ordained." Her mother closed her eyes and started to hum a hymn that was strangely familiar to Angie, yet she couldn't quite place it. That cold chill of dread crawled deeper.

"Which cathedral are you talking about, Mom?"

"It was snowing out," she said softly, "when they brought her back. Like a babe in a manger in a box, she was."

"Mom. Look at me. Please."

Her mother opened her eyes, and confusion chased through them as she struggled to focus on Angie. "Who are you? I . . . I *know* you . . ."

Angie smiled gently, yet her pulse was hammering hard and her skin turning slick with sweat. Confusion chased through her own brain—some sixth sense warning her that there was more to her mother's words than the ramblings of a cross-wired mind. "I know you too," she said, squeezing her hands. "But remind me who *you* are again?" she said, testing.

Her mother sat awhile, thinking. "I'm Angie's mother. I have a beautiful little girl."

Emotion burned fierce into Angie's eyes. "Yeah. You do."

"Do you know her?"

"I do."

This pleased her mother, and she seemed to drift, her features going serene as she shut her eyes and started to sing the words to the hymn in a soft mezzo-soprano.

"Ave Maria . . . Gratia plena, Dominus tecum . . ."

Angie swallowed, a strange chill of horror icing into her bones at the sound.

Her mother began rocking again, slowly, slowly. *"Benedicta tu in mulieribus . . ."*

"Mom?"

"Et benedictus, fructus ventris tui, Jesus . . ."

"Mom!"

"Sancta Maria, sancta Maria, Maria . . ."

Panic lashed through Angie. She had to get out of here. Stat. A woman's voice filled her head. She was screaming . . . in some foreign language, yet the words seemed to make sense . . .

Uciekaj, uciekaj! . . . Run, run! . . . Wskakuj do srodka, szybko! . . . Get inside . . . Siedz cicho! . . . Stay quiet!

"I . . . I'll be back," Angie said, lurching to her feet and eyeballing the exit door across the room. "I'll come visit again as soon as I can. It'll be better next time, I'm sure." Angie bent down and kissed her mom quickly on the cheek. She hurried for the door, heart slamming. *What the fuck?*

Maddocks sat waiting in the Mount Saint Agnes parking lot for Pallorino, engine turning to keep warm.

The passenger door swung open suddenly, and Pallorino entered with a blast of cold. She slammed the door shut and rubbed the knees of her jeans. "Thanks for waiting," she said, looking dead ahead.

"Jesus, you spooked me." He laughed. "I didn't see you coming— thought you'd exit out of those other doors."

She buckled up, still avoiding his eyes.

"All okay?"

She rubbed her mouth. "Yeah. Yeah, fine." She turned to him, her game face on. "Dropped the dog off?" she said.

He studied her. And she met his measuring gaze, unblinkingly, almost defiant. Something unspoken surged between them. Then he said, "Yeah, I dropped him off." And he engaged gears.

As he drove back to the station, he said quietly, "Got an update from Buziak while I was waiting. Leo and Holgersen found Hocking's apartment—it's been cleaned out."

"What do you mean, *cleaned out*?"

"Apparently Hocking called and gave notice eleven days ago. Moving van came and took all her stuff."

"So she was alive eleven days ago?"

"Or someone else claiming to be her called to cancel her lease. Holgersen and Leo also located the guy they believe to be her dentist." He shot her a glance. "Guess what his name is?"

"What is it?" she said, watching him intently.

"John Jacks. Except it's spelled J O N J A C Q U E S."

"The same name as Drummond's boyfriend?"

"Apparently Dr. Jacques has a son. Jon Jacques Junior. Twenty-two years old. Leo and Holgersen have been digging into Jon Jacques Senior's background. He's on the board of the Oak Bay Country Club, and he's been investigated in the past for organized crime connections. Allegations of laundering, tax evasion, bribery of a judge. Nothing stuck. Crown counsel has dubbed him Teflon Jon."

She whistled softly. "So the dentist and his son could be a nexus between our two dead girls—Gracie Drummond and Faith Hocking."

"And that *Sun* reporter, Merry Winston, was also at Faith Hocking's apartment, same time as Holgersen and Leo arrived there. Somehow she got wind of our floater's ID and address." Maddocks cast his partner another glance. "What are your thoughts about this leak being internal?"

"If it is internal, it's gotta be someone with a serious axe to grind," she said. "Winston's informant either wants to take someone inside the MVPD down, or he's hitting at the entire organization of the MVPD."

"Not necessarily a he. Could be a she."

"What are you saying?"

"Exactly what I said."

"You think it's *me*?"

"You're not the only female in the MVPD, Pallorino."

She glared at him, waves of hot energy crackling off her. "I'm the only female with this particular case information."

"No you're not. There's tech support staff. And there's the family and intimate connections of other officers. Cops talk at home—like it or not, it happens."

She fell silent, just the sound of wipers and the soft hum of the heater in the car.

"You trust me, right?" she said quietly after a while.

"You've got to trust a partner." He stole another glance at her. "Your partner is the guy who has your back."

CHAPTER 30

The incident room was hot and thick with the scent of bodies, wet coats, stale cigarette smoke that lingered in clothing and damp hair. Combined with the cheesy, yeasty, garlicky, pepperoni smells of the pizza slices softening their cardboard containers, it was making Angie feel sick. She poured herself a glass of cold water and took a seat up front, near the whiteboard, her mother's strange words churning around and around in her brain. And that hymn—a supposedly beautiful Christmas song of praise to the Virgin Mary. She'd looked up the English translation on her phone before entering the incident room.

> *Ave Maria*
> *Virgin of the sky*
> *Sovereign of thanksgiving and loving mother*
> *Accept the fervent prayer of everybody*
> *Do not refuse*
> *To this lost person of mine, love . . . .*

Was the discomfit that this song seemed to awaken inside her because of this case—the religious overtones? The Virgin Mary symbolism? Because Gracie Drummond had been laid at the feet of a stone Madonna? Or was everything—her hallucinations, the voices inside her head, her possible PTSD, her sexual conflict over Maddocks, her anxiety over her mother's mental illness—curdling with the facts of this homicide case and her past rape cases? Was her ever-increasing fatigue further scrambling her mind?

Her thoughts returned to her mother's odd mention of Italy. Combined with the discrepancies of the dates on the backs of those photos and the snippets of memory seemingly returning from the car accident when she was a child . . . it was eating at Angie. And those phrases that she kept hearing in her brain?

Uciekaj, uciekaj! . . . Run. Run! . . . Wskakuj do srodka, szybko . . . get inside. Siedz cicho! . . . stay quiet!

What in the hell language could that be? Why did she seem to understand what the words meant?

Buziak resumed his place in front of the whiteboard at the head of the room and rapped his knuckles on the table like a gavel. A large monitor had been brought in and mounted beside the board, which was accumulating more graphic photos and information as results came in from various aspects of the investigation. A male who looked to be in his late fifties—dark hair, John Lennon glasses—was fiddling with a laptop at a table near the monitor, gearing up for some kind of presentation as he brought a desktop image up onto the screen. Fitz was there, too. Sitting in his chair against the wall again, observing.

As the other detectives began to seat themselves around the room, the seat beside her remained vacant, as if she was some kind of pariah. It was Maddocks who eventually took it. As he sat, his arm bumped up against hers. Angie involuntarily tensed. She could *feel* his heat, his solidity beside her. And again a memory of him naked in the red room pulsed into her darker, twisting thoughts. She inhaled deeply.

Desire was a tricky beast.

Lust was her addiction. Anonymous sex was easy. But this . . . this other thing she was beginning to feel—this vulnerability, this need for his approval, this budding sense of . . . affection—she needed to get out of his proximity. She needed a new partner. She couldn't handle losing another friend. And she could certainly not find herself slipping into another intimate relationship with a colleague. Instinctively she knew she was not in a good headspace to deal with any of this right now.

"Okay," Buziak said. "What do we know so far? Let's start with the postmortem lab results . . ."

The heat and stifling atmosphere in the room thickened further as he spoke. Angie's brain began to buzz and her vision started to narrow. Buziak's words drowned into an unintelligible monotone. She tugged at the collar of her sweater, trying to pull his words back into focus.

". . . undigested gastrointestinal tract contents indicate that Hocking had eaten two to three hours before death," Buziak was saying. With shock, Angie realized she'd completely tuned out, and she had no idea how long she'd been absent. Panic kicked through her. *Focus, dammit.*

". . . DNA analysis on the contents of Hocking's GI tract indicate she consumed a meal that included *Tuber melanosporum*, black truffles—which are native to parts of southern Europe—and Kobe beef, specifically from the Tajima-gyu breed of cattle found in Japan's Hyōgo Prefecture." He glanced up from his notes. "Our floater ingested a very pricey meal two to three hours before she was killed." He scanned further down the pages of the report. "We're still waiting on further expert analysis, but the animal hair found inside the tarp is goat. Domestic. Both the outer winter guard hairs and softer underfur. There was also human hair trace found in Hocking's pubic combings. Nuclear DNA and mitochondrial DNA tests, plus light microscopy, show the hair to be Caucasoid, black, and originating from the pubic, lower abdomen, and thigh areas of two specific male donors. Neither of those two DNA profiles match anything in the system.

"Additional body hair from one of those profiles was also found on the decedent's body. So, two unidentified male subjects . . ." He pursed his lips as he skimmed more of the report and turned a page. He found what he appeared to have been searching for.

"The pieces of leaves—*Quercus garryana*—commonly known as Garry oak. And the seed found in the tarp is from an agronomic grass species. Combined with the Garry oak, it likely represents one of the rare scrub oak ecosystems found on shallow soils of the southern island and Gulf islands—we have a botanist attempting to narrow down an area for us."

He took a sip from a glass of water. "We got nothing more from a canvass of the area around the Blue Badger Bakery. The regular commuter who gets off at Drummond's stop checks out, has alibis. No one could identify the second passenger who also got off at that stop the previous Saturday evening. The forensic ident guys, however, did find hair and blood evidence in the gasworks alley that is a DNA match to Drummond, as well as a button from her coat. The trace from Drummond's clothing, including what appears to be some blonde head hair, is still being processed." He looked up.

"Various tire imprints were located in the adjacent lot, both sedan and SUV, recently made. This is all consistent with the theory that Drummond was surprised and attacked in the gasworks alley, subdued, and then transported by vehicle to the site where she was sexually assaulted and mutilated, before being transported once again and placed on the Ross Bay grave site. Video surveillance footage obtained from the 7-Eleven opposite the cemetery shows a dark SUV driving slowly past the top entrance shortly before midnight Sunday. Our experts have identified the model as a Lexus LX 570. Recent. High-end. Footage enhancement shows a partial plate—registration looks like it could start with BX."

A murmur rippled through the detectives. This could prove to be a breakthrough. Buziak stuck a grainy black-and-white of the Lexus up on the board. He followed this with a second even grainier image of the plate partial.

Something began to niggle at Angie's memory as she stared at the images.

"The 7-Eleven surveillance footage," Buziak said, "is consistent with witness evidence obtained during a canvass of the surrounding Ross Bay Cemetery residences. A female senior with insomnia was looking out of her window shortly before midnight and saw a dark SUV parked down near the side entrance of the cemetery, closer to where Drummond was discovered."

He placed his knuckles on the table and leaned into them, his dark eyes intent on his detectives. "Forensic techs are presently combing through footage secured from a new highways department camera mounted on the Johnson Street Bridge to see if they can pick up this Lexus and plate traveling west or east around the time Drummond was abducted in Victoria West."

Angie cleared her throat. "There was a black Lexus SUV with tinted windows parked across the street from Lara Pennington's residence when we interviewed her," she said. "It pulled off as I caught sight of it. I didn't see the plate, but Pennington had been watching the street from her window and seemed afraid."

Buziak stared at her a moment. "You didn't get a plate?"

"No, I didn't get the plate," Angie repeated coolly.

Maddocks turned to overtly stare at her, as if asking why she had not informed him of the Lexus.

She added, for his benefit, and to get in her own dig, "I only noticed the vehicle because I was waiting for Detective Maddocks to finish walking his dog."

His eyes narrowed sharply at her. Someone behind her whispered something.

"All right," Buziak said. "Also of significance, our so-called pastor, Markus Gilani, has a record and has served time. He was charged for driving while impaired eleven years ago. He had a minor with him in his vehicle. She was giving him oral sex when he struck and killed a female cyclist. Leo and Holgersen will be paying our pastor another visit. Now, I'm going to hand over to forensic psychologist Dr. Reinhold Grablowski, who I've brought in as a consultant on this case."

Again, murmurs rippled through the audience, and behind Angie, someone groaned.

The dark-haired man with the Lennon glasses came to his feet. He pressed a key on his laptop. The screen came to life with a Geographic Information System map of greater Victoria.

CHAPTER 31

Merry banged on the door to Harbor House, shivering and hugging herself against the cold. Pastor Markus opened the door, and his eyes went wide.

"Merry? What . . . on earth are you doing here? We've already allocated beds for the night, if—"

"I don't need a place to stay. I just need to see you. Can I come in?"

He glanced furtively down the street, then, voice lowering, he said, "You shouldn't have returned here. I told you, it's natural that you might feel . . . things, because of what I helped you go through, but I'm a married man. A man of God. Verity, my wife, is pregnant at last," he said. "I'm going to be a dad now."

"Fuck, it's not *that*! It's about those girls! It's about what happened before. To me. There's a fucking monster predator out there. He's back, and he got that Cemetery Girl, and might have gotten Faith, and he's been out there for a fucking long, long time."

"Come inside," he said quickly, probably more to quiet her down than anything else, because she was starting to get hysterical and she knew it, and she couldn't control herself.

He led her through the kitchen and into his small back office. He told her to sit near the heater, and he brought her a mug of hot tea. She cradled her hands around the ceramic mug that had been printed with the words *Repent thy sins, and thou shalt be forgiven*. She sipped, still shaking, from something far deeper than cold. He fetched her a sweater from the thrift store box.

"Give me your coat," he said, holding the sweater out to her.

She shrugged out of her wet coat and into the sweater. He hung the coat by the gas heater. He looked agitated.

"I heard the cops came to see you about Faith," she said. "What did you tell them?"

"Nothing."

"You didn't tell them about me? About the red crucifix on *my* face five years ago?"

"No. I respect my kids, the residents—"

"What happened to me, and to the girl in the cemetery, it's connected. It's him. He's back."

"You should go to the police, Merry—"

"And tell them what? That I was a runaway foster reject, a methhead junkie? That I was so high I can't even remember exactly what happened that night? I recall his eyes, and those words, and waking up in the ravine. And then seeing the red crucifix on my forehead when I looked in the mirror. And I knew I was sore and bleeding, but I wasn't one hundred percent sure of *anything* that had happened apart from that. I thought I could have been tripping out."

"Merry," he said gently. "Have you been using again?"

"Not yet."

He shifted uncomfortably in his chair. "Why did you really come to me, Merry?"

"I shouldn't have," she spat out bitterly. "I thought you could help. Now I know for sure you won't tell me, but I *need* to ask—have there been any others like me that you know of? Do you know of any street kids over the past years who spoke of a bad john, or a possible sexual assault associated with a crucifix? I want to know exactly how long he's been around, been doing this." She set the mug down and dragged her hands over her wet hair. "Fuck, I'm scared. I didn't know who else to talk to. He could be reading my stories in the paper and know that I was one of his victims. He could have been watching me all this time."

He returned her gaze steadily but remained silent, and her stomach kind of bottomed out.

"So there *have* been others."

Silence.

"Shit. *Tell* me."

Silence.

"If you won't talk to me, I'm going to your wife, and I *will* tell her what happened between you and me all those years ago. I'll tell the congregation. It'll be the end of you and your silence, *Pastor*."

He heaved out a sigh, looked away, got up, paced. Then he reseated himself and drew his hand down hard over his mouth. "Okay," he said softly. "There was a kid once, named Allison Fernyhough, who was assaulted in the same manner as you were. She was pretty messed up by it and ended up doing drugs on the street for a while, and she bunked here some nights, which is how I came into contact with her. She told me, and I suggested she tell the police, given your earlier experience. She did, but it was too long after the fact. There was no evidence they could use, and they weren't able to help. Allison said there were rumors on the streets about other victims, too, but I never heard more than that."

"And you never mentioned this to me?"

"Like I said, I met Allison well after your attack, Merry. And then no more. It all stopped. Like he disappeared."

"When, exactly, did this happen?"

"Two years after you."

She surged to her feet, grabbed her wet coat.

"Where are you going?" he said, getting up. "What are you going to do?"

"I'm going to get him. I'm going to find this sick fucking bastard and nail his dick to the wall, and I'm going to use my crime blog to do it. For Faith, and for those other girls, and for myself. I've got a freaking huge following now. Even if the paper does fire me, I won't need them in order to finish this. I don't need the *City Sun*'s bureaucracy and editorial board shit. I'll do this on my own."

I'm not going to let him drive me back into using, not going to let all my hard work go to waste. He will not put me back in the gutter . . .

"Merry, you *cannot* do this on your own."

"You know what? I *can*. No one has ever been there for me. Apart from you, that is. You picked me out of the gutter and wrung me out. Save the good girls, you said. You helped me after I was assaulted—you sold me your sorry story of a light at the end of the tunnel, and of God and heaven and all that, and for a while I actually believed you because it was all I had. But it was my own smarts that got me out of that hole I was in and cleaned me up. My own determination that stuck me through the night classes, and kept me holding down those fast-food jobs, and kept me studying for my journalism diploma at the same time. My own ability that swung me a nighttime gig on the *Sun* crime desk, because I *knew* the streets and where to find a goddamn good story, and I clawed up one rung at a time. And you know what else? Now I know you for what you are." She glowered at him, breathing hard, anger and hate and bitterness twisting through her body.

"There's always another path, Merry. A high road instead of the low road."

She snorted. "I was born to the low road, Pastor. Just like you. And I don't trust those cops. Clearly they couldn't help this Allison Fernyhough, and I know things about some of them. One of them is using me and my position at the paper, and I'm gonna use him straight back."

She dumped his sorry-ass thrift store sweater onto the floor, punched her arms into the wet sleeves of her own coat, and made for the door.

✝

CHAPTER 32

Dr. Reinhold Grablowski peered at the task force members with coal-black eyes set deep into sockets under thick brows. With his hooked nose, narrow face, and long neck, he reminded Angie of a vulture, a predator himself, picking at the brains of sick offenders. Her dislike for the doc was instant. But on some level, she knew that no one inside this room was much different from Grablowski. They all in one way or another tried to inhabit the brains of heinous villains in an effort to hunt and catch them. For whatever their personal reasons.

"From the evidence," Grablowski said with a slight Germanic accent that she couldn't quite place, "we're not looking for a rapist who kills his victims in order to avoid being identified, but rather a lust-based predator for whom the act of killing, and the associated ritual and sexual paraphilia, fulfills a psychosexual fantasy. In other words, these victims"—he pointed to the photos of the young women on the white-board—"didn't just happen to cross his path. They're not victims of opportunity or chance. They were chosen. Hunted, trapped, assaulted, and killed because these victims fit his psychosexual fantasy. He's also a psychopath—sadistic and organized. Methodical, cunning. The cruelty of his act excites him, and he may engage in torturing his victims. He will usually take a souvenir from his kills—a trophy, like the locks of hair—in order to relive his fantasy until the need grows so great that he is compelled to hunt again."

Way to go, genius . . . like none of us have already deduced that . . . If Buziak had let her finish speaking the other day, she'd have said almost the same.

"Statistically, the man you are looking for is likely to be of above-average intelligence, and a loner. He's more likely than not to own a car in good condition, so he's mobile, and he's also likely to travel longer distances than the average person. This offender is capable of using his verbal skills to manipulate and gain control over his victims until he has them within his comfort zone. However, his colleagues, if he has them, might consider him odd or somewhat socially inept."

The doc reached for the glass of water on the table in front of him and took a slow, deep swallow, his prominent Adam's apple bobbing in his long neck. Again, he reminded Angie of a strange predatory bird.

He set down the glass. "Most of his victims will share common traits. In this case, it might be physical appearance and age range. These victims"—again, he motioned to the board—"were all in their teens at the time of their attacks. All are Caucasian and have long, dark hair. They were probably strangers to the offender, and for some reason he identified them as women he could control, either through verbal manipulation or strength. Above that, they are 'right.' They fit his psychosexual fantasy. Thus, victimology in these cases becomes paramount, as in: Who were these women? What was going on in their lives at the time of the event? How did they first come to the attention of their assailant? Answers to these questions, and where the information intersects, will help narrow in on the subject."

"Wiseass," Leo whispered behind Angie. "Welcome to Homicide 101."

"All human sex is initiated through fantasies," Grablowski said. "Mental images that involve fulfilled or unfulfilled desires. We all have what is called a paraphilic love map, and these love maps begin to develop shortly after puberty. But the sexual predator, clinically speaking, has developed a love map where his lust is attached to fantasies and practices that are either socially forbidden, disapproved of, ridiculed, or penalized. And his fantasies usually involve aggression, domination, control. He becomes aroused by mere thoughts of sexual aggression, which he reinforces by using sadistic porn or fantasy stories that feature sexual sadism. In turn, he reinforces these stories, or porn, with masturbatory activities. This eventually forms a 'template,' or what we refer to in law enforcement as the signature of the offender."

He paused, took another sip of water, his wet lips shining, and Angie's mind went to her own love map—"love" was a dumbass word for this stuff, anyway. It should be called a lust map. There was no "love" in these sick, sadistic, violent acts of which the shrink was speaking.

"In this offender's case, his love map has a strong religious connection, and it was possibly formed around being punished for his own sexuality starting at puberty. In other words, sexual arousal was seen as a sin for which one had to be punished and cleansed. He likely has a Catholic background and has been baptized in the faith. He will likely be hunting his victims some distance away from his area of residence or work." Grablowski clicked a key on his computer, and red dots appeared on the GIS map.

"Ritter was attacked here." He pointed to a dot. "Fernyhough over here. Drummond appears to have been abducted here. All areas west of the city, and the Gorge. Hocking, we don't know yet where she was attacked. But going by what we have so far, your area of peak probability of finding this offender's place of residence is here." He tapped a key, and an area on the map washed yellow. It covered the suburbs abutting the city to the east. "His hunting zone is where his desire for anonymity and his desire to operate within his comfort zone meet. Which means his next victim is likely to be found in this area." He hit another key, and the map to the west of the Gorge went red.

Great help there, Doc . . .

226

"Given the timing of the recent two cases, he's likely to have recently experienced a major psychological trigger in his life, and this is causing him to devolve fast. He *will* kill again, and soon in my opinion. Bear in mind, also, that he's fully cognizant of the criminality of his acts. He takes pride in his ability to thwart police. He will be aware of investigative procedures and will avoid leaving behind evidence where he can help it. He will bring his own weapons and other tools of restraint, and he will attend funerals and other public events associated with his work. He is also likely to be closely following the course of this investigation via the media. Media coverage might make him change his patterns to avoid capture."

"Like we needed a fucking head shrink to tell us that," Leo mumbled behind Angie. And yeah, for once she agreed with the old misogynist.

Fitz stood up and crossed to the center of the room. Silence pressed down on the group as he started to speak in his strangely high, creaky voice.

"Considering our unidentified subject is likely following media coverage and being tipped off as to what we know, the consequences of these suspected internal leaks to the press are grave. Untenable. And they must be stopped. To that end, I'm informing you all that I have brought in an internal investigations team. Please be forewarned that no one is above scrutiny, and that each and every one of you could be under surveillance, or brought in for questioning, at any time." He paused, making eye-to-eye contact with each member of the task force in turn. His gaze lingered a fraction longer on Angie. "We *will* find you. And we *will* prosecute to the fullest extent of the law."

CHAPTER 33

TUESDAY, DECEMBER 12

"Angie," her father said as he opened the door. "What are you doing here so early? You look terrible—you okay?"

"I went to see Mom yesterday," she said.

"Come inside. Want some coffee? I got a pot on."

"I'd kill for some." She left her boots at the door and followed her dad in his checkered flannel housecoat into the kitchen, the underfloor heating warm beneath her socked feet. She set the photo album that she'd brought on the kitchen table and scooted a stool up to the counter. She perched atop the stool and watched her dad pour coffees. She felt beat. When she'd finally drifted into sleep last night, she'd woken in a cold sweat with a sense of a presence in her room. In the gloom she'd seen the child standing at the bottom of her bed in a soft pinkish glow, watching her. Then the girl had put her index finger to her lips and hissed the words . . .

Siedz cicho! . . . Stay quiet!

. . . or had it been the shush of the wind coming through a crack in her drapeless bedroom window?

She'd gotten out of bed and flipped on all the lights. Of course there'd been no child in her apartment. She'd self-medicated by drinking more vodka and googling the foreign-sounding words as best she could phonetically—guessing at spellings. She'd come up with various Eastern European and Russian sites and expressions, but nothing made sense. Then she'd reverse-typed into a translator site the English words which she believed held meaning for the foreign ones she'd heard inside her head: *Stay quiet!*

One by one she'd tried translating *Stay quiet* into the various Slavic languages. When she'd clicked on TRANSLATE INTO POLISH, she got a hit. *Siedz cicho!*

Knowing the Google translator's limits, before she'd come to see her dad this morning, she'd phoned and woken an old Polish friend from her college days, and she'd asked her friend to translate into Polish the phrases: *Run, run! Get inside! Stay quiet!*

The friend had confirmed what Angie was starting to believe. The words: *Uciekaj, uciekaj! Wskakuj do srodka, szybko! Siedz cicho!* meant: *Run, run! Get inside!*—in the context of getting into a car, or a box, or a bus. And, *Stay quiet!*

Either she was going mad, or she was remembering something in Polish.

Her dad cast a quick glance at her, and then his gaze touched briefly on the album resting upon the table. "How was she?"

"Not good." Angie accepted the mug he was handing her and took a sip. Steam warmed her face. "She didn't recognize me, and she said some weird things."

"She was in a really bad way yesterday. Hallucinating. They sedated her, and she was on other medication as well."

"I know, but . . ." She hesitated, set her mug down, and cradled her hands around its pottery warmth. "She told me that she had a little daughter once named Angie."

He smiled sadly. "She did. You were little once."

"But then she said her daughter was gone, just like that. Taken by angels. However, her daughter didn't belong in Italy, or in heaven, so she was brought back. Mom said she was returned at Christmas. It was snowing and she'd been singing at the cathedral." Angie paused. "Then she began to sing 'Ave Maria.'"

Her father's face changed. Slowly, he set his mug down on the granite counter. "Angie, we almost lost you in that car accident in Italy. Maybe that's what she meant. You . . . were unconscious, face cut, lost so much blood."

She held his gaze and saw something odd in his features. He was lying. She felt it in her gut, knew the tell signs. Being a cop for so long, you got a feel for a lie, or a cover-up, the various tics and other displacement behaviors when people were avoiding the truth.

"What about her mention of Christmas then, and snow? The accident was in March."

He dragged his big hand over his thick gray hair, looked away for a moment. "Maybe because you were only really fully on the mend come the following Christmas? You'd had the first cosmetic surgery to your mouth, and it looked like a second operation would finally get you back to almost normal, and we were home by then, and she was getting over it."

"Did Mom ever sing, in a choir, at a church?"

"What *is* this, Angie?"

She reached for the album, opened it, and took out the photos from Italy. She turned them over, showing her dad the tiny scrawl of her mother's hand on the backs.

"Look—it says, *Rome. Jan. 1984*. Then this one from Naples, which also says 1984. However, in this photo, taken in front of the Christmas tree, my mouth still needing the second surgery, it says, *Christmas 1987. Victoria*." She looked up. "There's missing time between the Italy pics and that Christmas. That Christmas photo was shot in 1986, wasn't it?"

"Like I said, your mother probably just made a mistake—the early signs of confusion—"

"Did anyone we know speak Polish to me when I was young?"

He frowned. "That's a strange question . . . I don't think so. But there could have been someone. Angie, please, tell me what this is all about?"

She replaced the photos. None of the others in the album had any dates on the backs. She'd dismantled the whole album last night. And she did not want to inform her dad that she was hallucinating, seeing a little girl in pink—no one was going to know that. Even just vocalizing it would put it out there into the air, make tangible and real the possibility that she was showing the same symptoms as her mother, genetically predisposed. She was searching for an easier answer, a way to explain it away. "I was just wondering, after what Mom said in that hospital. I always feel so awful around Christmas, around the sound of hymns and carols, the cold. Snow. Just . . . wondering."

His features softened, and he placed his big hand over hers. "You dig too much, Ange, your job, always looking to find something bad. You should take a rest, and yeah, *especially* after what happened in July, with that toddler and Hashowsky."

She got up, leaving the rest of her coffee. "Yeah, maybe. I should go. Long day ahead."

Driving to the station, Angie checked the time on the dash—it was just past the top of the hour—and she clicked on the radio to catch what was left of the news.

As she listened, a segment on real estate prices was cut short. "We have late-breaking developments in the story on the two gruesome murders that have rocked Victoria—" Her heart quickened. She reached over and turned up the sound. "*City Sun* reporter and crime blogger Merry Winston is reporting on her website that the recent sex killings are linked to several religious-oriented and violent sexual assaults over the last five years. She claims that there have been at least three, possibly more, local incidents where victims were raped and sodomized before crucifixes were drawn in red ink on their foreheads. Locks of hair were cut from all the victims from the same location on their heads. We'll have more on the story as it develops through the day. And following the news, Granger Paton will be talking with professor of criminology Dave Biggs, who asks: Do we have on our hands a local serial rapist who has now escalated to serial killing? And are other young women in danger?"

Shit!

She quickly pulled over onto the verge and scrubbed her hands hard over her face. *Shit shit shit.* She reached for her phone, dialed her partner.

"Maddocks, you heard the news?"

"Not yet. I—"

"Winston is apparently reporting on her blog that the Hocking and Drummond homicides are linked to earlier rapes. She's mentioned the red Sharpie crucifixes and the locks of hair. How the fuck does this stuff get out? From a closed task force? And she claims that there were three, maybe more, sexual assaults, and she's dating them back *five* years—Hash and I only had two. The first we knew of was four years back. Who in the hell were the others? Is this even for real?" She didn't give him a chance to answer. "I'm going to see her myself."

"No, wait, Pallorino! Don't do it. Brass is dealing directly with the *City Sun* publishers. They're getting legal involved. Don't undercut—"

"This is not the *Sun.* It's Winston on her personal crime blog."

"That's just a back door for the *Sun.* They know full well what their crime reporter is doing."

Something struck her suddenly. "How do you know that brass is speaking with the publisher and bringing in legal?"

A beat of silence. "Fitzsimmons told me."

"Fitz? You're in bed with Fitz now? When did he tell you?"

"We met over another issue. It came up."

"Another issue? You mean the internal investigation into the leak?"

"Angie—"

"It's Pallorino. And I'm going to talk to Winston. They're going to look at me for this leak anyway. Leo's already angling for it, and you know he is. If there *are* more incidents that this woman knows about, I want to know about them, too."

"Don't. That's an order."

She hung up and shoved her vehicle into drive.

CHAPTER 34

"What did you mean, three, maybe more assaults?" Angie said, trying to keep her voice low, level. She and Winston were tucked into a cubicle in a tiny English pub downstairs and around the corner from the *City Sun* offices. Benches with dark wood and high backs cushioned acoustics, keeping them private from other patrons clacking their knives and forks over full English breakfasts.

Winston eyeballed her over the rim of her coffee mug, assessing. Irritation sparked through Angie, like tiny bees bouncing against the inside of her skull, trying to get out. "You don't actually have anything, do you?"

"I have Allison Fernyhough and Sally Ritter," she said in barely a whisper. "Those were your two cases—ones you never closed. And there is at least one other confirmed incident that I can't name for you."

Every muscle inside Angie twitched. "Can't, or won't?" she said quietly.

"It's my scoop," she said.

"Where did you get this information?"

"I found and spoke to Allison Fernyhough last night. She told me what happened to her, the red crucifix, everything, how the cops— *you*—did nothing to catch the bad guy. Then she told me how Sally

Ritter had been raped the year before, and how you'd informed Allison that it was the same rapist. Same MO. She told me she'd heard on the streets that there could have been others."

"How'd you find Fernyhough—*who* told you about her?"

"I'm a good reporter, whether you want to believe it or not." Defensiveness crackled in her posture, her features.

Angie eyed Winston. Her bad teeth. Her constant twitchiness. The way her hands trembled ever so slightly. Her mind went to Faith Hocking's teeth. The effects of prolonged drug use.

Focus, Pallorino. Use what's in front of you . . .

She softened her voice. "Who is the other 'confirmed' victim, Merry?"

"I can't tell you that. Look, I'm not even going to print Allison and Sally's names. I made Allison that promise before she'd talk to me. I honor my promises, my sources."

Angie gave a soft snort. "Merry Winston has honor?"

Anger darted through the young reporter's eyes. "I know for a fact what happened to Allison and Sally, and my sources are one hundred percent good on the other victim."

"I don't believe you."

"Fuck you," she said quietly, then took another sip from her mug, eyes darting around the place.

"Who is your leak at MVPD?"

She gave a little laugh, said nothing.

Angie got up to leave, then suddenly reseated herself, setting Winston off-kilter. She leaned over the table, right up close to Merry Winston's funny little wrecked-pixie face that Holgersen said he thought was cute. "Whoever is feeding you police information, Winston, has a serious agenda. You gotta ask yourself what that agenda might be and who it's designed to bring down. Because if this agenda is designed to hit right up at the top of the MVPD and you get caught in the middle when heads start to roll, that informant could become cornered and very, very dangerous to you. Because you know who he—or she—is, and that person could start to worry that you could compromise or leverage him. Or her." A pause. "You're being used. And when you've been all used up, you might just wind up dead, kid. A loose end tied right up in a neat little bow and dumped into the Gorge. Like Faith Hocking."

She blinked.

"Enjoy your coffee." Angie plunked some cash on the dark wood table, got to her feet, and started to walk out.

"What do you care?" Winston called after her.

Angie stilled—this was what she'd been building up to. She turned, came slowly back to the table, and looked down at the reporter. "*What* did you say?"

"I . . . you're a fucking cop. You arrest people who are no better than you are—people who are down, addicted, just trying to survive. I seen cops on the street doing shit to underage kids, buying drugs. Same fucking cops that put others away for the same fucking shit. Yet you can't even catch a monster like this and lock him up, too busy busting kids and hookers who're just trying to get a fix while the fucking johns go back to their wives and their cop jobs."

Heart banging, Angie leaned over Winston, her hands braced apart, palms flat on the table. The kid was shaking, eyes glistening, hot spots riding high onto her cheekbones and redness developing around her nose.

Softly, Angie said, "I once spoke to a nine-year-old girl who told me that she slept with a knife under her pillow because her stepdad sometimes came in and raped her. Another time I was at a gas station when a truck pulled up, windows rolled down and the rap music turned up so loud, with lyrics all full of 'motherfucker this' and 'motherfucker that.' Two big men in muscle shirts jumped out of the truck, and what followed them into the convenience store made me want to cry." She paused, holding Winston's eyes, which were starting to water. "It was the cutest little girl with blond curls and a dirty dress. She was carrying her little doll, and she was trying to keep up with those big guys in their muscle shirts and tats." Angie paused again. "She couldn't have been any more than three years old, and all I could think about, and still think about, was what her home life must be like. What did she hear, day in and day out? What did she see? Who did she become in the end? And then, six months ago I held a dying toddler in my arms, her blood all over me. Killed by her own father, who had been raping her. Her name was Tiffany. I lost my partner that day." Her voice cracked, and she cleared her throat.

"See? I *do* care, Winston. I care enough to have become an officer, to have put my name in for sex crimes. I care enough to have stayed in the sex unit for six years, because I want to put away bad guys who hurt women and kids. Maybe I fail. Maybe I don't make any fucking difference at all. But I care enough to keep trying, and if you stop me from getting this bastard, if you stop me from doing my job by giving away proprietary law enforcement information that is going to make him change his MO, *you* are as guilty as him when he hurts his next victim, and I *will* care enough to put *you* away for it." She stood up and straightened her shoulders. "So don't stop me from doing my job, understand?"

"That a threat, *Officer?*"

"No, Merry Winston," she said softly. "It's a promise." She placed her card on the table and pushed it toward the reporter. "Call me when you're ready to talk." She turned and made for the exit.

"Pallorino," Winston yelled as Angie reached the door. "Don't think you can scare me into stopping doing my job, either!"

CHAPTER 35

"What do you guys want now? I told you everything I could last time," Pastor Markus said, stepping outside into the street and closing the Harbor House door firmly behind him. *No access this time,* thought Kjel.

"You didn't tell us yous had a criminal record, now did you, Gilani?" Kjel said.

"I did my time. It's no longer relevant."

"Yous was busted for driving drunk with your fly open and some minor female sucking on your cock, Gilani. You ejaculate before, during, or after you killed that mother of two young kids?"

A weird kind of calm overcame the man's face, and all he said was "I'd like you to leave now."

"Or what?" interjected Leo.

He gave a shrug. "Or I guess you'll get even wetter standing out here in the rain." He turned his back on them and reached for the door handle.

"What kind of vehicle do you drive, Gilani?"

"I take public transit. Or bike," he said, his back still to them.

"Do you own or have access to a vehicle?"

Slowly Gilani turned to face them. "If you detectives had done your homework properly, you'd have learned that not only did I do my time, I had my driver's license pulled. I never applied for another."

"So they kept yous off the road, yet they let you work with minors," Kjel said. "Soooo many vulnerable, transient young women coming through here, who, like you pointed out, won't go to the cops when they run into trouble. You could do anything to them. Trust, you said. They trust you like a father figure, eh, *Pastor*? Yous promise them a bed and warmth and comfort and even lets them sit on your lap while you play Santa Claus, eh?"

"Mine was not a sex crime, officers. Part of my restitution was to go into rehab. Part of my twelve-step rehab program brought me to God, and that in turn brought me here, to this haven, this parish, these children. I found my purpose here, and I work every day to atone for what I did, and yet, I know that as much as I ask God for forgiveness, the only peace I will ever find is to help others, selflessly, every minute of my life, repenting for my sins every second of the way. Because the moment I stop . . ." His voice faded for a moment as nightmares haunted his eyes. He cleared his throat. "Alcohol and subsequent loss of inhibition, bad judgment, was my problem. I was an addict. I'm not an evil person. And I'm certainly not a sex offender." He paused and met their eyes in turn. "We all have them—coping mechanisms, addictions, ways of running from things too uncomfortable to face. One man drinks. Another buys sex in the streets. Another falls prey to crystal meth. Another runs ultra-marathons. Or climbs one mountain higher than the next. My life is now one of sobriety, and my salvation is charity work here."

As they left, Kjel and Leo drove in silence for a while, an odd weight hanging between them.

"You buying it?" Leo said finally.

"Yeah, I thinks I'm buying it," Kjel said, smoothing his goatee. "He's not saving them kids. He's just trying to save himself."

Leo lit a smoke, and Kjel responded by opening the window to a blast of wet air.

Exhaling a cloud of smoke, Leo said, "So what's yours—your addiction, your coping mechanism?"

"I'm celibate."

"*What*—why? You got some disease I should know about?"

"Gives you control, you know? If yous can manage to master that most basic drive for sex, you can control all the other things in your life."

Leo stared at him. "You have gotta be kidding me? You *are* a fucking freak, you know that?"

"At least I don't go getting my cock sucked off by some tweaker in a back alley."

"What are you trying to say?"

Kjel gave a half shrug. "Nothing."

Leo smoked in silence for a while, then said suddenly, "Half the guys down at the station do it, you know? A blow job. Blows off some steam. Keeps all the work crap away from the missus. No harm, no foul. For Chrissakes. Don't tell me you've never even thought about it."

CHAPTER 36

The atmosphere crackled in the heavy silence between Maddocks and his partner as she drove them to the apartment of Jon Jacques Jr. He'd gone to interview Rick Butler solo while she'd abandoned him to confront Merry Winston against his orders as her senior partner in this duo. *If* one could call it a duo. They were in her Crown Vic now, because he'd managed to drop his Impala off to be detailed now that Jack-O had a sitter.

She shut off the engine in the lot outside the luxury complex where Jacques Jr., all of twenty-two years old, lived in a penthouse suite by himself.

"How did it go down with Butler?" she said.

He inhaled slowly, then released the air. "I struck out. Butler knew that we'd be coming, and he was prepared. All he gave was that he and Drummond had broken up, and he claimed that he'd had nothing to do with her since. He conceded that Drummond had met Jacques Junior at the club, and that he knew Lara Pennington. He said he did not know who Amanda R. was, nor could he think of any of Drummond's associates or friends with the initials J.R. or B.C. He said that Jacques Junior and he are not friends outside the club, and he claims to know nothing about Drummond's high-end possessions."

"Faith Hocking?"

"Claims he's never heard the name." Maddocks paused, looking up at the apartment block. "I have a feeling we're going to strike out here, too."

Silence.

He glanced at her—mouth tight, sexy scar, her gray eyes cool. Badass. And at this moment he wanted to lean in and kiss the shit out of her. Maybe it would relieve the frustration building inside him.

She broke eye contact, reached for the door handle.

"Don't do that to me again, okay?" he said quietly.

Slowly she met his gaze once more. "Do what? Listen to you because you rank higher? I made the right decision, Maddocks. I got to her."

"You got control issues, that's what you've got. Dominance issues. This much was evident from the first time I met you, Angie."

Heat flickered into her eyes at his use of her first name, and her jaw tightened.

"Maybe that's fine for a good fuck," he said, unable to stop himself now, powerless against the sexual tension and frustration that had been burning inside him since she'd left him naked with a hard-on on that bed and written her name on that piece of paper—an unspoken promise there would be more. "But not on the job. Homicide is for team players, and I need a partner who has my back and who doesn't go off half-cocked against my advice or orders."

She swallowed. A small vein pulsed near her temple. "Maybe," she said, very quietly, "I don't want you as a partner. Not if you're going to keep bringing up that we had sex—"

"It's not just sex, dammit. It's Russian roulette, going to that club and picking up strangers like that."

"So now you're my guardian? So it's fine for a guy? It's fine for *you* to go to the club and let an anonymous woman with a knife in her pocket cuff you naked to a bed and have her way with you? Are you going to keep raising this every time your male ego gets bruised?"

Blood beat hot and fast through his veins, and he told himself to stop. Right now. All he had to do was go back to the station and put in for a new partner. It could kill her goal of getting into homicide, but he owed her nothing. He didn't know why he should even be concerned about her apparent desire for self-sabotage. But he was like a fireball rolling downhill through a tinder-dry forest and just gathering speed and flame as he went.

"You want to make homicide, right? You know that I'm supposed to evaluate you while you're temporarily partnered with me?"

She blinked.

"Well, you're not going to get it this way, *Angie*. This is not just about the club. It's about character, and being a team player, and having a partner you can trust will not get you killed. And I owe it to my fellow officers to tell them the truth if I judge you to be a risk."

"You're threatening to sabotage me?"

"I think you're going to do that all by yourself."

She swore viciously. "So your ego gets bruised and you resort to revenge?"

"Listen to yourself. You already had an incident where you lost a partner. If I were you, if I wanted a promotion, I'd be kissing ass right now, not self-destructing."

She glowered at him. Electricity burned between them. And be damned if all he wanted to do was grab her and fuck her right here in this car.

"I'm not a baby, Maddocks. I don't need you to care for me." She flung open the door, got out, slammed it shut, and marched for the apartment complex entrance.

He cursed, exited the vehicle, and stalked after her. She broke into a run as an older male approached the complex doors and used an electronic fob to open them. The man entered, and the door began to swing shut behind him, but she caught up and slapped her hand on the open door. She showed the man her badge. The man shrugged and gave her access. She entered, allowing the door to almost swing shut and lock in Maddocks's face. He shoved through, caught up to her at the elevator.

Both breathing hard, avoiding eye contact, they rode up to the penthouse in fiery silence. Just before they reached the top floor, he said quietly, "Don't try me again, Pallorino. I'm not someone you want to cross."

Her gaze sparked to his. And he saw in her eyes, in her features, that she regretted her own impulsivity, her own quick flare to aggression. He regretted his own words, too. There was no textbook for this.

The elevator doors opened, and they both hesitated. He let her go first, and they made their way down the hall to the penthouse of Jon Jacques Jr., her leading the way.

Pallorino knocked on the door, her spine erect and her shoulders squared, her game face back on.

The door opened, revealing a young man of average height, blond hair fashionably cut around a boyish face. He wore a bathrobe and stood barefoot on the wood floor.

"Jon Jacques?" Pallorino said.

"Who are you?"

"Detectives Pallorino and Maddocks, MVPD homicide," she said, holding out her badge. Maddocks offered his. "Can we have a moment of your time?"

Jacques made a laborious show of carefully checking both their IDs. Behind him hardwood floors gleamed toward an expanse of windows that looked out over the city. His living room furniture was white. Music played inside. "What is it, J.J.?" came a female voice.

"Nothing, babe," he called over his shoulder. "Stay hot for me. I'll be right back." He returned their badges to them. "How did you get into the building without buzzing me first?"

"We understand you knew Gracie Marie Drummond," she said.

"Gracie? Yeah, from the tennis club, yeah." His body posture changed slightly, and his hand went to the doorknob, as if blocking entry.

"We're sorry for your loss."

A beat of silence. "I hardly knew her."

"Can we come in?" Maddocks said.

"No."

"You drive a black Bimmer," he said. It was not a question—he'd already checked. A BMW Z4 E89 Slingshot was registered to this punk.

"So what if I do?"

"You dated Drummond," Pallorino said. "That's a little more intimate than 'hardly knew her.'"

"Look, I have company right now, and I really don't like your questions, and I really don't have to answer them. My father told me that you cops had bugged him about someone else yesterday and that you might come around. He's put a lawyer at my disposal, and—"

"And your father just made a leap of logic that because cops asked him questions about 'someone else' that we'd come here and ask you about Gracie Drummond?"

He gave a laugh, but his eyes showed nerves. J.J. Jr. clearly was not the sharpest tool in the shed.

"Not at all. My father has just learned from experience that when you guys go on a fishing expedition, or on one of your witch hunts, that you attack his family from all angles—this is harassment, so unless you're going to charge me with some trumped-up thing, I have nothing to say." He began to shut the door.

Maddocks put his foot in the way. "Next time," he said, "we do this down at the station."

"Obnoxious little fuckhead," said Maddocks as they drove off, his partner at the wheel.

"Jacques, Pennington, Butler, that pastor Gilani from what Holgersen and Leo say—it's like there's a conspiracy of silence," Pallorino said.

"Except for the media and Merry Winston and her loose-lipped informant." He hesitated. "What did happen with her this morning?"

She cast him a sideways glance. "I told her to back off, and I asked her who her other rape cases were and who the leak was."

"She give anything?"

"No."

"No surprise there. What did you mean when you said you 'got to her'?"

Pallorino took a deep, slow breath, and he could see her hands tightening around the wheel. "I told her that I cared. About Fernyhough and Ritter. About justice for Drummond and Hocking. That I cared about protecting vulnerable young women and kids, and that's why I did this job. I told her that her reports using confidential information could put other young women in jeopardy." She paused, moistening her lips, and Maddocks got the sense she'd opened the window, just a crack, and he was getting a glimpse of the real Angie Pallorino inside. "But although she told me nothing concrete, I know I got through to her. And I did get something else, a feeling she's damaged goods. She's been in a bad place, and we need to look into her background, because the more we know about her, the closer we'll get to her informer. I'm sure of it. I'm going to have her run through the system."

"You think Fitz hasn't already done that? She doesn't have a record."

Her eyes flashed. "So you and Fitz really are in bed together?"

The only MVPD officer that I've been to bed with is you, Angie Pallorino . . . But he held his tongue and was saved by the ring of his cell phone.

He answered. It was Buziak.

"We got a break," Buziak said immediately. "Highways camera captured a black Lexus, license plate BX3 99E, heading west over the Johnson Street Bridge at 5:37 p.m. Saturday. The same Lexus was captured again, heading east at 6:52 p.m. I want you to handle this lead, and I need you to tread lightly. Very lightly. Everything by the book, understand? Because that Lexus is registered to Ray Norton-Wells."

Maddocks's pulse stalled, then kicked to a rapid staccato. *"The husband of the assistant deputy attorney general?"*

"The same. Address 5798 Stanley Road, Uplands. Keep this quiet for now. When talking to him, focus solely on the Lexus—don't link it to the murders yet. Just because that vehicle was seen in both places, it doesn't prove it was involved in the Drummond abduction. Again, I cannot reiterate this firmly enough—tread extremely carefully. If this does start to go anywhere, if this case is connected in any way to the ADAG and the office of the attorney general, we're going to need a special prosecutor on board. And that will blow sky-high in the media and political establishment. We need to have all our legal ducks in a fucking tight little row."

CHAPTER 37

Gravel crunched beneath Angie's boots as she walked with Maddocks slowly around a bronze Jaguar parked outside the front of the house. The doors to the garages at the side of the house had been left open. Rain redoubled efforts, and the wind whipped icy up from the sea into this subdivision of high-end estates. Tension still simmered hot and sexual between her and Maddocks. With it came unease, because she knew that she'd overstepped the mark, and it scared her that he was right, that he could read her like a book, that he dared say to her things no one else would. She *was* self-sabotaging. Like some kind of sick addict. And she couldn't seem to stop the slide, and she didn't know why or what was truly driving her. He was right about another thing—one word from him and her bid for homicide would be toast. She resented that he had that power over her right now.

"This is not a house," she said, stopping to look up at the three floors. "It's big enough to be a small hotel."

Inside the garage was a little red 2016 Porsche 911 Turbo and three vacant spaces. Not surprising. It was Tuesday afternoon. House occupants would likely be at work.

"Can I help you?" came a gruff voice from behind them.

They spun around. A man in a raincoat over a suit, briefcase in hand, shined shoes, stood next to the Jag.

"Ray Norton-Wells?" Maddocks said, approaching.

"Who's asking?"

"Detectives Maddocks and Pallorino, MVPD." He showed his badge. Rain was dampening Norton-Wells's hair, face.

"What's this about?"

"You have a black Lexus registered in your name. I don't see it parked here."

The man frowned. A movement up in a window in the left wing of the mansion caught Angie's eye. A young male in a white T-shirt stood there. Watching them.

"That's because it was stolen," said Norton-Wells.

A ripple of interest went through Angie.

"When?" said Maddocks.

"About two weeks ago. Look, I need to get back to my office—"

"Did you report the theft, Mr. Norton-Wells?" Maddocks said.

"My son, Jayden, did. I'd given him the Lexus for his use. He's had it for about six months now."

"But the insurance was in your name."

He irritably wiped rainwater from his brow. "Yes."

"But when the vehicle was stolen, you didn't cancel it?"

"Jayden said he'd taken care of it."

"Is your son home, Mr. Norton-Wells?" Angie interjected.

"I'm going to have to ask why you're interested in this vehicle."

"It might have been used in the commission of a crime," Maddocks said.

Norton-Wells stared at them for a beat, and then his glance flickered toward the window in the west wing. The young man was no longer standing there, and for a moment Angie thought Norton-Wells was going to lie.

"You caught him on a sick day. Which isn't unusual." The man jerked his head toward a door on the west side. "He lives in the suite. Entrance is over there. If you'll excuse me, I'm late." He turned and beeped the lock on his Jag. "If you need anything else from me, call my assistant." He folded himself into his Jag and fired the engine.

"Seems no love lost between father and son," Angie said as she and Maddocks walked toward the suite door.

"No kidding," Maddocks said as he knocked.

The door opened slowly. A younger mirror of the man they'd just been speaking to stood before them. But his eyes were feverish and his skin sheened with perspiration. His hair was damp and as blue-black as Maddocks's, she noted. Perspiration also stained the armpits of his fitted white tee. A gold chain disappeared into the neck of the shirt, gold watch on his wrist.

"Jayden Norton-Wells?" Maddocks said.

"Yeah."

Maddocks explained who they were and why they'd come. "Can we come inside for a moment?"

Jayden seemed lethargic. Angie wondered if he was on medication, drugs. He opened the door, padded inside on bare feet, and slumped onto a sofa. He put his face into his hands and rubbed, then looked up. "Sorry, I've got a flu bug or something. Been out of sorts for a few days."

Angie and Maddocks remained standing. The room smelled of sweat and stale alcohol. Heat had been set on high. Windows were closed. While Maddocks handled the questions, Angie walked up to a wall of framed images. One was of a graduation certificate for Jayden Royce Norton-Wells.

J.R. Norton-Wells? Her pulse accelerated slightly as she moved to another framed photo, this one showing a young Jayden—about eleven years old—sporting a white suit. He stood smiling with his mom, now the ADAG, his dad, and a bishop in robes. Under the photo: *Jayden Royce Norton-Wells, First Holy Communion.*

"Your father says you reported the Lexus stolen?" Maddocks said.

"I forgot to."

"A Lexus. And you *forgot?*"

"Been really busy with law school. I . . . I just hadn't gotten around to it yet."

Angie exchanged a glance with Maddocks.

"When, exactly, was it stolen?" he said.

Norton-Wells scratched his skull through damp hair. "I . . . ten days, fourteen days ago, maybe. Not sure."

"What day of the week was it? What were you doing? From where was it taken?"

"I . . . it was a Tuesday. Yeah, I remember now—November twenty-eighth, that's it, right at the beginning of the cold snap. We . . . were at a restaurant downtown, and I'd parked up the street in a pay lot. Stayed late. Had a lot to drink, so took a cab home. When I returned the next day to pick up the SUV, it was gone."

"Which restaurant?"

His eyes flickered, then he said. "The Auberge."

"Which lot?"

"The one a block up from the restaurant."

"Did you have a reservation?"

"No."

"How did you pay for the meal, credit card?"

"Yes, no . . . wait, I think I paid cash that night."

"Why?"

The guy shrugged. "I often do."

"You keep the receipt?"

"No, I did not. Look, what's going on? Why are you asking all these questions?"

"Your vehicle was possibly used in the commission of a crime."

He paled, his eyes going wide, pupils very dark. Definitely some sort of chemical in his system, thought Angie.

"What crime?" he said.

"I'm not at liberty to say at this moment," Maddocks replied. "Who was dining with you that night—you said 'we'?"

Norton-Wells stared at them a moment, as if trying to pull his story straight. Then he said, "I'm not going to drag my friends into this. If this vehicle was used in a crime, it's got nothing to do with me. I've got nothing more to say."

Tread lightly. ADAG's son . . .

"That's fine," said Maddocks benignly. "We'll need you to come down to the station to make a formal statement, though. Can you do that?"

"I . . . as soon as I feel better. I'm really not up to leaving the house right now."

"Fair enough. We'll be in touch. Soon."

As Maddocks and Angie made for the door, Angie swung suddenly back to face Norton-Wells as he was pushing himself up off the sofa.

"That chain you're wearing," she said with a nod to his neck. "A Saint Christopher?"

His mouth opened and hung for a beat. "Uh, yes, why?"

"Catholic family." She nodded to the photo of him in the white suit.

"That's a well-known fact."

She moistened her lips, turned to leave, then as if on second thought—but really just to unsettle him—she swung back to face him. "Your second name is Royce."

"Well, yeah."

"Jayden Royce. Anyone ever call you J.R.?"

He hesitated. "Some."

"You ever give anyone a Saint Christopher engraved with *Love from J.R.?*"

Blood drained from his face. "No. No, I did not. I'd like you to leave."

✝

Maddocks turned out of the Norton-Wells driveway and drew the Crown Vic up under an old oak tree along the curb on the opposite side of the street. Pallorino had given him the wheel—her way of a peace offering, he surmised.

"Good call," he said quietly, staring at the stone gateposts. On one post a bronze plaque had been mounted with the word AKASHA, all in caps. "But a close one. Buziak ordered us to focus only on the vehicle at this point."

"The photo of the holy communion ceremony was in plain sight," she said. "So was the graduation certificate with his full name. The leap was obvious—J. R. Norton-Wells, devoutly Catholic, wearing a gold chain around his neck. And magically, his Lexus goes missing. He's clearly in a bad way. We *should* have asked him if he knew Drummond and Hocking."

"It's how Buziak wants to play it."

"The ADAG's son," she said incredulously. "What are the odds? This could be huge."

As Maddocks was about to respond, the little red Porsche came roaring down the driveway and busted out of the gateposts, tires skidding as it cornered and sped down the street.

"He's bolting!" she said.

Maddocks rammed the Crown Vic into gear and spun the tires in a U-turn. They took off after it.

CHAPTER 38

"What the—? It's . . . Zach Raddison, the mayor's aide." Angie peered through the camera's telephoto lens, watching as the tall dark male rapidly exited city hall with Jayden Norton-Wells. The two men stopped and began to argue in the rain, arms gesticulating. She clicked off a rapid series of shots. Norton-Wells shoved Raddison in the chest. Raddison reeled back, then lunged forward, grabbing Norton-Wells by the shoulders, holding him firmly as he spoke intently, face up close to Norton-Wells. Angie shot more frames, the digital camera firing a fast staccato of *click click clicks*.

She and Maddocks were parked across the street from city hall. Norton-Wells, the guy who'd professed to be too ill to leave his house in order to come down to the station to make an official statement, had raced the Porsche straight here. He'd parked at a bad angle in an off-street parking space and run inside, wearing just his T-shirt and jeans despite the wintery cold. It was barely minutes before he exited with Raddison in tow.

"So," said Maddocks, "the ADAG's son, who might have given Drummond a Saint Christopher on a chain, and whose vehicle might have been used in the commission of a crime, has some sort of volatile relationship with the manager of Jack Killion's election campaign, Zach Raddison, who is now the mayor's right-hand man."

"Like they say, we all move within six degrees of separation from one another." Angie clicked again as Raddison gripped Norton-Wells by the upper arm and began marching him back to the badly parked Porsche.

"So, Norton-Wells is spooked by our visit, and he rushes here, presumably straight up to the mayor's office to find Raddison. Why?" he said.

Norton-Wells got back into his car. Raddison slammed the door shut on him. Norton-Wells pulled out into the street, driving slowly now. Raddison stood on the sidewalk in his shirtsleeves, in the rain, watching the Porsche disappear down the road, before turning and heading back into city hall. He looked visibly rattled.

Angie lowered the camera. "Do we follow Norton-Wells, or pay Raddison and the mayor's office a visit?"

Maddocks reached for the door handle. "Mayor's office. While Raddison is still shaken."

Zach Raddison was by all accounts a model-handsome kinda guy, thought Angie. Dark Mediterranean-type skin, liquid black eyes, an impossibly white and quick smile. And his looks came with the kind of arrogance that money and privilege and the adoration of too many women could bring. Angie and Maddocks stood in his office, which was in a kind of antechamber off Jack Killion's office. Rain ran in squiggles down the window behind him. He'd offered them both a seat, but they'd declined, so he perched his honed butt and tailored pants on the edge of his gleaming desk and folded his arms over his chest. He waited for them to tell him what they'd come for.

"Got a little wet, I see," Maddocks said with a jerk of his chin to the rain marks on Raddison's crisp white shirt and royal-blue tie.

Raddison smiled, not missing a beat. "We have an inaugural council meeting tonight where Jack Killion will officially be sworn in as the new mayor of this city. If you could get to the point, detectives, I can return to my business."

Angie did her meandering around the office thing, looking at his art, what was on his shelves, while Maddocks engaged the subject up close and personal. She burned to ask Raddison directly about Drummond and Hocking, but they had their orders from Buziak—stick with the Lexus. And she needed to play by the book for a while after her blowup with her senior partner.

"Do you know Jayden Norton-Wells?" Maddocks said.

Again, Raddison didn't hesitate. "He's a friend of mine. We go back to high school days. Our parents are well acquainted."

"Private school?"

"And this is going where?"

Angie came to a ceramic bowl on the shelf near the door—painted with some kind of First Nations art. It contained business cards and a few books of matches. She touched her fingers to the assortment, moving some of the cards aside, and she picked up a matchbook. Her pulse quickened.

"Could you not touch anything, Detective? Please. Thank you," Raddison called out over Maddocks's shoulder. Ah, she was finally hearing the beginnings of an edge in his voice.

"Sure." She replaced the matchbook and came to Maddocks's side, putting her hands into her coat pocket.

"Were you perhaps dining with Jayden at the Auberge on Tuesday, November twenty-eighth?" said her partner.

A quick flicker ran through his eyes. "No, why?"

"Apparently Jayden was eating there with friends, imbibed a bit much, left his Lexus parked in town, and it disappeared."

"Disappeared?"

256

"He claims it was stolen."

Raddison's brows lowered. "You don't believe him?"

"Did you know that it was stolen?"

"Of course. He told me."

"Outside, a few seconds ago?"

Silence. His Adam's apple moved. His eyes narrowed ever so slightly. *Bingo.*

"What did Jayden come and see you about? He looked a little . . . upset."

Raddison crossed his arms over his chest. "It was personal," he said quietly.

"Anything to do with the Lexus?"

"Like I said, it was a personal issue."

"Just as a matter of interest, Mr. Raddison, where were *you* on the night of Tuesday, November twenty-eighth?"

He wavered for the first time. "Look, I don't know where you're going with this, but frankly you're wasting my time. And consequently, the mayor's. So if you don't have—"

"What do the initials B.C. stand for?" Angie interjected.

"*Excuse* me?"

The door to the mayor's office suddenly opened wide, and Jack Killion himself appeared. "Zach—a moment of your time, please."

"I'll be right there."

Killion glanced at Maddocks, then Angie, then raised his brows at his aide.

"Metro's finest," offered Raddison.

The mayor's gaze narrowed as he measured them in greater detail. "About what?"

"They haven't told me yet."

The mayor hesitated, then said to Maddocks and Angie, "We have an inaugural meeting to prepare for, officers. I need my man. If you could speed things up?" He disappeared. The door shut.

Fuckhead, thought Angie, suddenly feeling much more kindly toward Chief Gunnar. If this was the new regime, it spelled trouble.

Raddison pushed off his desk and sauntered toward the door. He extended his arm toward the exit. "If you decide what it is that you wanted, or if you have any further questions, please do feel free to make an appointment with my secretary."

Angie stood her ground. "B.C.," she said again. "What do those initials stand for?"

"I have no idea . . . Before Christ? British Columbia? Bacon and cheese? One hundred other things?"

She lifted an open matchbook out of the bowl, the one she'd been examining earlier, and held it out to Raddison—a plain white cover with two curlicue letters intertwined—a B and a C.

He stared at it, shoved his hands into his tailored pants pockets and pursed his pretty-boy lips, then shook his head slowly. "Sorry, no idea. People drop business cards in there mostly. Looks like some matchbooks, too. Could have been left by anyone."

"You a smoker?"

"Occasionally."

She casually flipped open the matchbook cover to the number she'd seen scrawled on the inside flap. "Who gives out matchbooks these days anyways?" she said, studying the number again.

Anger darkened his face, and he snatched it from her hands. "You want to look at anything more in this office, you better come back with a warrant."

She looked up into his black eyes. His mouth was tight, neck taut. Raddison, it seemed, was not a young man who appreciated being crossed by a woman. Or maybe by anyone.

"Maybe we will, Zach," she said softly. "Maybe we will."

As they exited the building, Angie ducked under an awning out of the rain. She pulled her notebook out of her bag slung across her chest and quickly checked the number Drummond's mother had given her at Saint Jude's moments before her daughter had died. "Shit," she said softly.

"What?" said Maddocks.

She looked up, excitement fizzing into her blood. "It's hers," she said. "The phone number in that matchbook was for Gracie Drummond's cell. And it was written inside a matchbook with a logo that says B.C." Her eyes lanced his. "Like on her calendar—B.C.—the dates she had with Amanda R. and Lara P."

CHAPTER 39

Killion was standing in his office doorway when Zach turned around. There was a strange look in his boss's eyes.

"What was that about?" Killion said.

Zach inhaled deeply, his mind racing, questions crackling and sizzling along synapses and short-circuiting, then zipping right back to be asked again. "Those detectives had questions about a friend of mine, Jayden Norton-Wells. It seems they're looking for his Lexus, which was stolen about two weeks ago."

"So why come to you, why *this* office?"

"Like I said, Jay's my friend. They wanted to know if I was with him at a restaurant the night his vehicle was taken—seems Jay was a bit too drunk to recall who all was there."

Silence. A strange kind of energy rolled off the mayor. A disquiet crawled into Zach's chest.

"And this thing about the initials, B.C.?"

So Killion had heard the conversation. Zach fingered the matchbook now in his pocket. "I have no idea."

"If there's anything I should know—"

"There isn't."

The mayor held his gaze for a moment, then cleared his throat. "Have those council agenda updates gone out to the media?"

"A while ago."

The door closed suddenly. Zach stared at the shut door, and the dark disquiet in his chest deepened.

Jack Killion picked up his phone, glanced at his closed door, and quickly dialed a number. Their special number. As the phone rang, he swiveled his chair to watch the silvery rain beat against his window.

"What is it?" came the husky voice he loved so much.

He moistened his lips. "The police were just here."

"*Your* office?"

"Two MVPD detectives—one male, one female—asking Zach questions about a stolen Lexus and your son."

"*Jayden?*"

"Yes."

"What . . . why?"

"Did he have a Lexus stolen?"

"I . . . yes, I heard him talking to his father about it. I don't involve myself in issues between those two. It never ends well. At least the cops are doing their jobs looking for the darn thing."

"So why come and see Zach, and why in my office? At this time—on the eve of my inauguration?"

"You think it's posturing on the part of the MVPD, some vendetta?"

"I've not made friends among law enforcement with my campaign promises to sweep the MVPD clean. And I chair my first in-camera police board meeting tomorrow. They're all anticipating a change of guard."

A long pause. "I'll speak with Jay when I get home tonight. It's probably nothing more than it seems."

"Joyce, the optics of it—Metro investigating a criminal issue in connection with the ADAG's son is a big enough media event as it is. And detectives coming to the mayor's office links *me* to your family and a criminal investigation. Christ, given the way the MVPD can't control the leaks from within their own organization, we could see this on the front page of the *Sun* tomorrow or on that woman's blog. Next thing we'll have telephoto lenses pointing into our penthouse windows, with media watching us from a press boat in the harbor."

"Maybe it's time," she said quietly. "To cut Gunnar loose and put your man Antoni Moreno into place, where he can watch and handle things. Where he can roust out this inside informant. Your hand might just have been forced, Jack. You can set it all in motion at the police board meeting tomorrow, right? You have at least three board members on your side, no? Maybe four."

"Yeah."

"Do it, Jack. Start the process. It's time."

"What about this serial killer thing—the idea of holding off on Gunnar until they're close to catching him?"

"You'll have to spin it another way. This is you stepping up to the plate to take charge as soon as you take office. This is you putting better, fresh police management in place, stat, to take over this grave investigation, to get rid of the traitors on the force, and to make the city safer for all those young women out there who are terrified to go out alone at night now."

Angie sat with Maddocks at the opposite end of Buziak's desk. Buziak had shut his door and drawn the blinds across his window that looked out into the homicide bullpen. He clicked the back of his pen in and out as he listened to Maddocks and Angie update him on the Norton-Wells interview and their subsequent interaction with Zach Raddison.

Before their meeting, another check had been run to ensure there was indeed no record of the Lexus being reported stolen. There wasn't. A BOLO had since been put out on the plate.

Once they'd covered everything, Buziak leaned back in his chair, pen still in hand.

"So, we have a connection between Gracie Drummond, Jayden Norton-Wells, and Zach Raddison at the mayor's office. Both the men are Caucasian, black hair. Raddison has a matchbook in his office with Drummond's phone number and the letters B.C. on it—the matchbook may or may not be his. The B.C. logo may or may not refer to something on Drummond's calendar. But right after you'd questioned Jayden Norton-Wells about the Lexus seen on the bridge and outside the cemetery on the night Drummond was assaulted, Norton-Wells rushed straight to Raddison, where he argues with him. Norton-Wells, the ADAG's son, is a practicing Catholic who wears a Saint Christopher medallion around his neck. He also has the initials J.R., which match the inscription on the back of Drummond's medallion. Plus he never reported his father's Lexus stolen, nor canceled the plate and associated insurance, and we have found no proof that he was ever dining at the Auberge the night his vehicle allegedly went missing. Or that the Lexus was ever parked in the pay lot up the street from the Auberge." He clicked his pen again.

"And then there's his father, developer Ray Norton-Wells, supporter of the Killion campaign, who has Killion's backing for his planned waterfront development, and who alleges *he* was too busy to cancel insurance on the missing vehicle. He, like his son, has black hair. Plus there's the ADAG—mother and wife . . . what a clusterfuck." He leaned abruptly forward, started rapidly ticking his pen against the desk now.

Angie had to restrain herself from stopping him. The sound was making things zip around in her brain like little live electrical wires. As Buziak was about to open his mouth again, a knock sounded at his office door. He stiffened, and his eyes met theirs.

"This connection between the Norton-Wells family, the mayor's office, and a vehicle possibly used in the commission of a homicide stays in this room until further notice, just between the three of us for now. Got it?"

They both nodded. He glanced up. "Come!"

The door opened. It was Leo. The hoary detective did a small double take when he saw Maddocks and Angie in Buziak's office, and he scowled.

"What is it, Leo?" said their boss.

"Botanist's report has come in. That specific combination of the Garry oak and agronomic grass form part of a rare ecosystem—one where the native oak has adapted to shallow soil and developed wind resistance. And there is only one place with this ecosystem that also has goats—feral goats. Thetisby Island."

Angie and Maddocks exchanged a fast glance. Excitement rippled through her.

"Meteorologist also confirms that powerful currents, the recent onshore winds, and high tidal flow could push something like a body from the area of Thetisby into the harbor. This would be consistent with the sheep maggot evidence, too, if the body was kept on the island for a time before entering the water."

Angie sat bolt upright. "There's an abandoned homestead on Thetisby Island," she said. "From the 1862 smallpox epidemic. A group of people left the mainland and established a small community there in an effort to avoid the plague. It was a going farm concern with goats, other animals. When the pox got them anyway, it went to ruin, and there's been a colony of feral goats breeding there ever since." She paused. The excitement in the room was palpable.

"We just might have our Hocking murder scene," Buziak said, coming sharply to his feet. "Let's get the ball rolling!"

✝

CHAPTER 40

Angie stood in Tyvek boot covers beside Maddocks, Holgersen, and Buziak in the freezing and cavernous root cellar of the crumbling homestead ruins on Thetisby Island. In silence they watched as Barb O'Hagan worked the scene with the forensic ident techs, the photographer documenting every millimeter of their progress. Kitted in white boiler suits, caps, booties, and wearing nitrile gloves, the techs moved as if in slow freeze-frame images as the camera flashed white light. It lent the subterranean scene an otherworldly air. There was no noise apart from the click of the camera and the thin ghostly wail of the wind that sought entry through the broken rafters in the ruins upstairs.

They had not been able to set out first thing this morning as hoped. A new storm front, dense fog, and high surf had held them back until this afternoon. The trip to the island, which should have taken them twenty minutes in the MVPD harbor unit craft, had taken far longer as they'd battled onshore westerly winds and high seas. Leo was on the island, too, but he'd been felled by seasickness and remained outside, smoking and trying to stop himself from throwing up again, swearing like a sailor at not being able to come down into the cellar to observe, in case he puked his DNA all over the place.

When they'd arrived it had been close to pitch-dark in this under-floor hole dug into the black earth. And it was cold—"cold as a witch's tit," Holgersen had so succinctly informed them. Cold as a meat locker, Angie thought. Combined with the well-below-freezing arctic outflow temperatures that had locked them in a frigid grip over the last two weeks, it was no leap of logic to see how Faith Hocking's body could have been preserved for some time down here. Given this new context, O'Hagan figured PMI was ten days to two weeks. Hocking's body, she'd said, would have kept as well down here as any human flesh stored in the morgue cooler. Even now, with this stormy, wet, and warmer trend, the place still felt like a frigid earthen maw, exhaling breath from the ground below.

They'd brought in portable, battery-powered LED lighting systems, which had illuminated with stark, unnatural light, providing clues to the horrors that might have been perpetrated down here. As she watched, Angie tried to piece together what might have happened to Faith Hocking in this cellar.

They'd found fresh scrapes in the slimy detritus covering the wooden dock where they'd put in with the MVPD boats. It was their first sign that there'd been recent activity on the island—a boat had been moored against the wood. And it was unlikely that it had been tied up there for a pleasure trip, given the weather over the past weeks. Tracks had then been found leading up from the dock—footprints in previously frozen mud, along with strange drag marks that had chunked up moss and lichen that grew over the rocks.

Outside the homestead entrance, more tracks in mud had been evident. And inside the ruins of the home, they'd found a herd of feral goats seeking shelter. It was easy to see how goat hairs, plus old Garry oak leaves, seeds, and other detritus, could have ended up trapped in Hocking's tarp cocoon.

But it was down in the root cellar where they hit the real pay dirt.

Polypropylene ropes hung from a support beam overhead and swayed softly in the breeze that managed to punch down through the open trapdoor—the same kind of rope that had been used to truss Hocking up. Luminol had revealed evidence of human blood on the rough rope strands. And trapped in the strands, the techs had found human hair trace—black, brunette, and dark blond strands. Angie figured the longer brunette hair strand could be Hocking's. It was the other hair trace that was now of keen interest. Some looked to be pubic, or male body hair. It had all been bagged and logged, and she was itching to know if it matched any of the hair trace that had been found on Drummond's clothing, because that would link the donor to both homicide victims.

A tech crouched near the wall where he was working to scrape up bits of candle wax. Several candle stubs, burned to the ground, had already been bagged and logged into evidence and carried upstairs to a tented staging area that had been set up outside the house.

A sheet of the same kind of polyethylene tarp that had cocooned Hocking was bundled into a far corner of the cellar, near remnants of decayed sacking, old wooden produce crates, and little windswept piles of dried Garry oak leaves, acorns, bits of old grass and bark, and strands of witch's beard that had been ripped from the pines growing on the windward side of the island. Luminol had also revealed as blood the dark stains on the cedar planks that lay across the earthen floor.

O'Hagan crouched near the stains, examining the scene against a set of morgue photographs that she'd brought to the island with her. She pointed with her nitrile-gloved finger to the rough, bloodstained cedar. "The size and spacing of the planks matches lividity patterns on Hocking's back." She pursed her lips, resembling some strange Pillsbury Doughboy squatting in her oversize boiler suit and cap.

"What is it?" Buziak said.

The pathologist glanced up at the dangling ropes strung over the support beam. "The rope circumference is consistent with the size of some of the ligature marks around her neck, but . . ." She worried her bottom lip with her teeth. "It's the gastrointestinal contents. She consumed a gourmet meal to the extreme."

"And there is no evidence that she ate that here," Maddocks said.

"Gives new meaning to a last supper," Holgersen added. "I's always thought it was a waste, you know, that last fancy supper request stuff for death row inmates, the food sitting undigested in their stomachs when they kick the bucket."

Ignoring Holgersen, Maddocks said quietly, "She could have been killed somewhere else and brought here by boat shortly after her murder, before lividity set in, which could have happened when her body was left lying on those planks. Or she could have been brought here right after her meal and then strangled here, with those ropes." He tilted his chin toward the hanging ropes.

"Yeah, like, she could have eaten anywheres along the coast and gotten out here within the hour by boat," said Holgersen. "Or she was strangled on the vessel that brought her here. Doesn't exactly narrow things down."

The wind outside howled suddenly, and a visible shudder chased through the tech scraping up the wax near the earthen wall. He glanced up, wide-eyed, as if one of the ghosts from the eighteen hundreds pox epidemic had suddenly crossed his grave. The ropes swayed, and upstairs a floorboard creaked. Somewhere an old shutter banged.

And suddenly the little girl was there—she was standing next to the tech with the candle in a soft, shimmering wash of pink. Angie froze. She heard the voice inside her head again, like a singsong playground tune . . .

Come um dum, playam dum grove . . .

Then the woman's scream in Polish . . . *Uciekaj!*

The girl spun around and ran with flowing hair and dress right through the cellar wall of black earth. Angie stared at the place the child had vanished, sweat breaking out over her body, her heart beating a steady *thwump, thwump, thwump*. In the distance, as if down some distorted tunnel, she was aware of Holgersen talking.

"Yeah, so he brings her down here, where she either dies, or she's already dead when he brings her. Maybe he revisits her a couple of times, and once he's finished with his fantasy thing, and the cutting, and once he figures she's going a bit rank, he rolls her up in the tarp, drags her down to his boat tied to the dock, puts out to sea. He then tosses her overboard on the lee side of Thetisby Island. He thinks she'll go down, except . . . the currents and weather start her traveling toward the inner harbor. Then maybe she floats up some, and her ropes get hooked up in some boat prop." He paused. "Skipper probably thought he hit a log or something. God knows those logs are floating half-submerged everywhere out there—real boating hazard in these parts. And then this freak hookup drags her into the harbor, until the rope is severed, and she flows with the powerful tidal surge into the Gorge, just in time for the homeless dude to see her come up under the bridge."

His voice droned on and on, then drowned as if being swallowed in a tunnel. The cellar started to go black, all light narrowing to one little pinprick . . .

Pallorino . . . are you okay . . . Pallorino . . .

"Angie!"

Her eyes snapped wide. She came back into focus.

"You okay?" It was Maddocks; he had his arm around her, holding her up. Panic kicked in. She tried to swallow, but her mouth was dust-dry.

"Ah, yeah. I'm fine." She dislodged herself from his support, grabbing instead on to the ladder that led down from the trapdoor above, steadying herself as she swayed on her feet again.

"Your pupils are really dilated," he said. "You look waxen."

Buziak and Holgersen were staring at her, too. O'Hagan was also watching her intently from her crouched position. Concern creased the old doc's face, which frightened Angie. She needed air. She needed to get out of here, fast. Every molecule in her body was screaming, *Flee! Run! Uciekaj, uciekaj!* She blinked as a red flash cut across her vision, and she caught a glint of silver that somehow felt like ice searing across her mouth. Her hand shot to her scar, and she brought it away, examining her fingertips, half expecting to see blood.

"Angie?" Maddocks was using her first name and supporting her by the arm again. "Let's get you out of here and into some air." He was helping her onto the bottom rung of the ladder, his arms strong, his body warm. All she wanted right now was to just give in to his solidity, the realness of him, to be vulnerable, to allow him to care for her. But she snapped back and stepped out of his grasp and away from the ladder.

"I'm fine, really, thanks." She wiped her mouth, ensuring there was no blood there, but her scar hurt, which was unusual.

"What happened? Talk to me."

Everyone was still looking at her.

She yanked her wool hat down harder over her ears, feeling cold. "I said I'm fine." She turned back to face the scene. "So why did he bring her here, then?" She spoke quickly, trying to show that she hadn't lost a beat while she actually felt as though she'd been through a gap of hours, weeks, through some weird time distortion. "For some reason Hocking and this cellar fit our subject's paraphilic love map, as Grablowski called it. She and this location fulfilled his fantasy." She turned to her colleagues. "He might be a guy of means—wealthy. He either owns a boat or has access to one. Somehow he's connected to a demographic that can afford to serve black truffles and fly in Kobe beef from Japan."

"Or he works for rich people," said Buziak.

"He must have known about this place," Angie said softly. "For some reason he's likely familiar with this island, this old homestead, these waters. He must've felt safe enough to leave her here for a while, and whether he's wealthy or not, he likely has a skipper's license and sails well enough to negotiate these seas in foul weather."

"Hoi, over here!" one of the techs yelled suddenly as he pivoted one of the portable lights. "Got something stuck between the cedar planks." Using forceps, he carefully maneuvered a used condom out from between two planks. The tech glanced up, eyes sharp and bright with the impact of his find. "He might have tried to clean up behind himself, but he missed this one."

"We gots him," whispered Holgersen, staring at the condom.

"Only if he's in the system," said Maddocks.

"Yeah, but we gots his DNA profile now, man. Either fucking way, we find us a viable suspect, and he matches the semen calling card in that little baggie there, and we gots us our Baptist."

THE BAPTIST

. . . for all have sinned and fall short of the glory of God.
—Romans 3:23

Naked, he sits on a small metal chair in the center of the basement. He's turned the furnace up to max, and the space is hot as a devil's little hell, his pale skin slick with sweat. It's dark, but he's lit white candles for effect. Like the ones in church. Like the ones in the root cellar. They flicker now in little glass jars. Like they shimmered and danced those nights on the island.

He plants the soles of his feet squarely on the floor, splaying his muscular thighs wide to expose his groin. His mother is positioned in a more comfortable chair directly ahead of him so she can watch, but not so close that she can touch.

Softly, he feathers the lock of Gracie's hair across his penis. At the first tickle—the sensitive skin in that area already stinging from a topical application of a muscle-relief cream called Icy-Hot—his penis begins to stiffen.

He closes his eyes, and with a soft moan, he draws his trophy once more across the region, and now he can taste her and see her and feel her and smell her again. His burning erection rises like a proud, stiff sentinel between his balls, which are beginning to resemble prickly fruit as his hairs grow back in from his last pubic shave, because he does not want to leave pubic hair trace at a scene. He also shaves the rest of his body. Not his head. Too proud of his head of hair. He wears a tight cap for that.

He inhales deeply, squeezing his eyes tight as he grows, bigger, hotter, more painful—the sensations setting him afire and pounding like a giant beating heart. The blood whumps against his eardrums with the primal rhythm of the world as he takes himself in hand and jacks off in time to the beat, letting his mind go, back. Back. Back . . . he holds his breath. He's there again, with her. Suddenly his breaths come shorter, faster, and he moves his hand quicker, harder, his world narrowing, spiraling down into the cellar with . . . Faith . . .

He's there now . . . flinging the rope over the beam, tying it securely. Her body is limp and her flesh still firm and pliant beneath his fingers. He's dragging her toward the rope ends hanging down from the beam. Candles shake and shiver in a sneaky breeze seeking its way in from the outside. But he likes it. It's far away and desolate and romantic and underground and . . . sacrosanct. It is. Yes. It is. Hooking his hands under her armpits, he bends her at the waist and hefts her up into a sitting position. Her head lolls forward, her chin tucking into her chest, and her long hair falls across her breasts. The nipple ring catches the candlelight, and it excites him, that ring. Quickly, he feeds rope across her chest—above the bare breasts—then around her back, then around her neck. He feeds the rope back up over the beam and pulls. Like a pulley. She shifts into position, heels dragging a little across the cedar planks. Levering her up just a little higher, he ties the rope securely there.

He steps back to check his work, and pleasure swells his chest.

She's suspended in a way that makes it seem as though she's sitting on the floor, nice and lifelike, her heels down, toes up, her lean thighs splayed wide open like a doll.

He stares for a while at the snakes on her abdomen, the fanged Medusa mouth that opens wide and is vampire-toothed around her pink pussy. A gust of wind punches down into the cellar. The candles flicker, and for a strange moment the Medusa seems to come alive, the snakes writhing over her groin, the pussy mouth licking its wet lips. *Come inside, Johnny boy, I want to eat your erection, John, you peeping Tom . . . She's a bad girl, Johnny, she made you look. She made you watch . . . fix her good . . .*

He takes his fine-edged X-ACTO precision blade from its sheath, and he places it carefully near the candles. That's for after.

CHAPTER 41

Maddocks sat at the bar, sleeves rolled up, tie off, his left elbow resting on the beaten copper counter as he sipped his beer. His attention was riveted on Angie, who was shooting pool with Holgersen and two other detectives from the high-risk offender unit who'd been seconded to Operation Limpet. And yeah, he found himself thinking of his partner as "Angie" instead of Pallorino now. What that meant . . . hell, he didn't want to think about what it meant right now.

The music was loud—a boisterous Irish fiddle duo—and the mood raucous in the Flying Pig pub, just down the road from the MVPD station. The task force was jubilant after the discovery on Thetisby Island. And following a stormy return trip by boat and an intense debriefing where theories were hashed out, evidence debated, and next steps in the investigation identified, they'd all repaired to the "police bar," except Buziak. And Fitz—Maddocks couldn't see either of them among the crowd, although they'd said they were coming.

He knocked back the rest of his beer and motioned to Colm McGregor, the pub owner, for another. It was late, going on midnight. He hadn't eaten all day, and the pub kitchen was overwhelmed by the sudden influx of famished officers. His food was thus taking its sweet time to arrive. Which meant the beer was going to his head and that he had a nice buzz on.

McGregor slid him another cold one, and Maddocks tilted back the bottle. Enjoying the cool, prickling, soft explosion of foam in his mouth, Maddocks's attention went back to Angie bending over the pool table. His gaze settled on her butt in her slim-fitting black jeans, and the memory of her naked atop him was suddenly stark, hot, and unavoidable. He forced his mind instead back to the major finds today: the different sets of human hair trace—blond, black, brunette—and the used condom that had fallen between the cedar planks. This was a significant breakthrough. They should have the forensics analysis on the trace shortly.

Angie moved to the opposite side of the table. Bending at the hips, she leaned her pelvis against the edge of the table as she strained to reach the ball with her cue, her focus intent on her target, her red hair falling over her shoulder. It was hot in here, and the top of her button-down shirt was open, and suddenly Maddocks could see in his mind her bouncing breasts as she'd ridden atop of him. *Shit*—he couldn't erase the memory of their sex no matter how hard he struggled to obliterate it. He tilted back another swig of beer, his thoughts turning now to her odd fainting episode in the cellar. Something was going on with her, and it just deepened his curiosity about the woman. It was also giving him slight cause for concern. A grunt sounded suddenly at his left, jagging into his thoughts. He turned quickly to see Leo, two stools down, nursing a whiskey tumbler and watching him intently, a smirk on his lips. It shot a spark of irritation through Maddocks. "Enjoying yourself there, Leo?"

Leo slid off his stool and moved closer, perching himself atop the seat adjacent to Maddocks. He knocked off the remainder of his drink, plunked his glass on the counter, and called out to McGregor. "Hey, big guy, make the next one a triple, will ya? And bring our horseman here another of whatever he's having." Clearing his raspy smoker's throat, he turned back to Maddocks.

"Watching a nice piece of ass there, eh, Sergeant?" he said, jerking his chin toward Angie.

Maddocks ignored him and addressed McGregor instead as the owner placed the fresh drinks in front of them. "How's that burger and fries coming?"

"Two minutes, tops," said the giant of a redheaded Scotsman in his native brogue.

Leo put his fresh whiskey glass to his lips, his gaze still fixed on Angie. "I wouldn't bother trying to get into her jeans if I were you—I figure she sways the other way." He chuckled to himself. "Probably has a fanged cunt like that Medusa we saw on Hocking, and she'll eat your prick alive if you try to stick it in there."

Every muscle in Maddocks's body tensed with an explosion of rage. Mentally, slowly, he counted to three, and then he took another long, cold sip of his beer. But still, he couldn't help what came out of his mouth next. "Did you make a pass at her yourself, Leo? She turned you down and it got your fat, hairy-ass ego hurt—is that where this is coming from?"

Leo's smirk faded, his eyes narrowed, and his face turned florid.

"Yeah," said Maddocks, regarding him steadily. "I thought so. Why don't you loosen your tie up a bit there, Detective? You're looking kinda heated and frustrated tonight."

"Fuck you," Leo whispered under his breath, turning his attention instead to the hockey game on the TV screen behind the bar. But the old cop couldn't seem to help himself, either. "She's a fucking ball-breaker, and you know it. I figure she's the fucking department leak, if you ask me—just the kinda game she'd play. I reckon she's trying to hurt the old brass who won't let her into homicide. Out of sheer spite." He sucked back half the whiskey in his glass, coughed, wiped his mouth with the back of his hand, and said, "What happened to your wrists? Looks like you were tied up bad as our floater."

"I was."

His gaze shot back to Maddocks's eyes. "What for?"

"Sex."

He stared.

"Never been cuffed to a bed and taken advantage of, Detective?"

"You're shitting me."

"You wish."

Leo opened his mouth, but before he could shoot back a retort, McGregor arrived with the burger and fries and placed the food steaming hot in front of him. With relief, Maddocks immediately stuffed several fries into his mouth. As he chewed, the pub doors burst open. Doc O'Hagan blew in with a blustery blast of winter. Wearing her big, comfy-looking jeans, she waddled directly toward them at the bar.

Leo jerked his head toward her. "Here comes another ballbreaker. Maybe she and Pallorino are getting it on, what you say?" He sipped his drink.

"How you doing, Leo?" O'Hagan said, slapping the old detective so hard on the back that he was forced to cough up his whiskey as it was going down. Leo's eyes watered, and his face burned redder. Cheery-faced, O'Hagan grinned broadly and raised her hand to summon McGregor. She ordered a Guinness pot pie and a draft of pale ale. She turned to Maddocks.

"So, Detective Newbie, how've the first days on the job been so far?" She smiled a genuine gap-toothed smile.

"The way I like it," he said, returning her smile. "Big case, the hours flying by."

"You weren't looking for a desk gig, then—management?"

He picked up his burger. "I wanted to get down and dirty in the trenches again for a while." He bit into his food. She assessed him in silence for several beats as he chewed, probably reading a lot more in his statement than most would.

"Well, that it's been so far—down and dirty." She scanned the noisy and full establishment as she spoke. "Where's Buziak?"

"Gunnar called him in for some kind of meeting," Leo mumbled.

"A meeting with the chief? This late?" O'Hagan said.

Leo shrugged and returned to his drink, growing morose now. O'Hagan gave Maddocks a nod and went over to talk to Angie.

"Barbed fucking wire O'Hagan," Leo muttered into his drink.

Maddocks turned back to the counter and quietly ate his burger and fries, intending to clear out as soon as he'd finished. But in the mirror behind the bar he could see Angie putting her pool cue down. He watched as she joined O'Hagan in a booth. McGregor brought drinks over to them, and Angie smiled at something O'Hagan said, then she threw back her head and laughed as McGregor made some quip. And in that moment Maddocks thought she was the most beautiful woman he'd ever seen. It was the first time he'd seen her smile, laugh, and he ached suddenly to be on the receiving end of that smile. Shit. He was drunker than he'd thought. He needed to get out of here, stat.

Hurriedly, he finished his meal, plunked cash on the counter, waved a thanks to McGregor, and made his way to the men's room before leaving.

But when he exited the bathroom a short while later, he heard Leo's raspy voice in the corridor. "It's you, *you're* the fucking leak."

Maddocks came quickly around a partition and saw that the old detective had cornered Angie in the tiny passageway as she'd exited the ladies' washroom. "You're trying to take us *all* down because you fucking can't take us on like a proper cop—"

"Hey! Back off there, Leo," Maddocks called, coming quickly forward. But Angie threw Maddocks a sharp warning look that stopped him in his tracks.

"Look, Leo," she said, her voice going low and cool. "I'm going to let this slide tonight, okay? Because you've had a few too many, and I know that you're going to regret ever having said this. Now back off, nice and easy, and let me pass."

Admiration swelled in Maddocks.

But Leo poked his finger into her face. "It's *you* who's wrecking us—you who needs—"

"I said back off, Leo." As she spoke, she was positioning her right foot slightly to her rear, and Maddocks saw her shifting weight onto it. She was getting ready to clock Detective Harvey Leo. Maddocks tensed, his own fists balling and shoulders tightening instinctively.

"I heard you was seen with that little punk-ass reporter yesterday. What did you give her this time, Pallorino?"

"This is my last warning. Step aside. Now."

Leo snorted, leering his face yet closer. "Why? What you gonna do about it? Sue me for sexual *harassment*? Gonna go whining to the union, then?" He touched her breast. "Let's see what you're made—"

Before Maddocks could blink, Angie reached down and thrust her hand between Leo's legs, grabbing him by the balls. He froze. She held. Eyes locked with the old cop's, she squeezed.

"Fuck—fuck! Bitch!" he yelled, bending over in pain as she released him.

Angie then shouldered past him and parroted back at him as she went, "What you gonna do about it, Leo, sue me for sexual *harassment*?"

"Asshole," Maddocks muttered as he passed Leo, making after Angie along the small passageway that was hidden from the rest of the bar. But before he could reach her, she'd yanked her coat off the stand near the entrance and was shoving out of the pub doors. Leo barreled up suddenly behind him and bashed out of the doors after Angie like a bull with murder on his face.

Shit.

Maddocks stormed after him in his shirtsleeves, into the dark winter mist and rain.

Ahead of Maddocks, Leo reached Angie, and he grabbed her by the coat. She swung around, but before her elbow could connect with Leo's face, Maddocks reached Leo and hauled him backward by his shoulders. Leo staggered sideways under the force, and Maddocks delivered a sharp left hook that cracked across the man's jaw.

Leo lurched backward and went down onto the wet paving with a violent curse. He scrambled back onto his feet, bent double, and came back at Maddocks like a wounded and enraged wild animal. And like a matador, Maddocks pivoted his hips, sidestepping Leo's thrust, and the old cop went flailing drunkenly forward until he stumbled, tripped, and fell back down onto his hands and knees on the wet parking lot paving.

Maddocks went for him again.

"Whoa!" Angie grabbed Maddocks by the arm. *"Enough!"*

He swung around to face her, breathing hard, adrenaline pumping like a freight train through his blood. Their gazes met. Their faces were suddenly close, her breathing as rapid as his. She was still holding on to his arm. Rain was falling in a soft, icy mist around them, and his shirt was wet and plastering to his torso. Behind them Leo swore and staggered off into the darkness. And suddenly they were alone and all was quiet apart from the plop of water dripping from eaves and the distant hum of traffic.

"Let him go," she whispered, her mouth coming closer. Clearing her throat, she added, "Go home, Detective."

He looked down into her eyes, and in them he saw the same things he'd seen in her face that night in the club when he'd first met her—a luminosity. A hunger. A fierceness. A simmering, barely restrained sexuality that was more about power than submission. But now that he knew her better, he knew there was also something broken in her, and it both intrigued him and fed the lust mounting in him right now. It spoke to the detective in him, the problem solver, and the protector and savior. And more . . . He cupped the side of her face, which glistened pale in the rain. "Come with me, Angie," he said softly. "Come back to my boat. Let's finish what we started."

Her mouth opened, but before she could say anything, Maddocks leaned down and pressed his lips over hers.

CHAPTER 42

Angie went rigid, then a blind, primal ferocity imploded all logic as she suddenly opened to his kiss, coming up to him, her breasts, her pelvis, pressing against the solid mass of muscle that was his body. Her sex rules blurred distantly through her mind.

Never kiss . . . Never sleep with a colleague . . . Leave first. Leave early. No names. Never stay the night. Never breakfast the next morning. Never take one that makes you feel vulnerable in any way . . . Always stay in control . . .

The rules twisted down into a hot vortex of total oblivion as her mouth, her hunger, her aggression met his, tongues tangling, mating, rough, taking. He fisted her hair, tilting her head farther back, as his other hand slid down her spine. He cupped her buttocks and yanked her hard against him. His shirt was completely plastered to his body, and she could feel every inch of his muscular contours under the wet fabric. She could feel the long hardness of his big, gorgeous dick straining against his zipper as he pressed against her pelvis. Heat pooled molten between her thighs. Dizziness swirled, and her knees began to buckle out from under her. She wanted him. All of him. Inside. Deep and fast and hard and rough. Out here. Right now. She bit his lip, drawing blood as she fumbled for his belt buckle, undid it, found the tab for his zipper, but before she could yank it down, a sound distracted her. She slowed. Her heart hammered.

The pub doors opened, spilling light and voices and laughter out into the night. Angie jerked back and stared up into his face as reality came back into focus. His features had been etched by lust into something smoldering and powerful and dangerous. He licked the blood from his lip. For a moment she was speechless, breathless. Confused. And so was he, both shell-shocked by what had just exploded between them, by this Pandora's box they appeared to have opened back at ground zero of the Foxy Motel. Possibly they'd never stood a chance—not since the instant their eyes had met over that crowded dance floor—and she'd been kidding herself all along that she could control this. Because right now, right at this moment, she couldn't. Almost didn't want to. All she knew right now was that she had to step away. Fast. Process this.

"I . . . this can't happen again," she whispered, voice thick. She spun around and strode fast into the mist, leaving him standing there in his soaking wet shirt, no tie. Blood thudded against her eardrums. It pulsed in her groin. And as she reached her vehicle she began to shake.

She got inside, keyed the ignition, and sat for a moment, heater running, trying to warm up, but the shakes worsened, and tears filled her eyes, and she didn't want to think. Or feel. She leaned forward suddenly and engaged the gears. And she knew exactly where she was going.

Maddocks watched her disappear into a veil of rain and darkness. His heart drummed a beat in time with the drips coming from an adjacent awning. A far-off siren wailed. Traffic hummed in the distance. And out there somewhere, he knew, a killer hunted.

He also knew exactly where she was going.

His hands fisted at his sides as desire continued to slam through his body. His cock was hard and his head fucked up. And she was the drug he needed to fix it all. But like a drug, the fix would just make the addiction worse; this he knew, too.

She was right. They *had* to pull back, stop this while they still could. *If* they still could. Inhaling deeply, Maddocks turned and went back inside the pub. He grabbed his coat and made for his Impala.

But on the way home, he couldn't help himself—he turned onto the road that would take him onto Highway 1 instead of the marina. She was going to fuck someone else, and it was eating him alive. He didn't want to believe it. It wasn't his business. But his compulsion to prove it to himself took him onto that highway, and he kept his eyes peeled for the rear lights of her Crown Vic.

Rain came down heavier as he headed toward the mountains, but traffic also thinned as he left the city behind, and then, suddenly, he believed he could see her vehicle up ahead. He eased off on the gas, not wanting to be made as a tail.

As the Crown Vic up ahead indicated for the next off-ramp, his heart sank, and a bitterness fouled his mouth. He followed the Vic as it turned off the highway and into the cracked parking lot of the Foxy Club and Motel. The red Xs pulsed into the wet night with a promise of hot adult entertainment.

He drew alongside the curb across the side street from the lot. He watched the vehicle park. From this aspect he couldn't make out the plate, so held out hope that he'd made a mistake, that somehow the car was not hers . . . but then the door opened, and she got out.

Fuck.

Maddocks watched as she strode toward the motel office. A few minutes later she exited the office and made for the club door. She spoke to the bouncer outside, and he let her in. A strange hot stab seared through Maddocks's chest. He punched the dash of his Impala, hard, and swore again, his mind, his body, every inch of him humming with memories of their own liaison in that motel room for which she'd just gone and paid up-front. And now she was in there hunting for a conquest. Within a half hour she could be banging her victim in that room, on that bed.

He fisted his hands around the wheel, debating whether to go in there and haul her out. Or . . . go in there and take her to that room himself. A kind of madness swirled around and around and around inside his skull along with the firestorm of sexual frustration consuming his body. He bit down on it all, rammed his Impala into gear, and he hit the highway, driving home too fast, trying to outrun his feelings. And yeah, his burning jealousy. His anger at her for doing this, knowing at the same time it was really none of his bloody business.

Angie's nerves zipped and fizzed like loose electrical wires smacking wet ground. Since she'd tasted Maddocks's kiss, the shape of her lust had changed. It had grown into a bloodthirsty and fanged thing deep inside her chest, inside her belly, and it had driven her here, to her hunting ground in search of relief she knew she might not find. Not this time. Not after that kiss.

The words of the forensic shrink, Grablowski, drummed through her brain as she scanned the dance floor.

His hunting zone is where his desire for anonymity and his desire to operate within his comfort zone meet . . .

The parallels unsettled her deeply, because this was *her* comfort zone, just far enough out of town, but not too far. Anonymous enough at this hour of a weeknight. And here she was herself escalating in some way. Devolving.

The barkeep grinned at her as she took a seat at the bar. "The usual?"

She nodded. But there was nothing usual about this night, she thought as he placed a vodka tonic in front of her. The barkeeper was shirtless tonight—apart from a black bow tie around his thickly corded neck. He'd oiled his torso, and his muscles rippled like a beautiful animal under his tan-bed skin. She inhaled deeply, trying to appreciate the view, trying to erase the sensation of Maddocks's torso under her palm, his wet shirt . . . the glorious taste and feel of him. The need in his eyes. The barkeep turned to reach for a bottle, and she saw that heart-shaped pieces of fabric had been cut away to expose his butt cheeks. Christ. She looked away. *Find your conquest. Get this out of your system. Go home. Sleep. Start again tomorrow.*

Angie scanned the crowd. Not very busy. Tonight the club theme was in tribute to a rock star who'd overdosed, and as the disco ball spun it sparked purple light over dancers who moved like sick lovers, pelvises grinding to the slow, seductive songs. The lyrics were about making love . . . about being *engaged with a kiss, the sweat of your body covering mine . . .*

Angie shook herself and reached for her drink, sipped. But even the taste of her drink was off tonight. She stilled as a man at the far end of the bar caught her eye. Tall. Dark blond. Awesome body. Defined jaw. Nice wide mouth. Pale ice-blue eyes that reminded her of an Alaskan malamute. Her pulse quickened, and she inhaled slowly. This was the one. She took another sip, staring directly at him over the rim of her glass as she swallowed. Her brazen attention snared his interest instantly, and he began to make his way over.

This was the ritual—pick a victim. Feel the soft rush of power as he came over to do her bidding . . . but the power feeling didn't come tonight. Again, Grablowski's words snaked through her brain.

We all have what is called a paraphilic love map, and these love maps begin to develop shortly after puberty. But the sexual predator, clinically speaking, has developed a love map where his lust is attached to fantasies and practices that are either socially forbidden, disapproved of, ridiculed, or

penalized. And his fantasies usually involve aggression, domination, control.
He becomes aroused by mere thoughts of sexual aggression . . .

She shook herself again, but she was unable to obliterate the echo of Grablowski's words inside her skull, or the echoes she could suddenly see so starkly within herself, or the unease that these thoughts brought—because there was nothing weird in *her* childhood that could have made her this way. It was something that had evolved later, after her disastrous affair, and she'd come to like it. Need it.

The song changed to something more upbeat as her victim neared.

"Hey." He leaned his hand on the bar, slightly to the side, his body shadowing hers, just like Maddocks had done that night. "What're you having?" He nodded to her drink.

Angie looked up into his eyes. So ice-cool pale they almost seemed inhuman.

A chill trickled down her spine.

She suddenly placed both hands against the edge of the bar counter, gathering herself, and then she quickly pushed herself back off her stool. "Thanks, but I'm with someone." And with that, she navigated through the crowd and shoved out of the doors into the dark winter wetness. But as she made for her Crown Vic, frustration ripped at her, and she kicked violently at a garbage can along the side of the wall with her steel-toed biker boot. Not once, but several times, kicking her anxiety out of her system as the hollow sounds of crumpling metal clunked and crashed into the night. *Fuck fuck fuck.* Tears burned. She ached. *She* burned. For her fix. Like any goddamn junkie. But having been with Maddocks had rendered her incapable. He'd stolen her one avenue of release.

And he'd replaced it with the beginnings of a yearning for something, someplace that she knew she couldn't go . . . he was making her ache for something more. Making her want to be a person she didn't know how to be.

✝

CHAPTER 43

THURSDAY, DECEMBER 14

It was late afternoon when Maddocks pulled up with Pallorino outside Saint Auburn's Cathedral, adjacent to the Catholic-run Saint Jude's Hospital. And yes, from here on he was going to think of his temporary partner as "Pallorino." He would work with her on closing this case, then she could return to sex crimes, and he'd have nothing further to do with her.

They'd come to observe Drummond's funeral service. As Grablowski had noted, the type of offender they were hunting was likely to follow media, revisit his crime scenes, and he was statistically inclined to attend events like this in order to bask in the penumbra of his handiwork. They also planned to talk to the priest afterward. Ordinarily, this would be the time that the college choir rehearsed at the cathedral, but on this Thursday the choir would instead be performing at the service, to honor one of their dead members.

For the better part of the day, he and Pallorino had been skirting each other and avoiding eye contact as they'd handled paperwork and discussed theories, notes, and evidence. Maddocks had also met privately with Buziak and a trusted prosecutor to see whether they might have reasonable probable grounds to obtain DNA samples from Jayden Norton-Wells and Zach Raddison, who both had black hair, and who were both persons of interest. It was going to take more than they had to get a DNA seizure warrant that would hold up down the road in a court. Especially given the high profiles of the young men and their families—and the fact that Joyce Norton-Wells was the province's top prosecutor. They needed solid evidence, and they needed to have every *t* crossed and *i* dotted before taking this forward.

Hopefully the forensic analysis that was starting to come in from the Thetisby Island crime scene might yield them additional ammunition.

He and Pallorino had, however, ascertained that both Jon Jacques Senior and Junior, Zach Raddison, and Jayden Norton-Wells all carried valid pleasure boat operating cards—proof that they were knowledgeable at least in part about watercraft and potentially able to navigate local waters and islands. All had access to vehicles.

Still, it was tough to see any one of those four fitting Grablowski's profile of a lone-hunting, sadistic, psychopathic sex killer. Yet all were clearly hiding something.

Holgersen and Leo were off pursuing the Jon Jacques angles. Leo had come in silent and sullen this morning, nursing a bruised jaw and a mother of a hangover. He'd kept his head down, his mouth shut, and avoided interaction with either Maddocks or Pallorino. It was clear that no one was going to pursue the incident.

"We could just ask Norton-Wells and Raddison to voluntarily give DNA samples, for elimination purposes," Pallorino said as Maddocks parked his vehicle. She was overtly edgy now that she was alone with him in the car again. Her voice was clipped, and she wouldn't meet his gaze. "At least to see if their profiles are a match to the black hair evidence found on Hocking's body."

Maddocks turned off the ignition and inhaled deeply. Looking ahead out of the rain-smeared windshield, he said, "We considered that, since we don't have grounds for a warrant. But Buziak doesn't want to risk getting their legal counsel winding up for a fight to quash things before we're ready. It could send them into damage control mode, which in turn could stymie the investigation and shut down potential avenues of further inquiry. He wants additional evidence—he wants reasonable and probable grounds. And he still wants to keep a tight lid on the connection between the ADAG's son and the mayor's aide, because of the MVPD leak, in part."

"*When* did he tell you this?"

"Earlier this afternoon. We met with legal."

She stared. "Why was I excluded this time? Doesn't he trust me?"

"I don't know who he trusts. I'm lead investigator. It made sense to meet with me."

"So why didn't *you* tell me this?"

"I just did."

She swore, got out, slammed the door, popped up a black umbrella, and climbed the stairs to the cathedral entrance at a clip. Maddocks joined her there. From a vantage point next to the doors, they watched as people started to arrive and sift into the church. Other officers watched also—down the street in plainclothes. Two members were filming the crowd. The Cemetery Girl's funeral was expected to draw large numbers, including the media. Mayor Killion had also made a statement to the press that he would be in attendance to pay his respects. He of course took the occasion to hammer home that he would be taking immediate action to toughen up on crime and to make the city safer.

"There's Killion's vehicle pulling up now," Maddocks said with a nod toward a black town car.

"Bastard," Pallorino whispered as they watched the mayor alight from the car with Raddison. "They're using this poor girl's service as a political event."

As the crowd swelled, there was no sign of Norton-Wells or Jon Jacques Senior or Junior. Pallorino stiffened suddenly, and drawn by the motion, Maddocks snapped his attention to her.

"What is it?" he said.

"I . . . nothing."

"Nothing is nothing. What did you see?"

"That guy—the tall blond one standing near the west door, wearing the skullcap and black coat—I've seen him before." As if sensing the sudden scrutiny, the man glanced their way. He stilled as his gaze met Pallorino's across the crowd. Even from here, Maddocks could see that his eyes were the palest blue.

"Where?" he said quietly.

"Just . . . last night. I went out."

"Why'd you go? Why'd you hit the club?"

"What makes you think I went there?"

"I followed you."

"What? You *followed* me?" She cursed. "It's none of your business."

"You made it mine."

"Oh, fuck off," she whispered, eyes glittering with anger, hot spots riding high into her cheeks. "Just fuck the hell off out of my life, okay? You don't go following me."

"Did you screw him—that blond guy? Is that why he looked at you like that?" The man was moving away now, down the stairs and into a throng of people lining the sidewalk.

"I said, it's not your business."

Maddocks burned inside his gut. His neck was tight. He fought to not fist his hands, fought to keep focus on his job of watching the mourners. He could no longer see the blond Adonis in the crowd. He struggled not to picture her naked on top of him, and it just fueled his anger.

"Besides," she said under her breath, "you're no saint yourself."

"My going to the club that night was a one-off."

"Yeah, right."

"It was. My buddy was visiting from the mainland. He said I needed to get out more. He said he'd meet me there, that I needed a life. He didn't show. I was about to leave, but then there was you."

"And I was cheaper than a hooker."

"You made an offer I couldn't refuse. Sue me."

Fury burned into the cool mist between them. Palpable. Thick. Crackling with power and sexual tension. Darkness was also creeping in. The strains of an organ reached them outdoors, and the rain pattered down louder on her umbrella.

"Dad!" Both of them spun around.

"Ginny?" Maddocks had expected to see his daughter here, given her involvement with the choir, but not in the presence of her current company—Lara Pennington. Lara shot a hot glance at Maddocks, then Pallorino. She whispered something into Ginn's ear and went on ahead into the church.

"What are you doing here?" Ginny said to him, but while looking at Pallorino.

"It's my case—"

"It's a funeral, Dad."

"How long have you known Lara?" he said, trying to keep an eye on the thinning crowd at the same time. "How *well* do you know her?"

His daughter's brow lowered. "Why?"

"Just answer the question, Ginny."

"I just met her on the bus over here. She was a good friend of Gracie's. She's at UVic, too, and part of the choir. We—"

"Ginny, I don't want you mixing—"

"Excuse me?"

"Just until this is sorted. I want you to steer clear of her."

Her mouth dropped open, and she stared aghast at him. Pallorino also cast him a sideways glance.

"Ginn," he said quietly, "there's a bad guy out there, preying on—"

"Oh, and you think he's suddenly going to come after *me* now? Jesus." The cathedral doors were being closed. The service was about to commence.

"Listen, when this Mass is over, when you're done singing, please wait for me out here. I'm going to drive you home. Okay?"

"Sometimes," she said quietly, with a hot flick of another glance at Angie, "I really wish you hadn't come to live in Victoria." And with that, Ginny turned and disappeared up the stairs and into the church.

"You should cut her a break," Pallorino said softly.

"Oh, that's rich, coming from someone who's never had kids."

"I was seventeen once, and female. I have a father who was as paternalistic and overprotective as you are."

"And look how you turned out."

She glowered at him, then turned and marched up the stairs and into church. The door closed behind her.

Rain came down harder, almost turning to sleet now, but Maddocks chose to wait alone outside to see if anyone suspicious arrived late. Or whether that blond Adonis returned. As the minutes ticked by and the temperatures continued to drop, he turned up his collar and stuffed his hands deep into his pockets. And he cursed himself for the way he'd handled Ginny again.

He'd been distracted by his task at hand. Worried. She looked so much like the victim whose funeral they were attending. Same age range. Similar interests when it came to singing in the choir. And Lara Pennington was a nexus. She'd been Drummond's closest friend since elementary school. She was hiding something and scared of something. She was also possibly being watched by someone in a black Lexus. So how wrong was he, really, to want his daughter to steer clear of her?

THE BAPTIST

Hail Mary, full of grace,
the Lord is with thee;
blessed art thou amongst women,
and blessed is the fruit of thy womb, Jesus.
Holy Mary, Mother of God,
pray for us sinners,
now and at the hour of our death.
Amen.

It's dark. He awaits the girls near the corner where they will catch the return bus. It's nicely away from the main crowd and police presence. He followed Lara to campus this morning, and he waited for her to finish classes. He's still searching for the right place to take her, the right moment in her schedule, and it's getting more and more difficult because the MVPD have been sending patrol cars down her street every now and then.

He knows tonight is Lara's choir night. The papers were also full with the news of Gracie's funeral service. He wants to see for himself. Following Lara here was worth the risk he took to do it, just to absorb the sheer impact of what *he* has wrought. To feel the thrill.

Snatches of female voices carry in the wind—*they're coming*. His pulse quickens.

On the bus ride over he dared sit right behind Lara and her new friend. So close he could smell them, could have touched their hair if he wanted. Lara has been nervous of late, hyperconscious of her surroundings, constantly glancing over her shoulder. This, too, is making things challenging. But this evening, engaged in animated conversation with her new friend, she was definitely less observant.

And from his seat behind them he managed to listen to their chatter about the choir, about how they were going to Gracie's funeral in that big, beautiful cathedral with the burnished wood pews that he himself helped tend and polish in his youth while his mother came for confession and brought victuals for Father. And made him confess, too.

Bless me, Father, I have sinned . . . but I didn't tell Father I'm a peeping Tommy, bad Johnny who likes to watch the girls naked in the school locker room . . .

Saint Auburn's is where he started his vocation—through his volunteer work in the church, polishing the wood. *A noble vocation, son . . . Joseph, father of God himself, was a carpenter. Even Jesus performed the inherited trade before going into His ministry . . .*

The girls are almost at the corner. He steps back into a doorway recessed into the wall, and he stands in shadow, excitement rippling over his skin. Ginny is the other girl's name. When he learned from their conversation on the bus that Ginny's father is Detective Maddocks, the one working this case with Detective Pallorino—the man he saw outside Lara's house the other day—it was as if he was smote by the heavens, a sign.

And a plan—something bigger, something that reaches far beyond the circle of girls whom he needs to save, far more sublime—is fingering its way into his brain. And into his libido. A big, beautiful plan that will involve Ginny Maddocks.

CHAPTER 44

"Yes, I did know Gracie personally," Father Simon said as he removed his voluminous purple chasuble over his head. He smiled sadly, opened a closet, inserted a hanger into the garment, and hung it on the rail beside similar vestments in red, black, green, and white. "Lorna Drummond requested the violet," he said, smoothing down his hair that had become ruffled. "She felt the traditional black was too solemn for her Gracie's service. She wanted to focus rather on atonement and sorrow."

Angie knew from her family's past involvement with the faith that each color of the robes reflected different events in the liturgical year. Green was for ordinary Mass. White for occasions of victory, like the resurrection of the Lord Jesus. Red was the color of fire and blood symbolizing the Pentecost, tongues of flame, and blood shed by martyred saints in the name of God. Black was generally for somber masses of the dead.

She and Maddocks stood with the priest inside the sacristy, a room in an annex off the main part of the cathedral where priests' vestments were traditionally stored along with other church furnishings, sacred vessels, and parish records. Father Simon now stood before them in a classic white alb cinched at the waist with a cincture—a cord that represented chastity. He was surprisingly young-looking and chiseled-handsome, with the build of a triathlete and light hazel eyes. There was a brightness in those eyes and a vitality about him that Angie found sexual, compelling, and at odds with that symbol of celibacy around his waist. She'd bet her ass there were plenty of women in this parish, young and old, who found Father Simon similarly alluring, and perhaps even more so because of the fact he'd sworn off sex—the sins of the flesh—in order to devote his life wholly and completely to God.

What, she wondered, had turned this vital man to the faith? What was *his* story?

"Gracie first sought my counsel when she decided to fully recommit to the church," he said, untying his cincture and unbuttoning and removing the alb to reveal black pants and a black button-down shirt, and yes, definitely a honed body in there. He adjusted his white collar. "From that point onward she never missed a Sunday Mass unless she was gravely ill. And she sang here as part of the college choir."

"Do you feel that you played a role in saving Gracie, then, Father?" said Maddocks.

Father Simon weighed Maddocks a moment, his eyes going serious. "You mean, did I twist her arm and threaten her with hell and damnation unless she returned to the Catholic faith?"

Maddocks said nothing, just held the man's gaze.

Father Simon inhaled. "It was Gracie's will to return to the fold. It was the Lord's will." He hung up his alb.

"Did she ever express to you a concern about being followed, stalked, any fears?" Angie said, wondering again why her own family had basically stopped practicing the Catholic faith.

"No," he said, shutting the closet door.

"Is there anything at all you could tell us that might help us learn more about her?" Angie asked.

A slight darkness flickered through his eyes. Or had she imagined it? She met his clear gaze, watching closely for other possible tells, a repeat of the flicker.

"Not really. Other than she was kind, gentle. Devout. She had long-term plans for the future."

"Such as?" Maddocks said.

"Travel mostly."

"With any guy in particular, perhaps—any special male in her life that you know of?" he said.

"I can't say."

"Can't—or won't?" he said.

Father Simon studied Maddocks again for several beats, yet his posture remained benign. Benevolent, even. Still, Angie detected an undercurrent between the two men, or Maddocks was just being an ass because of his earlier altercation with her. "I do think she had a special person in her life, yes," Father Simon said. "I don't know who that was, though." Calmly, he waited for them to press on with more questions, as if indulging impatient children who would learn with time. The weight of the church, the sense of its age and history, seemed suddenly to start pressing down on Angie, and claustrophobia began to circle. She cleared her throat, fighting back the sensations, worried that it might be a precursor to another hallucination.

"Is there perhaps anyone in this congregation, or someone who does building maintenance, or tends to the gardens, or does something administrative for the parish, who might have expressed an unnatural interest in Gracie Drummond?" she said.

"You think someone from this parish hurt her?"

"Whoever did hurt her, Father, is acting out a lethal sexual fantasy within a powerful religious context, and likely a Catholic-specific one."

"Why Catholic-specific?"

She glanced at Maddocks, and he gave her a slight nod. "We believe that after sexually assaulting his female victims in a violent manner, he immerses them in water as a symbolism for baptism. Cleansing them in the name of the Lord. After which he adorns them with a sign of the cross and removes the parts of their bodies designed purely for female sexual pleasure. And in Gracie's case, he displayed her at the feet of the Virgin Mary." She held his eyes.

He didn't blink. "This symbolism—the crucifix, baptism—it doesn't mean it's Catholic. Many Christian religions use immersion for baptism, or used to."

Again, she glanced at Maddocks, ensuring he was on board with giving Father Simon what used to be holdback information, although just about everything of their cases had now been leaked to the press. He gave another small and tacit nod, his eyes still angry.

"He uses specific words during his attacks, and he forces his victims to make specific responses before he rapes them. These phrases and the responses are consistent with the script used in the official Catholic baptismal ceremony," she said. "As in, the celebrant asking the parents of the infant to be baptized the following questions, among others: 'Do you reject Satan? And all his works? Do you reject the glamour of evil and refuse to be mastered by sin? Do you reject Satan, father of sin and prince of darkness?'" She paused, watching his face. "Whereupon the godparents are supposed to answer 'I do' to each question before their godchild is anointed with holy water, and the priest then traces the sign of the cross on the child's forehead. Correct?"

The priest nodded slowly, and then he said, "But it doesn't mean he comes from this parish, does it?"

"This was Gracie's church, Father. She spent time *here*. Sang *here*. Given the religious and Catholic context of the crimes, it's conceivable she crossed paths *here* with someone of strong faith, possibly someone deeply conflicted about sin and lust." That discomfit she'd felt in the club about her own echoes in behavior started circling again.

The priest inhaled deeply and rubbed his jaw, and his eyes seemed to have narrowed ever so slightly, the light in them not quite as vivid.

"Is there anyone you know who might fit these characteristics?" she said.

He shook his head slowly. "I'm really sorry, but I'm afraid there is nothing here that I can help you with." He glanced at the clock on the wall. "And I do have an appointment in less than ten minutes, detectives. Will this take much longer? Or can I walk you out?"

Angie got a strong sense that he *did* know something that perhaps he was not at liberty to share, or refused to, and it quickened her pulse. "Just a few more quick questions, if we might, Father. Do you perhaps know a Jon Jacques?" As she spoke, she placed on the counter two photos gleaned from online news stories—one image of Jon Jacques Senior and one of Junior.

He studied them closely. "I can't say that I do, no."

"What about Jayden Norton-Wells?" She placed a photo of Norton-Wells beside the others, also obtained online.

"I do know the Norton-Wells family quite well," he said, looking at the image. "They don't worship at this church, but they're stalwarts in the greater Catholic community—big donors."

"Gracie never came here with Jayden?"

"Not to my knowledge."

"Did she ever mention who gave her a Saint Christopher medallion?"

His brow creased slightly. "No."

"Do you know Faith Hocking?"

"From the media." He sighed. "Bless their souls. Now, if you don't mind, I'll show you out?" He held his arm toward the door.

Angie and Maddocks exited the sacristy with Father Simon, who then walked them back through the cathedral and down the aisle between the rows of burnished wood pews. Panic began to hiss like steam through cracks into the fringes of Angie's brain.

Focus. Focus.

In the last row a woman knelt, her head bowed in prayer as she fingered the beads of her rosary. A faint memory darted into Angie's mind as she saw the two confessional boxes that flanked the last pew.

The lights over the doors of the confessionals glowed greenish white, which to Angie's knowledge meant they were open for confession. A red light meant someone was inside telling a priest of his or her sins.

Angie stopped and turned to the priest. "Did you ever take Gracie's confession, Father?"

He glanced at the woman praying and said softly, "Let's talk through there." He led them into the antechamber that served as a kind of entrance hall to the church. He stood beside the bowl of holy water. "Detective Pallorino, I'm sure you are aware that the Seal of Confession is sacrosanct. It's the absolute duty of clerics not to disclose anything learned from penitents during the course of the Sacrament of Penance."

Her pulse quickened slightly. He *did* know something. She felt it in her gut, saw it hidden in his eyes.

"If Gracie did tell you something that could help us find who did this, it would save other young women a terrible—"

"I would be excommunicated," he said crisply. "I will die before I break that seal of the confessional."

Her heart beat even faster, and she felt the shift in Maddocks's energy, too.

"Not even the highest courts can compel me to break that seal," he added. "I'm legally protected in this regard by confidentiality laws."

"Maybe so," Angie said, "but courts have also ruled that a clergyperson still has a mandatory duty to report any suspicious interactions he might have observed *outside* of the confessional. Possibly Gracie mentioned something through regular pastoral counseling, where confidentiality has limits."

Their gazes warred. And she felt a chink deepening in this handsome young man of the cloth.

"It's your job to catch a killer," he said quietly. "Mine is to save souls."

"Oh, so you *saved* Gracie's soul?" she said. "Think about what she endured—the fear, the torture, the pain as some sick and perverted man tried to 'save her soul' in his own deviant way. She suffered, believe me, Father, she suffered. You didn't save her from that. But you could save others if you are holding something critical back."

"We all have our suffering, our own crosses to bear, Detective."

Frustration whipped through her. She opened her mouth to fire off another question just as the cathedral bells started to toll, and she completely lost her train of thought. More bells joined the first ones, the sound growing monstrous as they pealed up high in the steeple and echoed down through the cavernous stone church. She felt confused. Maddocks glanced at her, his eyes narrowing in concern.

"I think we're done here," he said, watching Angie closely. "Thank you, Father."

As he opened the heavy wood door out to the dark winter night, Father Simon suddenly said, "Gracie was conflicted. I can say that much."

"Conflicted by what?" Maddocks said, still holding the door open. The peals seemed louder from the outside, the sound coming in through the gap in the door. And through that gap, under a halo of streetlight, Angie could see that sleet had turned to soft snowflakes. Her mouth grew dry. Her skin turned hot.

Father Simon's voice seemed to come from far, far away. "Through the giving of spiritual guidance, outside of the confessional, I can say that Gracie Marie was troubled by her own promiscuity."

Angie tried to latch on to this, tried to focus on the next question, but her mind was blurred, a panic licking to a fire inside her with the clanging of the bells, the sense of snow, the scent of it coming in through the door which Maddocks was still holding open. Time seemed to stretch, warping everything like elastic.

"Meaning?" Maddocks said.

"Meaning, I was led to believe she regularly had intercourse with many different partners, and it bothered her."

"She told you this? Outside of confession?" he confirmed.

"Yes."

"That's a rather intimate thing to tell a male priest, especially outside of confession. How did it come about? What kind of relationship *did* you have with Gracie?" Maddocks said.

"She tried her female charms on me."

"She tried to *seduce* you?" Bells clanged louder.

"When I asked her why she was doing this, I came to learn that Gracie was . . . needy. She craved love, acceptance. I think she felt abandoned by her father and lonely with a largely absent mother. She also had trouble as a younger child at school with being accepted. From what she told me, sex, giving her body, bought her relationships with boys and subsequent interest from the in-girls at school. It helped her feel that she belonged. At least, I believe this was the case with her previous boyfriend."

"Rick Butler?" said Maddocks.

"I believe that was his name, yes."

"Did she tell you anything about her new boyfriend, about these other males she allegedly slept with?"

"I've told you what I can, detectives. And now, I must go."

"When did you last actually see Gracie yourself?" Maddocks said.

The door to the inner part of the cathedral opened behind them. The woman who'd been saying her rosary exited. As the door swung slowly shut, the strains of an organist warming up were joined by a high, sweet voice—a young boy starting to sing . . . *Ave Marie—aaaah* . . .

Terror kicked through Angie.

She shot a glance at the gap between the exit doors, her heart banging hard against her ribs.

"Sunday before last," the priest said. "For Mass, during the sacrament of Holy Communion."

"Thank you, Father," she muttered quickly, and she shoved out the exit doors into snow. Fat flakes wafted softly in the misty halos of the streetlights. Outside the bells resounded in a clattering cacophony through the canyons of the buildings. Growing louder . . . louder . . . louder. Angie stared at the red emergency sign of the hospital across the street, through the madness of the swirling flakes, the bells, the sweet high sound of the hymn being drowned by bells, that glowing red sign, the cross, the snow . . . it all built to a blinding roar inside her skull . . .

Flee! . . . Uciekaj! Uciekaj!

Maddocks's voice reached her, as if from deep inside a tunnel. "What do you make of him, the celibate priest, and his relationship with Gracie, them talking about sex?"

They were walking beneath the gargoyles of Saint Jude's now toward the red hospital sign. How had they gotten here? Had they crossed the street? They were nearing the red emergency sign.

Get inside! Wskakuj do srodka, szybko!

Siedz cicho! Stay quiet!

A woman's shrill scream sliced through the noise. And everything went dead silent. Angie couldn't hear a thing. She couldn't see anything, just the red sign behind the falling flakes. She was blind. Danger. Pain. Everywhere. *They're coming . . .*

Her hand went under her coat, to her hip. With a rapid, well-rehearsed movement, she unsheathed her carbon-fiber knife, flicked it open . . . went into a crouch . . .

CHAPTER 45

Shock slammed through Maddocks. Beside him, Pallorino had frozen into a crouch, and it was as if her boots had rooted into the ground. Her complexion had turned ghost white. Her eyes, like big black holes, appeared to stare sightlessly at the hospital emergency entrance. She started to rock slowly side to side as she waved the blade of her knife in front of her.

"Pallorino?"

She shifted rapidly to face the sound of his voice, her mouth open. She was panting lightly and now brandishing the knife at him.

"Angie—you okay?"

She lunged forward with the blade, and he jerked back in surprise. "Jesus, Pallorino, what is it?"

A sheen of sweat covered her skin. Concern, worry stabbed through him.

"*Angie!* Can you hear me? Talk to me!"

She moved fast, gunning the tip of the knife straight at his gut. He grabbed her wrists, wrenching her arms to his right as he swung his body out of the way of the blade. He twisted her arms, hard. "Drop the knife!"

She yelled something unintelligible, foreign-sounding. Maddocks heaved his weight to the side while still gripping her wrists. This wrenched her off balance, and it forced her to bend at the waist. But she surprised him by suddenly moving along with his force instead of fighting it. At the same time her right elbow came up and cracked into his nose. Pain sparked through his skull. The taste of blood filled the back of his nasal passages. His eyes burned.

She broke free and jumped backward, resuming her stance. Again, she waved the knife at him, eyes wild, glittering. She now had him cornered in an alcove. She'd kill him if she could—he didn't doubt it. His mind went to his gun in its holster.

Instead, he put both palms up, eyes watering, gouts of blood gushing from his nose. At the same time he adjusted his stance so that he could go for his weapon in case he was forced to. "It's okay," he called out loudly. "It's okay. Just me. Maddocks. James Maddocks. Your partner, Angie. *Pallorino!* For Chrissakes, stand down!"

She lunged forward, swiped. The sharp tip of her blade cut through the sleeve of his thick wool coat. He used her motion to swing around and grab her again, and he smashed her shoulder-first against the stone wall, yanking her hands behind her back and twisting until her fingers released and the knife clattered to the sidewalk.

His heart thumped in his chest. He coughed and gagged, choking on his own blood. But he kept her pressed up against the wall as he groped in his pocket for plastic wrist restraints—the same kind she'd used to cuff him to the motel bed. He tightened them around her wrists, and still holding her in place, he reached down and retrieved her knife, closed the blade. He pocketed the knife, and then he took her service weapon out from her holster.

Her body began to shudder.

"Angie?" His voice was shaking. He coughed again. She turned her face sideways against the wall, as if searching for his voice.

Cautiously, he turned her body around to face him. Fear was wide in her eyes, but her pupils were going back to normal, her focus returning. She stared at his face, at the blood leaking down his front. Her gaze dropped down to her gun in his hand. Slowly, she looked up at his face again, a kind of horror entering her features. Tears began to wash down her cheeks. Her shakes turned into great big palsied shudders.

"It's okay, Angie," he said softly, pocketing her gun. "It's going to be okay." He gathered her into his arms, her hands still cuffed behind her back, his nose bleeding onto her coat, and she gave in to him, leaning herself into his body. He stroked her wet hair. "It's going to be okay." He glanced toward the emergency exit as he spoke. "Take it easy now, okay. I'm going to walk you slowly over to the hospital. We're going to get you some help."

She stiffened suddenly, and her head jerked up. "No," she whispered, voice hoarse. "No, please, not there." The wild look was starting to flood back into her eyes.

He gagged again on the blood going down the back of his throat, and he spat a gout of blood and phlegm to the ground.

"I'm not going in there," she repeated.

"Yes you are. For me. I need you in there for me, okay? I think you've broken my nose. I need your support, okay?"

"Oh God . . . fuck . . . fuck."

"Come—"

He put his arm around her shoulders and led her toward the emergency entrance to Saint Jude's.

CHAPTER 46

It was dark in the marina, apart from some strings of colored Christmas lights dotted along ropes and the light coming from cabin windows. Sleet battered down sideways, and the boats rocked on the swells surging into the small harbor, making water slap and chuckle against hulls, and halyards chink against masts.

"Careful, deck is slippery," Maddocks said as he held his arm out to Angie.

She stopped and stared at his outreached hand, suddenly overcome with a feeling that if she clasped onto that hand, it would be a point of no return. That if she allowed him to lead her down into his old, wooden-hulled yacht, she would be obligated to share with him secrets, insecurities, fears that she'd kept hidden from every single person on this earth. And it would cost her her job.

She also knew if she *didn't* go with him, it would cost her her job.

"Angie?" he said, using her first name. They were far beyond surface veneers and professional civilities now. She'd attacked and tried to kill him. She'd close to broken his nose, and it was swelling, deep-purple contusions forming beneath his eyes. And she couldn't thank him enough for not forcing her to seek medical attention herself tonight when he'd taken her into the hospital with him, for instead bringing her here, where he said he wanted to watch her while she considered her options . . .

Because you must *see someone, Angie . . . I can't work with you. I cannot trust you as a partner to have my back if you're going to flip out and try to kill me. You could be more of a danger to a partner than the bad guys you're after . . . This, I cannot let this slide—I won't.*

She inhaled and looked slowly up into his eyes, which were inky in the darkness, and she did it—she grasped his hand, stepped on board. He led her down into his cabin.

She climbed down the companionway ladder to find Jack-O curled on a little sheepskin rug in the cabin. He growled low in his throat, as if saying, *Stay in your area of the yacht and I might not attack.*

Maddocks seemed larger in the cozy confines of the main living area, which also housed a neat galley. He looked down into her eyes. His own were bloodshot above the bandage covering the bridge of his nose—it was going to take some explaining to his colleagues tomorrow. Her stomach clenched at what she'd done to him without even realizing it, and what he might tell them. "I'm so sorry," she said again.

Concern sifted into his eyes. And more. She hadn't spoken a word since they'd left Saint Jude's. He still had her knife and service weapon. On one level she'd wanted to resist him, to hate him for having seen her like this, to just walk away and pretend it had never occurred. On a more logical level, she knew that she really did need help now, and she didn't know how to go about getting it without jeopardizing her career.

"Take a seat," he said, putting on the gas heating system and opening a cupboard in the galley.

She blew out a heavy breath, pushed damp hair off her brow, and shucked off her coat. Seating herself on the bench sofa in the little living area, she removed her boots. He took out two glasses and a bottle of scotch. He poured a healthy shot of liquor into each and brought the glasses over. Jack-O watched them warily from his mat, growling again as Maddocks handed her a drink.

"Thanks." Angie had to hold the glass with both her trembling hands in order to deliver it to her lips. She managed to take a big, burning sip without spilling. She took another and closed her eyes as the alcohol went down. It settled her shakes. She opened watering eyes and looked straight up into his, which were still burning with questions, concern, compassion.

She opened her mouth to say something, then shut it again. He didn't push. Instead he removed his own coat and hung both his and hers up on hooks next to the ladder. He went back into his tiny galley, opened a container of dog biscuits, and clattered some into a bowl. He set the biscuits onto the floor next to a water bowl and gave a whistle.

Jack-O rose from his mat and scuttled over on his three legs, casting another leery glance at Angie as he did. He kept a beady eye trained on her as he crunched his doggie biscuits.

Wind gusted, the boat rocked, and halyards clattered. It felt cozy and safe inside, not at all claustrophobic as she'd anticipated. Photographs of him and Ginny covered his small fridge. Books and papers littered his dining table. He seated himself beside her and took a sip of his own drink.

"Has it happened before?" he said.

She cupped the glass between her palms, resting it on her lap. "Not like that. Never like that."

He waited.

Panic suddenly tightened, along with an urge to flee. She glanced toward the exit.

You have to face this . . .

"I've been having hallucinations, I think," she said finally. She described to him in detail the little girl in pink, where and when she'd appeared, what the child seemed to be saying and in what language. She told him about her mother's illness and that the onset of her mom's symptoms started around the same age Angie was now.

She took a sip and gave a soft snort. "I'm going crazy. There, I said it. It's my lot in life to wind up sitting in an old rocker staring at my own reflection in the locked wards of the Mount Saint Agnes Mental Health Treatment Facility, watched over by white-coated orderlies."

"So that's who you went to visit there?"

Angie nodded. Now it was out. She'd relinquished control of the information. That was the thing about secrets—you didn't tell one if you truly wanted it to be kept secret. The idea of "sharing" a secret was, to her, a joke.

He weighed her in silence, just the sound of the wind and water outside.

"It is possible that you're developing schizophrenia," he said quietly.

"Well, thanks."

He removed her drink from her grip and set both glasses on the small table in front of them. He gathered her hands in his. Gently, his thumb stroked her skin, and it sent soft strands of desire tingling to her nipples. Suddenly she ached to just fold herself into him, like a child, in a fetal position, to be held. Loved. This need to put herself into someone's care was an emotion Angie had not experienced since she was a child.

Jack-O finished his meal and came to lie at Maddocks's feet, his nose pointing toward Angie's socked feet.

"Or it could also be PTSD, Angie. That, to me, is more likely, given what you went through with Hash and that toddler—she's come back to haunt you."

"How much do you know about that incident with Hash?"

"I read the file."

"Why?"

He gave a half shrug.

"You were worried about me being your partner? Is that what you were really driving at, outside Jon Jacques's penthouse? You question my judgment because you think I could have done something to save Hash from being killed."

"On the contrary. I was intrigued about the woman who tied me to the bed at the Foxy Motel." He smiled. It didn't quite reach his eyes, and it made him wince.

"If you're trying for a joke, it's not funny."

He nodded slowly, features sobering.

"And what about the strange language, then?"

"Hmm. Have you considered that it might be related to memory, possibly buried?"

She looked away, chewing this over, running the past days over in her mind.

"Maybe the incident with Hash, PTSD, is surfacing something deeper, Angie."

"I don't know. I do think I might be remembering more of the car accident that happened when I was four. I was badly injured. Almost died."

"The scar on your mouth?"

She nodded.

"Tell me about it."

She explained the story. Italy. Her dad's sabbatical. "But looking at the photos, something about the timing seems off." She described to him about the dates inscribed on the backs of the Italy photos, the discrepancies she'd discovered. Then she mentioned her mother's strange comments about angels, and how "Angie" was returned on a Christmas Eve when it was snowing, and how badly she'd been shaken when her mother had started to sing "Ave Maria" in a soft mezzo-soprano.

His eyes narrowed. "So all these triggers came together in a convergence tonight? Is that what happened? The cathedral, the bells, the season being Christmas, the fact it had started snowing, the boy singing the same hymn as your mom?"

She heaved out a chestful of air and rubbed her face. "I guess. I . . . I felt panic. Terror, even, when I . . . we came out. I saw the red emergency entrance sign, and then I don't recall what happened next."

He snorted. "You tried to kill me, that's what."

"I'm sorry. I'm a fuckup." She reached for her glass and swigged back a gulp of scotch.

"You do need to talk to someone, Angie, a professional—"

"And lose my job when Metro PD discovers I'm some crackpot?"

He held her gaze, and she read the unspoken words in his eyes: *You're not safe to do the job while you* are *some crackpot.*

"You owe it to yourself," he said quietly. "And to everyone who might work with you in a high-risk situation."

Hearing him voice it again made her feel sick to her stomach. She was a liability. To herself. To others. She could have killed him.

He cupped her face. Gently, he thumbed her lip, her scar. "It might be quite simple, Angie," he said. "Memories—that's all it might be. Things you might have repressed as a kid. Something around the accident coming out now because of a convergence of circumstances that are stressful. Like your mother being admitted. Hash and the toddler dying on your watch. This Baptist case. They're triggers."

"And the girl in pink?"

"You said she has long red hair. Maybe she's some externalized version of yourself at an age where you experienced the violent accident. Maybe extrapolated with Tiffany."

"And the Polish language?" she said again.

"Again, maybe something locked in your memory. You yelled at me in what sounded like a foreign language outside the hospital. It could have been Polish."

She closed her eyes and yielded to the sensation of his caress on her face, the feel of his solidity beside her. The sense of cocooned comfort inside his boat. Even his gnarly little rescue dog had decided to nudge his nose up against her socked foot now, and it was snoring in an ugly little fashion that somehow relaxed her.

"What if I learn that I've inherited my mother's illness?"

"Then you need to know. Either way. Because as you mentioned, your mother apparently managed it for years, and you can get treatment, manage it, too."

"I'd have to quit being a cop."

"Being a cop is not what it's cracked up to be. Look at what it did to my life."

She glanced around the interior of his yacht, this testimony to his solo existence. She thought of him trying to repair this old boat, to somehow mend his old dreams of family, retirement. Her gaze went to the pics of him and Ginny stuck to his little fridge, and her heart opened big and sudden to this man. She fingered his ring. He looked down and watched her doing it. In silence, he withdrew his hand and removed the gold band. He set it on the table next to his glass, and his gaze met hers. She swallowed.

He leaned in and kissed her.

The touch of his lips against hers was soft, seductive, the stubble on his jaw rough against her skin as his mouth opened hers, and the tip of his tongue explored her scar, caressing it. She placed her hand against the side of his face, careful not to hurt his injuries, and she leaned back, angling for a deeper kiss. He began to undo the buttons of her shirt as his mouth moved over hers. He slid the fabric off her shoulders. She reached behind her back to unclasp her bra. Her breasts swelled free, and his breath caught in his throat.

"Come," he murmured against her mouth as he cupped her breast with his rough hand. "Come to my bed."

CHAPTER 47

Naked, Angie sat on the edge of the bed, Maddocks standing between her legs while she undid his pants, a lust building, boiling, deep inside her. She slid his pants down his hips and that gorgeous dick swelled free. She caressed him, taking him into her mouth, holding his hips as she worked him with her lips, her tongue. His hands clamped down hard on her shoulders, his fingers digging deeper and deeper into her skin as she stimulated him to the point that he groaned, fisting her hair. He stopped her suddenly, pulling her off his wet erection by moving her head back. His gaze, dark, dangerous, locked with hers, and he shoved her backward and hard onto the covers.

She fell back with a bounce against the mattress, hair spreading in a wild tangle around her head, thighs open. She ached for him. Was so ready for him. She raised her hips to him. Slowly—painfully slowly—he raked his gaze down the length of her body. He swallowed, his indigo eyes turning black with lust above his bandage, his carotid fluttering fast at his neck. She rotated her hips slightly in a come-hither-I-want-you gesture, burning for his penetration, to feel his length plunging deep inside her, his width stretching her. A slight smile of appreciation played over his lips. But he took his sweet time, reaching for his pants on the floor and taking a condom from a pocket.

Angie watched him sheath himself, and a slight unease began to whisper along the distant fringes of her consciousness. It was always she who brought a condom, rolled it on. But he had his own, in his pocket, and while that shouldn't really mean anything to her, it robbed her sense of being absolutely in control. He knelt over her, hands on either side of her head, and with his knees he widened her thighs as he lowered his mouth to her throat, licking, teasing, working his way down toward her left nipple. It tightened with exquisite sensitivity as he took the tip between his teeth. Heat snaked through her. Blood pulsed like molten fire into her groin, swelling her labia, making her clit hard and erect, tingling for his touch. He moved his mouth lower, down her belly, flicking his tongue into her navel, lower, down between her legs. His tongue, warm, wet, slicked in between her folds and encircled her clit. He nipped lightly with his teeth, pulling on the nub. A silent scream, a pressure, built inside her chest, inside her head, inside her vagina, and she felt as though she would explode as her vision, her entire world narrowed to just this moment, to him, on this boat, this bed. She opened her legs as wide as she could, arching her spine, lifting herself to him as his tongue sought deeper entry to her vagina, slipping in and out. She closed her eyes, rolling her head from side to side, moaning until she couldn't take it any longer. She needed the hardness of him, deep. She needed to fuck him, hard. In rising desperation, her body going slick with sweat, her muscles starting to shake, she moved her arms under his armpits, drawing his head out from between her thighs, and she raised her right knee, bringing her inner thigh up his hip as she twisted her body at the waist, struggling to flip him over onto his back so that she could straddle him and sink herself down onto the hot length of him, rock and rub her clit against the coarse hair of his groin, feel the delicious friction that she recalled from the night in the club. But he resisted her.

Instead, he grabbed her wrists and pinned her hands high above her head as he kneed her open even wider and put just the tip of his erection inside her. Angie stilled. Her heart jackhammered. Her breaths came light and fast and dizzying. He had her totally exposed. She wriggled, trying to free her hands, but he was strong. Far stronger than she was, than she could ever be. Angie closed her eyes, the sound of her blood booming against her eardrums, a cocktail of conflicted emotions suddenly raging like a cracking wildfire through her—submit, she told herself. It felt good. She wanted this.

He moved slowly at first, achingly slowly, and a tension of another kind built inside her as she wiggled to free her hands again but couldn't. And her eyes flared wide. She was struggling to breathe.

He gave a powerful thrust, and he was inside her, up to the hilt. She gasped, and he moved his hips harder, driving himself yet deeper. Her eyes watered as he began to fuck her, his heavy, muscled build pumping her deep into the bedding, her hands trapped high above her head. She was coming close. Yet fear also continued to build in her chest. Desperate, she fought him again, writhing wildly to free her hands, bucking under him, heat rising, tears building in her eyes, and he took it as pleasure, as mad hunger, and he thrust harder to meet her struggle, a low groan building in his chest, sweat breaking out over his body.

"Stop," she whispered suddenly. "Stop. *Stop!*" He stilled, and his eyes met hers, dark and wild. Confusion chased through his face. His erection was quivering inside her.

"Please, Maddocks," she whispered. "Please." He swallowed, his muscles beginning to shake against his battle to suddenly control himself, sweat slicking over his skin, and suddenly he gasped, and came powerfully, uncontrollably, inside her, his fingers digging into her flesh as his body took charge, shuddering him inside her. Tears filled her eyes as Maddocks, spent, lowered himself slowly down onto her, then rolled onto his side, withdrawing from inside her.

"Angie?" he whispered, his eyes refocusing.

Tears leaked out from the corners of her eyes, onto his covers. And she still ached with desire, and she felt shame, defeat, guilt. He stroked her cheek and moved a damp tangle of hair off her face. "Did I hurt you? What is it?"

She shook her head, unable to voice it, unable to tell him what was going on, unable to understand herself. And she was filled with embarrassment.

"I'm sorry," he murmured. "So sorry."

She shook her head again, wanting to say, *It's me. Not you. You're beautiful.* But emotion choked her attempt to speak, and she could see the hurt, the disappointment in his eyes. He leaned over and kissed her gently on the lips, then clicked off the bedside light. In the darkness he brought the covers over them both. And he simply held her, spooning her, as the boat rocked in the mounting wind, Jack-O snoring on his little mat in the cabin.

CHAPTER 48

Angie surfaced as if from a black swamp of molasses. The little girl was running through the blackness in a glow of pink, feet bare, hair flowing. She had a basket in her hand this time. There were trees suddenly, tall, reaching way, way up into the sky, and dappled light came through the leaves to make gold shapes on soft spring grass, and there were dandelions. They were in Italy, there was Rome, the shining ocean, yellow sunshine, and rolling Tuscan hills. Then the sky turned to ink. Sounds of a car crashing, the sensation of it rolling seized her. She struggled to get out of the crushing metal, away from the screaming . . . her mother's voice. *Flee! Get inside! No. Get out!* Fighting, she battled up to the surface of consciousness, and her eyes fluttered open.

A dream. Just a dream.

She was lying on something that was rocking slightly. The scent of fresh coffee reached her.

Shock slammed through her. *Cabin. Maddocks. Boat.*

Sex.

Oh Jesus. She sat bolt upright. The dog was sleeping on the covers near her feet. It looked up at her with little liquid-brown eyes. She stared into those doggie eyes, feeling every bit the wretched stray. She was another Jack-O, a broken thing that James Maddocks had peeled off the metaphorical road. Tentatively, she reached out, touched the animal's head. The fur was surprisingly soft. She smoothed it, and he did not growl. Jack-O just closed his eyes with a little sigh and dropped his head back onto the covers. It sent a funny punch to her gut.

Her attention moved toward the warm band of light seeping in through the partially open cabin door. She could hear him, Maddocks, knocking about in his tiny yacht galley. She could hear the wind still hammering, lashing at halyards and lines, sending in swells that rocked and smacked at the hull. Through the little porthole window she could see it was still dark.

Her attention flared to the clock. The digital glow showed 5:55 a.m. Friday. Work. She—they—needed to get to the station. Gathering her clothes up from the floor, Angie dressed quickly. She tied her hair back and entered the small living and galley area. Maddocks had his back to her. He was dressed in his work pants, shirt. A tie.

He turned. "Hey." A smile creased his gorgeous face, and then he winced again. Angie's remorse, shame, self-hatred—fear—was instant at the sight of the bandage still plastered across the bridge of his nose, the black-and-purple contusions below his eyes.

"Coffee?"

"I'd kill for some, thanks."

"Please don't," he said, deepening his smile, then wincing once more as it pulled at his swollen face. He turned, reached for a mug, poured. "How do you take it?"

Never sleep with a colleague.

Never kiss.

Leave first. Leave early. No names. Never stay the night. Never break-fast the next morning. Never take one that makes you feel vulnerable in any way . . . Always stay in control . . .

"Actually," she said quickly, "I think I'm good." She reached for her boots, sat, began tugging them on.

"What about coffee?" He stood there with the steaming mug in his hand.

She came to her feet, snagged her coat off the hook. "I'll grab some on my way."

"Angie?"

She stilled at his tone, the gravity in his eyes.

"Where do think you're going?"

"Home. Shower, change. Work." She remembered suddenly that he'd taken her service weapon. Her knife. His gaze remained locked with hers. Silence swelled between them, highlighting the outside noises of the marina, the engine of a boat chugging out to sea.

"No," he said quietly.

She stared, her heart beginning to race.

"We spoke about this, remember?"

Shit. This was real. She glanced toward the portlight above his tiny sink. A dull gray dawn was seeping into the darkness. She dragged her hand over her hair, smoothing her ponytail.

"Angie, look at me."

She inhaled deeply, then finally met his eyes.

"Call in sick. Take some time off. Go see someone."

"I can't just call in sick. The case—"

"I'm giving you two options, Pallorino. Call in sick, and see a professional. Or try to come in, and I'll have to hand over your service weapon and report what happened."

She glowered at him, tension thrumming into her body, her hands tightening at her sides.

"I don't want you on my team right now. On anybody's team."

Heat seared into her face as she focused on his bruised and bandaged one. The impact of what she'd done to him was undeniable. And she realized, as much as she wanted it to all just go away, to pretend it never happened, she couldn't shove it under the rug this time. He'd have to go in to work and offer some explanation as to what had happened to his face.

"Don't push me, Angie. Don't make me report this." He paused. "Let me help you."

So he was going to hide it, for now? He was going to make up some story for her?

"Why?" she said quietly. "Why are you doing this for me—risking things?"

He was silent a long while. Wind gusted, sending a clatter of raindrops against the thick glass of the portlight.

"Because I care," he said, in slow, measured words. As if working this out for himself. There was a sincerity in his tone that made her heart gallop up into her throat. She wasn't worthy of this. Of him.

Uciekaj! Run . . .

She could not handle it. Didn't want it. Him. Wanted independence. The panic noose tightened. She moistened her lips, turned her back to him, hesitated, then climbed the small ladder up to the companionway and pushed out of the doors onto the dark, wet deck. Angie wavered for a moment as the freezing rain spat against her face. Then she climbed overboard and made her way along the dock in the dark gray dawn, leaving him standing there in the warm galley with her coffee mug in his hand. And inside she was shaking.

CHAPTER 49

"So, like, where's Pallorino?"

Maddocks glanced up from his metal desk in the incident room. In front of him stood Kjel Holgersen wearing his narrow-legged, dirty-gray jeans that bagged around his skinny ass in that supposedly fashionable way. Even in stillness the man appeared fidgety.

"What?" Maddocks said, irritated at the interruption. He'd come in early to work on his notes from the Drummond funeral observation and the Father Simon interview. The priest had revealed something potentially key about Gracie Drummond's promiscuity. He was also trying to focus on work instead of Angie.

Holgersen took a small step backward as Maddocks raised his head from his work. "Jesus, man. What in the hells happened to your face—your nose? You look like shit."

"Yacht lines came loose in the storm last night—boom swung round in the wind, smacked me in the face while I was slipping around in the snow and seawater on deck in the dark trying to resecure things."

Holgersen regarded him in silence for several beats.

Maddocks met the detective's gaze square, unblinking, despite the throbbing pain in his face and his watering eyes. Given Holgersen's opening question about Angie, he was fishing for something and was reading him for tells. There was a reason this guy came highly recommended despite his oddities—he was sharp. He had an uncanny read on people, and most tended to underestimate him because of his speech, his dress, his quirky body language. And Maddocks was fast learning that this was Kjel Holgersen's advantage—and possibly he riffed off it to set people off-kilter.

"What's up your butt, Detective?" Maddocks said smoothly. "Can't you see I'm busy?"

Holgersen reached into his breast pocket, pulled out a packet of nicotine chewing gum. "I's said, where's Pallorino?"

"I don't know." Maddocks returned his attention to his notes. But his pulse had quickened. Holgersen remained there, making a crackling noise as he struggled to pop a square of gum out of its cellophane packaging.

"Christ, Holgersen," he said, looking up again. "What do you want? I need to get these notes wrapped before Buziak's a.m. briefing."

He freed the tablet of green gum from its cellophane prison, grinned, and popped it into his mouth. He started to chew as he dragged a chair up to the side of Maddocks's desk. He seated himself, pointed to his mouth. "Not giving up the smokes, just sos you knows. But the gum fix keeps me calm when I can't have a cigarette indoors. Been trying it out since Wednesday."

Two detectives entered the incident room along with the scent of the fresh coffees they were carrying.

Holgersen lowered his voice. "I phoned her. She didn't pick up."

Maddocks shrugged and returned to his notes one more time. But his shoulders were tensing.

"Like, several times."

"Okay, Jesus." Maddocks slapped down his pen and sat erect. "You're pissing me off now. It's early, okay. Maybe she doesn't want to take your call. Maybe she's in the damn shower. So wait for her to come in."

He smoothed his goatee, his twitchy, dull-brown eyes fixed on Maddocks's face.

"I heard she called in sick today," he said.

"Where'd you hear that?"

Holgersen's gaze twitched toward the two detectives who were now conversing in the far corner with another two investigators who'd also entered the room. He lowered his voice further. "Overheard Fitz talking to one of them suits from internal. They was inside Buziak's office. I figure from what Fitz was saying that he's gunning for Pallorino as the deep throat, and he wants her badge. And I's just wanting to be warning her about it. Funny thing—Buziak was not in his office. Just the inspector and the suit. Maybe Buze called in sick, too. Maybe something went down at that late-night meeting he was called into when we was all drinking and celebrating at the Pig."

Maddocks felt blood drain from his face and anger rise in his chest. "You and Leo cook this up? He trying to mess with Pallorino again?"

Holgersen snorted and was about to speak when the incident room door burst wide open.

"Sergeant Maddocks?" Inspector Frank Fitzsimmons called out in his scratchy, high-pitched voice, his hand on the door handle. Behind him loomed a skinny man in a bad suit—someone Maddocks did not recognize. "A word in my office, please, Sergeant?"

All attention in the room swung onto Maddocks and his bruised and bandaged face. His stomach muscles tensed.

"What I freaking tell you, man?" Holgersen muttered as Maddocks pushed back his seat, came to his feet, and smoothed down his tie.

"Good luck," Holgersen said, standing up himself.

Then, as Maddocks started toward the door, Holgersen murmured under his breath, "Guess Leo was also smacked by a boom Wednesday night, eh?"

And it struck Maddocks like a bolt—*Holgersen had seen Angie, him, and Leo fighting outside the Flying Pig*. He'd probably been lurking under the eaves, out of the rain, smoking in the dark shadows. He'd seen him and Angie kiss.

And he was warning Maddocks, too, not just Angie, that maybe the information was out there. And was going to be used.

Or was he playing some other dark game entirely?

CHAPTER 50

"This is Sergeant Charles Tillerman from internal," Fitz said, holding his tie against his stomach as he bent to take the seat behind his desk. Tillerman seated himself to Fitz's side. Maddocks took the lone remaining chair, positioned directly in front of Fitz's desk.

Fitz had shut the door behind them. Blinds were drawn against observation from the bullpens.

"Tillerman was originally Vancouver PD," Fitz offered. "Maybe you two knew of each other, given you both worked the greater Vancouver area."

"I was RCMP, integrated homicide, and while iHit does partner with VPD, we have not met." He glanced at Tillerman, who sat stony-faced and still.

"I see," Fitz said in his reedy voice, and Maddocks sensed he was being played, measured. His walls of caution went up higher. Silently, he half-thanked Holgersen for the warning, if that's what it was.

"What happened to your face, Sergeant Maddocks?" Fitz said.

He repeated the boom story.

"I see."

Maddocks waited in silence. People underrated silence.

Fitz cleared his throat. "And your partner, Detective Pallorino, she called in sick today?"

Tension ratcheted higher. "I've not yet been informed."

"Food poisoning." He waved his hand. "Or some such. Left a message on Sergeant Buziak's phone."

"I see," Maddocks said, mirroring Fitz, whose eyes flickered.

"Sir, all due respect, but if you could let me know why I'm here, I could expedite things for you. Otherwise, I need to be ready to present my aspect of the investigation at Buziak's briefing." He glanced at his wristwatch. "In six minutes."

"Yes. Well." Fitz rubbed his chin. "You, with Detective Pallorino on occasion, have been having private meetings with Buziak. Apart from the task force team."

Leo, Maddocks thought. It had to be him—Leo had opened the door on the three of them once.

"Correct. If that's all?" Maddocks made to get up.

Fitz raised his palm, motioning him to remain seated. "What was the subject of these private meetings?"

Maddocks met Fitz's beady eyes. "Again, due respect, sir, but why am I being asked these questions in front of an internal investigations officer when you could ask my superior, Buziak, himself? Unless of course I'm under investigation, in which case, I'd—"

"Oh no, no. Nothing at all like that." He flashed a tight smile. "I called you in because I'd like you to take over Sergeant Buziak's briefing this morning."

"Excuse me?"

Fitz leaned forward and clasped his hands atop his desk blotter. "In fact, I'd like to offer you the position as temporary task force lead."

"Where's Buziak?"

Fitz glanced at Tillerman. The man remained poker-faced but gave a small nod. Fitz continued. "Sergeant Buziak is on a temporary leave of absence pending the outcome of an aspect of the internal investigation."

"You think *he's* the deep throat? Giving away details of his own case?"

Fitz rubbed the side of his beaky nose. "Confidentially, there is . . . how shall we say . . . possible internal collusion occurring among old-guard MVPD officers to undermine the organization."

"A conspiracy?"

Silence.

Jesus.

"Additionally, we'd like you to formally evaluate Detective Pallorino's performance over the next few weeks, as she continues to work under you. We'd like a fortnightly briefing. Here in my office. She's had performance issues, including an incident that resulted in the recent death of her senior partner. Sergeant Hash Hashowsky was one of our longest-serving, most highly respected, and well-liked detectives. I called him a friend."

So *that* was Fitz's motive? He was a revenge guy—he blamed Angie for Hash's death. As Leo did. And some others. And Fitz wanted payback. He was taking her down, vigilante style, however he could, and he was going to use this internal investigation—and Maddocks himself— to find something, anything, he could use against Angie.

This was nothing like Buziak asking Maddocks to informally evaluate Angie for possible inclusion into the homicide unit. It was retribution. Unjustified. And possibly misogynistic to the core.

No wonder she was paranoid. She had reason. No wonder she was fighting that psych eval.

This guy was a viper.

Maddocks cleared his throat and said dispassionately, "I understood Pallorino was cleared of any breach of MVPD protocol."

"Officially." Fitz moistened his lips. "However, there remains contention that Detective Pallorino, a less experienced and junior investigative officer, made errors of judgment under stress, which cost her partner's life."

Shit.

If they now discovered that he was hiding Angie's recent breakdown on the job, covering for her . . . if they learned that he'd confiscated her knife and service weapon for fear that she'd kill him—yet another one of her partners—or use it on someone else . . . Conflict, sharp, stabbed down through his insides. With it came a fierce stab of protectiveness, a determination to stand by her. And it was coupled with pure-white hatred for this beaky, squeaky, reedy, ball-less, insecure little man who had a penchant for titles and couldn't just call anyone by their names. He needed to contact Angie. Stat. Tell her to sort herself and get back in here before Tillerman came looking for her. And nailed *him* in the process, too.

"Acceptable to you?" Fitz said. "To take over from Buziak until further course of action is determined? Salary, of course, shall be commensurate. Your résumé shows that you successfully assumed similar administrative roles in the past, within a larger force, and have worked on serial cases. You're ideally suited." He flashed another quick smile.

Maddocks's brain reeled as it weighed possible avenues of action, searching for ways out. This man was dangerous. He'd probably never trusted a soul in his life. The guys on the Limpet team were going to resent Maddocks, the new guy on the block, stepping into Buziak's shoes ahead of any one of them. For being in bed with Inspector Frank Fitzsimmons and internal. Christ . . . and then there was him being asked to spy on Angie, the woman he'd been sleeping with and for whom he was covering . . . talk about a no-win situation.

"Or . . . is there something I should know about?"

"Acceptable," Maddocks said, standing up. "If you'll excuse me, I need to get down to take over that briefing."

"Good, good. Pending outcome, there's always a potential for the position to become more permanent. I think we will work well together."

"Sir," Maddocks said with a benign nod. He made for the door. But just before leaving, he turned and said, "One condition. I'm not exclusively a pen pusher. I go out into the field with officers, as warranted. I get a better handle on my team that way."

Fitz's beady eyes bored into him for a moment too long. "Fine," he said slowly. "Sergeant Tillerman and I will see you again in this office in two weeks, seven a.m., for your first report on Detective Pallorino. Unless, of course, something arises that needs to be brought to our attention earlier."

"One other thing," Maddocks said. "I'll need you to announce the news to the team about Buziak, and to introduce me as a temporary stand-in until he returns. I'll delay the briefing by forty-five minutes so we can both prepare." He waited a beat, watching Fitz's features. "The news would be better received coming from you, sir. I need the support of the Limpet investigators."

"Fair enough. Oh, before you go—there was a BOLO put out on the black Lexus, which was found to be registered to developer Ray Norton-Wells, husband of the assistant deputy attorney general."

"Correct."

"And the Lexus has since been reported to have been stolen."

Maddocks felt his bile rise. He suddenly saw where this was going. "Yes."

"We're after that thief, Sergeant Maddocks. This has nothing to do with Ray Norton-Wells or his family. Correct?"

Maddocks's gaze bored back into those beady black hawk eyes. "There are sensitive aspects to the investigation, yes. Hence our closed-door meetings, especially given that we still have a leak."

"Hmm. I see. Well, let's keep those doors closed, then, shall we? And nothing happens on that front without my say. Understood?"

"I see," Maddocks said. He exited, shut the door quietly behind him, took a deep breath, then strode fast toward the fire escape stairwell.

As he took the stairs down to the bowels of the station two at a time, he dialed Angie.

She did not pick up. His call went to voicemail.

At the bottom of the concrete stairwell, he tried again.

Voicemail. He hesitated before wording his message, acutely aware now that he was using a police-issue phone and was probably under scrutiny himself, he said, "Pallorino, it's Sergeant Maddocks. I heard you called in sick. Check in and update me as soon as you are able."

CHAPTER 51

Angie's lungs burned raw as she thumped on her treadmill, feet pounding, arms pumping, sweat soaking her shirt. She was about six klicks into her run, hadn't dropped the pace for an instant.

Her mind looped back to Gracie Drummond, Faith Hocking, how she'd been forced to call in sick, how she was locked out of one of the biggest investigations at the MVPD, and what this mess in her head was going to mean for her in the long run. She could only imagine what Leo and Holgersen and the others were speculating, because only once before in her career had she been too sick to come into work, and that was the day after Hash died. And it was only for a day.

Run. Flee. Run . . . uciekaj, uciekaj . . .

She hit the speed button, making the tread move yet faster as she tried to outrace those wretched Polish words which she could not put into context.

Her phone rang again on the kitchen counter, and she slowed the machine gradually, sweat burning into her eyes. She dropped to a walking pace. Her calves ached. Her hips hurt. Her shoulders were painfully tight. Angie stepped off the treadmill and snagged her phone from the kitchen counter and checked the last incoming number.

Maddocks again.

She *couldn't* speak to him—not until she'd figured this out and gotten her narrative all straight in her head.

The earlier calls had been from Holgersen. Not on her life was she going to talk to him, either. She'd left a message on Buziak's phone, calling in sick, and that was it.

She shut her phone off and got back onto her treadmill, ramping up the speed quickly, and this time also increasing the incline. She went faster and faster. Higher. She felt like she was going to throw up. And went yet harder. Steeper.

Nausea washed through her and up into her throat. Struggling to keep down her stomach contents, she jumped off the treadmill and staggered to the bathroom. She clasped her hands on the sides of her toilet bowl, hanging her head down, gagging.

How much more could she push?

How had she come to this place?

When had it actually all started?

What all was she in self-denial about?

She cursed and gave another dry retch. She hurt. Bad. Physically. Mentally. Emotionally—deep inside her heart. It pained her to think about her mom. And her dad so alone. Hash, gone. She thought about what she'd done to Maddocks—how close she'd come to killing or critically injuring him. She couldn't do this anymore—she could no longer try to numb this shit with the chilled vodka in her freezer or mindless fucks at the club.

She owed Maddocks, too. And he was now the gatekeeper to her job, her continued involvement in the investigation, and it was killing her to be cut out of it. Policing was her life. Pure and simple.

Angie pushed herself upright from the toilet bowl and hobbled over to her sliding glass door that looked out over the Gorge. She opened it and stepped out into the cold air on her tiny balcony. Gripping the railing, she turned her face up toward the pale winter sun and closed her eyes.

Slowly, in the warming sun, listening to the sounds of the city and the waterway below—boats coming in, gulls squabbling, the *keeee* of an eagle up high, the blare of horns, the yells of coxswains giving orders to shells filled with rowers—she realized this was it.

She wanted to live. Really live. Be alive in this city. Be present.

She wanted her job.

And right now she was on the cusp of losing everything. Angie wiped the sweat from her brow, returned inside, and rummaged around in a desk drawer. She found what she was searching for. An old business card. She powered up her phone and punched in the number on the card, wondering if it would still work.

Angie tensed as it began to ring. She paced up and down her tiny apartment, trying to distract herself with the pain in her body. Her call connected. She caught her breath.

"Hello?" came the male voice.

For a second words eluded her. Then she cleared her throat. "Alex? Hey. It's Angie. Angie Pallorino."

"Angie . . . *Pallorino?* Christ." A pause. "How long has it been? How in the hell *are* you?"

"Got time for an old friend?" she said.

"Always." Another moment of hesitation. "Professional or personal?"

"I . . . maybe a bit of both. I don't know yet. I . . . just need to talk to someone, sound something out."

"Want to come to my home office? I'm out of town at the moment, but I'll be back tomorrow."

"Tomorrow morning would be good."

"I can manage early afternoon. How does two thirty sound? I'll have a pot of tea waiting. Like old times."

She smiled, fond memories of her old psychology professor—mentor, academic advisor, and friend—resurfacing, the copious

336

amounts of Darjeeling, Earl Grey, and Ceylon tea consumed during vigorous debates. "You still at the same address?" she said.

"Same cottage. James Bay. See you then."

"Thanks, Alex." She killed the call. Her heart felt lighter.

She'd taken the first step.

CHAPTER 52

The briefing this morning had gone as Maddocks had expected. A chilly reception to the news of Buziak. Mistrust for him. Audible grumblings from Leo. A sullen mood all around as the investigators headed out on their assignments for the day. Their only consolation was probably the fact that it would be Maddocks—the new guy—who went down as the scapegoat if they all failed spectacularly in their hunt to catch this killer before Christmas.

This witch hunt of Fitz's was wreaking the expected damage. The case was stalling because of it. Plus there remained a suspected deep throat among them—Maddocks wasn't buying that it was Buziak. Or some old-guard Gunnar-supporting conspiracy. Why would the old guard want to leak information that was politically damaging to Gunnar and feeding into Mayor Killion's clean-sweep-the-old-guard threats?

Add to this Maddocks's Gordian knot of conflicts over Angie and his problems on the home front with Ginny, and he was not a happy camper when he entered the forensics lab late on Friday evening. Head forensic technician Dr. Sunni Padachaya had agreed to meet with him at this late hour to discuss the forensics results that had come in for the hair trace found primarily in the ropes on Thetisby Island.

Maddocks pushed open the door. The place was empty at this hour, apart from a slight, dark-skinned woman in a lab coat hunched over a microscope at a bench on the far end of the room. She looked up as he entered, and smiled.

"Detective Maddocks," she said, coming to her feet and making her way over to him. And yeah, maybe it was because of her sunshiny-sounding name, or because of the genuineness in her smile and the subsequent light it put into her liquid black eyes, or how comical the scientist looked in the translucent blue shower-cap-style protection covering her black hair, but he felt himself returning her smile. This little scientist came with a sterling rep and was far younger than he'd expected.

"Thank you for staying late to walk me through the analysis," he said. "I'd shake your hand, but—" He nodded to her latex gloves.

"No worries. I always stay late. No life, obviously." She peeled off the gloves as she spoke and dumped them in a bin. "Come take a look."

She led him over to a light board onto which had been mounted enlarged images of hair shafts taken under the microscope.

She clicked on the light, bringing the images to vivid life.

"Since there is such a wide range of interpersonal variation in head and pubic hairs," she said, "most of the work in forensics to date has been in that area." She picked up a pointer. "However, we can also tell which parts of the body other hairs originated from, using general morphology—length, shape, size, color, stiffness, curliness, and microscopic appearance all contribute to the determination of body area. So does pigmentation and medullar appearance.

"So, here we've grouped the various sets of hair evidence under *Black-Haired Male One*—" She pointed. "*Black-Haired Male Two*. And *Blond Male* there."

"And that grouping over there?" Maddocks pointed to slides showing reddish-brown shafts.

"That's *Female Brunette*. She's a DNA match to Faith Hocking—so we'll just refer to her grouping as *Hocking*."

"Gotcha. And these are all from the Thetisby scene?"

"I'll get to that." She grinned like a little Cheshire cat, and he sensed she was going to save the prize for last. Maddocks liked her on the spot.

"'Kay, *Black-Haired Male One*—" She indicated the first set of images with her stick. "We've got head hair, body hair, pubic hair. *Black-Haired Male Two*. Similar set—pubic, head, body. *Blond Male*. Head only."

"All Caucasoid?"

"Correct."

"Now, these are the head hairs—usually the longest hairs on the human body." She motioned to the head hairs in all the groupings. "See how they're characterized as having a uniform diameter and, in these images over here, a cut tip?"

Maddocks nodded.

"Most of these head hairs have been forcibly removed. Hair that falls out naturally has a club-shaped root, like this one, here. But these others are stretched at the root area and have follicular tissue attached."

Which could indicate an altercation, Maddocks thought, or perhaps just hair getting caught up in rough rope strands while tying knots.

"These are the body hairs." She tapped the various slides in the *Black-Haired Male One* and *Black-Haired Male Two* groupings. "And these are pubic—generally coarse and wiry in appearance. They exhibit considerable diameter variation, or buckling, and often have a continuous to discontinuous medulla, which is the type of hair core. All of these pubic hairs have been forcibly removed and have follicular tissue attached."

"As in, from friction during rough sexual intercourse."

"That would have to be your determination, Detective. I'm just the scientist telling you what I see."

Yeah, he liked this little Sunni scientist. She was making his crap day feel just a tad brighter, and scientist or not, she was building his anticipation like a master storyteller.

"*Hocking.* Pubic trace from the floor in the cellar, here." She tapped her pointer on the slides. "Head hair evidence from the ropes, here. All forcibly removed. Evidence of chemical treatment on the head hair—she colored her hair a slightly darker shade."

Padachaya moved to the adjacent light board and clicked that one on, too. "So here we have the DNA profile of *Black-Haired Male One* and *Black-Haired Male Two.*"

"Bottom line?"

"Lay speak, bottom line—both *Black-Haired Male One* and *Black-Haired Male Two* DNA are a match to the two sets of postmortem hair trace found on Hocking's body—from pubic combings and from inside her tarp wrapping." She glanced up at Maddocks, a glint in her dark eyes. "And the DNA profile of *Black-Haired Male One* is a match to several hairs found on Gracie Drummond's clothing."

He whistled softly. "Nice work, Dr. Padachaya. You've just linked *Black-Haired Male One* to both homicide victims."

She laughed. "Please, call me Sunni. Everyone does. And it's my team you can thank—just doing their jobs."

Maddocks peered more closely at the hair images. "And from the looks of things—if those male pubic hairs were obtained from Hocking's pubic combings, both black-haired men potentially engaged in intercourse with Hocking."

"Pubic contact and probably rough friction in order to forcibly remove the hairs, at the least," she said.

"And Mr. Blond Male, he's not connected?"

Silence.

He turned and looked down at her. Maddocks's pulse quickened at the look on her features. "Okay, Doc, spit it out—what have you been withholding to the last?"

"He's a match to the semen DNA from the used condom. Hocking's DNA is also on the condom. Plus, techs found one of his blond head hairs on the exterior of Drummond's coat."

He stared at her, his brain spinning. "Holy cluster—"

"I know."

"Three men. One blond, two dark," he said quietly, staring at the slides on the board. "With the DNA profiles of Mr. Blond and Mr. Black One connected to both homicide victims."

"And so far," she said, "we still have no matches to any known subjects for those three unknown male profiles—nothing in the National DNA Data Bank, CODIS—they're not in the system."

Maddocks's mind turned to Jayden Norton-Wells, Zach Raddison—black hair. Jon Jacques Junior and Senior—both blond. Tension and adrenaline twisted through him. They needed DNA samples from those men. To rule them in or out.

But they still had no new evidence that would give them RPG—reasonable and probable grounds—for a DNA seizure warrant. They needed to find something that would show a judge that one of those men probably committed the designated offense or offenses. Or was party to the offense. *That* was their stumbling block right now. That was what they needed. They were a long way off.

"I owe you, Sunni," he said.

"I'll hold you to that, Detective." She grinned again.

CHAPTER 53

Merry shifted to ease the cramps seizing her leg, grateful for her down jacket and toque. While the clear Friday night was great for visibility, it meant cold.

The pregnant moon was waxing. It shone a path like beaten metal over the sea, and it made the white yachts in the marina gleam eerily. Zooming in with her telephoto lens, she clicked off another rapid series of shots, making sure she captured the name of the luxury mega-yacht clearly—the *Amanda Rose*—and the flags she was flying.

There was a fair bit of activity on board the big vessel—the silhouettes of people moving across the lighted windows, some occasionally filtering out onto the deck to smoke, cigarette ends flaring bright orange in the dark as they lit up or inhaled. Faint strains of music and snatches of laughter trailed up to where she squatted between a Dodge truck and a Kia Sorento parked along the road that curved around the northeast end of the small bay. Her VW Bug was parked just a few cars down, on the opposite side of the street, but she had a better sightline from here.

Action seemed to quiet down as the minutes ticked past midnight and into Saturday morning. Cold was crawling deep into her bones now. This must be what cops felt like on stakeouts. Hours of nothing, just waiting, getting cramps. Her mind went back to the altercation this afternoon, when she'd gone to find Damián Yorick.

Damián was the pimp Nina reported having seen Faith with some months ago. Merry had gone to ask Damián about the blond guy with the Bimmer.

She was with that pimp of hers from way back, Damián, and some other blond guy—rich prick who was driving a small, black BMW. Young, like in his twenties . . .

Damián, however, claimed to Merry that he hadn't seen Faith in almost two years. It was a lie. She'd believe Nina over that bastard pimp any day. She'd confronted him over his lie. The argument replayed in her head as she watched the *Amanda Rose.*

You fuck the hell out of my business, you little meth-head whore. You wanna end up floating in that gorge, throat slit, like your friend? This is big shit, too big for you, you little two-bit tabloid trash. Fuck off out of here now before I do something I'm going to regret . . .

She'd taped it . . . *my business . . . this is too big for you . . .* those words led Merry to believe Damián *was* somehow connected to Faith's death, that *something* was going on with the blond guy. So she'd waited outside his place until he'd left his premises around 10:00 p.m. She'd followed his car to this marina. He'd turned into the private marina lot, while she'd driven a little farther around the bay and parked. From her vantage point, she'd seen Damián making his way through the marina security gate and down along the dock, to where he'd boarded the *Amanda Rose.*

Merry tensed suddenly as another man came striding purposefully down the dock toward the luxury yacht. She zeroed in on him with her telephoto lens. Dark hair—black maybe. About the same age as Damián. Tall. Decent build. She clicked off a series of frames as he climbed the gangway and boarded the yacht.

The seconds ticked by. Things grew even quieter. Cold began to bite hard, and Merry started to shiver in spite of her down gear and toque.

She was about to pack it in, thinking that maybe she'd return tomorrow to see if she could learn more about the boat, when suddenly she saw Damián returning down the gangway with the dark-haired guy.

The two men walked together along the dock toward the exit gate, heads bent in close conversation. She shot images as they went up the gate and then up into the parking lot. She zoomed in closer over the distance. The guys paused at Damián's vehicle. The other male then turned his face her way, and she clicked. He then made his way over to a dark-colored Porsche. Looked red in this light. The stranger opened his driver's side door, got in. Merry's pulse quickened. She could run in a crouch behind the row of vehicles parked along the waterfront, get into her Beetle, and follow Damián as he pulled out of the private lot. Or she could follow that Porsche, try to find out who the stranger was. She chose the Porsche. Scurrying along, bent low, she opened her Beetle door, climbed in, fired the ignition. She pulled into the street and rounded the small bay as the Porsche sped out of the lot. Its brake lights flared red, and it turned onto the road that led into the ritzy Uplands neighborhood.

Because the streets were so empty and the night so clear, she held way back while still trying not to lose him.

He turned left, and then right again, climbing into a wide tree-lined street of estate homes. His taillights flashed red, and abruptly he swung into a driveway, disappearing from view.

Merry drove past the driveway entrance and drew up alongside the curb. She stared at the lit gold plaque on the stone pillar flanking the driveway, and her mouth turned dry with excitement.

AKASHA.

Pulse galloping, she photographed the name. But just as she fired off a rapid succession of clicks, another car—a white Audi—pulled into view and came to a stop under a streetlight several meters short of the driveway entrance. Merry slid down in her seat, peering up over the edge of the window. There was a man and a woman in the front of the

Audi. The man leaned over, and the two engaged in a long, passionate kiss. Slowly, Merry raised her lens, clicked. Again. And again. The Audi windows started to steam up. Then suddenly the interior light flared on as the passenger side door opened. A woman got out. Merry's heart stalled as the woman leaned down into the car to say something while holding the door open.

The man was Jack Killion. The freaking city mayor. And the woman was ADAG Joyce Norton-Wells.

Staying low, hands trembling with excitement, Merry fired off another series of shots. The ADAG shut the passenger door. The Audi pulled off, and Joyce Norton-Wells walked up the AKASHA driveway carrying her briefcase.

CHAPTER 54

SATURDAY, DECEMBER 16

It was 5:30 a.m. on Saturday morning. Maddocks had come in early, knowing things would be quiet at the station, just a handful of Operation Limpet guys coming in. Primarily, Fitz and the rest of management would not be there. And he didn't want Fitz around for what he was about to try—bringing Jayden Norton-Wells in to give a *voluntary* DNA sample.

The plan had come to him last night, as he'd lain in the grip of insomnia aboard his yacht, fretting about Angie and the case. She'd not returned his calls, and he'd not tried to go around to her place, either. He'd decided last night that whatever course of action she took, if it was to be of any value, if it was to work long term and be in *her* best interests, he had to do the most difficult thing of all—wait for her to come to him.

He shoved his hands deep into his pockets as he stood in front of the whiteboard. Chewing lightly on the inside of his cheek, he studied the new lines he'd drawn linking victims Drummond and Hocking to *Black-Haired Male One*, *Black-Haired Male Two*, and *Blond Male*.

A cough sounded behind him, and he spun around.

Holgersen. Quietly watching him.

"How long you been standing there?" he said, slightly rattled—hadn't heard the guy come in at all.

Holgersen came forward. Under the harsh fluorescent light this morning, the hollows beneath his eyes looked deep, and his cheeks gaunt. "You called, boss," he said, referencing Maddocks's new position on the task force. "You left me a message in the middle of the night. Told me about the black hair DNA profiles, told me to come in this morning to help with your plan. Remember?"

"I didn't say five thirty a.m."

He gave a halfhearted shrug. "Thought I'd come take a look at things and give it alls a think in the quiet myself." He tilted his chin toward the whiteboard. "But you gots here first."

Maddocks regarded the man in silence for a beat. "You get any sleep at all, Holgersen?"

Another shrug. "Ah, yanno, a case eats away at a person sometimes. So . . . you gots the DNA profiles up there, I see." He came close to the board, studied the new links and information. Without turning around, he said, "So, Fitz, eh. Buziak. You the new man-in-charge."

Maddocks remained silent.

Holgersen turned, crooked a brow. "How's Pallorino?"

"Don't know."

He nodded. "And I reckon Fitz isn't gonna be on board with this plan of yours?"

Silence.

"So what makes you think our Jayden-pretty-rich-boy is actually gonna wanna offer us up his body juices by choice today?"

Maddocks walked over to the counter where he'd put a pot of coffee on to brew earlier. He poured himself a steaming mug and held up the pot. "Want?"

"Nah, I'll get me some real shit later, thanks."

Maddocks returned to the board and sipped as he considered the photo of Jayden Norton-Wells. He pointed his mug at it. "He's the weak link. And the key link. The Lexus. The Saint Christopher medallion. Him fleeing to Raddison, who has a matchbook in his office with Drummond's cell number on it. He's connected. Don't know how—but he is. We nail him, I figure the dominoes will start falling."

"See, here's the thing," Holgersen said, fishing into his breast pocket for his pack of nicotine gum. "If Norton-Wells is connected, he's not gonna give us a DNA sample voluntarily. Plus, even if he's not connected, he's a law student. Them guys are big on shit like the Charter of Rights and Freedoms, privacy laws, personal rights—full of braggadocio blow and all."

Maddocks cocked a brow. "You been doing the daily jumble with Leo now?"

A grin slashed his tired face. He popped a tablet of green gum between his teeth, held it there, and said around it, "I do know some shit, boss."

Recalibrating. That's what Maddocks felt he was doing with each new interaction with Kjel Holgersen. The cop intrigued the puzzle-solver in Maddocks. What, he wondered, was Holgersen's motivation in becoming a detective? What made him tick? What was his motive in trying to tip him and Angie off about Fitz? It was part of the reason he'd picked Holgersen to go with him today. Keep your friends close, as they say, but your enemies even closer—and he wanted to figure out which Holgersen was. Friend or foe.

"Motive," Maddocks said slowly, watching Holgersen's face. "That's how I approach everything, everyone. Norton-Wells might be a law student, but he's also a disappointment to his father. I'm guessing his mother, too—a top prosecutor and politician. If he's a law student because he wants approval from his own parents, he's needy. Not in his wheelhouse. I'm betting he's probably not the smartest, or most strident, of law students, either." He sipped, returning his attention to the photo of Jayden Norton-Wells.

"He's devoutly religious," Maddocks said quietly, staring at the young man's features. "There's a clear morality at play in his head. Right and wrong. Good and bad. And in his faith, bad means you go to hell. And Jayden Norton-Wells is shit-scared he's going to hell. Because when we went to see him, right after the news broke about Drummond, he was a mess. Sick with stress, oozing fear. You could smell it on him."

"Yah, so, he fits the religious aspect of the killings maybe, and he *might* have known our Gracie, and he lied about the Lexus . . . but he don't fit no Grablowski lone-wolf, lust-based, cunning, *sadistic*, serial killer profile. Way I figure it, *if* he did give our Gracie girl a personally engraved Saint Christopher medallion, he cares about her. Them saints are supposed to look after people. Jayden-pretty-softy-rich-boy don't want to rape and cut and kill her and then risk hell and damnation by dragging his offering into the cemetery at midnight and leaving her bleeding and dying at the foot of the Virgin Mary. No way, José."

"Exactly. But he *does* know something. He's hiding something. He's shit-scared. And Norton-Wells panics when scared. He panicked into a really bad lie about that Lexus, the dinner at the Auberge, about the parking lot from where the Lexus was allegedly stolen, and he panicked into a wild dash to have something out with Raddison at city hall—couldn't even think to put his coat on, or who would see him. Now, *that* wasn't a lawyer thinking." Maddocks set his mug down. "Panic is like a wild horse without the jockey of logic to rein it in. You actually lose the ability to think at all—you just act from the primal brain. We go lean on Norton-Wells for the murder of his dear Gracie Drummond, we make him panic, he might just offer up his DNA sample to save his ass—because my bet is he *didn't* do those things to Gracie Drummond. But he might know—or suspect—who did."

"What if he bolts straight to Daddy and Mommy and they pull out all them big legal guns? Then we gets nada."

"I don't think he will. And even if we do find enough for a DNA warrant, those guns are coming out anyway. This way we head them off at the pass. And the clock is ticking on this one. Fast. It's worth a shot."

"Worth the wrath of Fitz?"

"We got nothing else right now." He paused and met Holgersen's eyes. "I'm running the investigation. Not Fitz."

Holgersen inhaled deeply, smoothed his goatee, then grinned heartily. "Let's go nab us a law-boy, boss."

CHAPTER 55

Dr. Alex Strauss handed Angie tea in a cup and saucer. Outside the bay window of his late-eighteenth-century James Bay home, the Saturday afternoon rain came down in a bleak and silvery curtain. "Ceylon," he said. "Remember those afternoons when we used to drink it?"

Angie smiled. "It's been a long time." She sipped, and memories flooded back—of being in his campus office, the hours of discussion. Dr. Strauss had been first her academic advisor, then friend. He'd left the university four years back and was easing his way toward retirement while editing a psychology journal.

"Too long to not see an old friend." He seated himself in a wing-back opposite her, sipped from his cup. Between them, a fire crackled in the hearth.

"You're looking good, Alex." And Angie meant it. He might be edging into his seventies now, but he really hadn't changed much. Being in his company was still like comfort food. For the soul. Why *had* she not come to visit him before now? "Still riding your bike?" she asked.

"And you, still flattering me, I see." His smiled faded. "Why so long?"

"Life, the job." She paused. "I don't know, Alex. I got busy."

He considered her for a moment. She had the urge to shift in her chair, but she refused to move.

"You never did make it clear to me why you decided to go into law enforcement," he said. "What drove you to leave academia behind for the world of policing?"

She moistened her lips. "You sound like my dad. I . . . wanted to help. To make a difference in the lives of the vulnerable. To put away those who abused and hurt them." Her thoughts spun back to Maddocks and what he'd said about his need to care for Jack-O—why he'd taken the stray on. About needing to make a tangible difference, because sometimes—often—the job didn't give that to you. He was a rescuer. A good guy. She didn't deserve a guy like him—

"Mostly putting men away—in the special victims unit, in particular," Alex said.

Angie pulled her thoughts back. "Sex crimes. Yeah, statistically it's the males who are the bad guys. That's the way life crumbles."

The psychologist nodded slowly, assessing her. "So, what precipitated this emergency visit, Angie? What's troubling you?" As always, he cut right to the chase. And she'd probably already given away more of herself than she'd intended. Possibly this was why she *had* avoided Alex. She'd become increasingly shuttered emotionally since leaving college, since joining the force, since learning to compartmentalize her life and stay objective on brutal, disturbing cases, since embarking on a life of increasingly anonymous sex encounters. So gradual had been the inner transition that she hadn't really noticed it happening. But she realized now, sitting with the old psychologist, that being with people like him, people who looked too deeply into her eyes and searched for the soul inside, and who saw things that others couldn't, had begun to unnerve her.

Carefully, she set her cup and saucer down on the small table beside her chair, and she began to tell him about her mother's illness and subsequent hospitalization, about her own fears that similar genetically predisposed symptoms might be surfacing in her—the visual and auditory hallucinations. The little girl in pink. The strange words and foreign language. And how, when these visions presented, she felt terror on a very primal level, a desperate urge to flee, as if for her very survival. She explained how she always felt uneasy at Christmastime and when it snowed. She explained how she'd reacted when her mother sang that hymn, and finally, how she'd blacked out and attacked a colleague outside the church.

Angie also told Alex straight-up that she was avoiding a psych eval following her experience with Hash and little Tiffy, and that she was afraid to go through any kind of official medical channels because it would leave a record, an evidence trail, of unsound mental health, which could cost Angie her job. Which was basically her world.

"Angie," he said gently. "I do know someone, a therapist, who comes highly recommended, and who—"

"I don't want *official* therapy, Alex. You're not hearing me. I want your advice, as a friend, first, before I decide on an official course of action." She fidgeted with her watch strap. "I met someone, and I . . . think I'm starting to care about him. He's the one I tried to stab outside the church. It rocked me very badly, and he convinced me that I owe it to him, to my fellow officers, to seek a diagnosis, to get the facts, and if I am indeed ill, that I need to pull myself out."

"So there's your conflict right there. You don't want help, yet you've been driven to it because of this man. So you came to me for a kinda therapy lite—an easy answer, a way out."

She held his gaze, and she felt her walls slamming up. "Yeah, maybe I made a mistake. I'm sorry." She came to her feet. "I should—"

"I've seen the news, Angie. I know from the media that you are involved in those sex-murder investigations. It's rough, that kind of thing. On anybody. It's enough to precipitate—"

"It's not the case. I'm not cracking under—"

He raised his palm. "Acknowledge it. In movies, sure, fictional cops are immune. Viewers are increasingly inured to violence. But this is real life. Real people. We're not built to deal with an incessant onslaught of the kinds of things that you deal with in sex crimes—certainly not without continual debriefing, without proper mental health care, without early recognition of post-traumatic stress symptoms." He paused. "That incident in July where you lost your partner, Hash, I did read about it, too. I saw the newspaper photos of you carrying that dead child, all covered in blood—the anguish on your face." A sad smile curved his lips. "I've followed your career."

Her guilt at not having visited Alex deepened. She bent down, picked up her bag, and hooked it over her shoulder. "I really should go. You're right. I wanted a way out."

"Sit, Angie. Put your things down. This might be more simple than you thought." She looked down at him, then slowly reseated herself.

He leaned forward. "With the caveat that this is *not* a therapy session, and from everything you have told me so far, and given the major stressor events in your life over the last six months—the joint impact of it all could be triggering suppressed childhood memories."

She sucked in a deep breath. "That's what my friend suggested. And maybe I am recalling some things—there are some discrepancies I've found around the car accident in Italy that nearly took my life and that scarred my face, and I think some of those memories could be rearing their heads from a four-year-old's perspective. But honestly, I had a pretty vanilla childhood, Alex."

He got up, reached for the fire poker, stoked the coals in the hearth, and added a log.

Returning to his chair, he said, "The classic 'possessions' view of memory has changed. There's a newer school of thinking that sees memories not as fixed, unchanging possessions that are stored like files in a filing cabinet and that can be retrieved, viewed, and replaced when needed," he said. "But rather, each time that we try to recall something, we create the narrative anew. When asked to remember an event, we take those key elements from our past, and we use those elements to reconstruct our experience." He leaned forward, held her eyes. "And sometimes, Angie, in this process of reconstructing our autobiographical narratives, we add things. Like feelings, beliefs, or even knowledge that has been acquired long after the event. We braid this new material into the narrative around the historic event, and we call this newly built story a *memory*." He reached for his cup and took another sip before replacing it in its saucer.

"And in trying to reconcile the stories of our pasts with the new demands of the present, errors, distortions can creep in. Whole false narratives can be implanted—all just part of the complex ways in which we humans try to make sense of our own existence. But—" He paused. "This process can also generate psychological dissonance if the narrative you are trying to tell yourself is greatly at odds with what really happened. Your subconscious, Angie, might be trying very hard to tell you something."

"You mean in the form of a little girl in pink."

"With long red hair?" He smiled. "Yes, of course I do, and I think you know it. Part of that dissonance I mentioned—when memories don't make sense with your perception of reality—the psyche can get very, very creative and illogical in its manners of avoidance."

He finished the last of his tea. "I'd like to try some hypnosis techniques, if you're open to it. Nothing heavy, just relaxation exercises where I will try to walk you back a little deeper into those scenarios with the little girl, go under the conscious layer a bit. Like taking a peek under the hood of a car, so to speak, to see what kind of engine is running things down there."

Angie felt a fresh clutch of anxiety. She pressed her hands down firmly on the armrests of the chair. "And you can bring me out anytime, right? I won't—"

"Get lost in there, trapped?" He grinned. "No. It'll be fine. I'll give you clear cues that will resurface you, should you start showing distress at any point."

✝

CHAPTER 56

"Mind if I smoke?"

"Chew the gum," Maddocks said.

It was late afternoon and already darkening. He and Holgersen were parked under leafless cherry boughs, watching the law faculty entrance on the UVic campus. Rain spattered the windows. Maddocks wondered where Ginny was right now, if she might happen across that lawn with its dead leaves. He'd decided Angie might be right. He was being overprotective. His plan going forward was to let Ginn be for a few days and then start over again with trying to be a better dad.

Holgersen crackled his gum wrapper, fiddling to get the green chiclet out of its childproof packaging, and Maddocks wished to hell that Norton-Wells would show up. He'd about had enough of being cloistered with Holgersen after all these hours. Because they'd not wanted to tip their hands to Norton-Wells's parents, they'd waited outside AKASHA this morning, until they got lucky and saw the little red Porsche exiting the estate. They'd followed it here.

"He could have gone out another entrance hours ago," Holgersen said, still crackling the packaging.

"But his vehicle is still parked down there."

"Maybe he left without it, made us."

"Betting he didn't," said Maddocks.

More crinkling of plastic sounded. Irritation spat through Maddocks.

"Thing about sex," Holgersen said, dropping his packet, then groping about for it on the passenger side floor. Maddocks's hands tightened where he was resting them on the wheel—this was it, where Holgersen was going to mention seeing him and Angie kissing and almost getting it off in the parking lot. Holgersen found his gum and recommenced fiddling with the packaging. "Messes with your head. Clarity and all that. You start cutting deals with the devil."

"What are you talking about?"

"Sex. I was saying—"

"Okay, Holgersen, whatever it is that you're trying to tell me, spit it out. You were outside the Pig in the dark. You saw Leo leaving—"

"Yeah."

"And?"

"I ams spitting it out. See? That's exactly what I mean—Pallorino . . . oooh, now she's a hot and dangerous one. Can't figure her out. But you want. You touch. You get burned. One taste messes you up. You want more. You can't get more. You end up doing deals with a Fitz-devil . . . and wham, you're smacked with a boom across your face in storm winds."

Silence. Maddocks's heart went *whump whump whump*. Angie. Even just talking about her. He was in far deeper than he thought. Heart and head and freaking body. And Holgersen had leverage.

"What do you want, Holgersen?"

"Don't worry, boss. I'ms a guy who keeps my lips zipped."

"Yeah. Right. Like when you came to me Friday morning and spilled on Fitz."

"Man's gotta have his loyalties, this is true. I happens to like Pallorino. All hard-ass and broken like. You sure I can't smoke? I can open a window—"

"No."

He fiddled again. Maddocks's gaze dipped to Holgersen's hands. A tool. That crackling paper. An interrogation tool. Fucking little genius. *He's interrogating me . . . getting under my hood to see what makes me tick . . .*

"Watch the damn building, would you?" Maddocks snapped. "The second you see him, we're on him. I want to get him in front of his friends, colleagues, profs, whatever."

"But not meeee. I's freeeee—" Holgersen started to sing in a soft and surprisingly good bass. "No deal with the devil for meee . . ."

Jesus. Maddocks dragged his hand fast over his hair. *Jayden, get out here already . . .*

"I's been celibate two years, one week . . . five days—" The gum popped out. "Ah, got it!" He held the green tablet up triumphantly. "They needs special adult instructions on how to open these things." He popped the gum into his mouth, checked his watch. "And six hours and twenty-seven minutes," he said, chewing.

Maddocks's head spun as once more he recalibrated his sense of Kjel Holgersen. He sat quietly for a while. Minutes ticked by. "Okay," he said finally, quietly, eyes fixed on the law faculty entrance. "So, you already did your deal with the devil. Now you're in a twelve-step program. Sounds like an addict talking—you're not 'cured,' just going minute to minute."

Holgersen said nothing, just started rapping his fingers on the dash, humming a tune. He stretched, cricking his neck.

Maddocks sucked in air slowly.

"So," Holgersen said finally. "Why'd you call me this morning, not one of the others?"

"Quality time, Holgersen. You and me. Thought it might be fun."

He snorted, then launched forward. "There! There he is!" He swung open the door and lurched into an incredibly fast stride across the lawn on his long, skinny legs. Maddocks scrambled to get out of the vehicle and rush after him.

✝

CHAPTER 57

"Your arms feel heavy, your eyelids are heavy—they're lowering. You're sinking, sinking, warm and comfortable, deeper, deeper into your chair."

Angie listened to Alex's low, calm voice, the soft crackling of the fire. He'd dimmed the lights and drawn the drapes. Her shoes were off, her phone silenced. She wasn't so sure this was going to work. Nevertheless, she closed her eyes, focusing on his cues.

"Your breathing is becoming more relaxed, slower, in, and out, in, out. Air is going deeper into your lungs, deeper. You feel sleep like a warm blanket around your shoulders. It's nice. You like it, and you're welcoming it, giving in to the soft caress of her arms as she takes you down, down, toward a comfortable place. A bed . . . you feel like a little child when your mother used to tuck you in after a long, happy day. She's reading to you, but you can't hear her words anymore because you're feeling sleepy, so tired . . ." His words droned on, and Angie was lying on her back. In a dark room. On her bed. There was a sense of a presence at her bedside. Someone keeping her comfortable in the dark room. Safe place. A hand holding hers. Words. A song filtering softly up into her consciousness. A gentle lullaby. It was a woman holding her hand. She was singing that lullaby. Warmth and familiarity blossomed through her, and Angie felt herself smile.

"What do you see?" he said gently.

"Darkness," she whispered. "All dark. She's holding my hand."

"Who is, Angie?"

"Safe. Looking after me. She's singing, softly, so that the others won't hear."

"What others?"

A clang of discord shattered the words. She shook her head. "I don't know. I can't see them. Just dark. She's stopped."

"Okay, breathe in, and out, and relax again. She's with you. Safe. No others now. She's singing again. What do you hear?"

Sweetly, ever so softly, the words came out of Angie's mouth, the sound of a child . . .

"A-a-a, a-a-a,

"byly sobie kotki dwa . . .

"A-a-a, kotki dwa,

"szarobure, szarobure obydwa . . ."

"What do those words mean, Angie? Are you aware of the meaning?"

She hummed the tune, and it made dapples of sunshine in her mind. "*There . . . were once two little kittens. A-a-a, a-a-, two little kittens . . . they were both grayish-brown. Oh, sleep, my darling. If you'd like a star from the sky, I'll give you one. All children, even the bad ones, are already asleep, only you are not . . .*"

"A lullaby," he said softly, and his voice seemed to come from so very far away, from another time and space. "It's making you even more sleepy. You're going to go deeper. Who is singing?"

"She is."

"And who is she?"

Light shattered the darkness like a breaking mirror. Her pulse quickened. She struggled to come up, fast. Not nice down there, not safe . . .

"It's okay, Angie, it's fine. You're fine. You *are* safe. She's singing the song. Can you hear it again—those words, that tune? Sing some more."

She nodded, the warmth coming back, and she whispered, *"Oh, sleep, because the moon is yawning and he will soon fall asleep. And when the morning comes, he will be really ashamed, that he fell asleep and you did not . . .*

"A gdy rano przyjdzie świt
"księżycowi będzie wstyd,
"że on zasnął, a nie ty . . ."
She stopped, feeling confused.

"What is she doing now?"

"Holding my hand."

"What does she look like?"

Angie started shaking her head side to side. Dark. Very dark. An image slammed her brain. "A man is in the room. On her. On top of her. He . . ." Tears burned. She gripped the armrests tight. "He's grunting like a dog. He's . . . like a dog on top of her. Breathing funny . . . not nice. *Not nice!*" She put her hands tight over her ears. "Go 'way. Get off! Stop it!"

"It's okay, let's get out of that room for now. Go to the door. Open it. Can you do that?"

She shook her head. "Locked." Her breaths came faster. "Go away."

"Okay, okay, I'm going to give you a magic key. I want you to use that key to open that door, and I want you to go through it."

Angie took the key that was suddenly in her hand. A big bronze key like the one in the picture of her fairytale book. She turned it in the lock and creaked open the big door. Light—so white it was blinding—came through the opening.

"Go through the door, Angie."

But she turned instead, looking back into the darkness of the room, and she held out her hand. "Come," she whispered.

"Come playum, dum grove." Suddenly there was a basket in her other hand. *"Jesteśmy jagódki, czarne jagódki,"* she said.

"What does that mean, Angie?"

She began to sing. *"We are small berries, little black berries . . . We are small berries, black berries."*

"Who are you singing to?"

"She must come, to play. We go to dum grove, down indum trees. Bring baskets. Berries."

"Who must come play? The lady who was singing?"

No, no, no . . . Angie's chest tightened. Her head felt as though it was going to explode. She shook it from side to side, getting more and more violent. Her legs were pumping, grasses and brambles scraping her skin open. She thrashed through the bushes, into the trees, then onto a cold street with snow, and there were Christmas lights . . . *flee, run, run!* Snowing. She began to pant rapidly.

"What's happening?"

"He's coming. The big red man and the other ones. Chasing."

"Where are you running to?"

"Dark. It's dark. Go. Get inside! I have to get inside and stay quiet like a mouse!"

"Okay, get inside, and tell me what you are getting into."

She shook her head, tears streaming down her cheeks now. She couldn't breathe. "A big shiny silver knife—he's got a knife . . ."

She screamed. Her hands went over her ears. Pain sliced across her face. "Blood! Everywhere—blood!"

Vaguely she heard a word. *Three.* Then louder. *Three!*

Two.

One.

"You're coming up, Angie," he said. "Waking up. Nice and easy. Comfy in the chair. You're in Alex Strauss's house. Safe. All safe."

Her eyes flared open. She stared at her hands. And the blood that had covered them all sticky and hot and wet was suddenly no longer there. Slowly, she glanced up at Alex.

He looked shaken.

Her hand went to her lip. "My mouth," she said. "I was cut. By a knife."

"Who?" he said quietly. "Who cut you?"

Her breath was shaky. Perspiration dampened her upper lip. "I don't know, Alex. I don't know what's going on. I was always told I was cut in the car accident."

He made more tea. She sat for a while, staring at the dance of the flames in the fireplace, feeling exhausted, trying to make sense of what had just happened, where she had gone in her mind.

"You've had no memories like this before?" he said, handing her another cup.

"Just that little girl. But it was more like a hallucination than a memory."

"And the woman, the songs?"

She shook her head. "Only those Polish words that come into my head when I see the girl in pink."

"Something happened, Angie. Something when you were a child, the same age as that girl you are seeing in a pink dress."

Her gaze snapped onto his. "You think my parents lied to me? About the accident?"

"Like I said, we construct our autobiographical memories anew each time we try to recall an event from the past, and sometimes false stories can be implanted, resulting in a false life narrative." He paused. "And cognitive dissonance."

She wiped her upper lip. Her hands shook slightly.

"We could always schedule another session, if you'd like. We could try to go deeper, for longer. But I did need to snap you out when I did. You were going into distress."

Absently, she sipped her tea, thinking of what she'd been told of the car accident. Of Italy. Her mind went to the dates on the backs of the photos in the album. The uneasiness that she'd witnessed in her father's features when she'd raised the discrepancies. Her mother's strange words in that hospital.

"I don't know," she said softly. "I'd always thought my childhood was normal. And if this is happening, why now?"

"Like I said, PTSD from the Hash and Tiffany tragedy could have been a trigger. Or it might all just have been building over time, increasingly exacerbated by the daily stresses of working in sex crimes."

Angie's thoughts turned to Grablowski and his words about the development of paraphilic love maps and sexual deviance. Was there something in her own prepubescent past that would explain her issues around sex and control? Her resistance to—fear of—love? The emotional walls she'd been erecting around herself over the years of being a cop?

Could it explain why she'd often felt so oddly distant from her parents and why she'd felt Hash had been more of a mentor and father figure in her life than her real dad had?

"I need to talk to my father again," she said quietly.

Alex nodded. "And here's another thing I can offer you. Something bad happened to that little girl in the past you've blocked out, and I suspect that subconsciously you've been spending your entire adult life trying to fix whatever it was. To save her. To make it right. I think it's why you became a cop." He paused. "And why you chose to work sex crimes in particular."

A chill trickled down the length of Angie's spine. Her thoughts wheeled to what she'd told Merry Winston, about how she *cared*. For that nine-year-old who'd slept with a knife under her pillow. For the little girl she'd seen at the gas station, carrying her doll. For Tiffy Bennett, abused and killed by her own father. The words had just poured from her mouth in a quietly passionate outburst. And she realized Alex Strauss might be right.

In everything she'd ever done as an officer, she was trying to save that little girl in pink with the long red hair.

And in losing Hash, she'd lost a father figure who was a true friend. In losing Tiffy, she'd failed the little girl in pink. And now that little girl wasn't going to hide inside Angie anymore. She wanted her place in the world.

CHAPTER 58

"What the fuck—are you *following* me? I don't have to talk to you guys anymore. I don't have anything to say. My dad's lawyers—"

"Oh, we think you have something to say, Jayden," Maddocks said as he and Holgersen reached Norton-Wells.

"This is harassment." Norton-Wells's pupils were already dilating as Maddocks and Holgersen hemmed in on either side of him, leaning in, and kept inching him backward toward the wall until he was backed into a corner.

The kid's gaze twitched in desperation toward other students exiting the law building, as if seeking a lifeline from one of them.

"Jayden!" a guy called, coming toward them.

"I . . . I gotta go—" Norton-Wells started saying.

But Holgersen stepped in front of Norton-Wells, blocking his line of sight to the approaching guy.

"Yous didn't come down to the station to make a statement about the stolen vehicle," Holgersen said, towering over Norton-Wells. "You says you was sick, but you looks all better to me, what you say, Maddocks?"

"He didn't come down because the Lexus wasn't stolen, now was it, Jayden?" Maddocks said.

"Jay?" said the male student as he neared. "You okay?"

"You want all your legal colleagues of the future to see you being arrested, Jayden?" Maddocks said.

Norton-Wells paled. He was starting to sweat—signs of stress, cortisol dumping into his system. "What do you mean?"

"For the rape and murder and mutilation of Gracie Drummond."

His eyes widened. "Go ahead," he yelled to his friend. "I . . . I'm good. I'll catch up with you guys."

The student hesitated.

"Go. I'm fine."

The other guy wavered a moment, then turned and left. Norton-Wells swallowed, his mouth clearly going dry. More stress. Good, thought Maddocks.

"We knows you were not at the Auberge—you know about CCTV, Mr. Law Boy?"

"They don't have—"

Holgersen laughed. "He thinks they don't have surveillance cameras, Maddocks, you hear that?"

"Sure did."

"Cameras everywhere these days. Restaurants. Overlooking parking lots up the streets. Can tell on what day, what people, drove what car. Or didn't. Like on the iron bridge—a Lexus went over the bridge just before Gracie was taken and back again just after." Holgersen stuck his mug right in Norton-Wells's face. "*Your* Lexus, Law-Boy. That was never taken from that lot."

Norton-Wells bumped up against the wall, legs giving out slightly, his face going white, his breaths becoming short and shallow. "Is . . . is that what you meant by . . . it was used in the *commission of a crime?*"

Holgersen snorted. "Someone bundled Gracie's body into that Lexus. We got you, Law-Boy." He lifted the medallion around Norton-Wells's neck. "Ah. Nice. Saint Chris. Just like Gracie's, right, Maddocks?"

"Just like it."

Holgersen flipped over the gold medallion in his hand. "'Cept on the back of Gracie's it says, *With love from J.R.*" He tutted his tongue. "He gave her a saint to watch over her, Maddocks. Now why would he do that? And then go grab her, and tie her up, and stick her head under water, and rape and sodomize and cut out all those pieces of her sweet pussy that make her want men over and over and over again . . . her clit, her—"

"Stop! Oh God, please . . . please . . . just stop." Tears filled Norton-Wells's eyes, and he leaned his head back against the wall.

Maddocks was watching closely, allowing Holgersen to go just so far, and they were getting there faster than he'd anticipated, because clearly it was a raw shock to Norton-Wells that his Lexus might have been used to help kill a woman he cared about.

"I tell you whys you did it," Holgersen said quietly. "Rage. Blinding rage. Because maybe you gots wind that your Gracie Girl likes to sleep around, eh? Like a lots. And you catched her with Mr. Blond and his Bimmer, or maybe City-Mayor-Boy Zach Raddison, eh? And you gets as mad as all hell, and you—"

"No!" He panted lightly. "No," he said again, so softly they barely heard. "It wasn't like that—I didn't do that." He gagged, shook his head. "I would never hurt Gracie. *I loved Gracie.*"

Bingo!

Maddocks and Holgersen exchanged a fast glance.

"Right, right," said Holgersen. "We knows you knew her. And cared for her. So you didn't do it? Kill Gracie, slice and dice her up?"

He shook his head.

"So here's the thing. We make your life real tough . . . arrest you, say, for obstruction of justice in a double homicide because you lied about the Auberge and the parking lot and the stolen Lexus, and it gets all in the papers . . . your moms and pops get all twisty up, lawyers . . . or we can eliminate you. And here's how—you come with us to the station now, and you voluntarily give a DNA sample to a qualified police officer. Easy peasy. Okay?"

He nodded. "Okay . . . okay . . . I'll do it." He heaved out a chestful of air. He was crying copiously.

"Do what?"

"I'll give a voluntary DNA sample."

The detectives exchanged another glance.

"Now, there's a boy." Holgersen put his arm comfortingly around Norton-Wells. "It's the right thing to do."

CHAPTER 59

Angie rummaged hurriedly through her dad's drawers, looking for the keys to his fire safe, in which he kept all his important documents. Wind was picking up outside, clouds boiling black across the water toward the house, trees bending along the shore, the sky darkening. Her phone beeped—yet another call, another message, and yet again she didn't care.

Her dad was not home, so she'd let herself into the house and come into his office. She was looking for papers, information, anything about her childhood. Italy. The accident. His sabbatical. Something . . . that might confirm dates.

I am not mad. I am not hallucinating. Memory. It's memory . . .

She clicked on the desk lamp as the light inside the office grew dim. Finally, she found the keys under a tray that held pencils in the bottom drawer of his desk. Angie grabbed them and moved to the closet below the bookshelves where her dad had always kept the small fire safe. She unlocked it. Putting on another lamp, she sat on the floor and began to empty the papers out over the carpet. She sifted through passports, insurance documents, copies and revisions of her parents' will, their antenuptial marriage contract, house purchase papers, medical bills . . .

She stilled suddenly—a newspaper clipping. In Italian. Tucked into a plastic sleeve.

Across the top of the text was a black-and-white photo of a mangled white sedan that had rolled down an embankment. And up on the road above the wreck, an ambulance and a fire truck were parked. Emergency personnel stood beside the vehicles. They were looking down at the smashed car. Angie read the cutline beneath the photo.

La bambina di due cittadini Canadesi Miriam e Joseph Pallorino è morta Mercoledì in un incidente stradale nella Toscana. La bambina, Angela Pallorino, aveva quattro anni . . .

She frowned at the word *morta*.

Embedded into the text, lower down in the story, was a picture of a toddler. The caption beneath this image read: *Angela Pallorino (4).*

The article was dated March 1984.

Angie's mouth went dry—1986 was when she'd been four going on five. Whatever this was—the date, the age of the child at the time—it didn't make sense. Wind smacked a branch against the big windows and she jumped. Rain started drumming on the metal roof. Angie reached into her pocket for her phone. She dialed the number for her favorite Italian restaurant where she regularly bought takeout. She asked for Mario, the owner.

He picked up.

"Hullo!" he yelled. She could hear the clatter of pots and kitchen pans and voices in the background.

"Mario." She spoke loud and fast and clear. "It's Angie Pallorino. I have a big, big favor, and I'm in a rush. Can I talk to you for a moment?"

"Hang on, Angie, I'm going to take this in my office."

When he came back onto the phone, the background noise was quieter, and there was no longer a need for him to yell.

"What can I do for you?"

"I need a translation from Italian into English—an old newspaper story."

"Ah, no problemo. You want to fax it over?"

"I . . . do you have a smartphone or an address where I could forward a photo of the article?"

He gave her an email address.

"And . . . Mario, it's personal. If—"

"No worries, Angie. No worries. What happens with Mario stays with Mario."

She smiled. "Okay. Hang on."

With the phone, she shot a close-up of the article and sent the image to him. She paced in her dad's office while she waited for him to read it, then tensed when her phone rang. She connected the call.

"This is really weird, Angie. What *is* this?"

"What does it say, Mario? Just tell me what it says."

"It says, *The child of Canadian citizens Miriam and Joseph Pallorino was killed in a car accident in Tuscany. The child, Angela Pallorino, was four years old.*" He paused. "It says the dead child's name was Angela Pallorino," he repeated. "Is this some mistake?"

A chill washed over her skin. She fell silent. Her brain swirled into a vortex, spinning everything she knew to be true into a wild whorl of color, and like water it was being sucked down a drain.

"Angie?"

"The . . . the date . . . when does it say the accident happened?"

"March 12, 1984."

"Mario, can you keep this to yourself? It's . . . very personal. And I . . . I need to figure it out."

"Of course, Angie. Like I said, what happens with Mario—"

"Thank you. I owe you." She hung up and stared blankly at the rain-streaked windows, at her own distorted reflection.

Angie Pallorino. Died. Age four. According to that news cutting.

That had to be a mistake, surely? Or whose reflection was she staring at?

Time ticked on, and still she stared, unable to fully compute this. She'd thought she'd begun to remember the accident—the pain on her mouth, trying to escape the crashing, mangling wreck. Were those memories false? What about the places her mind had gone with Alex during hypnosis—the men, the knife? What the *fuck* did this mean?

She lunged back down to the papers scattered across the carpet. On her knees, Angie rummaged through them until she finally found what she was searching for. Her birth certificate. She read the date.

February 14, 1980.

A sick sensation dropped like a cold, hard stone into the bottom of her stomach. This wasn't her birth certificate at all . . .

The door opened behind her. Angie swung around, startled.

Her dad stood in the doorway. White-faced, he stared at what was in her hands, the pile of documents littered across the floor.

"Angie?"

"Who was she?" Angie demanded. "Whose birth certificate is this, and who was the baby girl who died in the car accident? Why do I have the same name as her? Who in the hell am *I*?"

CHAPTER 60

Law-Boy, face as white as a sheet, opened his mouth wide. He winced as a police officer trained to collect bodily substances stuck a foam applicator into it and rubbed the inside of his cheek to collect skin cells. Kjel, who stood beside his new boss, felt a quiet implosion of relief as the officer finally placed the buccal swab carefully into an approved DNA Data Bank sample collection kit and labeled it.

Next came the blood sample—a quick jab with a lancet, and the drop of blood was pressed onto an evidence card. This too went into an approved kit, and the sample was marked. Norton-Wells had already had his prints taken. Eight of his head hairs had also been plucked out and had gone into their own designated DNA Data Bank sample collection kit.

Kjel stole a look at Boss-Man Maddocks. Fuck, he wanted to high-five the dude right here and do a freaking victory dance around the room with him. He'd gone the whole hog, and he even had the process video recorded for good measure. But the sergeant showed no emotion. He just watched. Like a statue.

Once the DNA sample kits had headed off to the lab and Law-Boy was back off to campus with a uniform in a squad car, they headed down the stairs to the incident room to grab their coats. As Kjel shrugged into his bomber jacket, he said, "Sos? How's about a beer or few at the Flying Pig, boss man?"

"I'll take a rain check, thanks," his boss said absently, buttoning his coat, as if deep in troubled thought.

"Got a date with a yacht boom, then?"

Those freaky dark-blue eyes snapped sharply to Kjel. For a minute the man looked dangerous, like he could kill. Then a smile cracked the intensity. "Sure. Why not. I might need a few to numb the coming wrath of Fitz."

"So, what's eating you?" Kjel said as they headed out of the station and ducked into the rain for the short walk to the Pig.

"The fact he gave it to us at all."

"He almost bailed—was touch-and-go there for a few hours. Seems he managed to screw his logic jockey back onto his panic horse a bit on the way over to the station."

CHAPTER 61

Her father walked woodenly toward the living room, where he crumpled into his chair and dropped his face into his big hands. Opposite him, on the other side of the hearth, her mother's chair sat empty. Angie stood there, waiting.

For a long while he said nothing. The storm lashed at the house, and branches swished and banged against the eaves.

"Dad, *talk* to me."

"Could you light the fire, please, Angie?"

She stared at him, dumbfounded, then did it, furiously cracking kindling and stacking wood and crumpling newspaper into balls, feeling as though she was in some kind of alternate universe, an empty pit gnawing away at her stomach. She put a flame to the paper. It whooshed to life, licking and gobbling up the kindling.

Once the fire was roaring, she poured them both whiskeys. Fat ones. She put a glass into his hands and took her mother's seat on the other side of the hearth. She sat there, watching him.

Finally, after a few sips of his drink, he spoke.

"I love her—your mother." He looked up and met Angie's gaze. And what she saw in her dad's eyes punched a hole right through her chest. It was a look of hollow, haunted emptiness. Of pain. Of love lost. She swallowed.

"I know you do, Dad, I know."

"She was driving that day. In Tuscany. It was a sunny day. A clear sky. Everything so perfect. You were in the backseat—" He wavered, taking a few moments to marshal himself. "Angie was in the backseat."

"Angie," she repeated. "I am Angie. My name is Angela Pallorino." The sick feeling deepened. "Right?"

He looked away, at the fire. "Your mother reached for her sunglasses, which she'd left on the passenger seat. She'd just come over a rise, and the sun was directly in her eyes. But she knocked the glasses onto the floor, and when she reached down for them . . . she was momentarily distracted, her attention not on the road. She hit a curve and lost control, and the car went through the railing. It tumbled down a steep mountainside." He stared at the fire, his mind going all the way back, as if he were there again, in Italy, all that time ago. He took another deep sip of his drink.

"She was badly injured in the crash, our little Angie . . . Oh God, Angie . . . Oh God . . . How do I undo this?" He met her eyes again. "I don't want to do this, say these things—I don't want to hurt you. *You* are Angie. You *became* Angie."

She tried to absorb his words, the whispering implications that underlay them. Part of her wanted to turn away, plug her ears, ignore what she was hearing. The other half was desperate for him to make it crystal clear, to tell her all at once, as brutally and honestly as he could.

"What do you mean, I *became* Angie?" she said coolly.

He shook his head and rubbed his brow hard.

"Dad, talk to me. That newspaper article said Angela Pallorino, aged four, died in a car accident in Tuscany. In eighty-four. You and Mom told me we had a car accident in Tuscany in eighty-six, that *I* almost died, and that's where I got this scar. That's when *I* was four going on five." She pointed to her mouth. Her father looked away.

"Look at me, Dad. *This* scar." Slowly, he turned his face back to hers. "*Who* died?"

"Our first baby, our first child."

She opened her mouth but couldn't speak. Lurching to her feet, she marched to the window, spun back, stared at her father sitting by the fire, next to the Christmas tree. A tree just like the one in the photo of the three of them when they were supposed to have returned from Italy after the accident.

"Who am I?" she said quietly.

"I loved your mother. I *love* her so much. I . . . it wasn't wrong, Angie. What we did was not wrong. It just . . . happened."

Her insides shaking, she returned to the fire and reseated herself facing him. "Just tell me," she said. "Just tell me in simple, chronological order. Bullet points if you must. I need to know. Whatever it is, it's been making me sick. Because I have . . . been having memories of things that don't fit into what I thought was my own childhood."

His shoulders rolled inward, and he nodded slowly. "My sabbatical was in eighty-four. The accident happened that year. Our four-year-old little Angie died in the hospital of injuries she sustained in that smash. Your mother suffered badly. Mentally. Terrible clinical depression. Then her hallucinations started. I tried. Everything. We came home to live in Vancouver, where she got good treatment. I took a position teaching at Simon Fraser University. But it was hard to leave her at home during the days. She was numb. Absent. Gone. Like part of her had died with Angie. It was when I took her to church that I began to find hope. She prayed for her lost child at church, and she seemed to liven up slightly, as if she'd found a contact again with her child. And the father there, Lord bless him, he got your mother volunteering and into singing again. She joined the Catholic church choir, and they often sang in the big cathedral in downtown Vancouver. Near the hospital." He reached for his whiskey and finished it. He sat in silence for a few moments, as if gathering his energy for what he had to say next.

"It was Christmas Eve. Two years after Italy and the accident."

Her mother's strange words sifted into her mind as her father spoke: *Christmas Eve she was returned. I was singing at the cathedral . . . such a beautiful cathedral. It was ordained . . .*

"Next to the cathedral downtown is Saint Joseph's Hospital. They have an Angel's Cradle there," he said. "It's a Catholic-administered facility, and the hospital staff, together with the police, wanted to put an end to the practice of young, unwed, fearful mothers dumping newborns to die in places like public washrooms or dumpsters. So they came up with the idea of a safe place where these mothers could leave their newborns without criminal repercussions. And police agreed that they would not pursue the mothers of those infants left abandoned in this safe place. A cradle was constructed for this purpose, or that's what they call it . . ." He wavered.

"Go on, please," she said quietly.

He cleared his throat and took in a deep breath. "The cradle itself is a tiny cubicle with a cot inside. It has a door at about waist level that opens onto the street. All a mother had to do was open the door in the street, right next to the hospital's emergency exit, place her baby inside, and close the door. She could then leave. Within a few minutes an alarm would sound inside the hospital, and nurses would open the cubicle from another door on the inside. They'd find and treat the baby. The infant would then go into the system and be adopted out."

The angels brought her back. They did. She didn't belong there. They returned her . . .

No. It couldn't be.

She could not have been left in the cradle as a newborn—not possible. The timing did not work.

Her father reached for the bottle Angie had left on the side table, and he topped up his glass. Cupping it in his hands, he regarded the play of firelight on the contents.

"That Christmas Eve in eighty-six, while your mother was sing-ing with the choir at the midnight Mass, some kind of violent gang fight erupted downtown, and it spilled down the street outside the church. From inside the cathedral, we heard gunshots, screaming, and tires screeching. Then nothing. When we came out, it was all quiet. So very quiet because it had started to snow. But we learned later through the media that the Angel's Cradle alarm had sounded that night, close to midnight. And inside the cradle they'd found a young girl, around four years of age, bleeding profusely from a slash across her mouth." He paused. "Knife wound, they thought. Associated with the gang fight."

Her hand went slowly to her mouth.

Uciekaj, uciekaj! . . . Wskakuj do srodka, szybko! . . . Siedz cicho! Run, run! Get inside!

"The child couldn't speak," he said. "Mute from shock, they thought. Then later, they wondered if you understood English—"

"Me?"

Emotion glittered in her father's eyes. "Long red hair. You had no shoes. It was *winter* and you had no shoes—just a little pink dress. Like a party frock, but old and torn and covered in blood." He drank more. It seemed to ease the words for him as they got harder for her to hear.

"When the story finally ran in the paper, when the details started coming out, and when the police couldn't find anyone related to you at all, you went into the system to be adopted out."

She blinked, unable to fully absorb what he was saying. His words were slotting like jigsaw pieces into a full picture that explained things with harsh clarity. But at the same time they didn't.

"It was a mystery, Ange. A case that went cold. But in the photos that your mother and I saw in the media, you looked *exactly* like our four-year-old Angie did when she was taken from us. The red hair. The right age. It was haunting, the fact that she—I mean, you—were found right outside the church where your mother was singing, where in her prayer she'd felt a link to you again—"

"To Angie, you mean," she said. "Not to me."

"She felt it *was* you, Angie. Arriving, returning, right on the cusp of Christmas Day, like a child in a manger. And your mother saw it as a sign. A very powerful sign. She believed you had been sent back by angels, and that we had to do everything in our power to claim you, adopt you, bring you rightfully home to us."

"That's crazy—that's insane."

He looked down into his glass again. "She wasn't well in her mind. I know. I . . . I don't expect you to understand what happened, how it happened, but in believing you were her baby come home, and in going through that adoption application process, in her desperate desire, her *need* to prove herself worthy to the authorities as a potential adoptive mother, she pulled herself together. She managed to appear normal again, and her depression of the past was put down to PTSD and sheer, all-consuming grief. We fostered you for a while. And when we were selected to be your parents—"

"Because no one else wanted me, right?" she interjected. "A four-year-old isn't exactly the easiest thing to adopt out. Plus there was my questionable history and inability to speak or remember on top of it all. So you got lucky."

He chose to ignore her jabs. "In finally bringing you home, your mother really did begin to shine again. She had purpose. She had love and laughter and energy. My Miriam came back to *life*, Angie. You brought her back to *me*. And I . . . I don't know if you can ever understand love like I have for her, but she . . . she's my everything. She's my world. And seeing her become whole again . . ." His voice drifted. He cleared his throat. "I just let it be. I let her believe."

"You called me *Angie*?" she said with disgust. "You gave me the same name as a dead child? How could you do that?"

"I didn't see the harm," he said, his voice suddenly small. "It made your mother better. And you were starting to thrive. Learning to speak, to sing. To laugh. I—"

"You inserted some abandoned kid into a dead child's life? How can that be *normal*? How can that do no harm?"

"It *didn't* do harm—you *did* start to thrive. We became a family. We moved out of town, to the island—to Victoria, just before Christmas in eighty-seven, and when we arrived here, you were just our Angie."

"And that's how you introduced me? As the child in the photo album? All those early pictures that led from birth up to Italy—that's not me? And then you just continued plunking in my pictures after the real Angie passed?"

Silence.

"And you were never going to tell me that you and Mom are not my biological parents?"

He rubbed his knee. "I thought we might, you know, tell you one day, when you were older. Or if some medical need arose. But . . . it didn't happen. You really did become our Angie in our minds, and why should we hurt you with such terrible news—the truth of where you really came from? No one knew anyway. All the leads to that case just dried up. There was no one to even test for paternal DNA. So why not just let it be?"

"Because it's not the truth." She lurched to her feet, dragged her hands over her hair, her whole world tilting dizzyingly on its axis. Everything she knew to be true suddenly was not. Her whole life would now have to be reexamined through a different lens. That person she saw in the mirror was someone else. Her sense of self had to be recalibrated. She wanted to run. To escape. She wanted to bust out of her own body, get blind drunk, go fuck herself senseless at the club.

"So I have real parents—biological parents—out there somewhere." It wasn't a question. She was just stating it out loud as a way to process this. "They might be dead. They might be alive." She paused, glaring at him, an anger rising fierce inside her, and it was cut through with pity, with sympathy, because he, too, was so alone now. It was like they'd shattered their entire past as a family on this night. And it was all over. Gone forever.

"Where do *you* think I came from? You must have a theory. Was my mother Polish? Did I ever say Polish words when I eventually learned to speak again?"

He shook his head. "No. Just English. You'd forgotten everything that came before the Christmas Eve that you were found in the cradle. No one knows, Ange. The local police, Interpol, other agencies—they all tried working at the case, but no relative ever came forward to claim you or to offer a DNA sample. And none was ever found. You were just there, Angie. The Angel's Cradle baby. Waiting for us."

Something struck her suddenly. "Tell me one more thing. Why did we stop going to church?"

"Because one Sunday service just before Christmas your mother saw a look in your face when the church bells rang, and she . . . I think she was worried that church might make you remember something. We never went back after that."

CHAPTER 62

Merry opened the door to her tiny apartment and stilled. The air felt changed. Someone had been inside. She clicked on the hall and living-room lights. A drape wafted in a slight movement of air.

Quickly, she moved to the window and drew back the drape. The window was open a crack, cold night air seeping in. Her heart kicked to a stutter. She had not left the window open. She rammed it shut, brain reeling. She spun around. Listened.

No other sound. Apart from the thud of blood against her eardrums, her own rapid breathing. She eyed her front door, across the living room, the expanse suddenly seeming huge. Maybe she should make a dash. In case someone was inside the bathroom, her bedroom . . .

Cautiously, she moved, and a floorboard creaked underfoot. She froze. Nothing. Then she saw it.

On her tiny dining table abutting the kitchen counter was a small baggie containing white crystals, a glass pipe, a Bic lighter.

She swallowed, her gaze shooting to the door to her bedroom. She waited, listening. When nothing sounded, she moved carefully across the room and edged open her bedroom door. Nothing. She checked the bathroom, behind the shower curtain, the closets, under the bed. Returning to the table, she stared at the baggie. There was a plain white envelope under it. She had to touch the bag in order to get to the envelope. Merry picked it up, opened it.

Inside were two grainy photos, taken at night. One of her VW Beetle driving along the bay at the Uplands Marina. The other was a photo of herself wearing a toque and down jacket, crouching between a truck and a Sorento, her massive telephoto lens aiming right at whoever shot this photo. She flipped it over.

YOU ARE DEAD

Merry began to shake. She stared at the baggie in front of her. The old, edgy hunger roared its head, fierce like a dragon reawakened from slumber. Panic tightened like a lasso across her throat. Hurriedly, she made her way to the door where she'd left her backpack. She fumbled to open the side pocket where she'd stuck Angie Pallorino's card. Merry found it and dialed the number.

It rang, then clicked over to voicemail. She killed the call, paced, stopped, stared at the drugs. *No. No. No.* With trembling fingers she punched in the detective's cell number again. Once more, it kicked to voicemail.

CHAPTER 63

It was near midnight when Maddocks parked in the West Bay Marina parking lot and made his way along the boardwalk to the marina gate in the blustery wind and rain. The beers with Holgersen and the guys at the Flying Pig had done zip to tamp down the effects of the cortisol still fizzing through his veins—helluva two days. And he remained worried about Angie. Hungry for Angie. Edgy about Angie. She was consuming his brain—he'd driven past her apartment block on the way home and looked up at the top floor at the corner unit where Holgersen had told him she lived. No lights had been on.

He reached the gate, but as he punched in his code, a movement in the shadows came from his left. He jerked around, his hand shooting into position near his holster. Shock rustled through him as a figure emerged from the wet blackness.

"Angie?"

She didn't say a word. Her coat glistened with rain. She wore a black ball cap, and her skin looked ghost-white against the darkness. Her eyes seemed wrong, too. Bigger, blacker, deeper, as if smudged with eye makeup. Worry sparked through him. On the back of his concern came a sinking feeling that she'd been to the club.

"What're you doing here at this hour? You okay?"

Without replying, she came right up to him, reached up, slid her icy-cold hand around the back of his neck, and threaded her fingers roughly into his hair. She looked up into his eyes—deep into his eyes.

Maddocks swallowed. "How long have you been waiting out here, Angie?" he whispered.

In silence, she drew him down to herself, and her cool lips—wet with rain—met his. She leaned up into him, pressing her body against his, and she moved her lips against his in a gentle, exploring, drowning kiss that clean stole his mind. His breaths came faster as he felt her hand going inside his coat, moving down his abs. She cupped him between the legs. A groan built low in his chest as he kissed her back, opening her mouth, wider, tasting her, his tongue twisting with hers. She massaged the growing length of his erection in his pants. But while she was blinding him, stealing his brain as all his blood flooded south into his cock, a small voice of caution in Maddocks said this was wrong. Her need was different. It was not the same hot, raw lust—the sexual aggression—that had fired her previously. He pulled back, breathing hard.

"Angie?" he whispered. "You haven't returned my calls. What's happened?"

"Are you going to invite me in, James Maddocks?" Her voice was thick, hoarse. Maddocks hesitated and then took her hand in his, unlocked the marina gate, and led her down along the dock, which rocked in the swells. His heart thumped with anticipation, promise. Fear. Conflict . . .

We'd like you to formally evaluate Detective Pallorino's performance over the next few weeks, as she continues to work under you . . . she's had performance issues, including an incident that resulted in the recent death of her senior partner. Sergeant Hash Hashowsky was one of our longest-serving, most highly respected, and well-liked detectives. I called him a friend . . .

"Want something to drink?" Maddocks said once they'd come down the companionway and entered his yacht.

She shook her head, slid his coat off his shoulders. Dropping it to the floor, she took both his hands in hers and led him backward into his sleeping cabin. His mouth turned dry. He half expected her to shove him backward onto the bed, rip at his buttons and zipper, strip him wild like that night at the club, straddle him, fuck him hard.

Instead, she seated him fully clothed on the bed and slowly undressed herself in silence, in front of him, lights on. As if she wanted nothing left to hide, no games left to play. She stood naked in front of him—pale breasts, nipples tight nubs, the hair between the apex of her thighs the same color as the long, dark-red hair spilling damp over her shoulders. A poignancy surrounded her, a vulnerability. A fragility that made Maddocks think of perfect glass—a thing of perfection that if he touched, would break. The beat of his heart boomed in his ears. He felt it in his erection. Tentatively, unsure, he reached forward to place his hands on her hips, but she moved them away. She began to undress him—painfully, exquisitely slowly.

When they were both naked, she lay down beside him and drew him atop her. Her pale-gray eyes were almost consumed by her dilated black pupils, making them look huge and dark. Haunted. Shock?

"Angie," he said again, fighting to concentrate, fighting the wildness crackling under his skin as she tilted her pelvis under him, and her hands guided his erection into her folds. "What . . . what in the hell happened?"

Her eyes began to glisten slightly, and she shook her head, as if to say *Not now.* She opened her thighs, arching her spine, an urgency entering her movements now as she strained for him, her breathing becoming faster, her skin warm.

His vision swirled as he thrust and entered her hot wetness. She sighed softly as if with relief. Maddocks moved slowly, tentatively at first, rocking into her, and she met each of his thrusts with soft, sure movements of her hips—a pace as old as time, a rhythm that matched the waves upon which his boat rocked. And inside him a blinding pressure began to build. He could feel her growing hotter, hungrier, beginning to move faster. He thrust harder, faster. She wrapped her legs around him, hooking her ankles behind him, taking him tight into her arms, as if she couldn't get him deep enough, as if she wanted to absorb and consume him wholly.

Suddenly, she gasped, went rigid. Her nails dug into his skin. She clutched onto him, unbreathing, unmoving. Then she cried out, and he felt her muscle contractions, wave after wave after shattering wave as she arched her head back, mouth open, eyes wide, and he couldn't hold back. One more hard thrust to the hilt and he came right inside those rolling waves, collapsing onto her.

For a while afterward they just lay there, entwined in each other, breathing hard, skin slick. Then he felt the wetness of her tears against his neck. His gaze jerked to her face. She was crying, her nose and cheeks pinked.

"Angie?"

She shook her head, cupped his jaw. "That was beautiful," she whispered, drawing his mouth down to hers, kissing him again through the salt of her tears on her lips. "So beautiful. Thank you," she murmured again, against his mouth. "Thank you."

CHAPTER 64

Angie looked up into those impossibly dark blue eyes that had drawn her so on that first night in the club, and a little faraway voice inside her whispered . . .

You could learn to love this man . . .

He'd slid out of her, rolled onto his side, and was propping himself up on his elbow as he studied her. He no longer wore the bandage over his nose, but the swelling was still evident. As were the bruises she'd put there. Her heart crunched.

You really could learn . . .

But at the same time, she knew she wasn't ready. Not yet. She first had to find herself, learn who she was. Those cops might have closed her case all those years ago, but she was determined to see it reopened.

You allowed yourself to be submissive and vulnerable in his arms, and it gave you pleasure, not fear. It was a gift . . . you could become a new person . . .

"Talk to me, Angie," he whispered, touching her lip, her scar, tracing the line of it across her mouth. "Tell me where you've been—what's happened."

"How's the case?" she replied instead, suddenly a little nervous of actually voicing it all to him, making it more real. "It's been killing me to be locked out of it. I've seen nothing in the media."

"Stalled," he said, his hand moving to her breast, tracing her nipple, so that it puckered and tingled all over again. She shivered slightly. He drew the blanket up over them both. "And you're stalling with me. What happened? What changed?"

She took a deep breath and said finally, "I went to see someone. Sort of unofficially. Dr. Alex Strauss. I was a psych major before I decided to go into law enforcement—Alex was my academic advisor, and he became a friend."

She explained to him all that had transpired with Alex and then with her father.

Maddocks listened, playing gently with her hair, an intensity in his eyes.

"So, I guess if Miriam Pallorino is not my biological mother," she said, "then I can't have inherited her genetic predisposition toward schizophrenia. I suppose that's something. Alex also offered to try further hypnosis sessions to see if I can remember more."

"How does all this make you feel?"

A wave of emotion surged through her, and she paused a moment to corral it. She turned her head away to look down at Jack-O, who was curled into a ball on his little sheepskin bed on the floor. The sight of the animal warmed her. "Determined," she said softly. "To search for my birth parents. To find out where I came from, who I am, what happened to me, how I got to be the Angel's Cradle baby. How I seem to know some Polish." She turned back to face him. "I think . . . something terrible was done to my birth mother—or to us both—which is why I could have suppressed all recollection of that period of my life."

Concern entered his features. And it gave her a sense of foreboding, because she wanted back on the drowned girls case. And Maddocks was the gatekeeper—she needed him to believe she was going to be all right now.

"Tell me about the case," she said in an effort to swing things back on course. "What did Leo and Holgersen say about my absence, and about your nose?"

"We'll talk in the morning."

The foreboding deepened—there was something in his eyes, something he was not telling her. "Why?"

"Have you seen the *time*, Angie? We sleep now."

"I want to return to work tomorrow, Maddocks—I *need* to. I've been off two full days. Any longer and there will be serious questions."

"What about that psych eval?" he said quietly.

Her stomach tightened. "I'll make it happen. I'll make an appointment—I'm going to be okay now."

"And the fact you could experience another flashback episode?"

"I won't. It's . . . it's like I've been under pressure my whole life, like this molten lava has been seething and boiling beneath the cool crust of my consciousness, which has been struggling to keep it in and hidden, and now that crust has been exploded open wide, and all that pressure is being relieved as that lava rushes out."

He regarded her for a moment in heavy silence.

"Maddocks," she said quietly. "I'm going to be fine. You *have* to believe me."

"We'll talk more tomorrow." He kissed her gently and clicked off the light.

But as Angie finally drifted off to sleep in his arms, naked and warm in the rocking boat, Jack-O snoring, the old propane heater clunking every time the thermostat registered that the cabin had grown too cold, a nursery-rhyme tune whispered into her mind. Then came tinny music. It grew louder and louder . . .

Two little kittens . . . Two little kittens . . . All children, even the bad ones, are already asleep, only you are not . . .

A deep and unspecified fear started to unfurl inside Angie at the sound of the music. With it came a cold, mental blackness. And she wasn't at all certain she *would* make it all work out fine.

✝

CHAPTER 65

SUNDAY, DECEMBER 17

Angie entered the galley wearing her clothes from yesterday, her hair tied back into a neat ponytail. She was desperate for a hot shower, but more anxious to talk.

Maddocks had set the little galley table for two. His back was to her. He was flipping an omelet and had a pot of steaming coffee on the brew. Jack-O was crunching his biscuits in a bowl at his feet.

"Hey," she said.

"Morning. Sleep okay?" He turned, frying pan in hand, went to the table, and lowered his gaze, focusing on the food as he slid portions of omelet onto two plates. Anxiety trickled instantly into Angie—he was avoiding her gaze.

"Yeah, fine," she lied. Her night had been tormented with dreams awoken deep in that place Alex had taken her.

"Grub's up," he said, taking a bench on one side of the table. He finally looked up and grinned. "My dad always used to say that. Come, sit. Eat while it's warm."

She remained standing, watching his face. His grin did not reach into his eyes. He wore jeans. Nice shirt. No tie. He was dressed for work, but a little more casual. She realized it was Sunday.

"Maddocks—"

"Sit," he repeated, pouring two mugs of coffee. Then, as if catching himself, he looked up again and said, "You doing okay this morning?"

"Peachy. You?"

His hand stilled. His smile sobered.

"We need to talk," she said quietly.

"I know. While we eat." His glance flicked to his watch, and he reached for his knife and fork.

Slowly, she seated herself opposite him. "You're going to work," she said. "You're watching the clock. Something's up with the case—you're anxious to get in there." She felt left behind—a gap yawing open. A sickish feeling filled it.

"Yeah." He reached for his mug, took a gulp of coffee, then cut into his food and delivered a forkful to his mouth. "Jayden Norton-Wells voluntarily gave a DNA sample late yesterday. Sunni said she'd have the profile for us this morning."

She stared. *What?*

"Eat," he said, motioning with his chin toward her plate.

"Why? Am I in a rush, too? Am I coming in with you—*Maddocks*?"

Carefully, slowly, he set down his knife and fork. He met her eyes. Lines furrowed into his brow and bracketed his mouth—an inner struggle evident in the tightness of his features.

"You're avoiding it. Me. This fucking elephant in the room . . . and you're scaring me, because I haven't seen you like this. I thought you were someone who hit things head-on, said things like they were. We've got shit to talk about."

"I . . . I'm sorry, Angie. I . . ." He inhaled deeply. Wind rocked the boat. "I don't know how to do this, either," he said finally. "I haven't been here before. I . . . I want to be there for you, and I'm . . ."

"Struggling with what to do with me? You've taken possession of my weapons. You know stuff about my state of mind that you *should* tell your superiors. We've slept together. Partners. And I've been accused of killing partners before, haven't I? Is that what they said back at the station? What *did* you tell them about your nose? About me? What did Leo and Holgersen and everyone say when I didn't show up? They shred me apart like jackals the first opportunity they had?" Her voice was going tight, her eyes burning. The crap thing about this metaphorical lava shit coming out her consciousness cracks was that it was making her *feel*. It was making her *vulnerable*. It was making her *need* his approval. His faith. His belief in her. And yeah, while she'd tasted vulnerability and submission last night, and it was a wonderful and shimmering and fragile thing—she didn't know if she could do this full-time. She felt herself beginning to close as she looked at him.

"I hate it," she said. "I fucking hate needing anything from anyone. I don't need you—I'm sorry I put you in this position . . . it's not fair, I know." She started to get up. "It's best if I take myself—"

His hand, big and warm, clamped over hers. "Angie."

Thump thump thump went her heart. She could hear her own blood beating. Could hear the chinking of halyards against masts in the wind outside. Could hear the slap of water against the hull. A sense of time pressed down. Past. Present. Future . . . uncertain.

"Just say it, Maddocks," she said quietly. "Bullet points, if you must—like I made my dad say it all. I can take it. I'd rather take it square, because I can't stand it any other way—the guessing, the innuendo. The not knowing."

His gaze lanced into hers. His features tightened further. Energy simmered off him in waves. He nodded, pushed his plate aside, heaved out a sigh, dragged his hand through his hair.

"Buziak is on leave pending outcome of the internal investigation."

She blinked, then slowly reseated herself. "Go on."

"I have no idea what they've got on him, but that news came down Friday. It's why I decided, in part, to go after Norton-Wells for the voluntary sample."

"Who's in his place?"

Silence.

"You?" Her world tilted again on its axis. The sense of betrayal was instant. "You're my *boss*?"

"I know how you must feel. I—"

"No you don't."

"I think I do. I've slept with you. I know things about you. I didn't tell you last night because my concern was about what had happened to you. And you had a lot to process, and I didn't want you to—"

"And now you're my keeper? Deciding what's good for me to hear?"

Loss of control, submission in sex was one thing, but . . . this. This was something else. She swallowed. Pressure was building in her ears. Claustrophobia circling. *Focus. Stay in control.* She started to get up, couldn't sit in this little cubicle, in this little bobble of a yacht . . . panic was rising.

"Fitz also asked me to spy on you."

It hit her like a sledgehammer. *"What?"*

Silence.

"You're in fucking bed with *Fitz*?"

"Would I have just told you this if I were in bed with him?"

She glowered at him. The old familiar anger, the spiciness of rage, began to swell inside her, pushing aside her fears, and she welcomed it. "Spy? Because of what happened with Hash?"

He nodded. "And because he's a misogynistic little prick with a Napoleon complex."

"So now I've done this to you, too—sharpened the conflict of inter-est. Put you in a situation where you've been asked to assess my mental fitness for the job, while you already know that I mentally cracked— almost killed you. Did you tell him *that*?"

"What do you think?"

"I don't know what to think anymore, Maddocks. I've put you in this position, and now I'm sitting here at your mercy. Fucking body, heart, soul . . ." She stopped at the sound of her own words.

Heart.

Soul.

Her eyes burned. She swallowed. He'd gone stone still. His eyes glistened, too.

It was out there now. Like a vibrating thing in the space between them—this thing they were beginning to feel for each other. The heavy implications. The shimmering possibilities. The challenges.

A sort of quiet tide of terror rose up inside her, swallowing away any teases of rage, leaving behind something far more complex.

"I have your back, Angie," he whispered. "You need to know that."

"It'll cost you, Maddocks." She looked away, fiddled with the knife next to her untouched plate of food. She turned the piece of silver cutlery over, and over, and over. She should just walk away. For his sake. Quit or something. This wasn't fair on him. But she also didn't want to step away from a fight. Angie did not like to lose. Ever. Conflict twisted, tore, warred inside her. Yesterday she'd glimpsed a way forward. She *wanted* that way forward, but the world wasn't suddenly going to make it easy for her now, was it? She looked back at him. Met those eyes.

She wanted him, too.

She couldn't walk away from him. As much as she should walk away from him.

"And I'm not alone," he said quietly.

"Meaning?"

"Holgersen, too."

"He *knows*?"

"Not about the incident outside the church. But he saw us, outside the Pig."

She swallowed. Memories of that kiss filled her mind. The club afterward. Her frustration. Her inability to take that blond ice-eyed Adonis to bed. Maddocks following her, unbeknownst to her . . .

"Holgersen's the one who warned me that Fitz was gunning for you. It's why he tried to call you. Several times." He paused. "Angie, you've got friends. You need to deal with that. Irascible as you might be, as much as you've tried to shut out and destroy and break your new partners, Holgersen *likes* you. O'Hagan likes you. I . . . I—"

"You trust Holgersen?" she said quickly.

He hesitated. "I think so. He's a dark horse, been bad places, maybe . . . but I think he's solid. Maybe more than solid." He leaned forward. "Look, it's not just you who Fitz is gunning for. He's after me, too, using me. Playing me. I'll bet my ass he's getting ready to throw me under the bus if this case is not wrapped by Christmas. And if we do close it, he'll personally take the kudos. He's a paranoid little control freak on a witch hunt all around—he's seen a gap, and he's taking it to push himself up the Metro PD ladder somehow."

"Do you trust me?" she said quietly.

Do you trust me enough to work with me again? Do you trust me to work with others?

He fell silent, the loaded question hanging between them. But as he was about to speak, her cell rang. Angie scrambled to fish it out of her pocket like it was a lifeline offering escape. She glanced at the caller ID. Unknown. But the same number had called several times.

"I need to take this," she said. Connecting the call, she put her phone to her ear. "Pallorino."

"Detective . . . it . . . it's Merry Winston." The voice on the other end sounded weak, odd, slightly slurred. Angie's spine stiffened. Her gaze twitched to Maddocks. He was watching her intently.

"What is it?" she said, turning away slightly.

"I've been calling and calling since yesterday. Can we meet? I've got something for you. It's . . . urgent."

"What's urgent?"

"I'll show you when you get here."

"Where, Merry?"

"There's this place at Ogden Point. The Wharf Bistro, at the top of the pier. It opens early. It's got a lot of windows—you can see anyone approaching from the street. And you must come alone. Promise me that you'll come alone, or I'm outta there, and you get nothing." The call ended.

"That was Winston," Angie said. "She . . . sounds odd. Scared. She wants to meet me, alone. The café at Ogden Point."

"Why?"

"Says she's got urgent information." Angie came to her feet as she spoke. "I need to go."

"You mean, information about the Limpet case?"

"I don't know."

Subtext simmered, the question still lingering in his gaze. *Do you trust me . . .*

"I need to go to her, Maddocks," she said softly. "I told you that I believe I got through to her when I went to see her the other day—it has to be me who goes, alone."

He inhaled deeply, got up, and went to open a compartment in the paneling on the wall. Inside was a gun locker. He opened it, removed her service weapon, ammo, and her knife.

He placed them on the table in front of her and met her eyes.

"Stay safe," he said quietly.

Her gaze locked with his. Intensity hummed off him. And Angie knew. This was it. He was crossing that line. He was betting the odds. On her. A team. And she wasn't ever going to let him down.

She picked up her gun, loaded it, holstered it, and pocketed her knife. "Thank you," she whispered.

CHAPTER 66

Angie found Winston hunched at a wooden table in the glassed-in porch area of the restaurant at Ogden Point. She was pressing her hands down flat on a brown envelope as she nervously watched the path that led from the road along the breakwater to the bistro. A fire crackled inside the main restaurant area, and the air was fragrant with the scent of freshly ground coffee and sweet pastries.

The other tables were all vacant at this early hour, apart from one near the washroom where a senior sipped coffee and turned the pages of his morning newspaper with his shaky liver-spotted hands. Angie guessed that it was his dog tied to the railing outside, black fur ruffling in the salt wind.

"Why here?" Angie said quietly, removing her coat and hat and taking a seat opposite the slight, dark-haired reporter. The woman's eyes were bloodshot, and they darted from point to point as if unable to settle or properly focus. There was an odd sheen to her skin, her complexion deathly pale. Drugs, thought Angie.

"Like I said, it's . . . open. Got a good view. Can see who's coming." As she spoke, she took two grainy black-and-white photographic prints from her envelope. She slid them across the table. "For you."

Angie turned her attention to the photos. One showed a dark-haired man in a leather jacket walking along a dock. The second was of the same man boarding a luxury yacht.

"What are these?"

Winston sucked in a shaky breath, rubbed her mouth, her eyes snapping between the window and the photographs. "Faith used to have a pimp. Way back. Damián Yorick. I heard from someone on the street some days ago that Faith had been seen with him again, fairly recently, along with a blond guy in a black BMW. That's him, Damián." She nodded to the photo.

Angie's pulse quickened. "Can you describe the blond guy he was seen with?"

"Young, apparently."

"How young?"

"Like early twenties young."

"And you're certain this blond guy was driving a black BMW? Did your contact note the plate?"

"No plate info—she's a crystal meth user, lives on the streets. But she was certain it was a Bimmer. One of those little sports models. Black."

"What's her name, your contact?"

"I . . ." Winston closed her eyes, as if fighting herself, then made a decision. "Nina. Sometimes she bunks at the Harbor House—it's where I met her and Faith." She cleared her throat, glanced nervously around. "I used to live on the streets, see? I was bounced around in foster care and ended up a runaway. Pastor Markus kinda took me under his wing. And Nina, and Faith. We grew close, looked out for each other on the streets. I got out. I came clean. Nina couldn't. Faith—she got into the escort business, with Damián at first, then I don't know who. Someone who introduced her into a much higher-end clientele, and she had what seemed like a regular big-paying gig on Tuesday nights." Winston sniffed and wiped her sleeve across her nose. "She wouldn't talk about

402

it, but she ended up in that nice apartment. Teeth fixed. Good clothes. Faith was still pretty, you know, once she got off the meth. She has— had—this really young look going on, and the older guys liked it."

Angie's adrenaline was pumping hard now. She knew it—she'd read Winston right. This kid had some big-ass issues and was still struggling to overcome her past. It explained her punchy, fuck-you attitude. Merry Winston had reason to hit back at the world, and she was using her keyboard to do it. A grudging admiration sifted into Angie's perspective on this little reporter with the bad teeth. Winston might have come clean, but meth-mouth was her legacy. "Go on," she said.

"I went to confront Damián, to ask him about the blond guy and Faith. But he lied about having seen Faith. He claimed he hadn't laid eyes on her in like over a year." Winston rubbed her mouth again. "So I waited, watching his place, and when he left, I followed his car to this place." She nodded to the photo. "Uplands Marina."

Angie's pulse dialed up another notch.

"What day was this?"

"Friday night into Saturday morning."

Angie looked more closely at the photo of Damián Yorick boarding the yacht. The *Amanda Rose*—the name was clear in the photo. And it struck her like a bullet to the brain. *Amanda Rose*. Amanda R. The name and initial on Gracie Drummond's calendar, along with Lara Pennington's, and the letters B.C. A reminder to meet those nights— usually a Tuesday.

"What was Damián Yorick doing visiting this yacht?"

"I don't know. But he's a pimp, right? He moves in questionable circles. He buys and sells women and sex, and he takes a cut. So I waited. There were people on board, some kind of party happening. Lights on inside, two guys who looked like they could be security up on deck, so I didn't want to go any closer. Then while I'm watching, this other guy comes along." Winston slid a third print out of her envelope. Another grainy nighttime shot, this one showing a second male boarding the *Amanda Rose*. Dark hair. Lean. Strong looking.

"Who is he?" she said.

Winston tightened her lips. She removed another photo and pushed it toward Angie. In this image the two young men were walking along the dock together, heads bent close as if in intense, intimate conversation. Angie's pulse ticked up a notch—the second male looked like Jayden Norton-Wells.

"They left in separate vehicles. I decided to follow the second guy to see if I could figure out who he was, where he was going. He drove this vehicle." From her envelope, Winston took a photo of a red Porsche. Angie's gaze flared to the reporter's.

"And where did he go?"

Winston placed in front of Angie a photograph of the red Porsche turning into a driveway flanked by two stone columns. On the column a plaque had been mounted. The name on the plaque was clearly visible—AKASHA.

Electricity crackled through Angie—it *was* Norton-Wells. She swallowed, staring at the image.

"Coffee? Anything to order?" said a server who'd materialized at their table. Quickly, Angie turned the photos over. "Could you give us another minute?" The server left.

Angie leaned forward. Lowering her voice, she said, "Do you know whose residence this is?"

The reporter nodded. In silence she placed another image in front of Angie. A photo of a man and woman kissing passionately in a white Audi parked under a streetlight.

"I'd pulled over across the street from the driveway when this couple in this Audi pulled up. The couple kissed, and then the woman got out." Winston placed another print on the table. Angie stared, mind reeling. *Joyce Norton-Wells*, her hand resting on top of the car door as she bent down to talk to the male sitting inside behind the Audi's wheel.

The vehicle's interior light clearly revealed the distinctly angular lines of the male's face.

Mayor Jack Killion.

"Clusterfuck, eh?" Winston said, her gaze flitting back to the path outside the window. She shifted in her seat. Her knee started to jiggle. "Those are for you."

Angie sifted slowly through the photos once more.

From the pocket of her jacket, Winston took a memory stick. She set it in front of Angie. "And this. It's a copy of the digital recordings I made of my calls from my anonymous source, who I believe is someone inside the MVPD."

Angie glanced up sharply. "Who is he?"

"I don't know. I don't even know whether it's a he or a she. They used voice distortion. I also have my recorded conversation with Damián on there."

There was a sense of finality to Winston's tone, and it set alarm bells clanging in Angie.

"Why, Merry?" she said, using the reporter's first name. "Why did you come to me with all of this now, when you could have just run with it, gotten a huge scoop, incredible mileage? That would have been more your style."

Winston's gaze darted back to the windows again. "Because I also got this." She shoved over the two last photos from her envelope. "That's me," she said, pointing to a small figure hunkering in a large, dark jacket between a truck and a sedan, a massive telephoto lens in her hands, a hat pulled snugly over her head.

"Someone on the boat saw me," she said. "They shot *me* while I was shooting them. Those security guys had to have known I was there, watching them the whole while."

"How did you get this?"

"Someone left that photo on the table in my apartment, along with this."

Angie studied the final image. A little baggie of white crystals, a pipe, and a Bic lighter.

"Someone broke into my home, Detective, and left crack and paraphernalia on my table and that photo of me. Read the back."

Angie flipped it over.

YOU ARE DEAD

Winston's eyes glistened suddenly. "I came to you because you said that you cared. And I believed you. I don't know what in the hell is going on, but I want you to nail those fucking bastards who hurt Faith." She shoved her chair back and got to her feet.

"One other thing. I *did* write my story—everything I know. About the deep throat. Faith. Her pimp. The blond guy and the Bimmer. How nice Faith got fixed up with her teeth and all. About the other rapes from years ago. The red Sharpie crucifixes. The words the rapist used about Satan being the father of sin and prince of darkness. About those—" She wrapped her arms tightly over her chest and jerked her chin toward the photos and memory stick on the table. "The *Amanda Rose*. The ADAG and the mayor. The red Porsche going up the AKASHA driveway . . . all of it. With photos. And I've scheduled the exposé to release on Christmas Eve." She turned and started to leave.

"Wait!" Angie reached for Winston's wrist, stopping her. "Why'd you preschedule the story?"

Her eyes met Angie's. "To give you a chance to get him. And in case something happens to me."

"Merry, what did you do with the drugs?" Angie said softly.

"I didn't use, if that's what you mean. I . . . I'm clean."

"What did you do with it?"

"It's at home."

"Get it out of your house, Merry. Bring it to me. It's evidence. We might be able to trace—"

But Winston jumped as the door opened. A couple entered, a little bird flying in behind them, becoming trapped inside as the door swung slowly shut. It fluttered into the glassed-in patio area and banged against the panes. Petrified, Winston jerked free of Angie's hold. "I gotta go."

"Come in, let us protect you—"

"No," she whispered. "No fucking way. That deep throat, I don't know who he is, but he's there, inside the Metro PD. It could have been him who left that shit in my apartment. He could be in with those guys on the yacht. If Damián and that yacht are mixed up with what happened to Faith, and if Damián is tight with the ADAG's son, and the ADAG is fucking the mayor—Jesus Christ—I don't know where the connections begin and end anymore. I don't trust anyone, especially the cops. I gotta look after myself. I'm all I got—me, myself."

"Yet you brought me those photos, that recording."

Her gaze twitched to the bird trying to get out. "Because of what you said the other day—" She swallowed. "You said you cared."

"What about those earlier rapes, Merry? You've *got* to give me details on those."

She shot another furtive glance at the windows and the pathway outside that led to the road. Then she leaned down toward Angie, lowering her voice to a barely audible whisper. "I know about them because *I* was one of his victims, okay? It happened to *me*. Five years ago. Red crucifix. Knife at the throat. Missing lock of hair. And it was why Allison Fernyhough agreed to speak to me. And she told me about Sally Ritter."

"What about the other—" A middle-aged male came along the path and up the restaurant stairs. Panic flared in Winston's face as he entered the door.

"I gotta go." She spun around and was gone. Out the door. Down the stairs. Through the windows, Angie watched Winston scurry along the breakwater path toward the road, her black hoodie pulled up over her head, hiding her profile. She approached a green Volkswagen Beetle, got in. Angie reached for her phone.

Maddocks answered on the second ring.

"I've got it," she said softly as she watched Merry Winston climbing into her Beetle. "*Amanda Rose.* It's a luxury yacht. And I have photographic evidence of Norton-Wells boarding that yacht with Faith Hocking's pimp on Friday night—a pimp who has been seen in the company of a blond male in his early twenties who drives a black Bimmer."

CHAPTER 67

Angie squared her shoulders, hesitated, took a deep breath, and entered the Operation Limpet incident room carrying the envelope Merry Winston had given her at the Wharf Bistro.

The place was abuzz, detectives shuffling through files, conversing with techs, who worked furiously at the computers on tables and desks arranged on one side of the room. The air was hot and smelled of burnt coffee and doughnuts that someone had brought in for Sunday breakfast. No one even looked up as she came in—her absence long forgotten in the excitement of the investigative discoveries now unspooling before them at warp speed. And they all knew from her phone conversation with Maddocks that the clock was ticking down toward Merry Winston's prescheduled exposé and photographs, which would launch on Christmas Eve. Relief was a punch to Angie's gut.

Maddocks looked up from where he was examining papers on a table at the front of the room with Holgersen. He motioned for her to come over, and he smiled as she approached. She read approval in his eyes. She'd set the ball rolling from the bistro, then gone home for a speedy shower and change of clothing—it was going to be a long day and then some, and she'd been nervous about returning to the station, of the scrutiny she expected to see in the eyes of colleagues like Leo. And she'd wanted to feel fresh and look her power-best.

He took the envelope from her and started spreading Winston's photographic evidence out on the table.

"Where's Leo?" she said, scanning the bustle in the incident room.

"Sent him with Smith to watch the *Amanda Rose*," Maddocks said, studying Winston's photos. "Got techs digging into the yacht's ownership history—she's registered in the Caymans, so that could be a problem—but I want to keep surveillance on her twenty-four/seven in case she decides to pull anchor. Don't want her heading into international waters before we've got a handle on this. Got Metro harbor units on standby in the next cove in case she bolts."

Angie smiled to herself and caught Holgersen's eye. Leo on surveillance duty. She could only imagine his grousing at being sidelined like that. One–zero to Maddocks. He glanced up from the photos.

"Well done. Thank you," Maddocks said.

Her eyes held his for a nanosecond, and she thought of the trust he'd placed back into her hands with her gun, at no small risk to himself. She had more to thank him for than he had to thank her.

He gave a small nod, pinned the Winston photos up onto the board, picked up a Sharpie, then turned to the room. "Okay, let's get to this. Gather around."

The team moved into position, focusing on the board.

"Are we going to try to stop that Winston interview from running sir?" someone from the group asked.

"We don't have cause," said another detective. "Freedom of speech and press and all that."

"Yeah we have cause, if what she says is going to compromise the investigation."

"We don't have evidence of exactly what she is going to say," added another.

Maddocks banged the table. "Here's how we play it. Christmas Eve and the scheduled Winston exposé is eight days away, counting today. We're going to focus on getting this wrapped before then. Got it?"

Murmurs.

"Right." With the back of his Sharpie he tapped Winston's photograph of Jayden Norton-Wells and Damián Yorick boarding the *Amanda Rose*.

"Norton-Wells, the ADAG's son. Black hair. Seen boarding the high-end Caymans-registered yacht with Faith Hocking's pimp, Yorick, on Friday, December fifteen. Yorick is known to police, has a record— street drugs, assault charges, has done time. Also black hair. He's allegedly been seen in the company of a blond male in his early twenties who drives a black BMW." Maddocks drew a line from the Yorick photo to the one of Jon Jacques Jr. and made a question mark under the image. "We're working on the assumption that the blond male is this man, son of a dentist, Jon Jacques Senior, also blond." He drew another line.

He tapped the photo of Faith Hocking. "Homicide victim Hocking, seen recently with Yorick and Mr. Blond Bimmer. Hocking had her meth-mouth fixed with expensive dentistry. She had a card for dentist Jon Jacques Senior in her apartment." He drew another line, linking the dentist and his son to both Hocking and the pimp.

"Mr. Blond Bimmer seems to have picked Gracie Drummond up at the Oak Bay Country Club after she was dumped by her boyfriend from school." He drew a line linking Drummond to the cluster through Jon Jacques Jr., and he turned back to face the room.

"After meeting Jacques Junior, Drummond seems to have come into money, makes many, very expensive, unexplained purchases. She also expressed to her priest that she had guilt issues with the number of men she was sleeping with. We're working on the assumption she was recruited into the sex trade."

"By Baby Jacques," said Holgersen. "He could be the scout. He brings girls like Drummond to the pimp, Yorick. I'm guessing he breaks them in. And the ones who need cleaning up, like Hocking, Daddy the dentist lends a hand."

"What's in it for the dentist?" said someone in the group.

"Maybe business share," offered another. "This is a dude who's been investigated numerous times for financial connections to organized crime and laundering, but nothing stuck."

Maddocks said, "We've got techs combing through the notes of that investigation. So far, Dr. Jon Jacques Senior appears to be linked to numbered accounts in the Caymans, and one of those accounts appears to share a business interest in the same account that is linked to the ownership of the *Amanda Rose*."

"Fuck me," whispered someone, and a rustle of energy moved like wildfire through the group—they were getting somewhere now. Somewhere big.

"So maybe there's some kind of high-end sex club on the *Amanda Rose*?" said another. "What about this Lara Pennington, also up on the board?"

Angie cleared her throat, thinking of her own club and the sex she routinely acquired there. "Drummond's calendar indicated that she had regular dates with Lara P." She picked a marker up off the table and wrote under Pennington's photo:

Lara P., Amanda R., B.C.

She turned to face the investigators. "We're working on the assumption that Pennington is also involved in a possible prostitution ring aboard the *Amanda Rose*. B.C.—we don't yet know what those initials stand for, but in the course of our investigation we came across a matchbook with a 'B.C.' logo on the front. That same book had Drummond's cell number scrawled on the inside of the cover." She paused, holding the attention riveted on her. "That book was seen in the office of Zach Raddison, personal aide to Mayor Jack Killion."

A whistle came from the back of the room, and again, that rustle of adrenaline as investigators physically shifted with the energy of the unfolding details.

"And Mayor Killion," said Holgersen, nodding to the photo Winston shot outside AKASHA, "is having an affair with ADAG Joyce Norton-Wells, mother of Jayden Norton-Wells, who was seen boarding the *Amanda Rose* with a known pimp."

"Holy clusterfuck," said someone.

"Yeah, becoming the go-to word for this investigation," replied another. "This is going to tank those two—the mayor and the ADAG—one way or another. Maybe the ADAG pressured her lover to push for those concessions he's making for that huge waterfront development of her husband's."

"And Law-Boy Jayden Norton-Wells—he's confessed that he knew and cared for Drummond, and that he *is* called J.R. by those who know him," said Holgersen. "And it's likely that he gave Drummond a Saint Christopher medallion for safe passage—whatever that means to him. He also lied about the mysteriously missing Lexus, which showed up on the iron bridge before and after Drummond's abduction near the Blue Badger Bakery and on the 7-Eleven surveillance camera outside the Ross Bay Cemetery where Drummond was found."

Angie crooked a brow and stared at Holgersen, stunned that the dude *could* actually speak in grammatically coherent sentences when it came down to it. Had he slipped? Was this the default Kjel Holgersen? Or was he just trying really hard to put on a show for these veteran investigators?

As if suddenly realizing his character slip, Holgersen continued, "An' when Law-Boy's confronted by police abouts his missing Lexus, he spooks and flees in his dinky red Porsche straight to city hall and Mayor-Boy Zach Raddison, here—" He pointed to the photo of Raddison. "With his black hair, B.C. matchbook, and Drummond's phone number."

"What do you figure the mayor's affair has got to do with this?" said Dundurn—who'd been brought in from the sex crimes unit along with Smith, who was now out with Leo at the Uplands Marina.

"Probably bad luck," said Angie. "One of those personal or family secrets that gets exposed when lives intersect with crime and the onion layers are peeled back by investigators."

A knock sounded, and the door to the incident room opened. Everyone swung around.

"Dr. Padachaya?" Maddocks said. And the crackle of anticipation was instant—they'd all been waiting for the DNA profile of Jayden Norton-Wells.

She came forward with a smile and a spark in her eyes that told Angie Sunni Padachaya had it—she had Norton-Wells.

She handed a folder to Maddocks. "Copies of all the results—from his hair, blood, and saliva samples."

He waited, ever the gentleman, allowing the small doc to drop her own bombshell.

"It's him," she said. "Jayden Norton-Wells is Black-Haired Male One. His body hair was found in pubic combings from our floater, Hocking, inside her tarp, in fibers of the ropes from the Thetisby Island crime, and on Drummond's clothing."

"Whoa, Law-Boy, we gotcha," said Holgersen with a victory pump in the air. "We gots him by the short-and-curly black ones. Let's go bring him in!"

"Not so fast," came a reedy, scratchy voice.

Everyone whirled around. Inspector Frank Fitzsimmons stood at the back of the room. Angie glared at him.

How long had he been standing there, the creep?

He came forward, thunder in his face, his hands tight at his sides, his focus lasered on Maddocks. As he neared, Angie saw he was actually vibrating with anger. He had papers in his hand that quivered with the tension emanating from his body.

"Sergeant Maddocks," he said, coming to a stop in front of Maddocks. "Ray Norton-Wells and his team of attorneys have received a motion from Judge Lofland to quash his son's DNA evidence. They claim he was forced to give it under duress. In no way, shape, or form can you use anything that comes from those DNA samples."

"That's bullshit," snapped Holgersen. "Whole fucking thing was recorded. He signed a—"

"Crown can appeal," retorted Fitz. "But right now, that evidence is off the table."

"Fucking hell," muttered Holgersen, looking at Angie.

"Sergeant, a word outside." Fitz spun and made for the door. As it swung shut behind him, Maddocks turned to face Angie.

"Get the vehicle ready. We're going to pick him up. Now. He'll be at church."

Her gaze spiked to the door. "Fitz?"

"Now!" He turned to Holgersen. "You take Dundurn, get a bead on Raddison. Don't touch. Just follow him. Anything unusual, I want to know stat. And you, Hazleton," he said to another detective. "Call Vedder. I want sex crimes fully on board with all its services on standby. Tell him we need an emergency response team. And I want that SWAT team on board the *Amanda Rose* tonight." He grabbed his coat off the back of a chair and stormed after Fitz.

Maddocks found Fitz waiting simmering outside the incident room door.

"I'm bringing him in," he told Fitz before the man could speak.

"Sergeant, I ordered you to inform me before—"

Maddocks flung his arm toward the door. "We could be sitting on an international sex ring there, a club selling underage women on a yacht registered in the Caymans with possible organized crime links via a local dentist whom the RCMP's commercial and organized crimes units has been investigating for years. And somewhere within that milieu, Hocking and Drummond crossed the path of a sick, lust-based serial killer. If we let this Norton-Wells slip out of our hands now—if he sends alarm bells out—the *Amanda Rose* could be in international waters by tonight, and that's a whole other ball game. That yacht could be taking the killer with it. And if there are any other young women on that boat, their lives could be in jeopardy—there could be an attempt to cover the crimes in international waters."

"We have no grounds to bring in—"

"Yes, we do. We have photographic and witness evidence that puts Norton-Wells on the *Amanda Rose* with Faith Hocking's pimp, who in turn associates with Jon Jacques Junior, who in turn was involved with Drummond. And we have his admission that Norton-Wells knows and cares for Drummond. And there's the Lexus. That photographic evidence could get us a DNA warrant now, thanks to Winston—we just start over with new samples."

"Sergeant," Fitz demanded in his high, scratchy voice, "I in—"

"I caution you before speaking, sir," Maddocks said, lowering his voice. "We have photographic evidence of Mayor Killion and ADAG Joyce Norton-Wells engaging in an extramarital affair." He paused, holding those beady little black hawk eyes. "Perception is often everything in politics, sir. Given the rumors that Mayor Killion is maneuvering to replace Chief Gunnar with his own man, and soon, and that there will be further internal MVPD firings and hirings—it would look most unfortunate if you were seen as the one who sabotaged this case, a case that implicates Killion himself. And the ADAG's son. Possibly in exchange for a promotion." He waited a beat. The man vibrated, glowering at Maddocks. And Maddocks figured his job with the MVPD was probably toast, but he was not letting that yacht sail away. Not on his life.

"The story is already scheduled to run," he said quietly, giving them an avenue out. "Complete with photos. On Christmas Eve. I'd like this case wrapped before that. Under your helm."

✝

THE BAPTIST

It's Sunday morning when he drives along the coast road. He needs the vehicle today. Today is the day he plans to take Lara, and he is tight with anticipation. He worked out with weights before dawn, then ran eight miles—all in preparation. He shaved his genitals last night. Lara is at church now. He's edgy, needing to do something until dark, so he takes the road past the Uplands Marina. Just to see if the *Amanda Rose* is still berthed there. He's come by often since Faith. He likes to watch the shining palace on the water at night and to wonder who is down in the cabins and with whom. And he imagines he's watching them again—Gracie, Lara, Faith . . . Eva . . . the others with the barcodes on the backs of their necks . . . He slows suddenly at the sight of a police cruiser.

It's parked to the side of the road. Two cops sitting in it. He swallows, keeps his eyes on the road, his hands at two and eleven on the wheel, indicates and quickly turns left, heading away from the water.

He pulls off the road and parks under a tree. His pulse is racing. His palms are damp. No. No need to worry. It's all good, all fine. But, because he's curious, because his senses are alert like a hunter in the wild today, he gets out of the vehicle and walks down a side alley toward the ocean road again. He pops out onto a knoll with long brown grasses under Garry oaks. He can see the marina. The *Amanda Rose* is there. In all her glory, her flags flapping gently in the winter breeze. He stills, just watching, scenting the air. The sight calms him. He thinks of all that glorious wood inside there. The women waiting with their pussies for the men to come . . . *That's when he sees them*—two men. One older, with white hair and a square head. The other is skinny and a little taller. They're sitting on a bench on the path above the marina. He watches them a while. One of them raises a small set of bird binoculars to his face. He's studying the *Amanda Rose* down in the bay.

His stomach goes tight. He swallows and steps back into the tangle of oak branches and shadows, and he watches them for a long, long while. They look wrong. Suits. Cops—they're cops.

He turns on his heel and makes hurriedly for his vehicle, his hands clenching and unclenching at his sides.

Stupid boy, Johnny boy, of course they're cops, Tommy, you silly Johnny . . . trying to catch Tommy . . . you better clear out, Johnny, closing in on Tommy . . .

By the time he reaches his vehicle, he knows what he must do. His plan has changed. He must move fast. Not Lara tonight. The other one tonight . . . end game tonight.

It's okay, Johnny. Just moving it ahead, Tommy . . . the only final sin is stupidity, boy . . .

CHAPTER 68

Angie chose to stand. She folded her arms over her chest and leaned her shoulder against the wall of the small interview room behind where Jayden Norton-Wells and his legal counsel were seated at a table bolted to the floor. Her design was to unsettle them.

The interior of the room was sterile—walls padded with off-white sound-absorbing tiles, a door to Angie's left, and a two-way mirror. From behind the mirror Fitz, Vedder, a Crown prosecutor, and Holgersen observed.

Maddocks sat at the table in front of Norton-Wells and his legal counsel. Angie and Maddocks had nabbed Norton-Wells coming out of his Sunday church service. He'd been docile, had not resisted arrest in any way, merely said he wanted his lawyer.

Now that his counsel had arrived—a top criminal attorney, funded by his father—they were proceeding with questioning.

"Why did you volunteer a DNA sample, Jayden?" Maddocks said.

Norton-Wells glanced at his lawyer—a woman in her late fifties with inscrutable features, her Mont Blanc pen and her writing pad resting on the table in front of her. "I didn't," he said blandly. "It was coerced."

Under the unforgiving fluorescent lighting, Norton-Wells's complexion was waxy. He looked exhausted and broken. Adrenaline coursed through Angie's blood.

Maddocks opened his file and slid the photographs of Norton-Wells boarding the *Amanda Rose* with Damián Yorick toward him.

He looked at his lawyer.

"Look at the photos, Jayden," Maddocks said. "That's you there." He tapped the first one. "You with Faith Hocking's pimp, Damián Yorick. And here's you with her pimp again. And this one—it's you getting into your red Porsche, license plate visible. And this one—you driving your Porsche up the AKASHA driveway after leaving the *Amanda Rose*." Maddocks leaned forward.

"We know you and Gracie were close, Jayden," he said. "We know about the Saint Christopher, that you made up the story about the stolen Lexus, that you were never at the Auberge. Never parked in that lot up the street—"

"Circumstantial at be—" began the lawyer.

"Not *those* photos," Angie said from behind them. "That's proof you were on the *Amanda Rose* with Faith's pimp. Was he Gracie's pimp, too? Did Faith die on that yacht, Jayden? After you finished screwing her?"

"Detective!" said the lawyer. "We have—"

"We're getting a DNA seizure warrant, Jayden," she said. "Based on what we have so far. And we all know what a new set of samples is going to tell us, don't we? It's going to tell us you had sex with Faith Hocking before she died. Maybe afterward, too. Fucked her real hard, eh, Jayden?"

His eyes started to water. He opened his mouth.

The lawyer placed her hand quickly on his arm. "You don't have to say anything, Jayden. We—"

"That's okay, Jayden," Angie said, walking slowly around to Maddocks's side. She stood beside Maddocks, her arms still folded casually. "You don't have to talk. Like I said, we're just waiting on that DNA warrant—your DNA will do the talking."

Norton-Wells's body spasmed. His lawyer's hand firmed on his arm. "That's enough, detectives. We're done here. Jayden, come with me." She began to rise from her chair, bringing Norton-Wells to his feet with her.

"Thing that puzzles me, though," Angie said quickly as they started for the door, "is why you volunteered your DNA in the first place, given what you did."

He stilled at the door.

"I think it's because he didn't kill Faith or Gracie," Maddocks said. "He might have paid for nice gentlemanly intercourse with Faith—and we know the courts go easy on the john angle. But brutalize and slice those girls? Shove their heads under water and hold them there? Leave little Gracie with her clit cut off, bleeding, her legs splayed open on that grave like that? Carving a crucifix into her face?"

Norton-Wells buckled at the knees, a little noise emanating from his throat.

"Jayden, come, now," said his lawyer. But he remained rooted to the spot, refusing to follow.

"Well, if he doesn't speak," said Maddocks, "his DNA will do it for him, and if so, he's going to go down for a double homicide—sexual serial killer Norton-Wells, wow, there's a thing. Going straight to hell, Jayden boy."

"I didn't do it. *I didn't do it. I didn't do it. I didn't do it!*"

He pulled away from his lawyer.

"Jayden!" She reached for his arm.

"No, leave me—I'm going to tell them! I *have* to tell them. I . . . I can't do this anymore. I didn't do it—it wasn't me."

"Who was it then, Jayden?" Maddocks said. "What *really* happened?"

"Zach did it. Zach killed Faith."

CHAPTER 69

"All I did was go to the club to have sex, pay for sex. That's all. That's how I met her. Gracie."

"What club?" said Maddocks.

"Bacchanalian Club. On the *Amanda Rose*."

"And the logo of this club is an ornate B and a C—intertwined?" Angie said.

He nodded, tears wetting his cheeks now. "They have little books of matches with their logo on them. It's a private gentlemen's club—that's what they call it. Super high-end clientele. Gracie wrote her cell number on a book of matches for me. They're not supposed to give out personal information, but . . . oh God, I can't believe this is happening."

"Go on, Jayden," Maddocks said with a quick glance at Angie. "Who is 'they'?"

"The girls."

"Sex workers?"

He nodded. "Companions, they call them. Gracie and I . . . we were getting close." He sniffed and wiped his face.

"You're a member of the B.C.?"

"I'm still a guest on probation. You need to qualify. Members can introduce friends as guests, and after a certain number of guest visits, and as long as all payments are cleared, and nothing goes wrong, and the girls have approved."

"And so, you were a guest when you met Gracie? It was a Tuesday night—Gracie wrote B.C. and Amanda R. on her calendar," Angie said.

"I got Gracie, yeah, on my first night. She was working PPN."

"What does that stand for?" Angie said.

He put his head back, eyes rolling into their sockets. He panted in short breaths, and he was sweating, as if he was about to faint. The lawyer, who'd reseated herself beside her client, came sharply to her feet again. "I'm going to have to call an end to this, detectives. My client is in medical distress. I need some help in here."

Angie and Maddocks exchanged another quick glance. They needed to close this deal, fast. Angie nodded toward the two-way mirror, where she knew Fitz, Vedder, a prosecutor, and a few other investigators were observing.

"Someone is fetching an EMT now," she said, placing her hand gently on Jayden's arm. "Jayden," she said softly. "If you really just made a mistake, the more you can tell us, the better."

He swallowed, nodded, wiped his face.

"Now, what is PPN?" she said.

"Plump Pussy Night." He choked on the words. "Usually Tuesdays. Masks for the men. Robes and other costumes if they want them. Sex toys and other equipment."

"Equipment like ropes?" Maddocks said.

He nodded. "It *was* a mistake, I swear it. I was just watching. The rope got too tight around her neck—Faith's neck. He didn't mean it. Then suddenly we noticed she wasn't breathing anymore. I . . . we panicked, tried to untie her. I couldn't loosen the ropes. Oh, God help me." He spun away from them.

"*Who* did you watch, Jayden?" Maddocks said.

"Zach," he said, voice small.

"Zach Raddison?"

"He's the one who took me there."

"Why'd he take you there?" said Maddocks.

"We . . . we've been friends since high school." Norton-Wells inhaled deeply. "Zach's always had a reputation for knocking women about a bit. He likes his sex rough."

"What kind of rough? Can you give me an example?" Maddocks said.

He swallowed, rubbed his knee. "One of his favorite things is to get a woman naked and down on all fours. He uses studded dog collars, and he makes the collar really tight around her neck. He affixes a leash to the collar, and he leads the woman around, verbally mocking and debasing her."

"Debasing? How so?" said Angie.

Clearing his throat, he said, "By calling them dog bitches in heat, dirty cunts, that kind of thing. And he likes to hurt them a bit, to make them cry, and then he tells them to whimper louder, like an animal, and then he takes them on all fours, mounting them from behind. Sometimes he would take a new date out for a fancy dinner and be all chivalrous and gentle, and he'd bring them home, close the door, then suddenly shove them hard up against a wall with his hand around their throats. He loved to see the raw shock in their eyes."

"And he's done this since high school?"

"Yeah." He sniffed, wiped his nose.

"Complaints filed?"

He shook his head. "There was a rumor once that the father of one of the women who was putting in a complaint was offered a top position at Raddison Industries. The complaint was dropped. There were also some sexual harassment complaints at his previous job, but they were also dropped for whatever reason. When he joined Killion's campaign, he knew he'd be in the media spotlight and that he'd have to keep it in his pants, or at least under the radar. That's when he heard about the Bacchanalian Club—a sex club, where you could get . . .

different things in an exclusive environment, for a price. Classy, clean girls. Excellent food and entertainment. Sadomasochistic stuff." He wiped his mouth.

"Zach went a few times as a guest, became a member, and then he took me. You get a bonus girl, something really special, if you bring in a new paying member."

"Why you?"

"It was a birthday gift. Zach figured I wasn't getting enough, or good enough." A moment of silence besieged him, and when he spoke again, there was a marked shift in his tone. He sounded utterly defeated. "I think . . . he just liked an audience. He wanted someone who was connected with his real world to see and know what he was doing at the club. It's the exhibitionist in him. It gives him a thrill. Sexual and ego." He cleared his throat, glanced at the two-way mirror, hesitated, and his eyes went to the door.

"Go on, Jayden," Angie prompted softly, adrenaline thumping in her blood. She also glanced again at the two-way mirror. She figured Fitz or Vedder would have given Holgersen the word by now to move on Raddison and bring him in.

Jayden scrubbed his face with his hands. His legal counsel had an odd look on her face. "Jayden," she said, placing her hand on his arm again.

He shook his head. "No. I don't care what my dad says. Or my mom. I . . . I *need* to do this. All of it. For Gracie." He heaved out a chestful of air. "Zach took me for PPN. Members who subscribe to the B.C. notifications receive a special text alert a few days before, if PPN is to happen. The message comes from an anonymous server, all mysterious. It makes members feel like they're part of some underground sex movement. At least that's what Zach says. The PPN girls are young."

"How young?"

"Gracie had just turned sixteen when she started. She said there are three others, at least, who are younger than she was. But those three aren't local. They came in on the *Amanda Rose*. The others maybe just look very young, and they play it up with makeup and pigtails, and they dress in school uniforms with really short skirts and no panties, and wear things like dildos shaped like baby pacifiers around their necks." He cleared his throat and stared at the table surface. "They sit around in the cabin using the pacifier dildos while some of the men watch and have drinks or whatever." He fell silent for a few seconds. "That kind of thing."

"And those young girls who are not local—where do they come from?"

"I don't know. They live on the yacht, I think. The *Amanda Rose* only stays in port for about three months at a time. She returns annually for what the B.C. club calls the Victoria Season. The previous stop was Vancouver, and before that it was Portland, I think. The *Amanda Rose* was off South America prior to entering US waters, according to Gracie. Those other young girls could have been picked up in any one of those ports. I never saw or spoke to those three."

"What about the local women who work on the yacht?"

"There was Gracie." He inhaled deeply and blew out a heavy breath. "Lara. Eva—I don't know if those were real names, but they're the two Gracie mentioned to me. She helped bring Lara and Eva in. She got a lot of money for that."

"And why did Gracie tell you all these things, Jayden?"

His mouth tightened, he gagged, and for a moment it seemed as though he was going to throw up.

"Like . . . I said, I . . . I was given Gracie that first night I went with Zach. We made love. I—"

"You didn't make love, Jayden," Angie snapped. "You paid for sex."

Maddocks shot her a hot glance. She gave a tiny shrug of her shoulder.

"It felt special. I . . . I returned with Zach the following week. For Gracie. And then every week that PPN was held, only for her. She liked me. We got talking. She saw my Saint Christopher and asked about my faith, and she told me about her own rekindled faith. Her choir. Some nights I paid and we just talked. She liked that." He looked down and began to trace little circles on the table with his index finger. "We began to talk about . . . after."

"After?"

"The future. After she quit the B.C. After she'd made enough money. We spoke about traveling, living abroad. The cities she wanted to visit. How we could go together once I'd finished my degree." He hesitated, looked up. "I wanted her to stop. To be with me. I told her I'd support her financially if she quit."

"You ever get jealous of her being with other men?"

"She was better than the job, and I told her so. She deserved more. I could have given her more."

"But she didn't trust you, did she, Jayden?" Angie said. "You were just another john."

"We were special."

Yeah, right. Nothing like an orgasm as reinforcement to make you think it was love.

"She *did* want to get out. But it wasn't so easy." His hands began to shake, and his voice quavered. "She was getting scared, because the B.C. was becoming more controlling, and it was being made clear that if she did speak, or violate their confidentially agreement in any way, she'd be dead."

"What did they mean, 'be dead'?" Maddocks said.

"I . . . I got the sense she felt they would hurt her."

"You mean, kill her?"

He nodded. "There was also talk about taking her overseas. They were really selling to her how lucrative it would be . . ." His voice choked on his emotions. He coughed. "That's why I gave her a Saint Christopher. To keep her safe as she negotiated this part of her . . . journey."

"How was Gracie introduced to the Bacchanalian Club? Did she tell you?" Maddocks said.

"Her boyfriend, or at least she thought he was her boyfriend at the time. A guy she called J.J."

Angie's gaze flashed to the recording light, just to be sure they were getting this.

"Jon Jacques?" Maddocks said.

"I think that was his name. He apparently met her at some tennis club where her old boyfriend from school practiced. After she broke up with her old boyfriend, this new guy dated her, gave her stuff, money. Lots of it. She said that he took her fancy places, made her feel really special. Then one night he brought a friend on one of their dates. He took her and this guy to a hotel. It turns out this friend was Damián. He—"

"Damián who?" Maddocks said. "For the record."

"Damián Yorick. Gracie's boyfriend wanted her to have sex with Damián while he watched. She didn't want to do it, but this J.J. coerced her into it, saying she'd be doing it for him, and it would show how much she loved and trusted him. So she did. Then she ended up having sex with them both. The next time she resisted, but J.J. knocked her about until she cried and gave in. And then he brought her huge gifts and was so sweet and all that. This happened a few more times. Then Damián took them both to the *Amanda Rose*, where J.J. plied Gracie with drinks—spiked—and he asked her to have sex in the lounge with one of the club members while a few men watched. He said it was a special nightclub. The club member paid her a huge sum, and the guys who watched paid, too. After that, J.J. and Damián treated her like a princess. Then they brought her back the following Tuesday to be with two more club members."

"And what about Zach? He liked Faith?"

"Yeah. She was up for the rougher stuff, for a price."

"He hurt her, then, like his others?"

"Slapped her around. Split her lip one time. Did his dog collar and leash thing. He used the equipment in a special room the B.C. provided. Whips. Ropes. Cuffs. Straps. Spikes—other sex toys that he said hurt her. He was trying to shock me with the details. Enjoyed it— watching my face when he recounted everything he'd done."

"The B.C. management okay with what he did?"

He fiddled with his thumbnail. "I guess. I mean, they gave him Faith, who was supposed to be up for it."

"Who's in charge of this club?"

"Madame. And her assistant."

"Madame?"

"Madame Vee. That's all I know. And her assistant, Zina—a big cross-gender person. Like seven feet tall. Funny skin color—sort of ash white. Colorless eyes. Hair dyed silver."

"This Madame Vee—old, young? Nationality? Accent?"

"I never saw her or her assistant until the night Faith stopped breathing. When that happened, Zina came in to clean things up, and he—I mean, they—sent us to Madame's office, where she made sure that we were going to be okay."

"How sweet," said Angie.

He glanced up at her. "I mean, okay to not tell the police."

"Ah, like a debriefing," she said. "As in, *If you tell, you go to prison for murder,* that kind of thing?"

He looked down at the table.

"Tell me about the night Faith was killed," Maddocks said. "When was that?"

"Tuesday, November twenty-eighth."

"What happened exactly?"

"Zach asked me into the cabin to watch him with Faith. He'd snorted coke and was high. He got off on being watched and said I might learn a thing or two. He hogtied her and had sex with her, and the ropes kept getting tighter. She tried to tell him to stop, and she started sobbing, and . . . and he kind of went berserkers. I yelled at him to stop. I swear, I did, but he grabbed a steak knife and made like he was going to hurt her if I came close enough to stop them. It was part of his game, his fantasy, I guess. And . . . next thing she wasn't breathing. He thought she was messing with him. Then he saw it was for real, and he panicked and tried to get the rope off her neck with the steak knife, but it just frayed the strands, and I tried to help him." Norton-Wells struggled for a deep, steadying breath. "Then we called for help."

"Steak knives?"

"From some fancy beef they'd served that night with black truffles. I . . ." He gagged suddenly at the memory, closed his eyes, sat in silence, trying to get past his nausea.

"So you handled the ropes?" Maddocks said, coaxing him before they lost him.

He nodded. "And again when Zina came in. Zina assessed the place and then told us to go to Madame's office up on the mid deck and to not say a word to anyone."

"What transpired in Madame Vee's office?"

"She gave us brandy from her special collection and kept us for over an hour, saying there was nothing to worry about. They'd handled situations like this before. And by the time we got home, it would all be cleaned up and long gone into the past, swept under the rug. And she said that maybe we should just lay low and take it easy awhile. Not return for a bit."

"And then?"

"We left."

"Straight home?"

"No. Zach and I reached the marina parking lot, and I started flipping out, saying that maybe we should report it. I . . . I was a mess. I was scared. He told me that I was being an idiot, that we'd both end up in prison. I tried to get into my Lexus, which was parked right beside Zach's Acura, and he grabbed me, worried I was going to drive straight to the cops, and we wrestled until he punched me in the jaw, and I just kinda broke down and cried. We sat in Zach's vehicle. I don't know for how long. Engine running. Drinking whiskey—he had a hip flask. It was cold, had started to snow. That arctic front was moving in. Snow was settling on the windshield, and the windows were misting up. Then suddenly Zach kinda . . . screamed. There was a face looking into the driver's side window, right up against the glass, just staring." He cleared his throat, and Maddocks pushed a cup of water toward him. He sipped.

"We realized it was one of the deckhands—a guy we'd seen before on the *Amanda Rose*."

"This deckhand have a name?"

"I don't know his name. I only saw him in passing, working up on deck. He stood out—super fit, ripped body. Good-looking, angular face." Norton-Wells inhaled deeply, and Angie could see that he was tiring. She glanced at her watch. From experience, she figured they didn't have much more time before he shut down fully. Tension twisted through her.

"Zach wound down the window and asked what the fuck the guy wanted, staring into the car like some moron. And this deckhand said he knew. He knew what had happened, what Zach and I had done to Faith. He described it in detail, like he'd seen it all for himself. Every detail. Down to the stuff Zach said to me, the steak knife, Faith sobbing. Zach fucking her hard, which opened her legs more, which made the ropes around her neck go tighter. This guy said he'd gotten rid of the body for us. Then he just waited, staring at us. Zach told him to get lost. But I could see that Zach was getting scared—this guy was freaking him out. Then the guy said, okay, if that's what we wanted, if that's all the thanks he was going to get, he might have to tell someone what we'd done. It was like he was messing with us, just to see how we reacted." He swallowed, sipped again from the cup Maddocks had given him.

"I got really scared, too—he was weird. I asked him what he wanted in order to just shut him the hell up, to make him disappear. He looked at my Lexus, parked right there beside Zach's vehicle, and said that he always wanted one of those." Norton-Wells paused, gathering himself.

"So I told him to take it, to just get the fuck away. I threw him the keys. He caught them, got into the Lexus, and I never heard from him again. Never saw him again. And I wasn't going to report the vehicle stolen for obvious reasons—if it was picked up, he'd tell the cops what we'd done."

Angie and Maddocks regarded him in silence, allowing tension to press down on the small, overly warm room.

Maddocks said, quietly, "And Gracie?"

His features twisted. He looked as though he was going to puke for real this time.

"I learned what happened to her on the news. And when I heard about Faith's body showing up, I figured right away that had to be him—the sick freak who took my Lexus. I mean, he worked on the boat. He knew everything that happened in that cabin with Zach and Faith. He took Faith's body. He had to have known about Gracie, too. And then you guys came around asking about the Lexus in connection with a crime."

"Does this guy live aboard the *Amanda Rose*?"

"All I know is that when I went to see Madame Vee on Friday, she told me that he'd originally been hired as a carpenter, and that he'd done double duty as a deckhand, but he'd vanished on the night Faith died—never came back to work."

"A carpenter?"

"Yeah. He maintained all the wood on the boat, and there's lots. Wooden decks, railings, paneling. He built and repaired cabinets, fittings, that kind of thing."

"Why *did* you visit the *Amanda Rose* on Friday, Jayden?" Angie shifted to lean on her other shoulder against the wall.

He scrubbed his hands hard over his face again, making it red and blotchy. "Because I was freaking out. It was *my* Lexus you were talking about. I knew it had to be him, the weird carpenter guy who took my vehicle. And I heard that psychologist talking on the radio, saying Gracie's killer would kill again, and soon, and he wouldn't stop until he was caught. And the newspapers were talking about this sex serial killer having links to earlier rapes. And no one was stopping him. Zach had quit returning my calls—like he'd cut me off. I . . . I *had* to tell the Bacchanalian Club that it was him—their carpenter, that he'd taken my car, that he was doing these things, and that they had to stop this monster. But Madame said to forget about it, that the carpenter was gone, not our problem. And that if I went to the police with this information, we'd all go down for the murder of Faith Hocking, and more." His glance flickered briefly to his legal counsel.

"Madame said her clientele is huge and comprised of incredibly powerful figures like a sitting judge, lawyers, top business execs, law enforcement, even. And I knew this was true because I'd seen faces on that yacht that I recognized from the provincial legislature and the media. Madame said they'd all be implicated, and my mother and father's careers would be toast. And then she looked at me long and hard and asked if I was going to be able to weather this storm."

He raised both hands and clamped them down hard on either side of his head, as if the information inside his skull was trying to explode outward. "I don't think she believed I could. That's when Zina called Damián in. They said he was a 'fixer' and that he'd be someone I could turn to after they pulled up anchor—they wanted me to meet with him."

"Pulled up anchor?"

"The *Amanda Rose* is sailing tomorrow."

Angie stiffened. Her gaze shot to Maddocks, then the two-way mirror.

"Where's she going?" Maddocks said, his voice suddenly clipped.

433

"I don't know. Across the Pacific, I think. Something about transporting the 'barcoded merchandise.' Usually they don't depart until Boxing Day, but I figure things are getting too heated with these killings linking back to the yacht. I figured that once they left port, Damián might try to . . . silence me. Which is why I can't sit out there anymore and not talk about this."

"You're scared."

He nodded.

"You should have come to us earlier, Jayden," Angie said.

He looked up and met her gaze. Pain. Remorse. Regret, twisting in his young face. Eyes shining, he said, "I'm here now."

"Pallorino." Holgersen pulled Angie aside as she exited the interview room. Maddocks kept moving fast down the corridor, making his way to the incident room.

"What is it?" she snapped, hot with adrenaline, hopping to keep pace with Maddocks. Then she saw the look in Holgersen's eyes. Ice trickled into her veins.

"Holgersen?" she said, voice suddenly thick.

"It's Winston. They's found her in a ravine near the Gorge. Half an hour ago. Looks like fentanyl overdose."

Blood drained from her head. She drew her hand down hard over her mouth. "How . . . is she?"

"She's dead."

Angie stared . . .

Someone broke into my home, Detective, and left crack and paraphernalia on my table and that photo of me. Read the back . . .

YOU ARE DEAD

I came to you because you said that you cared. And I believed you . . . I've scheduled the exposé to release on Christmas Eve . . . in case something happens to me . . .

"They certain it was fentanyl?"

"I'm sorry. But yeah. Officer who responded found a folded piece of paper with her body. He opened it, and white powder poofed into his face in the wind—started feeling sick right away. Had to call in paramedics for naloxone."

A powerful opioid antidote.

Yet another officer overdose—the stuff was an epidemic on the streets, being cut into all manner of drugs, too dangerous to touch, the reason officers were now being issued naloxone kits for vehicles.

She rubbed her mouth. "Yorick—they arresting him?"

"Yeah. As we speak. And Jacques. I already brought Raddison in."

"Get them to check Yorick's place. He's a dealer as well as a pimp. Get them to see if they can match the composition of that powder. Jesus." She turned away. "I should have brought her in."

Holgersen reached to touch her arm, but she spun away and marched toward the stairs. Before he could see the glittering in her eyes.

I should have brought you in . . . I let you down, Merry, I let you down. Fuck it . . . I let you down . . .

CHAPTER 70

Angie shifted to adjust the pinch of her bullet-suppression vest. It was just past midnight. Precipitation was holding off. Wind had lulled and ragged clouds dragged across the sky, playing peek-a-boo with a pale gibbous moon that shimmered on the water. Marina lights glowed. The parking lot was full, but quiet. She lay shoulder to shoulder with Maddocks behind a slight rise on a bank overlooking the operation, waiting for the all-clear signal from the ERT guys so that they could board the *Amanda Rose*.

The planning for the takedown had begun the moment she and Maddocks had gone out to pick up Norton-Wells. Fitz and Vedder were overseeing things from a command post.

She panned her night-vision scopes across the lot as a black town car drew slowly in. Three men alighted. The vehicle pulled out. The men, laughing and stumbling a little, made their way along the dock to the shining white ship. Others had come and gone earlier, via cab, limo, private cars. Those who left the marina were being stopped at roadblocks that had been set up along the exit roads.

Angie tracked her scopes across to the *Amanda Rose*. Behind the yacht, MVPD harbor unit boats were sliding into view—black shapes out at sea. Two high-speed boats hung back around the point, ready in the event the *Amanda Rose* crew might try to flee in the smaller boats they'd seen aboard the yacht. A chopper waited on standby. Anticipation crackled into her veins as she caught the shapes of the ERT guys moving like black ninjas toward the vessel, assault weapons at the ready.

Medical and social services were on standby.

Gunshots cracked suddenly into the night. A shrill scream sliced the air. Men started yelling, the sounds carrying across the water.

"They're swarming the decks," she said to Maddocks, who watched with his own binoculars. Shadows moved fast, men running. A flash of light exploded the darkness, and the *whumpf* of a small blast reached them. Another scream rent the air—female. More gunfire. Then things began to settle. She could hear the sharp bark of orders being given. Arguing. More men yelling. The sounds came in snatches on the night breeze.

Then came the all-clear signal. She and Maddocks surged to their feet and ran in a crouch down the embankment and along the dock toward the vessel. At the top of the gangway an ERT officer in full gear directed them toward the companionway stairs. The opulence inside the yacht was breathtaking—all burnished wood, fixtures of gleaming white and chrome, high-end art on the walls. Music was still being piped throughout. She could smell pepper spray.

Down one flight of stairs they found ERT guys cuffing crew members. Women wrapped in blankets were being brought up the stairs to be taken into a staging area on the upper deck. Several were crying. Men were being flushed out of the lower deck boudoirs, too, in various stages of undress. Some still wore grotesque, baroque-looking carnival-style masks to hide their identities—long, hooked noses, devil's horns, a bull's face.

As Angie and Maddocks reached a lower deck, ERT guys directed them afore, toward a cabin where "Madame Vee" and her bodyguard assistant were being held. An officer with an automatic weapon stood guard outside the door. He opened it for them, showing them into a cabin with a gleaming wood desk. Behind the desk another officer stood watch over a woman clearly into her sixties. She was seated with hands cuffed behind her back. Sitting beside her, hands also cuffed, was the transgender assistant whom Jayden Norton-Wells had described—a person who appeared as if from another dimension with silver-white hair, colorless eyes, and a strange ashen-hued complexion.

That colorless gaze met Angie's but gave no hint of emotion or tension. The woman's eyes, however, flashed in defiance, her bloodred lips tight with anger. Angie noted that beside her, a paper shredder had been stopped mid-shred.

"Give us a moment," Maddocks said to the ERT guy, who nodded, exited, and shut the door. While the ERT guys had been tasked with handling the *Amanda Rose* takedown, Angie and Maddocks had one goal—to get information on the carpenter. He was still out there, and the clock was ticking down fast toward his next kill if Grablowski was right.

"You can speak to my attorneys," the woman snapped, raising her chin. "You have no right to do this. You're disrupting a legitimate business—I run an exclusive gentlemen's club that facilitates encounters between paid members. They come for the cuisine, entertainment, and what they do in the privacy of their cabins is between consenting adults."

"I need an employee list," Maddocks said.

The woman flattened her mouth, turned her face away. Her bodyguard remained expressionless—a cold and dangerous animal, thought Angie.

"What is the name of the carpenter who recently worked for you?" Maddocks said, going through her drawers, seeking to unsettle her. "What's your legal name?"

"I repeat, you can speak to my *legal* counsel."

He swung her swivel chair around violently, shocking her. And he brought his face close to hers. "Just the carpenter's name. Withholding this employee's information is going to cost you in the courts. Big-time. Believe me. Whatever your operation is here."

Silence.

Frustration bit through Angie, and she had to tamp down a rush of mounting rage, a fierce urge to tear this female pimp apart limb from limb. Maddocks turned to Angie and jerked his head toward the door, indicating that they were done here—clock was ticking. Fast. He made for the exit. She followed him out.

"We're wasting time in there," he said, then turned to the man guarding the door. "Where's the rest of the staff being taken?"

"Being rounded up and corralled in a holding area on the lower deck, sir."

They ran down the stairs to the lowest deck. Outside, they found ERT guys leading crew members toward an area near the ship's stern. A female cop summoned Angie and Maddocks over.

"I got someone here who's willing to talk—one of the cleaning staff." She pointed out a female who looked to be in her early twenties. Quickly, they drew the young woman aside.

"I didn't know what was going on," she said, breathless, eyes wide with fear. "I swear. I'm new. I—"

"What's your name, hon?" Angie said, handing her a tissue from her pocket. Wind was cold off the sea on this side of the yacht, and it was picking up again as a new weather front mounted beyond the horizon.

The woman blew her nose, trembling like an aspen. "Katie Collins. I . . . I'm new on the yacht," she repeated.

"How new?"

"A month."

"Not too new, huh, to understand what was going on. You cleaned up the rooms?"

She nodded.

"So you had to see the results of the nights before. What was it? Used condoms, sex toys, maybe blood? Ever see the women? See them being beaten up?"

She swallowed. "I never saw the women, any of them. No staff apart from the few who worked club catering service were allowed into the lower cabins when the club was in operation. By the time we go in to clean, everyone has been moved out. The quarters where the girls bunk, too—they always move the girls to another part of the yacht if we need to clean there."

Angie shot a hot glance at Maddocks. "So there *are* young women kept on board?"

Collins nodded. "They . . . I heard them referred to as the barcode girls. I heard they were all foreign. They remain on the yacht at all times. I've never seen them myself. And there are three even younger women kept in another area. Then there are the other women who come in with drivers provided by the club, and they leave the same way." She looked at her feet. "I . . . the money was so good. I . . . wasn't sure. I just tried to keep my head down."

"Just help us out here, Katie, and you'll be helping yourself. There was a crew member who worked on the *Amanda Rose* until about two weeks ago—a deckhand and a carpenter. Blond guy, maybe midthirties. Good-looking, but possibly seemed just a little off. You recall someone like that who doesn't work here any longer?"

"Ah . . . yeah. He quit. They told us he quit. Spencer."

Adrenaline kicked through Angie. "Spencer *who*?"

"I don't know."

"Know where he lives?" Maddocks said. "Foreign? Did he come in with crew from other ports?"

"I don't know—" She pointed suddenly to a cuffed crew member in chef whites being led to the processing area. "That guy, he knows more."

Angie and Maddocks pulled the man out of the line. He was big, pock-faced, rough features. Blood stained the front of his chef's jacket.

440

"I want a lawyer," he said immediately.

"Listen, buddy, I don't want you—not interested in you," Maddocks said curtly. "I want to know about Spencer. You tell me about Spencer, and things are going to go a hell of a lot easier for you. Keep silent, and I'm going to make your life pure living hell."

His eyes flickered at the mention of Spencer. "Can we go in there?" he said, motioning to a door. Angie opened it to find a small area with seating. Staff break area, she guessed.

The man entered with them, glancing over his shoulder. "Spencer left," he said once they'd shut the door.

"We know he left. Why did he go?"

"Something happened in one of the club cabins a few weeks back. I don't know what—something bad. Spencer was called to help. We never saw him after that."

"Spencer got a last name? You know where he lives, where he comes from, how long he's worked on the *Amanda Rose*?"

"Addams. His name is Spencer Addams. He's local, from Victoria. He's worked on the yacht for a few years—done some of their trips down in the Caribbean and the Med. Seasonal stuff. He told me he answered an ad for a yacht carpenter a couple of years ago. Lives in James Bay with his mother. Never spoke much—kept to himself. Very talented with the carpentry. Loved his work—it was like . . . a religion to him. He was a bit . . . weird. Often quoting passages from the Bible."

Angie's pulse hammered. "Where in James Bay?"

"I don't know."

The door opened. It was one of the male ERT officers. "Hoi, detectives, you're going to want to see this."

The officer led them to what appeared to be a supply closet inside the yacht on the lower deck. He opened the door, showing them into a cubby maybe eight by eight feet. "We had to break the lock to gain access," the SWAT officer said.

Angie and Maddocks stepped into the tight space. The walls were paneled with wood. A padded swivel stool was positioned in the center. A small counter, under a foot wide, ran around the walls at about waist height. Wires fed from holes in the paneling. USB ports attached to the ends of the wires had been plugged into a laptop that rested on the narrow shelf.

Maddocks snapped on gloves. He ran his hand along one of the wires up to the hole in the wall. "There's a removable plug of wood around the wire," he said, opening the little cover that had been carefully recessed into the paneling. He swore softly and removed another wood plug.

"Cameras," he said, his gaze snapping to the laptop on the tiny counter. "These wires all feed from cameras to that computer."

Angie took a pair of latex gloves from her pocket, pulled them on, and opened the laptop. She hit the ON key, and it fired to life.

"Shit," she whispered as she opened consecutive files, each showing footage of different cabins, men in various stages of having sex with women. "He was spying from here. The bastard watched it all, filming everything." She looked up. Four walls. Holes in each. Wires all leading to this laptop station. "He can see into several cabins from here. It's like a little nerve hub in the belly of the *Amanda Rose* beast," she said, opening another file. Video footage came to life—a black-haired, naked young man leading a naked woman around on all fours by a rope. Angie's heart stalled. She hit FAST FORWARD.

"We got him," she whispered, feeling sick to the pit of her stomach as she watched the young man hogtying, then hammering himself into the woman from the rear, her hair falling over her face, which was pointed toward the camera. Tears stained her cheeks, and her features were twisted in anguish as the rope tightened around her throat. Behind them, in the far right corner, was Norton-Wells. "We got them both," she said softly. "With Faith Hocking."

The camera's time-date stamps showed November 28. As they watched the footage, Hocking began to gasp, her eyes bulging at the camera. Her body slumped. Raddison kept at it. Bile rose into Angie's throat as they watched the young woman die, the footage turning into bona-fide snuff.

"He must have fled in a rush to have left this here," Maddocks said, watching by her side.

"Or he just uploaded all of this to a cloud from where he could download it and watch it somewhere else at leisure." She wiped her sleeve across her mouth, the depravity suddenly getting to her. "If what Norton-Wells told us was legit, this Spencer Addams guy was summoned by his bosses right after this happened, to get rid of Hocking's body. Once he'd dumped her on Thetisby Island, he returned to the *Amanda Rose*, presumably via smaller boat, and as he was leaving the marina, he saw Raddison and Norton-Wells up in that parking lot, and he worked the opportunity that presented itself. He secured the Lexus, with which he later abducted Drummond. Then, when Hocking's body finally surfaced, with evidence of her mutilation getting into the press, linking her to Drummond's abduction and mutilation, he *couldn't* come back." She met Maddocks's eyes in the tiny space. "Because his employers would know by that point that it would have had to be him who'd mutilated Hocking postmortem. They were the ones who'd entrusted him to properly dispose of her body, but he didn't."

Maddocks turned to the SWAT guy waiting right outside the door. "Have this room sealed off. We'll get the crime scene techs in here as a priority." He reached for his phone and called Fitz.

"We need a residential address, stat," he said into his phone, his gaze locked on Angie's. "Spencer Addams. He's our guy. James Bay. Apparently lives with his mother. We're heading toward the subdivision now, will be on standby for the address and for backup."

CHAPTER 71

The second tactical team had come quietly, no sirens. The James Bay house had been in darkness. The ERT guys had broken in the door, but Spencer Addams and his mother were gone. The forensics ident unit was en route.

Receiving the all-clear, Angie and Maddocks entered slowly through the garage, which fronted the quiet, quaint street of period houses and white picket fences and neat little flower beds. It was dark and windy out, the waxing moon shining silvery on the slumbering neighborhood. A black bank of cloud was building in the distance. The homes in this area were all within walking distance from the sea, and from the pier where Angie had met Merry Winston, and from the legislature buildings and inner harbor—the bustling core of the city. The location was made all the more stark and horrific by the notion that a violent sex killer had been raised right here, nurtured in their midst, gone to school and lurked and festered, growing ever more sick and sadistic over time.

Angie nodded to the faint oil stain on the concrete garage floor where a vehicle had been parked. The interior of the garage felt warm, and the faint scent of exhaust and hot engine lingered on the stale air, as if the occupants had only very recently departed the house by vehicle. Metal shelving units lined the walls. Plastic boxes containing gardening tools, household cleaning equipment, and other supplies rested upon the shelves. From a corkboard affixed to the wall, tools hung from hooks in symmetrical rows.

"He's a neat freak," said Maddocks as they moved toward the door at the rear of the garage. It opened onto a stone path that led to the main house.

Angie stalled. "Wait, over here," she said. "Gun safe."

The door to the safe hung open. It was designed to hold long guns but was empty. An overturned ammunition box rested on the counter. Also empty. "Twenty-two caliber," she said, reading the box. "He's out there, and he's armed with a rifle."

They exited the rear door, made their way up the small path to the white, gabled house with stained glass detail above the windows. The exterior lights had been put on, and they revealed a well-kept lawn, shrubs neatly trimmed.

While they'd waited for backup, Vedder had started techs running searches and checks on the name "Spencer Addams." His middle name was John. He had no criminal record. His DNA and prints were not in any database. His mother's name was Beulah Lee Addams, née Cartwright. And this house was in her name. Spencer had been raised here. His father, John Addams, had been reported missing when Spencer was five years old. That case had eventually gone cold—the father was never found. Spencer had thereafter been raised by a single mother, had attended local schools, worked as a carpenter's apprentice. Beulah appeared to have a long history of active engagement with Catholic-based charities and had been a member of Father Simon's parish. And that was as much as the guys back at the station had managed to unearth so far.

The forensics unit was pulling up outside as Maddocks and Angie entered the house wearing crime scene booties and gloves. It was warm inside, and it looked as though the occupants had definitely left in a hurry, because the television was still on, playing a recorded episode of *Coronation Street*. Embers glowed orange in the old fireplace, and a menthol cigarette had been left burning, its long column of intact ash resting on an ashtray full of butts, all stained with bright-red lipstick. Beside the ashtray was a box of blue latex gloves and a shopping bag with a logo that said **Druggie Mart**. They'd passed that store on the corner down the street on their way in.

Coats hung on hooks by the door. A woman's flower-patterned umbrella rested in a stand alongside a pair of men's Salomon running shoes and a smaller pair of women's Rockport walking shoes. The air was laden with the acrid, minty stink of the menthol cigarettes.

Angie's heart raced softly as she took it all in.

While crime scene techs would comb carefully through this place, she and Maddocks had a more immediate goal—go through the house quickly, looking for any sign that might tell them where the occupants had gone. The clock was still ticking. Their subject was on the run and armed. He could be feeling cornered, and thus dangerous. Whether his mother had gone voluntarily with her son remained a key question.

Maddocks and Angie moved down the hallway and entered a small bathroom on the left. Angie caught her breath.

Pasted down the side of a mirror above a white basin were photos of a naked Gracie Drummond engaged in sex acts with various men. Across the top of the mirror, scrawled large in bright-red lipstick, were the words *Save the Girls*. Right beside the lipstick scrawl, a red arrow pointed down to an image of another naked young woman engaging in intercourse with a bearded male who looked to be in his late fifties.

"Lara Pennington," said Angie.

Under the image of Pennington and the male, smaller text had been scrawled: *Next. To be baptized in the name of the Lord. Save them all. Out with Satan.*

Her pulse quickened. "They're stills," she said, leaning closer. "Taken from his recordings on the yacht. Addams watched Drummond, Hocking, and Pennington, along with other women working at the club—that's what fixated him on these girls. He went after Drummond, perhaps, after tasting his thrill with Hocking's body."

"He wanted a live one," Maddocks said softly.

"And Pennington is next," Angie said, her gaze dropping to a pair of exfoliating bath mitts lying inside the basin. With gloved fingers, Maddocks lifted one. The fingers of the mitt were crumpled and stuck together with a dried substance.

"Semen?" he said.

Along the rim of the basin lay a selection of open safety pins, a razor. A tube of cream called Icy-Hot—for muscle pain relief. And what looked like some blood.

Maddocks's attention went from the mitt, to the pins, and the razor, then back up to the images of fornication. "You thinking what I'm thinking?"

She inhaled, a dark sense of foreboding, of worse to come, filling her mouth. "Looks like he jacked off here, using those pictures of Drummond and Pennington with other men as stimulation. If he did it wearing those gloves, and if he also used that cream on his private parts, it would have burned like all hell."

"And there's the pins and razor," he said. "Pain gets this bastard off. Wonder what his mother thought of these photos on the mirror. If they were living together, she had to have seen them."

"Maybe she was a part of it," Angie said, nodding toward the red scrawl. "That looks like her lipstick—same color as the lip prints on those menthol cigarettes. And she's vanished with him."

They moved down the hall to the first bedroom and entered. It was austere—the walls unadorned apart from a wooden crucifix that hung above a simple twin bed with navy-blue duvet cover and pillows. Bare wood floors. No drapes.

That dark sense of foreboding sank deeper as Angie followed Maddocks into the second bedroom.

This one was bigger—frilly and flowery. A queen-size bed was covered in pillows and pink floral linens. A crocheted throw had been neatly folded and placed near the footboard. A framed Emily Carr print of an old church hung on the wall. A mirrored dresser—dark wood and shaped like a kidney—was positioned under a window that was covered by scalloped sheers. On the dresser a rosary curled among framed photos and a jumble of lipstick tubes, a blush compact, blue eye makeup, face powder, and a half-eaten bag of Hattie's Candies from the Olde Sweet Shoppe. The sales slip indicated that the candies had been bought five days ago. Angie picked up one of the frames and studied the photo. It showed a cute-looking kid around ten years of age, tousled blond hair, an urchin smile. Bright-blue eyes. Skinny little legs with knobby knees stuck out of baggy shorts. The woman with him was somewhat pinch-faced. Cat's-eye glasses.

"This could be Spencer when he was a boy, with his mother," she said, replacing the frame.

There was no sign of a male in this room, nor in the en suite bathroom.

Passing the crime scene techs entering the house, she and Maddocks quickly made their way down into the basement. A swinging lightbulb above wooden stairs lit their way.

Both stilled at the bottom of the stairs. The basement ran the entire length of the house. At the far end was a makeshift gym complete with bench press, barbells, exercise bike, and treadmill.

They entered slowly, a cold sensation pressing low into Angie's stomach. It was as if she could *feel* him in here, his shed skin cells still hanging in the air, getting into her mouth, into her nasal passages and bronchia.

A laundry and bathroom led off the gym area. Inside the laundry was a stainless steel trough large enough to have pushed Gracie Drummond's head under water. At the other end of the basement was a fridge and a large chest freezer. In the center of the room a simple metal chair had been positioned. It faced a more comfortable-looking, padded wingback. Ropes strung from a support beam along the roof hung down to the floor around the wingback—reminiscent of the rope structure in the root cellar on Thetisby Island. Beside the wingback was a television screen and video equipment. Maddocks switched it on.

The screen made a soft static crackle as the image came to life. Angie stared. Gracie Drummond. Bound. Her mouth duct-taped. A blond, well-honed, naked male forcing himself into her. Angie looked away, sweat breaking out over her skin as Alex Strauss's words hammered through her.

It's rough, that kind of thing. On anybody . . . acknowledge it. In movies, sure, fictional cops are immune. Viewers are inured to violence. But this is real life. Real people. We're not built to deal with an incessant onslaught of the kinds of things you deal with in sex crimes . . .

She moved away from the screen toward the counter that ran the length of the wall between the fridge and the freezer. On it was a large concertina sewing box. She lifted the lid and was greeted by a bright array of spools of colored thread. Opening it wider, the top compartment slid back to expose the bottom layer. She stilled.

"Maddocks."

He came to her side. "Trophies," she said, staring at the locks of hair—all lacquered together at the top of each lock and tied with different colors of thread. "There have to be more than twenty different strands in here. And they have names, dates, places tagged to them." She leaned closer, not wanting to touch or mess with this evidence. She tried to read the tiny hand-printed text on one of the minute tags. "It says 'Malaga,'" she said. "And one that says . . . 'Toulon,' and that one says 'Nice.'" She looked up at Maddocks. "Places along the Cote D'Azur and the French Riviera? He's been at this, collecting, for years."

The sound of people coming down the stairs reached them. Angie moved quickly to open the fridge. It was filled with bottled sparkling water, vitamin water, sports drinks. She closed it. As she moved to open the freezer, Maddocks's cell rang. He stepped aside to answer it as the crime scene techs and a photographer entered the basement. Angie lifted the freezer lid.

"Fuck!" she gasped, pulling back and almost dropping the lid closed. Her stomach contracted violently.

The blue, frosted face of a woman stared up at her with sightless, frozen eyes. Her lips were painted in the same bright-red lipstick that stained the cigarette butts and the mirror upstairs. The head was attached to the naked torso of a senior. But her legs and arms were stashed separately alongside her.

"His mother?" she whispered, horror rising up into her throat. "Beulah Addams? Jesus. How long has she been in here?" Her gaze shot toward Maddocks as the techs came up to the freezer.

His face had gone bloodless. He wasn't looking at the freezer. He was clutching his phone.

"It's Ginny," he said, voice rough. "She needs my help."

"What?"

"She . . . says she went out with friends, had too much to drink, and she thinks her drink was spiked."

Angie motioned quickly to the techs to take over the freezer, and she went over to Maddocks. He looked ill.

"She's frightened . . . she sounds in a bad way, Angie. She needs me. Now. She asked me to come." His eyes glittered. "I've neglected her—I thought I'd just give her time and that she'd come back to me. But . . . not in this way."

Urgency and conflict crackled through them both.

"It's your biggest case, Maddocks," she said quietly.

"And it's my daughter. It's why I'm here. I came to be here for her. This is my world, Angie. I came to be a better dad, to make up for all the lost time." His gaze went to the freezer, to the crime scene photographer now taking photos of the body inside. "Can you handle it from here? Can you get a unit to pick up Lara Pennington, take her in before this monster gets to her, if he hasn't already? Find out who else might be in jeopardy?"

Her mouth tightened. She regarded her partner, her boss. Her lover. This beautiful man. He was a rescuer. And she believed she loved him. And she hurt at the pain she saw in his features. Emotion burned into her eyes, and she nodded. "Yeah. I've got it. Go. Go look after her."

And he was gone, up the stairs, the flip of his black coat hem the last thing she saw.

CHAPTER 72

Maddocks drove too fast in the unmarked MVPD vehicle he'd taken from the crime scene. Ginny's small, slurred voice, her words, tumbled and tumbled through his mind.

"Daddy . . . can you come? I screwed up . . . I . . . I'm so, so sorry . . ."

Emotion burned into his throat as he swerved up against the curb outside her converted apartment block. He left his car door open, took the stairs three at a time, banged hard on his daughter's door, then tried the knob. It opened. Inside her apartment it was dark. Dank. He could smell sweat—male sweat. Alarms began to clang inside his head.

"Ginny?" He smacked on the lights, then stilled as the living room came into focus. Upturned chair. Mug on the floor. Spilled liquid. Ginny's purse—her phone lying next to it. He rushed madly through the small apartment. *"Ginny!"*

His heart jackhammered.

She wasn't here.

Maddocks rushed back to the table, opened her purse, rummaged through it. Her apartment keys, wallet, ID, everything still there. A sick, cold feeling dropped like a stone into his bowels. He spun around. And that's when he saw it.

A note. Written in black marker. On the kitchen counter. Beside it, a lock of dark-brown hair. A spear of dread sliced his heart.

Maddocks lunged for the note.

Come alone,
And you might have time . . .
To say goodbye . . .
To watch her die . . .
Old rail trestle at Skookum Gorge.
Tick tocks . . . Detective Maddocks
See you there, or be square.
Johnny the Baptist

Oh God, please, no. Had he already assaulted her? Mutilated her? That was his modus operandi—to sexually assault first, baptize, *then* take his trophy. He stared at the lock of his daughter's hair.

Breathe. Focus. Think.

He scanned the note again.

. . . you might have time . . . to say goodbye . . .

Time. Spencer Addams had taken a rifle, spare ammunition. He was luring Maddocks, using his own daughter as bait. *Why?* Because he wanted a confrontation? He wanted to kill one of the cops hunting him? Because they'd cornered him, and now he was devolving into something else—entering some kind of spree phase? Or was this going to be a negotiating tool to escape? Maddocks *had* to believe this—that Ginny was okay—that she was going to be okay. He just had to reach her in time.

He dialed Angie's number as he made rapidly for the door.

She answered right away.

"He's got her—Spencer Addams has taken Ginny to the old trestle bridge over Skookum Gorge. He left a note in her apartment." Maddocks ran down the stairs and got into the unmarked vehicle, firing the ignition as he spoke.

"It's a trap, Maddocks," she said. "He's luring you into a trap—"

"I know. Get another SWAT team—everyone out there. We're thin on the ground right now with the yacht and James Bay house takedowns, so bring in neighboring jurisdictions, military if we have to. Medical backup. This is not just about my daughter, Angie," he said, swerving out into the street and hitting the gas. "This is an armed and dangerous serial offender who's killed and attacked women in several countries." He blew through a red light and swerved onto a main street, tires skidding. Horns blared and brakes screeched as he narrowly missed oncoming traffic. Even at high speed and on an empty highway it would still take over half an hour to reach Skookum by vehicle.

"I'm coming—"

"No! And that's an order, Pallorino. Remain with the forensics unit at the Addams house. Help me by coordinating response from your end—the ERT teams will come into Skookum via chopper. They'll reach the inlet well before you could, and do far more. Use your time, nail this bastard from the evidence end." He killed the call, flicked on his siren and lights, and floored the accelerator, both hands tight on the wheel. He was *not* putting Angie in jeopardy as well.

Please, please . . . don't let him have time to hurt her, to rape her, to mutilate her like those young naked female bodies on the morgue slab . . .

He finally hit the exit that fed off the highway and onto the narrow, twisty, darker road hemmed in with huge, dripping, moss-covered trees. It was the only route along the coast to Skookum Gorge, an inlet famous for its roaring rapids and whirlpools caused each day as tides forced massive amounts of seawater through the narrows, raising the water level more than ten feet within minutes and creating currents that could exceed sixteen knots. The Skookum tidal rapids were famous.

For drownings.

Angie made the calls. Rapid-response action was being mobilized in coordination with various jurisdictions. She'd taken eight minutes to set things in motion, and she was now on the line with Fitz, updating him on the Addams house crime scene—the dismembered body of a woman who appeared to be Beulah Addams in the freezer. Pathologist Barb O'Hagan and coroner Charlie Alphonse were en route. "We found more photos in the basement," she said, her mind cleft between this house of horrors and Maddocks racing toward his daughter and into a trap. She glanced at her watch. Nine minutes now since Maddocks had called.

"Several of those photographs show the frozen female corpse propped in the wingback chair in the basement," she told Fitz. "He used ropes from a support beam to string her into place, to make it appear as though she's sitting there of her own volition, her frozen legs balanced against the base of the chair." Angie nodded to a tech and pointed him toward the basement door. She was upstairs in Addams's living room now.

"It appears he took her out of the freezer and propped her there for company as he seated himself on the metal chair opposite her, from where he could watch footage he'd shot from his peepholes into the Bacchanalian Club cabins."

From the living room window, Angie saw the coroner's van pulling up under the streetlight. The entire block had been cordoned off. News choppers *thucked* overhead in the dark hours of this early morning.

Nine and a half minutes since Maddocks had called . . .

"Pallorino," Fitz said quietly, his reedy tone shifting in a way that made her tense. "I want you to stay away from the Skookum narrows, understood? Remain on scene."

She held the phone tighter. He'd read something between her and Maddocks. Probably everyone had. He was anticipating what she might do now—rush out there, guns blazing—anything in order to *not* lose another partner for whom she was beginning to care.

"What is the ERT ETA?" she said. "What time did they get up into the air?"

"Pallorino—"

"They haven't taken off yet, have they?"

"Back off. Do your job."

"Sir." She killed the call and folded her arms tightly over her chest, clutching her cell as she watched O'Hagan and Alphonse coming up the path toward the house in their black jackets with the word CORONER emblazoned in yellow across their backs.

They seemed to be moving in slow motion under the glare of the portable lighting that had been brought in. Everything around her felt slowed. Even sound was reaching her brain in low, long, distorted tones.

Sometimes, Angie thought once again, the difference between heaven and hell was people. Sometimes, no matter how hard you tried, you made no difference at all. Her mind turned to Gracie Drummond and the anguish on her mother's face.

You think you have all the time in the world, and then . . . then you wish . . .

Then you wish you'd done something.

Outside, branches wagged in mounting wind, and a fog was blowing in, making halos around the lighting—another huge weather front roiling in from the sea. A chopper was going to have trouble in this.

She knew Skookum Provincial Park, too. She'd hiked and camped there throughout her college years. There was nowhere to land a helicopter near that trestle bridge. Not unless the pilot tried to balance his skids on the ancient wood and stone structure itself, while still managing to keep rotors free of old-growth trees and cliffs hemming in on either side. It would require incredible skill in good weather, let alone bad. Trying to get there in fog would mean potentially risking the lives of all members on board—a call the team captain would have to make. Alternatively, members could be lowered in by long line. Again, that would be delicate and require exceptional skill from all parties, especially in dense fog.

And it would take time.

Time Maddocks and his daughter might not have.

Outside more vehicles were pulling up. Holgersen and Leo climbed out of one. Both looked toward the house. Fitz got out of another vehicle with two veteran homicide detectives from the Operation Limpet force. A uniformed officer pointed them to the Addams residence. Angie sucked in a deep breath.

He was her partner. He was alone out there. No one was coming. Not with this weather.

She checked her watch. Eleven minutes since Maddocks had called.

She heard O'Hagan and Alphonse entering the hallway.

In a split-second decision, Angie spun and hurried toward the back entrance of the house.

She ran down the stairs into the yard, crossed the lawn, and ducked out via the back alley.

I want you to stay away from the Skookum narrows, understood? Remain on scene . . .

"Fuck it," she muttered to herself. Maddocks had laid every-thing on the line for her. What would that be worth if he lost his life now? Or if he lost his daughter? She broke into a sprint when she hit the sidewalk, aiming for her vehicle parked farther along the side of the road.

Thirteen minutes after he'd called, Angie was gunning along the highway, one thing on her mind.

Help her partner. Her lover.

CHAPTER 73

Maddocks's tires crackled on the wet paving as he drove as close as he could to the trailhead that led to the narrows. His wipers struggled to keep the windshield clear of the gelatinous slush now falling. Mist drifted thick among the old-growth trees.

The Skookum Provincial Park lot was large enough to accommodate busloads of tourists who came in to watch the salmon spawn from viewing platforms built high on the rock cliffs above the rapids. It was now deserted and desolate.

A lone vehicle was parked at the trailhead—his beams hit it as he turned the corner. *Lexus.* The plate read BX3 99E. Addams was here.

Anxiety balled in Maddocks's throat as he swerved to a stop alongside the Lexus. He checked his sidearm, then popped the trunk. He got out of the vehicle. Sleet pummeled down on his head. He could hear the distant roar of surf—waves crashing against rocks as the tide surged. With the moon on the wax, the tide would be pushing even higher than normal. He found a flashlight and a rifle and ammunition in the trunk. He loaded the gun and pocketed the flashlight and spare ammunition. He slung the rifle across his back.

He was already wearing his bullet-suppression vest from the Amanda Rose takedown. Before heading down the trail, he checked the

Lexus. Locked. He shone his beam inside. Empty, apart from coils of rope and some other tools.

Guided by the powerful beam of his flashlight, he entered the woods and moved fast down the narrow hiking trail, his boots sucking in thick mud and slipping over areas of wet, moss-covered rock. The scent was of soil and pine and old-fall detritus and the brine of the ocean. There was evidence of tracks in the mud, but it was hard to tell anything from them in the dark and wet.

He moved faster.

As he ran, his beam bounced off trees. Shadows loomed and ducked and darted. Mist sifted through the trunks like tattered wraiths, alive, grasping for him, then retreating. A sense of the vastness of this place— the sheer size and scope of this old-growth forest—pressed down on him. No humanity for miles and miles. The trail started to rise, the incline becoming severe as he reached a rock knoll. The sound of surf grew louder.

Maddocks scrambled to the top of the knoll and came out onto a wooden viewing platform. A metal railing ran along the perimeter. Beyond the railing the earth dropped sheer away to the water. Far below him, the tide had started its push with white-capped, rolling waves marching insidiously forward, as if in a series of stairs, toward the narrow cliffs that formed a gateway to the estuary that fanned out beyond. Wind hit Maddocks as he crossed to the far railing. To his right, through the mist, he could make out the shape of the old railway trestle bridge crossing from cliff to cliff at the narrowest choke in the waterway.

Then he saw it—a small light bobbing in and out of the trees along the clifftop on the opposite side of the water. Quickly, he clicked off his own flashlight. Addams was armed with a .22 rifle at the very least. He took his own rifle from his back, chambered a round, and using railings to guide himself as his eyes adjusted to the dark, Maddocks moved slowly along the platform, changing from his last spotted position in case Addams fired blind.

He peered into the darkness and fog, trying to catch another glimpse of the light. But it was gone. Another movement caught his eye. His gaze shot down to the water below the bridge where foam on the waves glowed white with fluorescence. As mist parted, he saw a shape above the water.

His brain scrambled, trying to make sense of what he was seeing, then suddenly his blood turned to ice. Addams had used ropes. Like he had on Thetisby Island, like he had in the basement of his house—he'd wrapped Ginny up in a tarp and strung her down from the rotting bridge so that she hung just above the water. The tide was rising fast to meet her.

And he'd brought Maddocks here to watch her drown.

CHAPTER 74

Maddocks moved in a crouch to the north end of the platform. From here, an almost vertical path appeared to lead down the cliff. It looked as though another trail cut back a short way into the forest, and it possibly led around to the trestle bridge.

But as Maddocks moved toward that trail, a shot cracked through the air. He ducked. A bullet whirred past him and thunked into a tree behind him. Bark exploded. His heart pounded. So this was the trap.

If he tried to access the bridge to rescue his daughter hanging below, he'd be picked off from the other side of the narrows. He'd be shot dead, and Ginny would drown.

Or he could sit here safely and watch her drown anyway.

And he *had* to believe that she was still alive.

His brain raced. He checked his watch. Had Angie managed to mobilize response teams? He was running out of time. The tide was rising. Time and tide—it waited for no man. It could never have felt more true, more stark. Mist swirled in again, completely obscuring the opposite cliff. The sound of a chopper somewhere up high in the clouds suddenly reached him. Maddocks said a silent prayer of thanks before the reality of the situation struck hard.

With the cliffs, the soaring height of the old-growth trees, and the dense soup of fog, there was nowhere to bring a chopper in.

Even so, the beat of the rotors grew louder, the sound bouncing off the rock canyon in a growing roar. Another shot rang out, and another.

Maddocks swore. Addams was firing on the helo. The chopper began to rise again, the sound growing less intense as it moved higher into the cloud and toward the west. His sense of aloneness could not have felt more profound.

Help was out there, but just beyond reach. And time was against them.

The minutes continued to tick down. The chopper was silent. He checked his watch again. He couldn't wait any longer. He had to do this on his own.

But how?

A crack of a branch snapped his attention to the forest behind him. He whipped his rifle toward the sound.

"Maddocks?" came a whisper. "Are you there?" A shape with a headlamp and flashlight emerged from the trees. *Angie.*

The shot was instant. Bark shrapnel exploded and pinged off the metal railing.

"Kill your lights!" he hissed. "Get down!"

She did, but not before another shot zinged across the platform as she dived. Then all fell silent. He could hear her breathing heavily.

"You okay?" he said.

"Where is he?" she said as she scrambled across the wood floor of the platform to where he crouched in the corner.

"Opposite side of the gorge."

"And Ginny—with him?"

The act of having to voice it hammered home the sick reality of the situation, made the horror of the nightmare all the more bleak.

"He's suspended her from the trestle bridge. Just above the rising water."

Angie wriggled herself up into a sitting position beside him, her breath misting, her shoulder pressing against his as he pointed out where Ginny had been strung. She'd been running and Maddocks could feel her warmth. It released a faint fragrance of flowers and something soapy fresh from her skin. Never had a woman's touch, her scent, felt more human, more welcome than Angie Pallorino right now. To have an ally suddenly meant the world.

"What in the hell are you doing here anyway?" he said.

"I'm your partner." She unhooked coils of rope from her shoulder as she spoke. "I left almost right after you. I got your back—and that ERT team is not going to be able to get in here." She shrugged out of the pack on her back, opened it. "We're going to have to do this on our own."

"Angie, you're not—"

"Shut the fuck up, okay? They're not going to risk killing a helo full of men in a doomed attempt to save one detective and his daughter, and you know it. They're fully aware Addams is out there somewhere. They know they can track him for days with dogs, bring in military equipment, man trackers. They'll get him in the end, flush him out. Or he'll die in the wilderness. They can afford to wait for the best possible conditions. We can't."

He stared into her eyes, dark and glistening in the faint light of dawn beginning to lighten their world as they approached the shortest day of the year. And at that moment Maddocks believed he loved her. Wholly. And he did not want to—could not—risk her life. He wasn't even certain Ginny was still breathing.

As if reading his mind, she said, "She's alive, Maddocks. She is. You have *got* to believe that. And we're going to save her. This is how—" Before she could finish, another shot rang out. They both ducked instinctively.

Crouching together, faces close, breath misting around them, they listened, waited. A swath of thick mist blew in again, buying them a few moments. Not only was the tide rising, but the light of dawn would soon make them sitting targets each time the shroud lifted.

"I know this place," she said, digging back into her pack. She took out a tangle of carabiners. "I used to hike and camp here when I was at college. And when I was a kid, my dad—" She hesitated, her fingers working fast to separate the carabiners. "Joseph Pallorino used to bring me here. We'd pump for shrimp, collect clams from the mud flats when the tide was out. I know how fast it comes in." She got up into a crouch, met his gaze. Intensity crackled off her.

"Are you a strong swimmer?" she said.

"Strong enough."

"That's stronger than I am." She handed him a coil of the climbing rope she'd brought, along with a link of carabiners.

"You go down. Use the *via ferrata* cable that runs off the end of this platform. Hold on to the cable and kick your feet into the cliff sides in order to work down to the water. Just above the high tide level you'll reach a wide slab of rock that runs all the way to the bridge. It's been scoured out by years of tidal action. If you can get down there, work your way along that platform to a point several meters before the bridge, where you will find an iron ring that someone drilled into the rock years back for some kind of moorage. At least I hope it's still there. People used to tie rafts to it when the water was low and calm. If you can hook your rope into that ring and secure the other end to yourself, you can feed yourself out into the water and hold yourself against the currents. The rope should be long enough for you to reach Ginny." She scrambled to her feet and hooked her pack onto her back, then scooped up the other coil of rope.

"I'm going out onto the trestle bridge. I'll try to cut Ginny free from the top. There's a path around the back of this knoll that leads there."

"He'll pick you off the second the mist clears."

"He'll pick you off going down the cliff face, too. Pray the mist holds. I'll try to provide a distraction from the top while you get out there at the bottom. Here." She handed him a whistle from her pack. "Two sharp blasts and I'll know you're under her. The instant you blow that signal, I'll try to sever her loose from the top. Give me your rifle."

"Angie, I can't let you—"

"Stop," she whispered, pressing her gloved fingers to his lips. "Please, stop. And focus." Then she said, "Maddocks, I've got nothing else. I *need* to do this." She paused. "I need to try."

And he heard the subtext. She'd lost one partner. She'd lost the toddler. She'd lost Merry Winston, whom she felt she'd needed to protect. She'd lost her own identity. And she could not bear losing again.

"I'm going to do it with or without you, Sergeant James Maddocks, you hear me? But I could use that rifle. I can put it to better use from up on the trestle than you can while you're neck-deep in rapids."

He handed her his long gun and the extra magazines. She pocketed the ammo and slung the gun and the coil of rope across her body. "Be safe," she whispered, before disappearing into the forest and mist. His heart slammed against his ribs as he watched her vanish. The rushing sound of waves rising reached him. He slung the other coil of rope over his own body, spun around, and carefully lowered himself over the edge of the platform, reaching for the iron cable. One slip of his feet or hands and he'd plunge to his death.

So would Angie on that rotting rail bridge if she made a slip on her end.

Or if the old rail ties gave in under her.

CHAPTER 75

Angie checked her watch. Just after 7:00 a.m. and still dark. Using her headlamp and flashlight, she negotiated the gully trail, protected from view by the knoll of trees above her.

She reached the end of the trail, switched off her lights, and crouched down. The old trestle bridge stretched ahead of her into the dark and mist. From where Maddocks had pointed, Ginny had been strung down just over midway across that bridge. Angie shrugged off the coil of rope. She'd have to forsake fashioning a harness in favor of creating a temporary distraction. It would draw Addams's attention to the bridge and away from Maddocks, who was negotiating his way down the cliff.

Removing her headlamp, she fed one end of the rope through the strap and fastened it. Hooking the rope holding her headlamp to her shoulder, Angie edged out into the darkness and onto the bridge.

The rail ties had gaps between them. If she slipped, she'd go straight through. Space yawed below her, and it made her head spin. Her heart hammered up into her throat. She paused, eyes adjusting, and she breathed in deep. Very deep. Then, exhaling in a slow, controlled fashion, she got down onto her hands and knees and began to crawl onto the bridge. She hated heights—she'd endured them for one of her recent

Justice Institute courses, and it's why she still had the ropes in the back of her Crown Vic. But she was even worse at swimming. Gradually, she inched out, trying to keep to the side where the ties adjoined the bridge structure in a solid stretch of wood. But the surface of the wood was slick with the slimy detritus of decay, and her hand slipped. She gasped, steadying herself, and she shut her eyes for a moment, marshaling her control. She resumed her crawl out into the chasm between the cliffs. Wind picked up the farther she moved into the void of mist and darkness. From below came the roar of surf.

When she judged she was about a quarter of the way in, Angie stopped. Carefully, she shrugged off the coil of rope. Breathing in, then out, using a steady rhythm to calm and distract herself from the gaping maw below, she secured the free end of the rope around a rail tie. Then, holding the end with the headlamp affixed to it, she continued inching her way to the center of the bridge. Her hand came into contact with what felt like thick polyester rope. Her pulse leaped.

Angie felt along the polyester rope. It was tied to a trestle, and it stretched taut below the bridge.

Ginny.

Angie swallowed and reached for the knife in her pocket. She opened the blade and clung there, waiting for Maddocks's whistle signal. Seconds ticked by. Time stretched. Her muscles started to cramp, then shake. She prayed Maddocks had managed to get down to the water, find the iron ring, feed himself out into the rapids far below her. She prayed the fog would hold and keep them all hidden, because a dull gray dawn was beginning to almost imperceptibly lighten the forest.

She heard it. One sharp blast, then another. Emotion sparked into her eyes.

Quickly, she switched her headlamp on to flash mode and dropped it into the void. Attached to the rope, it swung down and back toward where she'd tied the other end, light pulsing into the mist.

The gunshot was instant. Then another. Addams was firing on the moving flashlight. Sweat prickled over her lip as Angie frantically sliced at the rope with the same blade she'd used to cut the cuffs off Maddocks that first night in the motel—the same blade with which she'd tried to kill him. Now she prayed that blade would save his daughter. Another gunshot sounded as her flashlight swung and pulsed below the bridge. She worked faster. Addams would wise up to the distraction trick sooner or later.

It happened sooner. Another gunshot cracked through the canyon. This time he was aiming not at the bridge, but at the water below where he'd strung Ginny. A scream—a woman's bloodcurdling scream—sliced the air as the last strands of polyester rope snapped free and the cut end of the rope dropped into the dark. Angie clung to the rail ties, listening. There was another shot. Then nothing but the sound of the surf.

Her gaze flared to the dark forest as a light appeared in the trees. The light bobbed and moved slowly down the cliff. Addams. He was making his way toward the water on the opposite side. Balancing carefully, heart in her throat, Angie reached for the rifle on her back. Easing into a flatter position on the trestles, finger curling around the trigger, she aimed carefully at the moving light. And fired. The butt kicked against her cheek and shoulder. She swallowed. The light was still there, moving faster, but uphill now, away. She'd missed, but she'd set him on the run. She aimed, fired again. The light bobbed even faster. He was climbing a trail that she knew would take him west and up into even more remote wilderness. He was fleeing. Angie scrambled up onto her hands and knees. She hooked the rifle back over her body and crawled as fast as she could along the rest of the bridge toward the forested cliff on the west side.

CHAPTER 76

The bullet slammed like a mallet into his chest. Dazed, winded, Maddocks heard a scream as he sank down into the churning surf. Unable to breathe or thrash against the water engulfing him, he saw Ginny's cocoon coming down beside him. She landed with a splash. Every instinct in his brain screamed to grab her before she went under and drowned, unable to save herself with her arms bound into that tarp. He fought to suck in a breath, the pain in his chest crushing. Managing to move his arms, he flailed pathetically in the rolling surf to grab the loose end of Ginny's rope that had come snapping down atop of them both. He snagged the rope and pulled himself along it, simultaneously pulling her closer toward him. Her cocoon reached him. He latched on to his daughter just as they washed into deeper water, faster, currents swirling. He kicked his legs like an eggbeater, struggling to keep them both afloat and hold her head above water, his wet clothes, boots, conspiring to drag him down. He saw her face. White like paper. Blood came from her brow. But her eyes . . . her eyes were wide open and wild with terror, and her mouth, too. She was screaming. The sound was all around him and being drowned by surf. His Ginny was alive and screaming and bleeding. The current snatched at them, suddenly whirling them in a mad fairground ride into a powerful set of roaring rapids as they were swept up toward the estuary.

Angie reached land on the far side of the bridge. She wobbled up onto her feet, limbs trembling from the effort of keeping her balance and her focus. She felt sick with fear that Addams had killed Maddocks. Or Ginny. Or both. That they had drowned below her.

She clicked on her flashlight. A trail of mud and rock and moss led steeply up into the trees. A fresh print showed in the mud. She swung her beam a little farther up the trail. More tracks. Leading farther up into the woods.

There was no way she'd be able to climb down the cliff in time to save Maddocks or Ginny. She'd cut Ginny's cocoon loose, dropping her into the water. Both she and Maddocks would have been swept up toward the estuary within seconds. If Maddocks was secured to the rope and still able, he might be able to pull himself and Ginny back to the safety of the rock ledge. She chose to believe this was the case as she dropped her pack and struggled with numb fingers to undo the side strap that held her two-way radio. The radio would be useless if there was no one in range, and it was unlikely the ERT guys would be close enough yet—that is, *if* they were even trying to access the area on foot. However, someone *might* hear her.

She engaged the radio. "Mayday, mayday. Trestle bridge, Skookum narrows. Mayday, mayday, Skookum narrows."

She waited. Tried again. Nothing. She tried once more, and still no response. Replacing the radio, she swung the pack and gun back up onto her back. Aiming her flashlight beam ahead of her, she started up the trail, moving as fast as she could. Sleet came down hard, and the mud was slick. She fell again and again but kept on getting up. Her breath began to rasp in her throat, and sweat drenched her body under her jacket and clothes, but all she could focus on was getting him. Stopping him before he could disappear forever into the wild.

Her advantage was that Addams didn't know yet she was tracking him.

Angie moved like this for hours. Her muscles cramped. Her toes went numb. Her heart beat like a rapid, deep drum in her chest. Daylight filtered into the forest, but beneath the old-growth canopy and with the low clouds, visibility was poor. She stumbled more and more. But she kept going, following his tracks, losing all sense of time. The forest grew darker again.

Suddenly the prints ended.

She stilled, tensed. Then clicked off her flashlight. Too late. A crack of a rifle snapped her attention upward and to the right, but at the same time she felt a slam in her arm. The impact spun her sideways, and her boot caught under a root. She went down hard into rock and mud. Pain screamed through her upper left arm. She heard the crash and crunch of brush breaking, of him fleeing. Rage exploded into her blood. Using her good arm, she grabbed on to branches to pull herself back up onto her feet. Retrieving her rifle from where it had fallen on the ground, she stumbled after him.

Angie's eyes watered with the pain. She felt her own blood soaking hot into her sleeve, going sticky down her arm. Her breathing became labored. Dizziness made the darkening forest spin. She stopped. Panting, she listened carefully. She heard him again, crashing through deciduous scrub. Suddenly she saw his light bobbing ahead. He was moving away from her and up a steep, mossy incline that exposed him.

With her good arm and some limited movement from her injured one, Angie maneuvered her rifle stock into the socket between her shoulder and her jaw. She tried to inhale deeply as she sighted down the barrel. She aimed for the dark bulk of his center. Curling her finger around the trigger, she exhaled, and on the last of her breath, she fired. Her weapon kicked. Sound boomed through the forest. Sweat, melting slush, leaked into her eyes, blurring her vision. She saw him stagger, fall. But he didn't stay down. He crawled a little farther up the incline, and then he swayed back up onto his feet. He started wobbling uphill again.

A wild, unthinking animal came alive and roared inside Angie's chest. In her mind she saw Drummond's body on that morgue slab, Faith Hocking's corpse cut wide open. She saw in her head what he'd done to them. Because they were women. Because they fit his sick sexual fantasy.

I came to you because you said that you cared. And I believed you . . .

She'd let Merry Winston down.

And all those other girls before Merry . . . and Ginny and Maddocks . . .

And suddenly, there she was again—the little girl in a wash of luminous pink. She floated with the mist in the trees. The forest was completely dark again—had night fallen once more?

Words—like a rushing river, like the wind, like the sound of crashing ocean surf—boomed into Angie's head. The noise seemed to come from within her skull, from the forest all around her, from the cloud . . .

Come um dum . . . dem grove . . . come . . .

The little girl chuckled, turned, and raced up into the trees, behind Addams.

Angie could see nothing but the pink glow. It tugged her forward, as if with strings attached directly to her heart. Panting, she scrambled and staggered and fell and crawled and got up again and again as she was pulled forward by that pink glow and her desperate urge to protect it, to stop it from getting any closer to the evil that was Addams.

She reached the top of the incline. And saw him.

Addams.

He sat on a rock, holding his thigh, his head bent. His weapon lay on the ground by his boots. She'd wounded him.

"Spencer Addams!" she screamed.

His head shot up.

She saw his face, white in the light of her headlamp. His eyes met hers. He remained motionless for a moment. She raised her rifle stock to her shoulder, oblivious now to pain, to any physical sensation at all.

"Step away from that weapon—get down on the ground! Now!" She moved forward as she yelled. "On your stomach!"

Very slowly, with his gaze locked onto hers, he moved, lowering himself to the earth.

The little girl ducked behind him, behind his rock. Angie blinked, trying to keep focus. Rain and sweat leaked into her eyes. He kept looking right back at her, just kept looking. Time stretched and warped. "Move it! Now!" she yelled, her voice cracking. Her finger curled tighter around her rifle trigger. That tinny nursery rhyme music began inside her head—quiet and distant at first, then loud and discordant and crashing, like a bad fairground ride . . . *There . . . were once two little kittens. A-a-a, a-a-, two little kittens . . .*

Angie swallowed. Her finger was tense on the trigger. She kept staring into those devil's eyes as reality seemed to blur. He moved suddenly, snatching up his rifle. He rose into a squat. She squeezed.

His head blew back. He dropped the gun. His body seemed to hang motionless as he kept looking at her. Blood, black in the light of her headlamp, bloomed white around his mouth, making him look like a mad, laughing clown. He slumped backward.

Panting hard, she moved quickly toward him.

He was on his back, just in front of the rock, writhing in the mud. She'd hit him in the jaw, on the left side of his mouth. He reached a hand out to her, like a claw, as if to plead for mercy, to grasp onto her. He was saying something . . . yelling something with that bloody maw . . . trying to scoot and wriggle backward in the mud.

Ice filled her heart. Rage mushroomed through her body, stealing all logic that remained in her exhausted mind. *Two little kittens . . . there were two little kittens . . .*

Angie raised her gun. She fired. Again. Into his face. And again. And again. She emptied the rest of her ten-round magazine and dropped to her knees in the mud, shaking.

Tears streamed down her face.

CHAPTER 77

Angie became gradually aware that she was lying in a bed. Her body hurt. She tried to open her eyes. Light was bright—pain. She shut them again quickly, nausea washing into her stomach. Her mouth felt dry, tasted bad. Confusion swirled thick in her brain. The memory struck her suddenly. Her pulse quickened. *Spencer Addams.*

Hunting him through the woods.

Her eyes flared open wide, heart racing. Hospital—she was in a ward. Angie struggled to sit up. Dizziness swirled, and she collapsed back onto the pillow with a groan.

"Whoa, easy there. Take it easy."

Slowly, she turned her head. Blinking, she tried to bring the speaker into focus. He was sitting in a chair in the corner of the room.

"Holgersen?"

He tossed aside the blanket covering him and came to his feet.

"Where am I?" She managed to pull herself up into a quasi-sitting position against the pillow. She realized her upper left arm was bandaged. It throbbed like all hell. Her head, too.

Holgersen came up to her bedside. "Bullet ripped through muscle and flesh, but missed bone. Doc says yous should regain full use of that arm, but it'll take a while. And plenty of physio."

Her hand went to her head. She tentatively touched a sensitive area that felt like a golf ball.

"Guess yous got a bash on the head, too, eh? Maybe when you passed out."

"What . . . what happened to me?"

"All's I know is you was lying there bleeding, unconscious, hypothermic, dehydrated, when the SAR guys found you and Addams's body."

Her brain reeled. She closed her eyes, trying to remember, struggling to bring it all into focus. She recalled tracking him. For how long she didn't know. Catching up. Yelling at him to lie facedown. Then . . . then nothing. Blackness. She opened her eyes.

Holgersen was smoothing his goatee, watching her closely.

"Addams?"

"You got him good. Real good. He's dead."

"Maddocks? Ginny?"

"They's here in the hospital." He smiled. "They's gonna be fine, Pallorino. Washed up the estuary. Bit beat up—Maddocks was shot in the chest, but the bullet-suppression vest saved him. Lung collapsed, broken ribs, but on the mends. Ginny—gots her head cut. Dislocated shoulder. Her injuries are gonna be more mental than physical. They's brought in victim counseling."

"Did he . . . did he sexually—"

"Addams did not assault her. He did not carve a crucifix. He was using her for something else."

Emotion flooded her eyes. She closed them for a moment as she strained to remember the series of events that had landed her here.

"How'd Addams get her?"

"He was waiting in her apartment when she came home."

"What day, what time is it?"

"Wednesday morning. By the time they brought you down the mountain, it was almost midnight Monday. SAR guys found you lying passed out. They stabilized you up there, then carried you down. Weather was still too bad to get a chopper anywhere near there. Like pea soup—couldn't even land in the Skookum parking lot. Doc operated on your arm Tuesday morning, gots the bullet out. Rehydrated and warmed yous up. Then you was in and out all day yesterday. They says it's quite a marvel that yous lived."

Angie fought to pull the last few days into focus.

"Media shit-storm out there," he said. "Lots of questions . . . and shit."

"What do you mean?"

"About how Addams died and all. MVPD issued a statement that said the suspect wanted in connection with the deaths of Drummond and Hocking has been located and has been found dead. That's alls they said—no mention of your name and that you shot him, but you gots him real good, Pallorino. In the face. In the neck. In the chest. Like point-blank, man. Emptied your clip into the bastard."

Darkness swirled the shards of images through her mind. "His face?"

"Yeah . . . he was like lying there on his back, it looks like. From the photos."

A sickening cold fingered into Angie's chest as reality clarified. Officer-involved shooting. "They've opened an investigation?"

"Yeah. Right away. There was two officers with the SAR guys, and they secured the scene when they saw what had happened. Gots the IIO investigators in the next day to examine the scene—the IIO has asserted jurisdiction over the incident." He paused. "They's waiting with questions."

Angie sat in silence. The Independent Investigations Office. They would decide now whether she'd committed a criminal offense. If so, her case would be passed to Crown counsel. "So am I still on active duty?"

"I guess that's ups to Fitz and brass."

A sick, anxious feeling dropped into her belly. "I don't remember shooting him," she said quietly.

Holgersen nodded but said nothing.

She threw back her covers suddenly and swung her legs over the side of the bed. "I want to see Maddocks." But dizziness slammed her in the side of her head, and she wobbled.

"Whoa, not now—you needs rest."

"I *have* to see him. Get me a wheelchair, Holgersen. Give me my clothes."

He snorted. "Your clothes is done, Pallorino. IIO investigators took them." He went to the small closet against the wall and took out a plastic grocery bag. From the bag he pulled a gray sweatshirt and sweatpants. He placed them on the bed. "I broughts you something from my place. For temporary." He paused. "I'll go get that wheelchair." He yanked the curtain across, giving her some privacy.

Angie reached for the clothes, removed the hospital gown, and struggled to insert her limbs into Holgersen's baggy, pale-gray sweats. She had to roll up the legs and sleeves and was exhausted by the time he returned, pushing the chair.

He helped her into it in silence and then wheeled her out of the room and down the hall.

"Ginny?"

Slowly her eyes opened, and she turned her face in search of his voice.

"Daddy?"

Emotion punched through Maddocks. He reached for her hand. It was slender and cool in his. His baby girl. His child. Now a beautiful young woman. This was what he'd made in life—the one good,

479

true thing that had come from his marriage. And he realized that this alone was worthwhile. That the years had *not* been wasted. That she was alive, and so was he, and the future could still shimmer in front of them. Addams had not sexually assaulted her. It would be a rough road forward for her, he knew that. But they were going to do this together. They still had each other.

"I'm so sorry, Daddy."

He straightened his spine, struggling to keep his emotions under check. "You did nothing wrong, Ginn. It's going to be okay."

"Thank you for coming," she whispered. "For saving me. He . . . he made me phone you. He was luring you, and I . . . I knew he was going to try and kill you. I didn't know what to do, and—"

"Shh." He smoothed hair back from her face where doctors had stitched up the cut along her brow. When he'd first seen it, he'd thought it was a crucifix—he'd thought the worst. "You did good, Ginn. He's gone now."

"Angie?"

"She's still out, sleeping." He'd checked on her dozens of times already. "She's going to be fine."

"She saved us—she got him."

"She did. He can't hurt anyone else, ever." He hesitated, swallowed, then said, "Your mother is here. The nurses told me that she's waiting outside to see you. Shall I bring her in?"

"With Peter? Is he here, too?"

"I don't know."

His daughter's gaze locked with his. "I'm sorry for all the things I said."

"I understand."

"We're going to be good, Dad. I promise. I—"

"I know, Ginn. I know we will."

"I love you."

He could no longer tamp down the rush of emotion, and his voice choked as he said, "I love you, too, baby. I've got your back. Always."

Tears pooled in her eyes. The same color as his. Her mouth pressed into a tight line, and she nodded, squeezing his hand.

✝

Maddocks was not in his room, his bed empty, covers thrown back.

Anxiety twisted tighter inside Angie as she stared at the vacant bed. She just needed to see him with her own eyes, touch him, see that he was okay. *Fuck.* This was going to cost her. She'd disobeyed direct orders in going after him alone. But she also knew that she'd do it again in a heartbeat—he and Ginny would probably be dead right now if she hadn't.

"I figure he's with Ginny," Holgersen said.

"Where's Ginny's room? Same floor?"

"Yeah."

"Take me there."

"Maybe it's not the best idea—"

"Jesus, Holgersen, just push me, will you? I can't make my arm work right now or I'd freaking do it myself."

"Glad to see yous back, Pallorino," he said, grabbing the wheelchair handles and swiveling her around. "You'd make a wretched senior, you know."

Angie swallowed as guilt reared inside her chest and her thoughts turned to her mother. With it came hurt, a deep sense of betrayal. She had a long road ahead and no idea how to navigate it right now.

They arrived at Ginny's room. Through the ward window Angie caught sight of Maddocks standing by her bed. He too was wearing sweats. With him was a woman. Slender, tall. Blonde. "Wait," Angie said. "Stop."

She stared at the woman—extremely well dressed in tailored pants and a soft coral-colored jacket. Impeccably cut shoulder-length hair. She turned her head. Very attractive, classic profile. She looked to be in her early to mid forties.

"Who's that?" Angie said.

"Mrs. Maddocks."

She swallowed slowly. "What's her name?"

"Sabrina."

Angie watched the small family unit for a moment through the glass. Ginny, with her dark hair spread on her pillow—their daughter. The two parents, worried for their child. United in this tragedy. Sabrina Maddocks lifted her hand and placed it on Maddocks's shoulder. He turned and looked down at her. Sabrina—his wife—not yet an ex-wife—reached up and gently wiped something from his eyes, then she leaned, kissed him on the cheek.

Angie's stomach did a sickening somersault. Her hands firmed on the wheelchair armrests.

"Go," she said to Holgersen. "Just go."

"You sure you—"

"I said go, dammit. Now. Faster."

"Jesus, Pallorino," he said, pushing her speedily down the corridor.

"Stop. Right over there. Push me there—by those chairs, by the window."

He acquiesced and brought her to a halt in a small seating alcove.

Her heart was hammering, and she hated that her body had reacted like this.

"You should have told me she was here."

"I told yous it wasn't best—"

Angie tried to stand, but dizziness slammed her back down into the chair. Her breaths were short.

"Pallorino, just sits, okay. Just relax."

Angie closed her eyes and struggled once more to recall the events leading up to her alleged shooting of Spencer Addams. She caught a flash of the bridge. In the mist. The shots. Getting to the other side. Tracking him through mountainous old-growth forest slaked in mist for hours . . . Her heart stilled. The little girl—*she'd seen the ghost of the girl again.*

Ice chilled in her veins.

She'd followed the girl . . . then . . . just blackness.

Holgersen's phone rang, and he answered it. Angie looked out of the window as he took his call. Outside, tiny flakes of snow shimmied against gray sky. Unusual winter, she thought.

"Yeah, she's awake now," Holgersen was saying. "Yeah, okay." He handed her his phone.

"Vedder. He wants to talk to you."

"IIO investigation?"

He nodded.

She reached for his phone and said, "Did he—the MVPD—send you to watch me? To tell them when I'd come around?"

"Fuck no, Pallorino."

"Don't lie to me, Holgersen."

He dragged his long fingers through his dull brown hair. "Okay. So they wanted someone here. They was going to send a uniform, but I came myselves, okay. Just take the damn phone."

She put it to her ear, shivering a little from cold.

Angie listened to Vedder asking the right questions about how she was feeling, offering the expected platitudes, and then he told her that he would be functioning as the liaison officer between the IIO and the MVPD on her case, and that she'd need to speak to the outside investigators as soon as she was able.

"Understood, sir," she said coolly. "I'll be in tomorrow. I'm sure I'll be fine tomorrow."

She killed the call and held the phone out to Holgersen.

This was her second serious incident in six months. And she had no recollection of the actual shooting. She was in shit.

"Any one of us woulda done it," Holgersen said, taking the phone from her. "Shot the crap out of him."

"Is that what I did?"

He held her eyes.

"Fuck," she whispered, pushing her tangle of hair back off her brow and looking away.

"At least they's alive—Maddocks and Ginny."

"Yeah." She stared at her reflection in the window. "At least."

Mirror, mirror, on the wall, who are you, for I know you not at all?

CHAPTER 78

Thursday, December 21

Angie sat opposite Vedder at his desk. It was after 7:00 p.m., and she was physically, emotionally, and mentally beat after spending the entire day answering the IIO investigators' questions about the Spencer Addams shooting and the sequence of events leading up to it . . . *Why did you defy a direct order from Inspector Frank Fitzsimmons and go after Sergeant Maddocks? What happened on the bridge? How long did you track Addams? What happened when you found the Affected Person? Did you warn him? Did you tell him to drop his weapon? Did you believe he posed a significant threat to your safety? Did you use all other means to effect an arrest? Did he resist? How did he resist? Why did you shoot? What did you do then?*

It was not helping her at all that she couldn't recall the actual shooting.

Neither was it helping to know that Maddocks and Fitz and anyone else involved in the lead-up to her "incident" were being questioned, too, as witnesses. And that a pathologist other than Barb O'Hagan was conducting the autopsy on Spencer Addams.

The union had assisted her with legal counsel, and a rep had been present. Angie, as the Subject Officer, and who thus faced jeopardy in the investigation, had had the option of invoking the Charter of Rights and Freedoms, which included the right to silence. But she knew the other officers being questioned as witnesses did not have that right. And while she might have overkilled Addams, she did not believe what she did was criminal. It was a risk she was prepared to take in order to be officially cleared.

The investigators had shown her diagrams, crime scene photos, shell casings—she'd apparently emptied her magazine into Addams's face, neck, chest while he'd been lying prone on his back. The rage evident in those images—the overkill—it frightened her. She had a wild beast inside her, and it had taken over her mind, and she didn't know if she could ever trust herself in a similar situation again.

Vedder had taken possession of her service weapon and had relieved her of active duty, pending a separate internal MVPD review. And Angie did not have a good feeling about that outcome. He'd called her in, working late as usual, to ask how she was doing.

"You handling okay?" Vedder said, compassion in his eyes. He'd always been good to her. He'd been the one to go to bat for her in a hostile environment when she'd first joined his sex crimes unit. She owed him, and she wasn't holding this against him now.

"I suppose. How're things going with forensics and the Addams house?" she said. "Anything on all those hair trophies?"

He rubbed his chin, as if considering how much he should—or could—tell her now. "So far we've matched hair samples to Merry Winston, Allison Fernyhough, and Sally Ritter. We're working with Interpol and going back to possible assaults in ports around the Med where Addams crewed."

"So you think Drummond was his first homicide?"

"That's the working theory—that the others were all sexual assaults, until he was afforded the opportunity to experiment with mutilating Hocking's body."

"And his mother?"

"O'Hagan's postmortem report is pending, but preliminary indication is that she likely died a natural death, and because Addams was fixated on her, he kept her. The investigation around Beulah Addams is obviously going to take time, but she probably abused him as a kid."

"Punished him for sexual arousal."

"That's Grablowski's take."

"The scrubbing mitts?"

He nodded. "She likely used those on her son. And it was both arousing and painful—"

"And thus grew his sick paraphilic map."

"As Grablowski would put it. Her death could have been a trigger, in conjunction with having to deal with Hocking's body, that set him off."

"So *she* was the real monster."

"She certainly helped breed and raise one. Nature–nurture and all that, it seems. Forensics also found a male skeleton beneath the concrete flooring in the basement, possibly Spencer Addams's father. Forensics and postmortem results on that are also still pending."

"The mother maybe killed the father?"

He gave a half shrug. "Again—it's the working hypothesis."

"So, missing student Annelise Janssen is no part of this?"

"So far. Her case remains open. But she's a blonde—doesn't fit the victim profile. Nothing ties her to this."

"What about the *Amanda Rose*, Bacchanalian Club, Madame Vee, the johns, the other girls—"

"An interagency task force including agencies from abroad is being formed to handle the ongoing details of that investigation. It's going to be a long haul. Could be years before parts of the case start going before the courts."

"Winston's case?"

"We found crystal meth cut with fentanyl in Damián Yorick's apartment. Techs also found his prints in Winston's home—on the window, on the table. Kitchen counter. Yorick will be charged, and he's not alone. He'd have to have received that photo of Winston from the *Amanda Rose* security guys. There's indication of a conspiracy to silence Winston."

"And her deep throat recording? And Buziak—I hear he's not back yet. What do Fitz and internal have on him?"

Vedder hesitated and broke eye contact for a moment. When he met her gaze again, he said, "That's all still under investigation, Angie. I'm not at liberty to discuss details at this point."

She stared at him, a cool feeling of isolation beginning to encircle her. She was being cut out. She was persona non grata on the force right now. She nodded and came to her feet.

"Thanks for what you did share, Vedder." She made for the door.

"Angie—you look like shit."

She paused, hand on the doorknob. "Yeah. I know. Thanks."

"What are you going to do?"

"While I wait to see if I'm going to be fired?"

He said nothing.

"I don't know—I have a . . . cold case, something personal that I want to look into. Night, Vedder."

She exited, shut the door, took a deep breath, and made her way down the row of bullpens, mostly empty at this hour. As she neared the station entrance, a woman got up off the chairs near the door.

"Detective Pallorino?"

Lorna Drummond. A box in her hands.

Angie stopped dead in her tracks and tensed, bracing for another assault—verbal or otherwise.

Drummond came forward. "Gracie left me a Christmas gift. I found it under her bed." The woman paused, overtly struggling to marshal her emotions. Clearing her throat, she held the box out to Angie.

"I want you to have it. Gracie would want you to have it. For everything you did for her. And for Faith. And all those other girls."

Angie stared at her.

"Please, take it."

Carefully, Angie took the box from Lorna Drummond. She opened it. Inside was what looked like an ornately carved cream-colored jewelry box. Angie looked up.

"Open it," Lorna Drummond said, her eyes swimming with moisture.

Angie lifted the box lid. A tiny dancer in a pink tutu popped up and started to wobble in a pirouette as lullaby music tinkled—made by a revolving cylinder with a set of pins that plinked at a comb of metal tines to create the sound.

"It's an antique," Drummond said. "I used to have a similar one when I was a little girl. My father gave it to me. He died that year, and not long after, the jewelry box was lost in a house fire. I often spoke to Gracie about that box and how it was the last thing I had of my dad. I was with Gracie when I saw this one in the antique store on Government Street a few months ago. I . . . I was moved by it, and she saw. She must have returned and bought it—" Her voice choked. She fiddled in her pocket for a tissue and blew her nose. "She'd . . . hidden it . . . under her bed. Waiting for Christmas."

Which would never come for Gracie Drummond.

We all lie.

We all guard secrets—sometimes terrible ones—a side to us so dark, so shameful, that we quickly avert our own eyes from the shadow we might glimpse in the mirror.

Instead we lock our dark halves deep in the basement of our souls. And on the surface of our lives, we work industriously to shape the public story of our selves . . .

Angie stared at the halting dancer. The music slowed to a plink then a plunk, then died. She swallowed, unable at that moment to look up and meet Lorna Drummond's eyes for fear of what she'd reveal in her own.

"I can't take it, Mrs. Drummond." Her voice came out in a hoarse whisper. "I just can't."

Lorna Drummond touched Angie's hand. "Please. I can't keep it, either. I want . . . I want you to have it. To remember her, and all girls like her." She fell silent. Angie glanced up.

Tears sheened down the woman's face. "Keep doing what you do, Detective," she whispered. "People like you . . . it's all we have between what is good and right, and what is wrong." A pause as she struggled to go on. "Thank you for finding him, for stopping him before he could hurt anyone else."

And she turned and was gone. Out the doors into the rainy dark.

Angie stared after her, unable to move, the box with the little dancer in her hands.

FRIDAY, DECEMBER 22

"Angie? Is that you?"

A rush of conflicting emotions flooded Angie's chest as she seated herself in front of her mother's rocker. Her dad's words filled her mind . . .

My Miriam came back to life, Angie. You brought her back to me. And I . . . I don't know if you can ever understand love like I have for her, but she . . . she's my everything. She's my world. And seeing her become whole again . . . I just let it be. I let her believe . . .

Her mom reached out, touched Angie's hand, her skin cool. "It's so good to see you, Ange."

"I brought you something, Mom."

"A Christmas present? What is it?" she said with glee and a childlike clasp of her hands.

Angie smiled, her old love for her mother warring with the new information, the secrets revealed, her complicated feelings around it all. She still felt a lingering *need* for this woman to be her mother, and she also felt a new hole in her heart knowing that her biological mom was still out there. Dead or alive. Unknown. An unsolved mystery.

"Sort of a present," she said. "It's something special to me, from a very special young woman—I thought you might like to look after it for me and enjoy it for a while."

Angie could not keep the jewelry box in her apartment—that little dancer in a pink tutu. It was too close to her little girl in pink who lived deep inside her mind. And giving the box to her mom felt right. It met a need in Angie to share something of herself— her work, her life—with her adoptive mother, who could no longer understand things with a simple telling. Angie hoped this symbol, this gesture, might fill that role somehow. Mothers and daughters. And the tricky love they shared.

Her mother frowned in confusion. "But it is from Angie?"

"Her name was Gracie."

She opened it. The music tinkled, the little dancer wobbling in her pirouette. Tears filled her mother's eyes. She clasped her hands together again, both a child and a woman confused in her own memories.

Angie took her leave from her mother, feeling hollow.

"Merry Christmas," the orderly said on her way out.

She nodded. Yeah. "Merry Christmas."

At least she understood her own emotions around Christmastime now, Angie thought, stepping out into the cold night.

SUNDAY, DECEMBER 24

They were holding a service for Merry Winston on a promontory that jutted out into the sea between two bays. It was a place where Winston apparently used to go sometimes, to just sit and watch the water.

On her way to the service, Angie pulled into the driveway of her childhood home. She sat in her vehicle a moment, looking at the shell of a house, the vessel of so many memories. True ones. False ones. Lies. Love misguided and misunderstood. Inhaling deeply, she got out of the car and took a big wicker basket from the backseat.

Wind tugged at her hair and coat as she set the basket at the front door. She was about to leave when the door swung open.

"Angie?"

"Dad. Hey." She dug her hands deep into her coat pockets. He looked old. He was wearing baggy jeans and his oversize comfy sweater with the leather patches on the elbows. Seeing him big and familiar was yet another emotional punch to her gut.

"I . . . uh . . ." Angie looked up at the sky as if gravity might hold it all in or show her answers. Everything felt so goddamn close to the surface right now. "I brought you a small turkey and fixings and stuff." She jerked her chin to the basket. "I . . . know you're going to visit Mom this evening. The orderlies told me. They said some families like to bring a festive meal to the center, share." She swallowed, that old picture of them all in front of a Christmas tree shimmering into her mind, along with a fresh sense of betrayal.

"Come with me tonight, Angie," he said.

Her mouth tightened, and she shook her head. "I can't. Not now . . . not yet."

He looked at her long and hard. "We didn't mean harm."

She nodded, stuffed her hands deeper into her coat pockets. "I know."

"We loved you . . . we still love you."

She nodded again. Cold wind whipped hair across her face. "I need to go."

"Work again."

"A funeral service. For a friend."

"Merry Christmas, Angie."

"Yeah. Take care, Dad."

✝

The knoll that jutted out into the sea was full with ancient history, long gold grasses, a totem pole that stood silent sentinel. A bald eagle perched atop the pole, feathers ruffling in salt wind as it peered down at the tiny gathering of people below. Angie stood among them, alone and a little to the side.

"Leaves should not wither and die in early spring," said the pastor from the United Church as Merry Winston's ashes were scattered to the wind, blowing toward the pale, wintery horizon. "Winter should not come before its time . . ."

Pastor Markus from Harbor House was here. So was Winston's street friend, Nina, and a few other ragged-looking women, rubbing noses and shivering in the cold. But no Holgersen. No Leo. No one else from the MVPD. And at this poignant moment, Angie felt a kinship with this motley group—she too was a fringe dweller of sorts right now. Left out in the cold. Lonely.

". . . for there is no answer to death, especially premature death, but to live vigorously and beautifully . . ."

Angie turned and made her way along the little grassy path up toward the parking lot.

A figure waited there. Tall. Black coat. Blue-black hair ruffling like those eagle feathers in the salt wind.

Maddocks.

Angie stalled, gathered herself, and went up to him.

His complexion was bloodless, the hollows under his eyes and cheekbones dark.

"You've been avoiding me," he said as she neared. His voice was stern, angry almost. Frustrated, maybe. "You haven't answered or returned any of my calls. Why?"

"I'm giving you space. I—"

"Don't shit me, Angie. I don't need space, and you know it."

"How's Ginny?"

"Ginny's fine, and don't change the subject."

"Sabrina?"

"Angie—"

"I saw you with her, Maddocks, at the hospital."

"She's Ginny's mother—she always will be."

"I know. You needed to be together. I . . . don't want to come between that. I know how you wanted to salvage the dream, the past. I've screwed up before, Maddocks, messed with a married man, and it killed his marriage, and I've regretted that every moment of my life. It's . . . why—"

"The club?"

And her sex rules . . .

She snorted and turned to look at the sea, the small group of people threading up through the long grasses from the knoll. "Yeah."

"Do you always have to go to such extremes?"

She cast him a sideways glance.

"I signed my papers, Angie," he said. A pause. "My divorce is final."

Her gaze ticked to his empty ring finger, then up to his face. His eyes bored hot into hers. She swallowed.

"I want you in my life."

"Don't, Maddocks, not now. I—"

"When this is all over, when you're back at work, we let management know that we're seeing each other, and they can make assignments accordingly. It's standard. It can be done."

Her heart tumbled over itself into a tight ball. Anxiety rippled over her skin, and it came with a dark whisper of promise.

"I've got a lot to work through. There's still going to be an internal review. Maybe even an inquest. It could take—"

"Angie." He placed both his hands firmly on her shoulders. "Look at me. I'm here for you. I owe you my life. You saved Ginny's life. And I need you there for me. Jack-O, too. He misses you."

She smiled in spite of the emotions burning through her.

"Where is he?"

"With his sitter. Because we have plans for tonight."

She tried to pull back. She was afraid of what she felt for this man—the power of it. "I don't think—"

"Come." He put his arm around her shoulders, turned her, and led her up to his vehicle in the parking lot. "We can leave your car here and pick it up later."

He opened the passenger door. She hesitated.

"Get in, Angie."

"Where are we going?"

"It's Christmas Eve. We're going to do something to honor that. I want to do something to honor the fact you saved my life, Ginny's life—you put your own life and career on the line. For me. For my daughter. Against all orders. I owe you."

He shut the door behind her and went round to the driver's side.

As he got into the driver's seat, she said, "I made an appointment. Police psychologist." He stilled, met her gaze for a moment. Emotion glistened in his eyes.

"We'll work through this, Angie," he said quietly.

We.

Angie held tightly to that word as he pulled out of the parking lot and drove back toward the city.

CHAPTER 79

As Maddocks turned onto the road that led around the inner harbor, Angie looked at him and said, "Did you tell the IIO investigators that you ordered me not to come after you?"

"It sort of didn't come up."

She regarded his profile in silence, and she realized that once again, he was trying to cover for her, protect her. At risk to himself. Her heart swelled painfully. She looked away, out of the window that squiggled with rain.

"So, you're busy on the ongoing investigations—the outfall?"

He hesitated a moment too long, and Angie felt a little clutch in her stomach.

"Yeah. The team is growing, prosecutors on board. My focus is the barcode girls . . ."

"Go on."

He cast her a fast glance. "Between you and me."

"Christ, Maddocks, who am I going to tell?"

"There were six of them found on the *Amanda Rose*. Four of Eastern European origin and two Syrian—we think they were refugees, bought out of some camp and trafficked to the owners of the *Amanda Rose*. We're guessing they're aged between thirteen and seventeen. None of them will talk—been abused, brainwashed. Terrified. All have been tat-tooed with a barcode."

Frustration sparked through Angie. "I should be on that case—sex crimes," she said quietly.

"It'll be there when you return. You'll be back faster than you think."

"Don't patronize me, Maddocks. I can see the reality of my situa-tion. You owe me more than platitudes."

He snorted, turned down Government. "I'm sorry. But I do believe it's going to work out. You have support, friends."

"Doesn't change the facts of the case . . . *wait*, what are we doing here?" He'd pulled up outside the Flying Pig pub and grill.

"I'm not going in there," she said.

"Oh, yes you are."

Maddocks held the door open for Angie. Music, boisterous, ema-nated from inside. She hesitated. "I can't believe you're forcing me to do this," she said.

He grinned, and a wicked little twinkle lit those gorgeous deep-blue eyes of his.

"Force *you*? I don't think anyone *forces* Angie Pallorino to do anything."

Angie entered, nerves flitting about her stomach. The place was packed, a live band playing on the small stage area in the far corner.

Maddocks took her coat. Angie tensed as Leo caught sight of them. Leo's hand shot straight up into the air. The band stopped. Everyone turned around. He brought his hand down, and the band started another tune as balloons released from the ceiling. Everyone began to sing . . .

497

For she's a jolly good fellow, for she's a jolly good fellow . . . and so say all of us! Three cheers for Pallorino!

The pub erupted into cheers, and Leo came up, slapped her hard between the shoulder blades. "Welcome back, Pallorino!"

Angie quickly swiped tears from her eyes, embarrassed at showing her emotions like this. "Jesus, Leo, I'm *not* back. I'm fucking suspended."

"Ah, good as back. This round's on me—what you having?"

Angie stared at him, stunned. She shot a glance at Maddocks. He was grinning like a stupid Cheshire cat. "Is this *your* fault?" she snapped at him.

"This is you on friends, Pallorino," Maddocks said. He turned to Leo. "Get us a bottle of nice red, will ya?"

"Comin' right up."

"Yo, man," said Holgersen as he joined them. *"You gots a tribe in blue that's a rootin' for yoooo!"* He sang the words in an astounding bass, then his face turned serious. "Good to see yous, partner."

"You've been drinking."

"Aye—" He held his hands out to his sides and angled his head. "Guilty as charged. But no sex. Still celibate all the ways down the line."

"Freak," muttered Leo as he shoved his way toward Colm McGregor behind the packed bar.

Barb O'Hagan waved from a booth at the back, quieter end of the pub. Above the booth tables hung streamers of Christmas tinsel. The whole place smelled like beer, and turkey cooking, and boozy Christmas pudding.

Maddocks escorted Angie through the crowd toward the booth. Seated with O'Hagan was Sunni Padachaya from the lab, coroner Alphonse, and Dundurn and Smith from sex crimes.

"Hey, lady," O'Hagan said with a gap-toothed grin. "Pull up a pew."

Leo brought the wine and glasses over, and Holgersen scooted in beside Angie with a full mug of beer.

"So, did you hear the rumor about Fitz?" Leo said.

"What rumor?" Maddocks said.

Leo leaned closer. "Have a friend in tech—you know that voice recording Winston made of the deep throat?"

"Spit it out, Leo," Holgersen said, lifting his mug and taking a frothy swig.

"It's a match to Fitzsimmons."

They all stared at him in silence.

"Fitz?" Holgersen said.

"Yeah. Unique speech patterns and his little weirdly scratchy voice—they reckon it's him. Matches what they got on file."

"Nothing's proved yet," Maddocks said quietly. "Give the guy the benefit of the doubt—innocent until guilty."

Leo snorted, sat back, and took a sip of his whiskey. "Never thought I'd hear *you* supporting him—not after that little set-to the pair of you had outside the incident room door the other day."

"Why would Fitz leak information?" said Padachaya.

"He's sick in the head, I tell ya—freak," retorted Leo.

O'Hagan snorted softly. "He's been around same length of time as Gunnar. He's been overlooked for one promotion after another while Gunnar climbed steadily to the top. He's a bitter little man."

"A revenge guy," Maddocks said with a glance at Angie. "Let's stay mum on this—wait and see how it plays out, okay?"

Leo mumbled. "Between you and me," he said, "that fucker's got what's coming to him—sure would explain why he wanted to quash that mayor–ADAG stuff and curry favor with Killion and the new police board." He gave a harsh laugh. "Probably figured it would unseat Gunnar and get him all the way up into the chief's chair himself, eh?"

Maddocks poured Angie a glass of wine. She scanned the rest of the room as she sipped. She caught sight of a dark-haired, hawk-like man in a booth at the opposite corner.

"Grablowski's here," she said.

"Yep," Holgersen said. "All's invited." Then he added, "He's the only guy really spinning his wheels over the fact that you shot Addams dead."

O'Hagan chuckled. "True. Angie, you apparently robbed the doc of an opportunity to study a locally bred monster firsthand, right in his own backyard. He already had a book deal in the works, but that's tanked now."

"Well," Angie said, taking another sip of her wine, "I'd love to say there'll be another time . . . I'm sure he'll still spin something out of it."

Music ramped up, and the crowd grew noisier. Dancing started in front of the small bandstand. Angie had to raise her voice. "What's the news on Buziak—is he ever coming back?"

"You didn't hear?" Maddocks said near her ear.

Her gaze ticked up and met his. His mouth was so close. She felt his warmth. Heat stirred low in her belly. "No," she said quietly. "Vedder wasn't about to tell me anything."

"He got caught in Fitz's net—internal was going through office devices, looking for external communications, anything that might clue them in to someone leaking information. Buziak, it appears, had a problem with online gaming, sites not legal here, and he was routinely accessing them from work."

"Oh man," Angie said. "Shit. He was a good cop."

"Fucking good cop," Leo added. "Had respect, that guy."

Colm McGregor, followed by two of his kitchen staff in chef whites, came muscling through the patrons toward their table. They carried trays laden with turkey and fixings and steaming gravy.

These were set on their table, and more trays were brought to other tables. Hungry law enforcement and allied personnel dug in all round as the music quieted slightly.

Glasses were raised, and there were cheers, and spills, and laughter. Maddocks met Angie's eyes and lifted his glass. "Merry Christmas, Angie."

She felt a clutch in her chest at the look in his eyes. "You too, Detective." And that night she'd taken him in the club felt like a million miles away.

"It's here!" McGregor called out, waving a newspaper in the air as he returned to the table. "Christmas Eve special edition—hot off the press." He plunked a copy of the *City Sun* in front of them all. The headline blared:

Mayor and ADAG Caught in Serial Killer Net

Below the headline was Winston's photo of Jack Killion and Joyce Norton-Wells embracing in a car outside the ADAG's estate, the name AKASHA clearly visible on the stone pillar.

"Shit," whispered Holgersen. "Winston's scheduled blog exposé has posted—it's all out there now." He regarded the photo. "Think either one will survive that? They's both married."

"Norton-Wells has already stepped down as ADAG," noted Padachaya. "Whether she'll bounce back eventually—who knows? She was badly rocked by the arrest of her son, from what I hear. Ironic—the top prosecutor having her son prosecuted by her own office."

"Media always goes harder on the woman having the affair," O'Hagan said. "Killion will probably manage to make a comeback, or maybe spin this somehow. We'll have to see how it plays out over the next few months, whether his wife and kids stand by him."

"C'mon, read it out loud, Holgersen," Leo slurred, waving his glass at the front page.

"Not him," O'Hagan said, reaching for the paper. "You'll never understand a word." She scanned the text. "It's a basic recap of everything we thought she'd put out there . . ." She paused. "And a personal footnote." O'Hagan began to read.

"'Killion's affair with Joyce Norton-Wells drives home the risks that one takes to satisfy sexual desire. Their illicit liaison is a mere point along a spectrum of lust. On the one end lies pure, healthy human intimacy. But move along the spectrum and the lines grow darker. Lust crosses into deviance, dysfunction, addiction. Crime. And at the very far black end lies what is lethal—violent, sexually motivated homicide.'"

Silence hung over them all. Angie thought of her own addiction to the sex club. Holgersen looked into his empty beer glass. "Shit. Kid was deep."

"She's right, though," O'Hagan said. "That lust spectrum plays out daily on my morgue slab."

"It's what it means to be human," Padachaya said.

"Or *in*human," Angie added.

Another moment of heavy silence.

"Well," said Leo, "I call it job security." He raised his glass. "So let's drink to that, eh?"

"Here's to Merry Winston," Angie said, lifting her glass. "Tough kid. May she finally rest in peace."

Maddocks placed his hand over Angie's as the group made another tipsy toast. They all saw his hand on hers. He was not afraid—not hiding his affection. He cared.

You got friends . . .

Violent death is not a one-person mission . . .

And in that moment Angie made herself a promise—she resolved to fight her way back, to be with this tribe, these brothers and sisters in blue. To be a better team player.

And she was going to find her biological parents, learn how she came to be the Angel's Cradle kid. She'd lost so much in discovering the dark deceit in her family. And yet gained so much in meeting Maddocks.

She still didn't know why she understood those Polish words, or what those other childlike utterings in her mind meant, but they would lead her forward into the new year.

Come . . . playum dum grove . . . Come down dem . . .

. . . come.

A SNEAK PEEK AT THE NEXT ANGIE PALLORINO NOVEL—COMING SOON

EDITOR'S NOTE: THIS IS AN EARLY EXCERPT AND MAY NOT REFLECT THE FINISHED BOOK.

FLOTSAM

To give the nameless back their names...
—The Doe Network

MONDAY, JANUARY 1

"Ty, dammit! Get your butt away from there, will ya!" Betsy Champlain, all of eight months pregnant, stood on the verge of the road and yelled into the wind for her son to come back from the water's edge. It was raining, clouds low, and dusk was rolling in fast with a fog from the sea. She could barely see him now, chasing their little family Maltese into the gloam along the strip of dark pebbled beach. Panic licked through her stomach.

She spun around. Behind her, along the man-made causeway that jutted out into the water, ferry traffic was lined bumper-to-bumper for miles. Four sailing waits long, and then some. Most of the earlier sailings between the mainland and the island had been canceled throughout the day because of the storms that had ridden into the polar jet stream on the coattails of Typhoon Shiori, blasting the Pacific Northwest with a roller coaster of foul weather. Plus it was New Year's Day—a holiday in this part of the world. Which meant tomorrow was the first day back at work in the new year, and everyone was trying to get home. She was never going to make it from the Vancouver mainland back to the island tonight, and frustration ate at her. She shouldn't have come solo to visit her mom with the two kids and the dog. Ferry traffic was always insane over the holiday period.

They'd been cooped up in the car for hours, and Chloe, their little dog, had needed a bathroom break. Betsy had left the Subaru in the lineup with the window down and Emily, her three-year-old, inside, sleeping. She'd crossed over the road to where she could watch her eight-year-old relieve the dog down the riprap embankment.

But Ty had been busting with frustrated energy after being imprisoned in the vehicle all day. He'd scuttled down the riprap, slipping and dropping Chloe's leash. Chloe had hightailed it straight down to the water.

"Ty! Get back here! Now!" Conflict stabbed through Betsy. She shot a look back at the Subaru, then glanced at Ty's little ghost-shape in the mist. She turned and waddled fast back to the car.

"Emily," she said, shaking her baby girl. "Wake up. You have to come with me."

Betsy grabbed her half-asleep child's hand and dragged her at a run back over the road. They negotiated the wet, slippery riprap down to the beach. Emily began to fall and cry. On the beach, Betsy scooped Emily up onto her hip and stumbled over the rocky strip to where she'd seen Ty vanish. She was breathing hard. She needed to pee—her bladder felt like it was going to burst.

"Ty!" she called. She couldn't see him. "Tyson Champlain, you get your butt over here right now, or—"

"But Ma—" He popped up from behind a rocky outcrop, holding a driftwood stick. Relief cut Betsy like a knife.

"Chloe's found something—I'm just taking a look." He disappeared again, behind his rock knoll.

Heaving out a sigh of exasperation, Betsy readjusted Emily's weight on her hip and negotiated her way over a carpet of small rocks encrusted with barnacles. She came around to the seaward side of the knoll. The tide was far out, revealing a wide expanse of silt covered in slime and scalloped with dirty brown foam. Along the lace of foam lay lengths of seaweed fat as her arm, along with other detritus that had been tossed up or blown in with the storm. A stench of rot and brine and dead fish filled her nostrils.

Ty was crouched over something and poking at it with his stick. Chloe growled, trying to wrestle it away from him. Unusual for the dog.

She frowned, a sense of foreboding creeping into her bones.

"What is it, Ty?"

"A shoe."

Betsy set Emily down, took her hand, and came closer to see. The mist was thicker down here. Emily stopped crying and peered with interest.

"It's got something inside," Ty said, trying to shove Chloe away as he jabbed the contents with his stick.

A memory suddenly chilled Betsy to the core—a news show she'd watched recently about severed feet in sneakers that had been washing up all over the BC coast and in Washington. Sixteen in all since 2007. No other body parts. A baffling mystery.

"Leave that alone!" She grabbed her son by his jacket and pulled him back. "Pick up Chloe's leash—now! Get her away from that shoe."

Ty's eyes went round in shock at her tone. For once in his life he obeyed fast and in silence. He grabbed the dog's leash.

Together, they stared at the shoe. It was a pale lilac in color beneath the grime and seaweed that entangled it. Small. Stubby. A high-top sneaker with a fat, air-filled base for a sole.

Betsy turned and looked back up at the rows of cars, blurred behind a screen of rain. What should she do? Run up there and bash on windows to see if anyone could help her? Help her do what? Police. She needed to tell the police.

"Hold on to your sister, Ty," she said, fumbling in her jacket for her cell phone. "And you hold on to my jacket with your other hand—don't let go, either of you."

He didn't.

Betsy had never called 911 before. No need, thank God. But . . . did this constitute an emergency? Or would she look dumb? Her gaze shot back to the little shoe lying in the silt. There was definitely something inside—like the photos she'd seen on the news.

She knew about the hoaxes, too. The runner found with a partially skeletonized animal paw inside. And others with raw meat stuffed inside. But the cops would want to know, too, if this was a hoax. Right?

"Mom?"

"Quiet."

Fingers shaking, she pressed 911.

"Nine-one-one, what is your emergency?"

"I . . . uh, I . . ." Betsy's voice stuck suddenly on a ball of phlegm. She cleared her throat. "I found a shoe. I think there's a foot inside. I think it washed up in the storm."

"What is your location—where are you?"

"The causeway beach at the Tsawwassen Ferry Terminal. About . . . halfway up, I think."

"What is the number you are calling from?"

"Cell phone." She gave her number.

"And what is your name, ma'am?"

"Betsy. Betsy Champlain." The pressure on her bladder was suddenly intense. She needed a washroom bad. For some reason she also needed to cry. She swiped the back of her hand across her nose, sniffed.

"Are you safe? Everything else all right?"

"Yes. Yes, I'm out here with my kids and my dog. In the rain. My dog found the shoe, and there seems to be a bit of old sock and something inside. I know there are hoaxes, but—"

Up on the causeway engines started growling to life, headlights going on. The line of cars started moving. Someone began honking at her stationary Subaru.

"Oh God, I need to go move my car—the ferry lineup is moving."

"Ma'am, could you please stay with the shoe? I've got RCMP on their way. There's a vehicle in your area now. They'll be there shortly."

"My car is in the lineup. They're honking—"

"We'll contact BC Ferries. They'll get someone out there to direct traffic around it. Ms. Champlain? Betsy?"

"I'm here. I'll wait." She paused. "I . . . know about the dismembered feet," she said quietly, her attention returning to the little lilac high-top. "But this one's not adult." She reached down and gathered her children closer. "It's a child's size nine or ten."

"Does it show the size?" said the operator.

"No. But it's the same size as my daughter's."

Betsy hung up, shivered, rain soft against her cheeks. She sat down on a rock and clutched her kids tightly to her body. Too tight. So tight—because suddenly everything that was precious and ever would be was right here in her arms. She stared at the child's shoe lying in the silt. "I . . . I love you, sweethearts."

"I'm sorry, Mom." Tears glittered in Ty's big brown eyes. "I . . . I'm sorry I didn't listen."

She sniffed and rubbed her nose. "Not your fault, Ty. It's not your fault—it's going to be okay."

"Whose shoe is it?"

"I don't know."

"Where's the rest of her?"

She looked up toward the shadows of land barely discernible through the mist across the bay—Point Roberts in the United States. Behind her, traffic inched along the causeway that stretched a mile into the ocean to the ferry terminal, which lay just five hundred yards short of the US water border—the ferries crossed through American waters each time they traveled from the mainland to Vancouver Island.

That little foot could have come from anywhere. *Off a boat? Washed from land out into the sea during the storm?*

"I don't know," she said. "They'll find her."

"Who will?"

"I don't know, Ty."

ACKNOWLEDGMENTS

To Marlin Beswetherick, again, thank you for walking the streets of Victoria with me on that frigid winter weekend, our breath misting on air, salt wind sharp off the ocean—for the peeks into the cathedral, the tiny eateries, for your stories of the clubs and the people, and the university. You sparked the Angie Pallorino series to vivid life. And while the city of Victoria is real, Angie's Victoria is one of an augmented reality, and her police force should be no reflection on Victoria's fine law enforcement organizations.

Thank you also to Ewa Drozdel for the nuances of Polish, and Dario Cirello for the Italian.

On the editorial side, a deep appreciation goes to Alison Dasho, Charlotte Herscher, and the rest of the Montlake team who work tirelessly behind the scenes to make the business of publishing happen. And to the indomitable Jessica Poore, who keeps all of us authors ridiculously happy and placated. Also, a special thanks to Rex Bonomelli for capturing the tone and the metaphor of *The Drowned Girls* so beautifully in his lush cover art.

While Angie might say that violent death is not a one-person mission, neither is producing a book.

ABOUT THE AUTHOR

Loreth Anne White is an award-winning, bestselling author of romantic suspense, thrillers, and mysteries. A three-time RITA finalist, she has also won the Romantic Times Reviewers' Choice Award, the National Readers' Choice Award, and the Romantic Crown for Best Romantic Suspense and Best Book Overall, in addition to being a Booksellers' Best finalist, a multiple Daphne Du Maurier Award finalist, and a multiple CataRomance Reviewers' Choice Award winner. A former journalist and newspaper editor who has worked in both South Africa and Canada, she now resides in the mountains of the Pacific Northwest with her family. When she's not writing, you will find her skiing, biking, or hiking the trails with her Black Dog. Visit her at www.lorethannewhite.com.